Thomas de Quincey

Protestantism and other Essays

SALZWASSER
VERLAG

Thomas de Quincey

Protestantism and other Essays

Reprint of the original, first published in 1863.

1st Edition 2022 | ISBN: 978-3-37500-075-2

Verlag (Publisher): Salzwasser Verlag GmbH, Zeilweg 44, 60439 Frankfurt, Deutschland
Vertretungsberechtigt (Authorized to represent): E. Roepke, Zeilweg 44, 60439 Frankfurt, Deutschland
Druck (Print): Books on Demand GmbH, In de Tarpen 42, 22848 Norderstedt, Deutschland

DE QUINCEY'S WORKS.

VOLUME VII.

PROTESTANTISM

AND

OTHER ESSAYS

BY

THOMAS DE QUINCEY

EDINBURGH

MDCCCLXIII

CONTENTS.

PREFACE.

THESE Papers, which first of all took their station in the periodic journals of this country, which were secondly transplanted into the literature of the American United States, and are now, for the third time, published at home in a new form with many emendations, may be supposed to have suffered by errors of hurry and inadvertence, from their original adaptation to a service very nearly extemporaneous. It was natural that they should do so. But my own experience, in common with that of many other writers, has taught me that the disadvantages of hurry are not without their compensations. Performers on the organ, so far from finding their own *impromptu* displays to fall below their more careful and premeditated efforts, on the contrary, have oftentimes deep reason to mourn over the escape of inspirations born from the momentary fervours of improvisation, but fugitive and irrevocable as the pulses in their own flying fingers. Something analogous there is in the effects of that inexorable summons which forces a man to write against time, when racing along to intercept the final closing of a weekly or monthly journal. It is certain, howsoever it may be explained psychologically, that the fierce compression of mental activities which takes place in such a struggle, though painful and exhausting, has the effect of suddenly unlocking cells in the brain, and revealing evanescent gleams of original feeling, or startling suggestions of novel truth, that would not have obeyed a less fervent magnetism. Pain, and conflicts with suffering, are ministrations of development to the human intellect even in the youngest infants, much more frequent than is commonly observed.*

I believe that there is no great call for preliminary explanations as to any difficulties in the following papers, except, perhaps, as to these six cases:—

I. The suggesting-ground of the paper entitled "Protestantism" was really a pamphlet, or rather book, judging by its careful and erudite composition; and this work, if now forgotten naturally after a lapse of a dozen years, was really ascribed to two separate bishops of distinguished literary pretension. I know not who it really was that I commented upon, but certainly he was no ghostly creation of mine: he was *incarnate* at that time, and I hope still continues to be so.

II. In speaking of the equation between the expenditure of a family in two remote times, or two remote places (as France and England), on the suggestion of the "Chronicon Preciosum," I omitted to fix the reader's attention (as properly I should have done) upon a common oversight affecting such equations—viz., that very often a large share of the difference forms no exponent of the mere price scale ruling in the two countries compared; since much of the difference should be often charged upon varying usages of life. For instance, about twenty-five years ago I saw a letter from a poor baronet, who had fixed his residence in Southern France, vaunting the prodigious cheapness of his own neighbourhood by comparison with any part of Great Britain. He had a large family of daughters, and an income of very little more than £500 per annum; and yet he described himself as keeping (and ordinarily using for the benefit of his five daughters) a coach-and-four. But, on further explanation, it came out, that the usage of that province allowed him a large social intercourse without the cost of dinner-parties. Otherwise, in several points, Eng-

* I have elsewhere mentioned, as a fact which ought to have a powerful interest for psychologists, that on the morning next after a severe paroxysm of "griping" pains, every infant manifests a striking advance, a bound forwards *per saltum*, in its apprehensiveness, and generally in its intellectual development.

land was the cheaper land. To *A*, *therefore*, on a review of all the circumstances—personal as well as local—France might be much the cheaper. To *B*, with very different habits, or a household very differently composed, England.

III. and IV. In the paper on "Oracles," and in the closing paper on "Greece under the Romans," there occur two suggestions that will be pronounced by many possibly in a high degree paradoxical. But in any bad sense (however erroneous a sense) neither of these suggestions is paradoxical. To the Delphic Oracle, as amongst Greeks—to the Byzantine Empire, as a great barrier standing through eight centuries, breaking and sustaining the assaults of Mahometanism, else too strong on that quarter for infant Christendom in the West—I have assigned majestic functions. So far as the ordinary current of history is not confluent with my view, so far the reader will see cause, perhaps, to remodel his opinion, and to amend his appreciation of two mighty organs working through ages on behalf of human progress, and only not historically acknowledged, because not truly understood.

V. "Schlosser on Literature" was not written with the slight or careless purpose to which the reader will probably attach it. The indirect object was, to lodge, in such a broad exemplification of German ignorance, a protest against the habit (prevalent through the last fifty years) of yielding an extravagant precedency to German critics (on Shakspere especially), as if better and more philosophic (because more cloudy) than our own. Here is a man, Schlosser by name, bookmaker by trade, who (though now perhaps forgotten) was accepted by all Germany, one brief *decennium* back, as a classical surveyor and reporter on the spacious fields of British literature through a retrospect of a hundred and fifty years. But the Schlegels were surely not so poorly furnished for criticism as Mr Schlosser? Why, no: in special walks of literature, if they had not arrogantly pretended to all, they were able to support the character of well-read scholars. What they were as philosophers, or at least what Frederick Schlegel was, the reader may learn from Schelling, who, in one summary foot-note, demolished his pretensions as by a pistol-shot. For real serviceable exposition of Shakspere's meaning and hidden philosophy, I contend that our own domestic critics have contributed very much more than Germany, whether North or South, whether Protestant or Catholic. And, in particular, I myself find, in Morgan's brief essay on the character of Falstaff, more true subtlety of thought, than in all the smoky comments of Rhenish or Danubian transcendentalists. Then, as to those innumerable passages which demand a familiarity with English manners, usages, and antiquities, provincial dialects, &c., naturally the very gates of entrance must be generally closed against all but native critics.

VI. In the little paper on "Miracles," the reader, who is new to the subject, must understand that no question is raised (as too probably he will be supposing) on the possibility of a miracle. That question is left entirely untouched. The discussion commences at a point lower down—viz., after assuming the possibility of a miracle, then next as to its *communicability;* meaning, whether a miracle, if it should actually take place, could have any power to propagate its own existence amongst mankind; that is, whether it could translate itself upon the wings of *testimony* from the little theatre of spectators or auditors, before whom it had been exhibited, to the great theatre of the world, and the still greater theatre of posterity.

WALKING STEWART.

He was a man of very extraordinary genius. He has generally been treated by those who have spoken of him in print as a madman. But this is a mistake, and must have been founded chiefly on the titles of his books. He was a man of fervid mind, and of sublime aspirations: but he was no madman; or, if he was, then I say that it is so far desirable to be a madman. In 1798 or 1799, when I must have been about thirteen to fourteen years old, Walking Stewart was in Bath—where my family at that time resided. He frequented the pump-room, and I believe all public places—walking up and down, and dispersing his philosophic opinions to the right and the left, like a Grecian philosopher. The first time I saw him was at a concert in the Upper Rooms; he was pointed out to me by one of my party as a very eccentric man who had walked over the habitable globe. I remember that Madame Mara was at that moment singing: and Walking Stewart, who was a true lover of music (as I afterwards came to know), was hanging upon her notes like a bee upon a jessamine flower. His countenance was striking, and expressed the union of benignity with philosophic habits of thought. In such health had his pedestrian exercises preserved him, connected with his abstemious mode of living, that, though he must at that time have been considerably above forty, he did not look older than twenty-eight; at least the face which remained upon my recollection for some years was that of a young man. Nearly ten years afterwards I became acquainted with him. During the interval, I had picked up one of his works in Bristol —viz., his "Travels to discover the Source of Moral Motion," the second volume of which is entitled, "The Apocalypse of Nature." I had been greatly impressed by the sound and original views which, in the first volume, he had taken of the national characters throughout Europe. In particular, he was the first, and, so far as I know, the only writer who had noticed the profound error of ascribing a phlegmatic character to the English nation. "English phlegm" is the constant expression of authors, when contrasting the English with the French. Now, the truth is, that, beyond that of all other nations, it has a substratum of profound passion: and if we are to recur to the old doctrine of temperaments, the English character must be classed, not under the *phlegmatic*, but under the *melancholic*, temperament; and the French under the *sanguine*. The character of a nation may be judged of, in this particular, by examining its idiomatic language. The French, in whom the lower forms of passion are constantly bubbling up from the shallow and superficial character of their feelings, have appropriated all the phrases of passion to the service of trivial and ordinary life: and hence they have no language of passion for the service of poetry, or of occasions really demanding it: for it has been already enfeebled by continual association with cases of an unimpassioned order. But a character of deeper passion has a perpetual standard in itself, by which, as by an instinct, it tries all cases, and rejects the language of passion as disproportionate and ludicrous where it is not fully justified. "Ah Heavens!" or "Oh my God!" are exclamations, with us, so exclusively reserved for cases of profound interest, that, on hearing a woman even (*i. e.*, a person of the sex most easily excited) utter such words, we look round, expecting to see her child in some situation of danger. But in France, "*Ah Ciel!*" and "*Oh mon Dieu!*" are uttered by every woman if a mouse does but run across the floor. The ignorant and the thoughtless, however, will continue to class the English character under the phlegmatic temperament, whilst the philosopher will perceive that it is the exact polar antithesis to a phlegmatic character. In this conclusion, though otherwise expressed and illustrated, Walking Stewart's view of the English character will be found to terminate: and his opinion is especially valuable—first, and chiefly, because he was a philosopher; secondly, because his acquaintance with man, civilised and uncivilised, under all national distinctions, was absolutely unrivalled. Meantime, this and others of his opinions were expressed in language that, if literally construed, would often appear insane or absurd. The truth is, his long intercourse with foreign nations had given something of a hybrid tincture to his diction; in some of his works, for instance, he uses the French word *hélas!* uniformly for the English *alas!* and apparently with no consciousness of his mistake. He had also this singularity about him, that he was everlastingly metaphysicising against metaphysics. To me, who was buried in metaphysical reveries from my earliest days, this was not likely to be an attraction, any more than the vicious structure of his diction was likely to please my scholar-like taste. All grounds of disgust, however, gave way before my sense of his powerful merits; and, as I have said, I sought his acquaintance. Coming up to London from Oxford about 1807 or 1808, I made inquiries about him; and found that he usually read the papers at a coffee-room in Piccadilly: understanding that he was poor, it struck me that he might not wish to receive visits at his lodgings, and therefore I sought him at the coffee-room. Here I took the liberty of introducing myself to him. He received me courteously, and invited me to his rooms, which at that time were in Sherrard Street, Golden Square —a street already memorable to me. I was much struck with the eloquence of his conversation; and afterwards I found that Mr Wordsworth, himself the most eloquent of men in conversation, had been equally struck, when he had met him at Paris between the years 1790 and 1792, during the early storms of the French Revolution: In Sherrard Street I visited him repeatedly, and took notes of the conversations I had with him on various subjects. These I must have somewhere or other; and I wish I could introduce them here, as they would interest the reader. Occasionally, in these conversations, as in his books, he introduced a few notices of his private history: in particular, I remember his telling me that in the East Indies he had been a prisoner of Hyder's; that he had escaped with some difficulty; and that, in the service of one of the native princes as secretary or interpreter, he had accumulated a small fortune. This must have been too small, I fear, at that time to allow him even a philosopher's comforts: for some part of it, invested in the French funds, had been confiscated. I was grieved to see a man of so much ability, of gentlemanly manners and refined habits, and with the infirmity of deafness, suffering under such obvious privations; and I once took the liberty, on a fit occasion presenting itself, of requesting that he would allow me to send him some books which he had been casually regretting that he did not possess—for I was at that time in the heyday of my worldly prosperity. This offer, however, he declined with firmness and dignity, though not unkindly. And I now mention it, because I have seen him charged in print with a selfish regard to his own pecuniary interest. On the contrary, he appeared to me a very liberal and generous man: and I well remember that, whilst on his own part he refused to accept of anything, he compelled me to receive as presents all the books which he published during my acquaintance with him. Two of these, corrected with his own hand—viz., the "Lyre of Apollo," and the "Sophiometer"—I have lately found amongst other books left in London; and others he forwarded to me in Westmoreland. In 1809 I saw him often. In the spring of that year I happened to be in London; and Wordsworth's tract on the Convention of Cintra being at that time in the printer's hands, I superintended the publication of it; and, at Wordsworth's request, I added a long note on Spanish affairs, which is printed in the Appendix. The opinions I expressed in this note on the Spanish character, at that time much calumniated on the retreat to Corunna, then fresh in the public mind, above all, the contempt I expressed for the superstition in respect to the French military prowess—a superstition so dishonouring to ourselves, and so mischievous in its results—which was then at its height, and which gave way, in fact, only to the campaigns of 1814 and 1815, fell in, as it happened, with Mr Stewart's political creed in those points where at that time it met with most opposition. In 1812 it was, I think, that I saw him for the last time: and, by the way, on the day of my parting with him, I had an amusing proof, in my own experience, of that sort of ubiquity ascribed to him by a witty writer in the "London Magazine." I met him and shook hands with him under Somerset House, telling him that I should leave town that evening for Westmoreland. Thence I went, by the very shortest road (*i. e.*, through Moor Street, Soho—for I am learned in many quarters of London), towards a point which necessarily led me through Tottenham Court Road: I stopped nowhere, and walked fast; yet so it was, that in Tottenham Court Road I was not overtaken by (*that* was comprehensible), but overtook, Walking Stewart. Certainly, as the above writer alleges, there must have been three Walking Stewarts in London. He seemed nowise surprised at this himself, but explained to me, that somewhere or other in the neighbourhood of Tottenham Court Road there was a little theatre, at which there was dancing, and occasionally good singing, between which and a neighbouring coffee-house he sometimes divided his evenings. Singing, it seems, he could hear in spite of his deafness. In this street I took my final leave of him; it turned out such; and anticipating at the time that it would, I looked after his white hat at the moment it was disappearing, and exclaimed, "Farewell, thou half-crazy and most eloquent of men! I shall never see thy face again." At that moment, I did not intend to visit London again for some years: as it happened, I was there for a short time in 1814; and then I heard, to my great satisfaction, that Walking Stewart had recovered a considerable sum (about £14,000, I believe) from the East India Company; and, from the abstract given in the "London Magazine" of the memoir by his relation, I have since learned that he applied this money most wisely to the purchase of an annuity, and that he "persisted in living" too long for the peace of an annuity office. So fare all companies, East and West, and all annuity-offices, that stand opposed in interest to philosophers! In 1814, however, to my great regret, I did not see him; for I was then taking a great deal of opium, and never could contrive to issue to the light of day soon enough for a morning-call upon a philosopher of such early hours; and in the evening, I concluded that he would be generally abroad, from what he had formerly communicated to me of his own habits. It seems, however, that he afterwards held *conversaziones* at his own rooms, and did not stir out to theatres quite so much. From a brother of mine, who at one time occupied rooms in the same house with him, I learned that, in other respects, he did not deviate in his prosperity from the philosophic tenor of his former life. He abated nothing of his peripatetic exercises; and repaired duly in the morning, as he had done in former years, to St James's Park, where he sat in trance-like reverie amongst the cows, inhaling their balmy breath and pursuing his philosophic speculations. He had also purchased an organ, or more than one, with which he solaced his solitude, and beguiled himself of uneasy thoughts, if he ever had any.

The works of Walking Stewart must be read with some indulgence; the titles are generally too lofty and pretending, and somewhat extravagant; the composition is lax and unprecise, as I have before said; and the doctrines are occasionally very bold, incautiously stated, and too hardy and high-toned for the nervous effeminacy of many modern moralists. But Walking Stewart was a man who thought nobly of human nature: he wrote, therefore, at times, in the spirit and with the indignation of an ancient prophet against the oppressors and destroyers of the time. In particular, I remember that, in one or more of the pamphlets which I received from him at Grasmere, he expressed himself in such terms on the subject of Tyrannicide (distinguishing the cases in which it was and was not lawful) as seemed to Wordsworth and myself every way worthy of a philosopher; but, from the way in which that subject was treated in the House of Commons, where it was at that time occasionally introduced, it was plain that his doctrine was not fitted for the luxurious and relaxed morals of the age. Like all men who think nobly of human nature, Walking Stewart thought of it hopefully. In some respects his hopes were wisely grounded; in others, they rested too much upon certain metaphysical speculations which are untenable, and which satisfied himself only, because his researches in that track had been purely self-originated and self-disciplined. He relied upon his own native strength of mind; but, in questions which the wisdom and philosophy of every age, building successively upon each other, have not been able to settle, no mind, however strong, is entitled to build wholly upon itself In many things he shocked the religious sense—especially as it exists in unphilosophic minds: he held a sort of rude and unscientific Spinosism; and he expressed it coarsely, and in the way most likely to give offence. And indeed there can be no stronger proof of the utter obscurity in which his works have slumbered, than that they should all have escaped prosecution. He also allowed himself to look too lightly and indulgently on the afflicting spectacle of female prostitution as it exists in London and in all great cities. This was the only point on which I was disposed to quarrel with him; for I could not but view it as a greater reproach to human nature than the slave-trade, or any sight of wretchedness that the sun looks down upon.

I often told him so; and that I was at a loss to guess how a philosopher could allow himself to view it simply as part of the equipage of civil life, and not less reasonably making part of the establishment and furniture of a great city as police-offices, lamp-lighting, or newspapers. Waiving, however, this one instance of something like compliance with the brutal spirit of the world, on all other subjects he was eminently unworldly, child-like, simple-minded, and upright. He would flatter no man: even when addressing nations, it is almost laughable to see how invariably he prefaces his counsels with such plain truths, uttered in a manner so offensive as must have defeated his purpose, if it had otherwise any chance of being accomplished. For instance, in addressing America, he begins thus:—"People of America! since your separation from the mother-country, your moral character has degenerated in the energy of thought and sense; produced by the absence of your association and intercourse with British officers and merchants: you have no moral discernment to distinguish between the protective power of England and the destructive power of France." And his letter to the Irish nation opens in this agreeable and conciliatory manner:—"People of Ireland! I address you as a true philosopher of nature, foreseeing the perpetual misery your irreflective character, and total absence of moral discernment, are preparing for," &c. The second sentence begins thus:—"You are sacrilegiously arresting the arm of your parent kingdom, fighting the cause of man and nature, when the triumph of the fiend of French police-terror would be your own instant extirpation." And the letter closes thus:—"I see but one awful alternative—that Ireland will be a perpetual moral volcano, threatening the destruction of the world, if the education and instruction of thought and sense shall not be able to generate the faculty of moral discernment among a very numerous class of the population, who detest the civic calm as sailors the natural calm, and make civic rights on which they cannot reason a pretext for feuds which they delight in." As he spoke freely and boldly to others, so he spoke loftily of himself. At p. 313 of the "Harp of Apollo," on making a comparison of himself with Socrates (in which he naturally gives the preference to himself), he styles the "Harp," &c., "this unparalleled work of human energy." At p. 315, he calls it "this stupendous work;" and lower down, on the same page, he says, "I was turned out of school, at the age of fifteen, for a dunce or blockhead, because I would not stuff into my memory all the nonsense of erudition and learning; and if future ages should discover the unparalleled energies of genius in this work, it will prove my most important doctrine—that the powers of the human mind must be developed in the education of thought and sense in the study of moral opinion, not arts and science." Again, at p. 225 of his "Sophiometer," he says, "The paramount thought that dwells in my mind incessantly is a question I put to myself—whether, in the event of my personal dissolution by death, I have communicated all the discoveries my unique mind possesses in the great master-science of man and nature." In the next page, he determines that he *has*, with the exception of one truth—viz., "the latent energy, physical and moral, of human nature as existing in the British people." But here he was surely accusing himself without ground; for, to my knowledge, he has not failed, in any one of his numerous works, to insist upon this theme at least a billion of times. Another instance of his magnificent self-estimation is, that in the title-pages of several of his works he announces himself as "John

Stewart, the only man of nature* that ever appeared in the world."

By this time I am afraid the reader begins to suspect that he was crazy: and certainly, when I consider everything, he must have been crazy when the wind was at NNE; for who but Walking Stewart ever dated his books by a computation drawn—not from the creation, not from the flood, not from Nabonassar, or *ab urbe conditâ*, not from the Hegira—but from themselves, from their own day of publication, as constituting the one great era in the history of man by the side of which all other eras were frivolous and impertinent? Thus, in a work of his, given to me in 1812, and probably published in that year, I find him incidentally recording of himself that he was at that time "arrived at the age of sixty-three, with a firm state of health acquired by temperance, and a peace of mind almost independent of the vices of mankind—because my knowledge of life has enabled me to place my happiness beyond the reach or contact of other men's follies and passions, by avoiding all family connections, and all ambitious pursuits of profit, fame, or power." On reading this passage, I was anxious to ascertain its date; but this, on turning to the title-page, I found thus mysteriously expressed: "In the 7000th year of Astronomical History, and the first day of Intellectual Life or Moral World, from the era of this work." Another slight indication of craziness appeared in a notion which obstinately haunted his mind, that all the kings and rulers of the earth would

* In Bath he was surnamed the "Child of Nature;" which arose from his contrasting, on every occasion, the existing man of our present experience with the ideal or Stewartian man that might be expected to emerge in some myriads of ages—to which latter man he gave the name of the Child of Nature.

confederate in every age against his works, and would hunt them out for extermination as keenly as Herod did the innocents of Bethlehem. On this consideration, fearing that they might be intercepted by the long arms of these wicked princes before they could reach that remote Stewartian man or his precursor to whom they were mainly addressed, he recommended to all those who might be impressed with a sense of their importance to bury a copy or copies of each work, properly secured from damp, &c., at a depth of seven or eight feet below the surface of the earth; and on their death-beds to communicate the knowledge of this fact to some confidential friends, who, in their turn, were to send down the tradition to some discreet persons of the next generation; and thus, if the truth was not to be dispersed for many ages, yet the knowledge that here and there the truth lay buried on this and that continent, in secret spots on Mount Caucasus—in the sands of Biledulgerid—and in hiding-places amongst the forests of America, and was to rise again in some distant age, and to vegetate and fructify for the universal benefit of man,—this knowledge at least was to be whispered down from generation to generation; and, in defiance of a myriad of kings crusading against him, Walking Stewart was to stretch out the influence of his writings through a long series of *λαμπαδηφοροι** to that child of nature whom he saw dimly through a vista of many centuries. If this were

* "*λαμπαδηφοροι*:"—Lamp or torch bearers, the several parties to an obscure Grecian game. The essential point known to us moderns is, that, in running, they passed on to each other a lighted torch, under what conditions, beyond that of keeping the torch burning, is very imperfectly explained. But already this feature of the game, without further details, qualifies the partakers in it to represent symbolically those who, from generation to generation, pass onwards the traditions of gathering knowledge.

madness, it seemed to me a somewhat sublime madness: and I assured him of my co-operation against the kings, promising that I would bury the "Harp of Apollo" in my own orchard in Grasmere at the foot of Mount Fairfield; that I would bury the "Apocalypse of Nature" in one of the coves of Helvellyn, and several other works in several other places best known to myself. He accepted my offer with gratitude; but he then made known to me that he relied on my assistance for a still more important service—which was this: in the lapse of that vast number of ages that would probably intervene between the present period and the period at which his works would have reached their destination, he feared that the English language might itself have mouldered away. "No!" I said, "*that* was not probable: considering its extensive diffusion, and that it was now transplanted into all the continents of our planet, I would back the English language against any other on earth." His own persuasion, however, was, that the Latin was destined to survive all other languages; it was to be the eternal as well as the universal language; and his desire was that I should translate his works, or some part of them, into that language.* This I promised;

* I was not aware until the moment of writing this passage, that Walking Stewart had publicly made this request three years after making it to myself: opening the "Harp of Apollo," I have just now accidentally stumbled on the following passage:—"This stupendous work is destined, I fear, to meet a worse fate than the aloe, which, as soon as it blossoms, loses its stalk. This first blossom of reason is threatened with the loss of both its stalk and its soil: for, if the revolutionary tyrant should triumph, he would destroy all the English books and energies of thought. I conjure my readers to translate this work into Latin, and to bury it in the ground, communicating on their death-beds only its place of concealment to men of nature."

From the title-page of this work, by the way, I learn that "the 7000th year of Astronomical History" is taken from the Chinese tables, and coincides (as I had supposed) with the year 1812 of our computation.

and I seriously designed at some leisure hour to translate into Latin a selection of passages which should embody an abstract of his philosophy. This would have been doing a service to all those who might wish to see a digest of his peculiar opinions cleared from the perplexities of his peculiar diction, and brought into a narrow compass from the great number of volumes through which they are at present dispersed. However, like many another plan of mine, it went unexecuted.

On the whole, if Walking Stewart were at all crazy, he was so in a way which did not affect his natural genius and eloquence—but rather exalted them. The old maxim, indeed, that "Great wits to madness sure are near allied," the maxim of Dryden and the popular maxim, I have heard disputed by Mr Coleridge and Mr Wordsworth, who maintain that mad people are the dullest and most wearisome of all people. As a body, I believe they are so. But I must dissent from the authority of Messrs Coleridge and Wordsworth so far as to distinguish. Where madness is connected, as it often is, with some miserable derangement of the stomach, liver, &c., and attacks the principle of pleasurable life, which is manifestly seated in the central organs of the body (*i. e.*, in the stomach and the apparatus connected with it), there it cannot but lead to perpetual suffering and distraction of thought; and there the patient will be often tedious and incoherent. People who have not suffered from any great disturbance in those organs are little aware how indispensable to the process of thinking are the momentary influxes of pleasurable feeling from the regular goings on of life in its primary function; in fact, until the pleasure is withdrawn or obscured, most people are not aware that they *have* any pleasure from the due action of the great central machinery of the system: proceeding in uninterrupted continuance, the pleasure as much escapes the consciousness as the act of respiration: a child, in the happiest stage of its existence, does not *know* that it is happy. And, generally, whatsoever is the level state of the hourly feeling is never put down by the unthinking (*i. e.*, by 99 out of 100) to the account of happiness: it is never put down with the positive sign, as equal to $+ x$; but simply as $= 0$. And men first become aware that it *was* a positive quantity, when they have lost it (*i. e.*, fallen into $- x$). Meantime the genial pleasure from the vital processes, though not represented to the consciousness, is *immanent* in every act, impulse, motion, word, and thought: and a philosopher sees that the idiots are in a state of pleasure, though they cannot see it themselves. Now I say that, where this principle of pleasure is not attacked, madness is often little more than an enthusiasm highly exalted; the animal spirits are exuberant and in excess; and the madman becomes, if he be otherwise a man of ability and information, all the better as a companion. I have met with several such madmen; and I appeal to my brilliant friend, Professor Wilson of Edinburgh, who is not a man to tolerate dulness in any quarter, and is himself the ideal of a delightful companion, whether he ever met a more amusing person than that madman who took a post-chaise jointly with him and myself, from Penrith to Carlisle, long years ago, when he and I were hastening with the speed of fugitive felons to catch the Edinburgh mail. His fancy and his extravagance, and his furious attacks on Sir Isaac Newton, like Plato's suppers, refreshed us not only for that day, but whenever they recurred to us; and we were both grieved when we heard some time afterwards, from a Cambridge man, that he had met our clever friend in a stage-coach under the care of a brutal keeper.——Such a madness, if any, was the madness of Walking Stewart: his health was perfect; his spirits as light and ebullient as the spirits of a bird in spring-time; and his mind unagitated by painful thoughts, and at peace with himself. Hence, if he was not an amusing companion, it was because the philosophic direction of his thoughts made him something more. Of anecdotes and matters of fact he was not communicative: of all that he had seen in the vast compass of his travels he rarely availed himself in conversation. I do not remember, at this moment, that he ever once alluded to his own travels in his intercourse with me, except for the purpose of weighing down, by a statement grounded on his own great personal experience, an opposite statement of many hasty and misjudging travellers which he thought injurious to human nature: the statement was this, that, in all his countless rencounters with uncivilised tribes, he had never met with any so ferocious and brutal as to attack an unarmed and defenceless man, who was able to make them understand that he threw himself upon their hospitality and forbearance.

On the whole, Walking Stewart was a sublime visionary. He had seen and suffered much amongst men; yet not too much, or so as to dull the genial tone of his sympathy with the sufferings of others. His mind was a mirror of the sentient universe—the whole mighty vision that had fleeted before his eyes in this world: the armies of Hyder Ali and his son Tippoo, with oriental and barbaric pageantry; the civic grandeur of England; the great deserts of Asia and America; the vast capitals of Europe; London, with its eternal agitations, the ceaseless ebb and flow of its "mighty heart;" Paris, shaken by the fierce torments of revolutionary convulsions; the silence of Lapland; and the solitary forests of Canada; with the swarming life of the torrid zone; together with innumerable recollections of individual joy and sorrow that he had participated by sympathy —lay like a map beneath him, as if eternally co-present to his view, so that, in the contemplation of the prodigious whole, he had no leisure to separate the parts, or occupy his mind with details. Hence came the monotony which the frivolous and the desultory would have found in his conversation. I, however, who, by accidents of experience, am qualified to speak of him, must pronounce him to have been a man of great genius, and, with reference to his conversation, of great eloquence. That these were not better known and acknowledged was owing to two disadvantages—one grounded in his imperfect education, the other in the peculiar structure of his mind. The first was this: like the late Mr Shelley, he had a fine vague enthusiasm, and lofty aspirations, in connection with human nature generally and its hopes; and like him he strove to give steadiness, a uniform direction, and an intelligible purpose to these feelings, by fitting to them a scheme of philosophical opinions. But unfortunately the philosophic system of both was so far from supporting their own views, and the cravings of their own enthusiasm, that, as in some points it was baseless, incoherent, or unintelligible, so in others it tended to moral results from which, if they had foreseen them, they would have been themselves the first to shrink, as contradictory to the very purposes in which their system had originated. Hence, in maintaining their own system, they found themselves painfully entangled, at times, with tenets pernicious and degrading to human nature. These were the inevitable consequences of the πρωτον ψευδος * in their speculations; but were naturally

* "πρωτον ψευδος:"—The first (or fundamental) falsehood.

charged upon them by those who looked carelessly into their books as opinions which, not merely for the sake of consistency, they thought themselves bound to endure, but to which they gave the full weight of their sanction and patronage as to so many moving principles in their system. The other disadvantage under which Walking Stewart laboured was this: he was a man of genius, but not a man of talents; at least his genius was out of all proportion to his talents, and wanted an organ, as it were, for manifesting itself, so that his most original thoughts were delivered in a crude state, imperfect, obscure, half-developed, and not producible to a popular audience. He was partially aware of this himself; and though he claims everywhere the faculty of profound intuition into human nature, yet, with equal candour, he accuses himself of asinine stupidity, dulness, and want of talent. He was a disproportioned intellect, and so far a monster: and he must be added to the long list of original-minded men who have been looked down upon with pity and contempt by commonplace men of talent, whose powers of mind, though a thousand times inferior, were yet more manageable, more self-interpreted, and ran in channels better suited to common uses and common understandings.

THE MARQUESS WELLESLEY.*

It sounds like the tolling of funeral bells, as the annunciation is made of one death after another amongst those who supported our canopy of empire through the last most memorable generation. The eldest of the Wellesleys is gone; he is gathered to his fathers: and here we have his life circumstantially written.

Who, and of what origin, are the Wellesleys? There is an impression current amongst the public, or there *was* an impression, that the true name of the Wellesley family is Wesley. This is a case very much resembling some of those imagined by the old scholastic logicians, where it was impossible either to deny or to affirm: saying *yes*, or saying *no*, equally you told a falsehood. As if, being asked whether you killed your wife by strychnia, then to reply *yes* would be directly to own the crime; but, on the other hand, to reply *no* would be indirectly to own it—since it would be argued that you admitted the killing, by denying that you did it by strychnia. The case as to the Wellesleys is briefly this: The family was originally English; and in England, at the earliest era, there is no doubt at all that its name was De Wellesleigh, which was pronounced

* Suggested by Mr Pearce's "Memoirs and Correspondence."

in the eldest times just as it is now—viz., as a dissyllable* —the first syllable sounding exactly like the cathedral city *Wells*, in Somersetshire, and the second like *lea* (a field under some modification). It is plain enough, from various records, that the true historical *genesis* of the name was precisely through that composition of words which here, for the moment, I had imagined merely to illustrate its pronunciation. Lands in the diocese of Bath and Wells, running up almost to the gates of Bristol, constituted the earliest possessions of the De Wellesleighs. They, seven centuries before Assaye and Waterloo, were "seised" of certain rich *leas* held under the Dean and Chapter of *Wells*. And from these Saxon elements of the name, some have supposed the Wellesleys a Saxon race. They could not possibly have better blood: but still the thing does not follow from the premisses. Neither does it follow from the *de* that they were Norman. The first De Wellesley known to history, the very tip-top man of the pedigree, is Avenant de Wellesleigh. About a hundred years nearer to our own times—viz., in 1239—came Michael de Wellesleigh, of whom the important fact is recorded, that he was the father of Wellerand de Wellesleigh. And what did young Mr Wellerand perform in this wicked world, that the proud muse of history should condescend to notice his rather singular name five hundred and fifty-five years† exactly after his decease? Reader, he was—"killed:" that is all; and in company with Sir Robert de Percival; which again argues

* *"As a dissyllable:"*—Just as the *Annesley* family, of which Lord Valentia is the present head, do not pronounce their name trisyllabically (as strangers often suppose)—viz., Ann-es-ley—but as if *Anns* (in the possessive case)—ley. In Scotland, this ancient English name is altogether transfigured into the Scottish name of *Ainslie*.

† *"Five hundred and fifty-five years:"*—*i. e.*, not in the year of original publication, thirteen years ago, but now, in the year of revisal and republication—viz., in 1858.

his Somersetshire descent; for the family of Lord Egmont, the head of all Percivals, ever was, and ever will be, in Somersetshire. But *how* was he killed? The time *when* —viz., 1303—the place *where*, are known; but the manner *how* is not exactly stated. It was in skirmish with rascally Irish "kernes," fellows that (when presented at the font of Christ for baptism) had their right arms covered up from the baptismal waters, in order that, still remaining consecrated to the devil, those arms might inflict a devilish blow. Such a blow, with such an unbaptised arm, the Irish villain struck; and there was an end of Wellerand de Wellesleigh. Strange that history should make an end of a man before she had made a beginning of him. These, however, are the *facts;* which, in writing a romance about Sir Wellerand and Sir Percival, I shall have great pleasure in falsifying. But how, says the too curious reader, did the De Wellesleighs find themselves amongst Irish kernes? Had these scamps the presumption to invade Somersetshire? Did they dare to intrude into Wells? Not at all: but the pugnacious De Wellesleighs had dared to intrude into Ireland. Some say in the train of Henry II. Some say —— but no matter: *there* they were; and *there* they stuck like limpets. They soon engrafted themselves into the County of Kildare, from which, by means of a fortunate marriage, they leaped into the County of Meath; and in that county, as if to refute the pretended mutability of human things, they have roosted ever since. There was once a famous copy of verses floating about Europe, which asserted that, whilst other princes were destined to fight for thrones, Austria—the handsome house of Hapsburg—should obtain thrones by marriage:

"Pugnabunt alii: tu, felix Austria, nube." *

* "*Nube:*"—One must wink at blunders where royalties are concerned;

So of the Wellesleighs. Sir Wellerand took quite the wrong way: not cudgelling, but courting, was the correct line of policy in Kildare. Two great estates, by two separate marriages, the De Wellesleighs obtained in Kildare; and by a third marriage, in a third generation, they obtained, in the County of Meath, an estate known by the name of Castle Dengan (otherwise Dangan), with lordships as plentiful as blackberries. Castle Dangan came to them in the year of our Lord 1411—*i. e.*, four years before Agincourt; which memorable battle was fought exactly four hundred years before Waterloo—*ergo* in 1415. And in Castle Dangan did Field-Marshal the Man of Waterloo draw his first breath, shed his first tears, and perpetrate his earliest trespasses. That is what one might call a pretty long spell for one family. Four hundred and thirty-five years* has Castle Dangan furnished a nursery for the Wellesley piccaninnies. Amongst the lordships attached to Castle Dangan was *Mornington*, which, more than three centuries afterwards, supplied an earldom for the grandfather of Waterloo. Any further memorabilia of the Castle Dangan family are not recorded, except that in 1485 (which surely was the year of Bosworth Field?) they began to omit the *de*, and to write themselves Wellesley *tout court*. From indolence, I presume; for a certain Lady Di. le Fleming, whom once I knew, a Howard by birth, who had condescended so far as to marry a simple baronet (Sir Michael le Fleming), told me, when a widow, as her rea-

---

else, between you and me, reader, *nube* is not the right word, unless when the Austrian throne-winner happened to be a princess. *Nube* could not be applied to a man, as an old dusty pentameter will assist the reader in remembering:

"Uxorem *duco; nubit* at illa mihi."

* "*Four hundred and thirty-five*"—but now (1858), on republication of this paper, hard upon four hundred and forty-seven years.

son for omitting the *le*, that it caused her too much additional trouble. She was a very good and kind-hearted woman; yet still, as a daughter of the Howards (the great feudal house of Suffolk), she regarded any possible heraldic pretensions of an obscure baronet's family as visible only through powerful microscopes.

So far the evidence seems in favour of Wellesley, and against Wesley. But, on the other hand, during the last three centuries the Wellesleys themselves wrote the name Wesley. They, however, were only the *maternal* ancestors of the present Wellesleys. Garret Wellesley, the last male heir of the direct line, in the year 1745, left his whole estate to one of the Cowleys, a Staffordshire family, who had emigrated to Ireland in Queen Elizabeth's time, but who were, however, descended from the Wellesleys. This Cowley or Colley, taking, in 1745, the name of Wesley, received from George II. the title of Earl Mornington; and Colley's grandson, the Marquess Wellesley of our age, was recorded in the Irish peerage as *Wesley*, Earl of Mornington; was uniformly so described up to the end of the eighteenth century; and even Arthur of Waterloo, whom most of us Europeans know pretty well, on going to India a little before his brother (say early in 1799), was thus introduced by Lord Cornwallis to Sir John Shore (Lord Teignmouth, at that time the Governor-General), "Dear sir, I beg leave to introduce to you Colonel Wesley, who is a lieutenant-colonel of my regiment. He is a sensible man, and a good officer." Posterity (for *we* are posterity in respect of Lord Cornwallis) have been very much of *his* opinion. Colonel Wesley really *was* a sensible man; and the sensible man, soon after his arrival in Bengal, under the instigation of his brother, resumed the old name of Wellesley. In reality, the name of Wesley was merely the abbreviation of indolence, as Chumley for Cholmondeley Pomfret for Pontefract, Cicester for Cirencester; or, in Scotland, Marchbanks for Majoribanks, Shatorow, as commonly pronounced, for the Duke of Hamilton's French title of Chatelherault. I remember well from my days of childhood a niece of John Wesley, the Proto-Methodist, who always spoke of the second Lord Mornington (author of the well-known glees) as a cousin, and as intimately connected with her brother, the great *foudroyant* performer on the organ. Southey, in his Life of John Wesley, the pious founder of Methodism, tells us that Charles Wesley, the brother of John, and father of the great organist, had the offer from Garret Wellesley of those same estates which eventually were left to Richard Cowley. This argues a recognition of near consanguinity. Why the offer was declined, is not distinctly explained. Certainly it requires explanation, being a problem of very difficult solution to us sublunary men. But, if it had been accepted, Southey thinks that then we should have had no storming of Seringapatam, no Waterloo, and no Arminian Methodists. All that is not quite clear. Tippoo was booked for a desperate British vengeance by his own desperate enmity to our name, though no Lord Wellesley had been Governor-General in the penultimate year of the last century. Napoleon, by the same fury of hatred to us, was booked for the same fate, though the scene of it might not have been Waterloo. And, as to John Wesley, why should he not have made the same schism with the English Church, because his brother Charles had become unexpectedly rich?

The Marquess Wellesley was of the same standing, as to age, or nearly so, as Mr Pitt; though he outlived Pitt by almost forty years. Born in 1760, three or four months before the accession of George III., he was sent to Eton, at the age of eleven; and from Eton, in his eighteenth year, he was sent to Christ Church, Oxford, where he matriculated as a nobleman. He then bore the courtesy title of Viscount Wellesley; but, in 1781, when he had reached his twenty-first year, he was summoned away from Oxford by the death of his father, the second Earl of Mornington. It is interesting, at this moment, to look back on the family group of children collected at Dangan Castle. The young Earl of Mornington, future Marquess Wellesley, was within a month of his majority; his younger brothers and sisters were these: William Wellesley Pole (since dead, under the title of Lord Maryborough), then aged eighteen; Anne, since married to Henry, son of Lord Southampton, then aged thirteen; *Arthur*, aged twelve; Gerald Valerian, now in the church, aged ten; Mary Elizabeth (since Lady Culling Smith), aged nine; Henry, since Lord Cowley, and British ambassador to Spain, France, &c., aged eight. The new Lord Mornington showed his conscientious nature, by assuming his father's debts, and by superintending the education of his brothers. He had distinguished himself at Oxford as a scholar; but he returned thither no more, and took no degree. As Earl of Mornington, he sat in the Irish House of Lords; but not being a *British* peer, he was able to sit also in the English House of Commons; and of this opening for a more national career, he availed himself at the age of twenty-four. Except that he favoured the claims of the Irish Catholics, his policy was pretty uniformly that of Mr Pitt. He supported that minister throughout the contests on the French Revolution; and a little earlier, on the Regency question. This came forward in 1788, on occasion of the first insanity which attacked George III. The reader, who is likely to have been born since that era—at least I hope so—will perhaps not be acquainted with the constitutional question then at issue. It was this: Mr Fox held that, upon any incapacity arising in the sovereign, the regency would then settle (*ipso facto* of that incapacity, and, therefore, in defiance of Parliament) upon the Prince of Wales; overlooking altogether the case in which there should *be* no Prince of Wales, and the case in which such a prince might be as incapable, from youth, of exercising the powers attached to the office, as his father from disease. Mr Pitt denied that a Prince of Wales simply *as* such, and apart from any moral fitness which he might have manifested, had more of *legal* title to the office of regent than any lamplighter or scavenger. It was the province of Parliament exclusively to legislate for the particular case. The practical decision of the question was not called for, through the accident of the king's sudden recovery: but in Ireland, from the independence asserted by the two houses of the British councils, the question grew still more complex. The Lord-Lieutenant refused to transmit their address,* and Lord Mornington supported him powerfully in his refusal.

Ten years after this hot collision of parties, Lord Mornington was appointed Governor-General of India; and now first he entered upon a stage worthy of his powers. I cannot myself agree with his biographer, Mr Pearce, that "the wisdom of his policy is now universally recognised;" because the same false views of our Indian position, which at that time caused his splendid services to be slighted in many quarters, still preponderates. All administrations alike have been intensely ignorant of Indian

---

* Which adopted neither view; for, by *offering* the regency of Ireland to the Prince of Wales, they negatived Mr Fox's view, who held it to be the prince's by inherent right, whether offered or not; and, on the other hand, they still more openly opposed Mr Pitt.

politics; and for the natural reason, that the business of home politics leaves them no disposable energies for affairs so distant, and with which each man's chance of any durable connection is so exceedingly small. What Lord Mornington did was this: he looked our prospects in the face. Two great enemies were then looming upon the horizon—viz., Mysore and the Mahrattas—both brutally ignorant of our real resources, and both deluded by our imperfect use of such resources as, even in a previous war, we had possessed. That one of these enemies who first came into play was Tippoo, the Sultan of Mysore: him, by the crushing energy of his arrangements, Lord Mornington was able utterly to destroy; and to distribute his dominions with equity and moderation; yet so as to prevent any new coalition arising in that quarter against the British power. There is a portrait of Tippoo, of this very tiger, more than tiger-hearted, in the second volume of Mr Pearce's work, which expresses sufficiently the unparalleled ferocity of his nature; and it is guaranteed, by its origin, as authentic. Tippoo, from the personal interest investing him, has more fixed the attention of Europe than a much more formidable enemy: that enemy was the Mahratta confederacy, chiefly concentrated in the persons of the Peishwah, of Scindia (usually pronounced Sindy), of Holkar, and the Rajah of Berar. Had these four princes been less profoundly ignorant, had they been less inveterately treacherous, they would have cost us the only* dreadful struggle which in India we have stood. As it

* "*The only dreadful struggle.*"—This was written thirteen years ago, when the Sikh empire of Lahore was only beginning to be dangerous; and the *Lion* of Lahore, Runjeet Sing (the Romulus of the Sikhs), was but dimly appreciated by our own officers, when presented to him on their march to and from Affghanistan. *Sing* means *lion*.

was, Lord Mornington's government reduced and crippled the Mahrattas to such an extent, that in 1817 Lord Hastings found it possible to crush them for ever. Three services of a profounder nature Lord Wellesley was enabled to do for India: first, to pave the way for the propagation of Christianity—mighty service, stretching to the clouds, and which, in the hour of death, must have given him consolation; secondly, to enter upon the abolition of such Hindoo superstitions as are most shocking to humanity, particularly the practice of Suttee, and the barbarous exposure of dying persons or of first-born infants at Saugor on the Ganges; finally, to promote an enlarged system of education, which (if his splendid scheme had been adopted) would have diffused its benefits all over India. It ought also to be mentioned, that the expedition by way of the Red Sea, against the French in Egypt, was so entirely of his suggestion and his preparation, that, to the great dishonour of Messrs Pitt and Dundas, whose administration, great by its general policy, was the worst, as a *war* administration, that ever feebly misapplied or lazily non-applied the resources of a mighty empire, it languished for eighteen months purely through *their* neglect.

In 1805, having staid about seven years in India, Lord Mornington was recalled; was created Marquess Wellesley; was sent, in 1821, as Viceroy to Ireland, where there was little to do; having previously, in 1809, been sent ambassador to the Spanish Cortes, where there was an infinity to do, but no means of doing it. The last great political act of Lord Wellesley was the smashing of the Peel ministry in 1834—viz., by the famous resolution (which he personally drew up) for appropriating to the great purpose of general education in Ireland whatever surplus might arise from the remodelled revenues of the Irish Church. Full of honours, he retired from public affairs at the age of seventy-five; and, for seven years more of life, dedicated his time to such literary pursuits as he had found most interesting in early youth.

Mr Pearce, who is so capable of writing vigorously and sagaciously, has too much allowed himself to rely upon public journals. For example, he reprints the whole of the attorney-general's official information against eleven obscure persons, who, from the gallery of the Dublin theatre, did "wickedly, riotously, and routously"* hiss, groan, insult, and assault (to say nothing of their having *caused and procured to be hissed, groaned, &c.*) the Marquess Wellesley, Lord-Lieutenant General, and General Governor of Ireland. This document covers more than nine pages; and, after all, omits the only fact of the least consequence—viz., that several missiles were thrown by the rioters into the viceregal box, and amongst them a quart-bottle, which barely missed his excellency's temples. Considering the impetus acquired by the descent from the gallery, there is little doubt that such a weapon would have killed Lord Wellesley on the spot. In default, however, of this weighty fact, the attorney-general favours us with memorialising the very best piece of doggerel that I remember to have read—viz., that upon divers (to wit, three thousand) papers the rioters had wickedly and maliciously written and printed, besides, observe, *causing* to be written and printed, "No Popery," as also the following traitorous couplet:—

"The Protestants want Talbot,
As the Papists have got *all but*;"

meaning "all but" that which they got some years later

* *Routously*:—This is not altogether lawyers' surplusage: for, let the hot-blooded reader understand, that to be *routous* is nothing like so criminal in law as to be *riotous*. *I* never go beyond the routous point.

by means of the Clare election, in favour of Dan O'Connell. Yet if, in some instances like this, Mr Pearce has too largely drawn upon official papers, which he should rather have abstracted and condensed, on the other hand, his work has a special value in bringing forward private documents, to which his opportunities have gained him a confidential access. We are indebted to Mr Pearce also for two portraits of Lord Wellesley, one in middle life, and one in old age, from a sketch by the Comte d'Orsay, felicitously executed.

Something remains to be said of Lord Wellesley as a literary man; and towards such a judgment Mr Pearce has contributed some very pleasing materials. As a public speaker, Lord Wellesley had that degree of brilliancy and effectual vigour, which might have been expected in a man of great talents, possessing much native sensibility to the charms of style, but not led by any personal accidents of life into a separate cultivation of oratory, or into any profound investigation of its duties and its powers on the arena of a British senate. There is less call for speaking of Lord Wellesley in this character, where he did not seek for any eminent distinction, than in the more general character of an elegant *litterateur*, which furnished to him much of his recreation in all stages of his life, and much of his consolation in the last. It is interesting to see this accomplished nobleman, in advanced age, when other resources were one by one decaying, and the lights of life were successively fading into darkness, still cheering his languid hours by the culture of classical literature, and in his eighty-second year drawing solace from those same pursuits which had given grace and distinction to his twentieth.

One or two remarks I will make upon Lord Wellesley's

verses—Greek as well as Latin. The Latin lines upon Chantrey's success at Holkham in killing two woodcocks at the first shot, which subsequently he sculptured in marble, and presented to Lord Leicester, are perhaps the most felicitous amongst the whole. Masquerading, in Lord Wellesley's verses, as Praxiteles, who could not well be represented with a Manton having a percussion lock, Chantrey is armed with a bow and arrows:

> "En! trajecit aves una sagitta duas."

In the Greek translation of "Parthenopœus" there are as few faults as could reasonably be expected. But, first, one word as to the original Latin poem: to whom does it belong? It is traced first to Lord Grenville, who received it from his tutor (afterwards Bishop of London), who had taken it as an anonymous poem from the "Censor's book;" and with very little probability, it is doubtfully assigned to "Lewis of the War Office," meaning, no doubt, the father of Monk Lewis. By this anxiety in tracing its pedigree, the reader is led to exaggerate the pretensions of the little poem; these are inconsiderable: and there is a conspicuous fault, which it is worth while noticing, because it is one peculiarly besetting those who write Latin verses with the help of a gradus—viz., that the Pentameter is often a mere reverberation of the preceding Hexameter. Thus, for instance:—

> "Parthenios inter saltus non amplius erro,
> Non repeto Dryadum pascua læta choris;"

and so of others, where the second line is but a variation of the first. Even Ovid, with all his fertility, and partly in consequence of his fertility, too often commits this fault. Where, indeed, the thought is effectually varied, so that the second line acts as a musical *minor*, succeeding to the *major* in the first, there may happen to arise a peculiar beauty. But I speak of the ordinary case, where the second is merely the rebound of the first, presenting the same thought in a diluted form. This is the commonest resource of feeble thinking, and is also a standing temptation or snare for feeble thinking. Lord Wellesley, however, is not answerable for these faults in the original, which, indeed, he notices indulgently as "repetitions;" and his own Greek version is spirited and good. There are, however, some mistakes. The second line is altogether faulty.

Χωρια Μαιναλιῳ παντ' ἐρατεινα θεῳ
'Αχνυμενος λειπων

does not express the sense intended. Construed correctly, this clause of the sentence would mean—"*I sorrowfully leaving all places gracious to the Mænalian god;*" but *that* is not what Lord Wellesley designed: "*I leaving the woods of Cylene, and the snowy summits of Pholoe, places that are all of them dear to Pan*"—*that* is what was meant; that is to say, not *leaving all places dear to Pan*—far from it—but *leaving a few places, every one of which is dear to Pan.* In the line beginning

Καν ἐθ ὑφ' ἡλικιας,

where the meaning is—*and if as yet, by reason of my immature age,* there is a metrical error; and ηλικια will not express immaturity of age. I doubt whether, in the next line,

Μηδ' ἀλκη θαλλοι γουνασιν ἠιθεος,

γουνασιν could convey the meaning without the preposition ἐν. And in

Σπεϱχομαι οὑ καλεουσι θεοι

—*I hasten whither the gods summon me*—οὑ is not the right word: ὁυ is *where*, or *in* what place; but the call is for *whither*, or *to* what place. It is, however, difficult to write Greek verses which shall be liable to no verbal objections; and the fluent movement of these verses sufficiently argues the off-hand ease with which Lord Wellesley must have *read* Greek, writing it so elegantly, and with so little of apparent constraint.

Meantime the most interesting (from its circumstances) of Lord Wellesley's metrical attempts, is one to which his own English interpretation of it has done less than justice. It is a Latin epitaph on the daughter (an *only* daughter) of Lord and Lady Brougham. She died, and (as was generally known at the time) of an organic affection disturbing the action of the heart, at the early age of eighteen. And the peculiar interest of the case lies in the suppression, by this pious daughter (so far as it was possible), of her own bodily anguish, in order to beguile the mental anguish of her parents. The Latin epitaph is this:

"Blanda anima, e cunis heu! longo exercita morbo,
  Inter maternas heu lachrymasque patris,
Quas risu lenire tuo jucunda solebas,
  Et levis, et proprii vix memor ipsa mali;
I, pete calestes, ubi nulla est cura, recessus:
  Et tibi sit nullo mista dolore quies!"

The English version is this:

"Doom'd to long suffering from earliest years,
  Amidst your parents' grief and pain alone
Cheerful and gay, you smiled to soothe their tears;
  And in *their* agonies forgot your own.
Go, gentle spirit! and among the blest
  From grief and pain eternal be thy rest!"

In the Latin, the phrase *e cunis* hardly expresses *from your cradle upwards.* The second line is faulty in the opposition of *maternas,* an adjective, to the substantive *patris;* whilst the repetition of the *heu* in two consecutive lines is ungraceful. In the fourth line, *levis* conveys a false meaning: *levis* must mean either *physically light—i. e.,* not heavy —which is not the sense, or else *tainted with levity,* which is still less the sense. What Lord Wellesley wished to say was *light-hearted:* this he has *not* said; but neither is it easy to say it in good Latin.

I complain, however, of the whole, as not bringing out Lord Wellesley's own feeling—which feeling is partly expressed in his verses, and partly in his accompanying prose note on Miss Brougham's mournful destiny ("her life was a continual illness"), contrasted with her fortitude, her innocent gaiety, and the pious motives under which she supported this gaiety to the last. Not as a direct version, but as filling up the outline of Lord Wellesley, sufficiently indicated by himself, I propose the following

INSCRIPTION FOR THE GRAVE OF THE HON. MARIA BROUGHAM:—

"Child, that for thirteen* years hast fought with pain,
Prompted by joy and depth of filial love,
Rest now at God's command. Oh! not in vain
His angel ofttimes watch'd thee—oft, above
All pangs that would have dimm'd thy parents' eyes,
Saw thy young heart victoriously rise!
Rise now for ever, self-forgetting child!
Rise to those choirs, where love like thine is blest,
From pains of flesh, from filial tears assoil'd—
Love which God's hand shall crown with God's own rest!"

* "*For thirteen:*"—*i. e.*, from the age of five to eighteen, at which age she died.

SCHLOSSER'S LITERARY HISTORY OF THE EIGHTEENTH CENTURY.

In the person of this Mr Schlosser is exemplified a common abuse, not confined to literature. An artist from the Italian opera of London and Paris, making a professional excursion to the French or English provinces, is received deferentially and almost passively according to the tariff of the metropolis; no rural judge being bold enough to dispute decisions coming down from the courts above. In that particular case, there is seldom any reason to complain—since really, out of Germany and Italy, there is no city, if you except Paris and London, possessing musical resources for the composition of an audience large enough to act as a court of revision. It would be presumption in the provincial audience, so slightly trained to good music and dancing, if it should affect to disturb a judgment ratified in the supreme capital. The result, therefore, will be practically just, if the original verdict was just; what was right from the first cannot be made wrong by iteration. Yet, even in such a case, there is something not satisfactory to a delicate sense of equity; for the artist returns from the tour as if from some new and independent triumph, whereas all is but the reverberation of an old one; it seems a new access of sunlight, whereas it is but a reflex illumination from lunar satellites.

In literature, the corresponding case is worse. An author, passing (by means of translation) before a foreign people, ought *de jure* to find himself before a new tribunal; but *de facto* too often he does not. Like the opera artist, but not with the same propriety, he comes before a court that never interferes to unsettle a judgment, but only to re-affirm it. And he returns to his native country, quartering in his armorial bearings these new trophies, as though won by new trials, when, in fact, they are due to servile ratifications of old ones. When Sue or Balzac, Dumas or George Sand, comes before an English audience, the opportunity is invariably lost for estimating the men at a new angle of sight. What is thought of Dumas in Paris? asks the London reviewer; and shapes his notice to catch the *aroma* of the Parisian verdicts just then current. But exactly this is what he should prudently have shunned. He will never learn his own natural and unbiassed opinion of the book when he thus deliberately intercepts all that would have been spontaneous in his impressions, by adulterating with alien views—possibly not even sincere. And thus a new set of judges, that might usefully have modified the narrow views of the old ones, fall by mere *inertia* into the humble character of echoes and sounding-boards to swell the uproar of the original mob.

In this way is thrown away the opportunity, not only of applying corrections to false national tastes, but oftentimes even to the unfair accidents of *luck* that befall books. For it is well known to all who watch literature with vigilance, that books and authors have their fortunes, which travel upon a far different scale of proportions from those that measure their merits. Not even the caprice or the folly of the reading public is required to account for this. Very often, indeed, the whole difference between an extensive circulation for one book, and none at all for another of about equal merit, belongs to no particular blindness in men, but to the simple fact, that the one *has*, whilst the other has *not*, been brought effectually under the eyes of the public. By far the greater part of books are lost, not because they are rejected, but because they are never introduced. In any proper sense of the word, very few books are published. Technically, no doubt, they *are* published; which means, that for ten or twenty times they are *advertised;* but they are not made known to *attentive* ears, or to ears *prepared* for attention. And amongst the causes which account for this difference in the fortune of books, although there are many, we may reckon, as foremost, *personal* accidents of position in the authors. For instance, with us in England, it will do a bad book no *ultimate* service that it is written by a lord, or by a bishop, or by a privy counsellor, or by a member of Parliament; though undoubtedly it will do an *instant* service—it will sell an edition or so. This being the case—it being certain that no rank will reprieve a bad writer from *final* condemnation—the sycophantic glorifier of the public fancies his idol justified; but not so. A bad book, it is true, will not be saved by advantages of position in the author; but a book moderately good will be extravagantly aided by such advantages. "Lectures on Christianity," that happened to be respectably written and delivered, had prodigious success in my young days, because, also, they happened to be lectures of a prelate; three times the ability would not have procured them any attention, had they been the lectures of an obscure curate. Yet, on the other hand, it is but justice to say, that, if written with three times *less* ability, lawn-sleeves would not have given them buoyancy, but, on the contrary, they would have sunk the bishop irrecoverably; whilst the curate, favoured by obscurity, would have survived for another chance. So again, and indeed more than so, as to poetry. Lord Carlisle (not of this generation, but the earl of fifty years back) wrote tolerable verses. They were better than Lord Roscommon's, which, for one hundred and fifty years, the judicious public has allowed the booksellers to incorporate, along with other rubbish of the seventeenth and eighteenth century, into the costly collections of the "British Poets." And really, if you *will* insist on odious comparisons, they were not much below the verses of an amiable prime minister (John Woburn) known to us all. Yet, because they wanted vital *stamina*, not only they fell, but in falling they caused the earl to reel much more than any commoner would have done. Now, on the other hand, a kinsman of Lord Carlisle —viz., Lord Byron—because he brought dazzling genius and power to the effort, found a vast auxiliary advantage in his peerage and his very ancient descent. On these double wings, he soared into a region of public interest far higher than ever he *would* have reached by poetic power alone. Not only all his rubbish—which in quantity is great—passed for jewels, but also what *are* incontestably jewels more gorgeous than the Koh-i-noor, have been, and will be, valued at a far higher rate than if they had been raised from less aristocratic mines. So fatal for mediocrity, so gracious for real power, is any adventitious distinction from birth, from station, or from accidents of brilliant notoriety. In reality, the public, our never-sufficiently-to-be-respected mother, is the most unutterable sycophant that ever the clouds dropped their rheum upon.

She is always ready for Jacobinical scoffs at a man for being a lord, if he happens to fail; she is always ready for toadying a lord, if he happens to make a hit. Ah, dear sycophantic old lady! I kiss your sycophantic hands, and wish heartily that I were a duke for your sake!

It would be a mistake to fancy that this tendency to confound real merit and its accidents of position is at all peculiar to us or to our age. Dr Sacheverell, by embarking his small capital of talent on the spring-tide of a furious political collision between the Whigs and Tories, brought back an ampler return for his little investment than ever did Wickliffe or Luther. Such was his popularity, in the heart of love and the heart of hatred, that he would have been assassinated by the Whigs, on his triumphal progresses through England, had he not been canonised by the Tories. He was a dead man, if he had not been suddenly gilt and lacquered as an idol. Neither is the case peculiar at all to England. Ronge, the *ci-devant* Romish priest (whose name pronounce as you would the English word *wrong*, supposing that it had for a second syllable the final *a* of "sopha"—*i. e., Wronguh*), has been found a wrongheaded man by *all* parties—and in a venial degree is, perhaps, a stupid man; but he moves * about with more *eclat* by far than the ablest man in Germany. And, in days of old, the man that burned down a miracle of beauty—viz., the Temple of Ephesus—protesting, with tears in his eyes, that he had no other way of getting himself a name, *has* got it in spite of us all. He's booked for a ride down through all history, whether you and I like it or not. Every pocket-dictionary knows that Erostratus was that scamp. So of Martin, the man that parboiled, or par-

* Not at all. He *did* move when this was written; but that was in 1847. He is now as sedentary, or as stationary, as a milestone.

roasted, York Minster some twenty years back; that fellow will float down to posterity with the annals of the glorious cathedral: he will

> "Pursue the triumph and partake the gale;"

whilst the founders and benefactors of the Minster are practically forgotten.

These incendiaries, in short, are as well known as Ephesus or York; but not one of us can tell, without humming and hawing, who it was that rebuilt the Ephesian wonder of the world, or that repaired the timehonoured Minster. Equally in literature; not the weight of service done, or the power exerted, is sometimes considered chiefly —either of these must be very conspicuous before it will be considered at all—but the splendour, or the notoriety, or the absurdity, or even the scandalousness, of the circumstances * surrounding the author.

Schlosser must have benefited in some such adventitious way before he ever *could* have risen to his German celebrity. What was it that raised him to his momentary distinction? Was it something very wicked that he did, or something too clever that he said? I should rather conjecture that it must have been something inconceivably absurd which he suggested. Any one of the three achievements stands good in Germany for a reputation. But, however it were that Mr Schlosser first gained his reputation, mark what now follows. On the wings of this equivocal reputation he flies abroad to Paris and London.

* Even Pope, with all his natural and reasonable interest in aristocratic society, could not shut his eyes to the fact that a jest in *his* mouth became twice a jest in a lord's. But still he failed to perceive what I am here contending for, that if the jest happened to miss fire, through the misfortune of bursting its barrel, the consequences would be far worse for the lord than the commoner. There *is*, you see, a blind sort of compensation.

There he thrives, not by any approving experience or knowledge of his works, but through blind faith in his original German public. And back he flies afterwards to Germany, as if carrying with him new and independent testimonies to his merit, and from two nations that are directly concerned in his violent judgments; whereas (which is the simple truth) he carries back a careless reverberation of his first German character, from those who have far too much to read for declining aid from vicarious criticism when it will spare that effort to themselves. Schlosser has simply had his old passport *vise'd* up and down Europe; fresh passports he has none to show. Thus it is that German critics become audacious and libellous. Kohl, Von Raumer, Dr Carus, physician to the King of Saxony, by means of introductory letters floating them into circles far above any they had seen in homely Germany, are qualified by our own negligence and indulgence for mounting a European tribunal, from which they pronounce malicious edicts against ourselves. Sentinels presented arms to Von Raumer at Windsor, because he rode in a carriage of Queen Adelaide's; and Von Raumer immediately conceived himself the Chancellor of all Christendom, keeper of the conscience to universal Europe, upon all questions of art, manners, politics, or any conceivable intellectual relations of England. Schlosser meditates the same career.

But have I any right to quote Schlosser's words from an English translation? I do so only because this happens to be at hand, and the German not. German books are still rare in this country, though more numerous (by one thousand to one) than they were thirty years ago. But I have a special right to rely on the English of Mr Davison. "I hold in my hand," as gentlemen so often say at public meetings, "a certificate from Herr Schlosser, that to quote Mr Davison is to quote *him*." The English translation is one which Mr Schlosser "*durchgelesen hat, und für deren genauigkeit und richtigkeit er bürgt*" [has read through, and for the accuracy and propriety of which he pledges himself]. Mr Schlosser was so anxious for the spiritual welfare of us poor islanders, that he not only read it through, but he has even *aufmerksam durchgelesen* it [read it through wide awake], *und geprüft* [and carefully examined it]; nay, he has done all this in company with the translator. "Oh, ye Athenians! how hard do I labour to earn your applause!" And, as the result of such Herculean labours, a second time he makes himself surety for its precision; "*er bürgt also dafür wie für seine eigne arbeit*" [he guarantees it accordingly as he would his own workmanship]. Were it not for this unlimited guarantee, I should have sent for the book to Germany. As it is, I need not wait; and all complaints on this score I defy, above all from Herr Schlosser.*

---

* Mr Schlosser, who speaks English, who has read rather too much English for any good that he has turned it to, and who ought to have a keen eye for the English version of his own book, after so much reading and study of it, has, however, overlooked several manifest errors. I do not mean to tax Mr Davison with general inaccuracy. On the contrary, he seems wary, and in most cases successful as a dealer with the peculiarities of the German. But several cases of error I detect without needing the original: they tell their own story. And one of these I here notice, not only for its own importance, but out of love to Schlosser, and by way of nailing his guarantee to the counter—not altogether as a bad shilling, but as a light one. At p. 5 of vol. ii., in a foot-note, which is speaking of Kant, we read of his *attempt to introduce the notion of negative greatness into philosophy. Negative greatness!* What strange bird may *that* be? Is it the *ornithorynchus paradoxus?* Mr Schlosser was not wide awake *there*. The reference is evidently to Kant's essay upon the advantages of introducing into philosophy the algebraic idea of *negative quantities*. It is one of Kant's grandest gleams into hidden truth. Were it only for the merits of this most masterly essay in reconstituting

In dealing with an author so desultory as Mr Schlosser, the critic has a right to an *extra* allowance of desultoriness for his own share; so excuse me, reader, for rushing at once into angry business.

Of Swift, Mr Schlosser selects for notice three works—the "Drapier's Letters," "Gulliver's Travels," and the "Tale of a Tub." With respect to the first, as it is a necessity of Mr S. to be for ever wrong in his substratum of facts, he adopts the old erroneous account of Wood's contract as to the copper coinage, and of the imaginary wrong which it inflicted on Ireland. Of all Swift's villanies for the sake of popularity, and still more for the sake of wielding this popularity vindictively, none is so scandalous as this. In any new Life of Swift the case must be stated *de novo*. Even Sir Walter Scott is not impartial; and for the same reason as now forces me to blink it—viz., the difficulty of presenting the details in a readable shape. "Gulliver's Travels" Schlosser strangely considers "spun out to an intolerable extent." Many evil things might be said of Gulliver; but not this. The captain is anything but tedious. And, indeed, it becomes a question of mere mensuration, that can be settled in a moment. A year or two since I had in my hands a pocket edition, comprehending all the four parts of the worthy skipper's adventures within a single volume of 420 pages. Some part of the space was also wasted on notes, often very

the algebraic meaning of a *negative quantity* [so generally misunderstood as a *negation* of quantity, and which even Sir Isaac Newton misconstrued as regarded its metaphysics], great would have been the service rendered to logic by Kant. But there is a greater. From this little *brochure* I am satisfied was derived originally the German regeneration of the Dynamic philosophy, its expansion through the idea of polarity, indifference, &c. Oh, Mr Schlosser, you had not *geprüft* p. 5 of vol. ii. You skipped the notes.

idle. Now the first part contains *two* separate voyages (Lilliput and Blefescu); the 2d, *one;* the 3d, *five;* and the 4th, *one;* so that, in all, this active navigator, who has enriched geography, I hope, with something of a higher quality than your old muffs that thought much of doubling Cape Horn, here gives us *nine* great voyages of discovery far more surprising than the pretended discoveries of Sinbad (which are known to be fabulous), averaging *quam proximè* forty-seven 16mo pages each. Oh, you unconscionable German, built round in your own country with circumvallations of impregnable 4tos, oftentimes dark and dull as Avernus—that you will have the face to describe dear excellent Captain Lemuel Gulliver of Redriff, and subsequently of Newark, that "darling of children and men," as tedious. It is exactly because he is *not* tedious, because he does not shoot into German foliosity, that Schlosser finds him "*intolerable.*" I have justly transferred to Gulliver's use the words, "darling of children and men," originally applied by the poet* to the robin-redbreast; for it is remarkable that "Gulliver" and the "Arabian Nights" are amongst the few books where children and men find themselves meeting and jostling each other. This was the case from its first publication, just one hundred and thirty years since. "It was received," says Dr Johnson, "with such avidity, that the price of the first edition was raised before the second could be made—it was read by the high and the low, the learned and the illiterate. Criticism was lost in wonder." Now, on the contrary, Schlosser wonders not at all, but simply criticises; which we could bear, if the criticism were even ingenious. Whereas, he utterly misunderstands

* "*By the poet:*"—viz., Wordsworth.

Swift; and is a malicious calumniator of the captain; who, luckily, roaming in Sherwood Forest, and thinking, often with a sigh, of his little nurse,* Glumdalclitch, would trouble himself slightly about what Heidelberg might say in the next century. There is but one example on our earth of a novel received with such indiscriminate applause as "Gulliver;" and *that* was "Don Quixote." Many have been welcomed joyfully by a class—these two by a people. Now, could that have happened had it been characterised by dulness? Of all faults, it could least have had *that*. As to the "Tale of a Tub," Schlosser is in such Cimmerian vapours, that no system of bellows could blow open a shaft or tube through which he might gain a glimpse of the English truth and daylight, or we gain a glimpse of Schlosser sitting over his German black-beer. It is useless talking to such a man on such a subject. I consign him to the attentions of some patriotic Irishman.

Schlosser, however, is right in a graver reflection which he makes upon the prevailing philosophy of Swift—viz., that "all his views were directed towards what was *immediately* beneficial, which is the characteristic of savages."

---

* "*Little nurse:*"—The word *Glumdalclitch*, in Brobdingnagian, absolutely *means little nurse*, and nothing else. It may seem odd that the captain should call any nurse of Brobdingnag, however kind to him, by such an epithet as *little;* and the reader may fancy that Sherwood Forest had put it into his head, where Robin Hood always called his right hand man "Little John," not *although*, but expressly *because* John stood seven feet high in his stockings. But the truth is, that Glumdalclitch *was* little; and literally so; she was only nine years old, and (says the captain) "little of her age," being barely forty feet high. She had time to grow certainly, but, as she had so much to do before she could overtake other women, it is probable that she would turn out what, in Westmoreland, they call a *little stiffenger*—very little, if at all, higher than a common English church steeple.

This is undeniable. The meanness of Swift's nature, and his rigid incapacity for dealing with the grandeurs of the human spirit, with religion, with poetry, or even with science, when it rose above the mercenary practical, is absolutely appalling. His own *yahoo* is not a more abominable one-sided degradation of humanity, than is he himself under this aspect. And, perhaps, it places this incapacity of his in its strongest light, when we recur to the fact of his *astonishment* at a religious princess refusing to confer a bishoprick upon one that had treated the Trinity, and all the profoundest mysteries of Christianity, not with mere scepticism or casual sneer, but with set pompous merriment and farcical buffoonery. This dignitary of the church, Dean of the most conspicuous cathedral in Ireland, had, in full canonicals, made himself into a regular mountebank, for the sake of giving fuller effect, by the force of contrast, to the silliest of jests directed against all that was most inalienable from Christianity. Ridiculing such things, could he, in any just sense, be thought a Christian? But, as Schlosser justly remarks, even ridiculing the peculiarities of Luther and Calvin as he *did* ridicule them, Swift could not be thought other than constitutionally incapable of religion. Even a Pagan philosopher, if made to understand the case, would be incapable of scoffing at any *form*, natural or casual, simple or distorted, which might be assumed by the most solemn of problems—problems that rest with the weight of worlds upon the human spirit—

"Fix'd fate, free-will, foreknowledge absolute"—

the destiny of man, or the relations of man to God. Anger, therefore, Swift *might* feel, and he felt it* to the end of his most wretched life; but what reasonable ground had

* See his bitter letters to Lady Suffolk.

a man of sense for *astonishment* that a princess, who (according to her knowledge) was sincerely pious, should decline to place such a man upon an episcopal throne? This argues, beyond a doubt, that Swift was in that state of constitutional irreligion—irreligion not from intellectual scepticism, but from a vulgar temperament—which imputes to everybody else its own plebeian feelings. People differed, he fancied, not by more and less religion, but by more and less dissimulation. And, therefore, it seemed to him scandalous that a princess, who must, of course, in her heart regard (in common with himself) all mysteries as solemn masks and mummeries, should pretend, in a case of downright serious business, to pump up, out of dry conventional hoaxes, any solid objection to a man of his shining merit. "*The Trinity*," for instance, *that* he viewed as the password which the knowing ones gave in answer to the challenge of the sentinel; but, as soon as it had obtained admission for the party within the gates of the camp, it was rightly dismissed to oblivion or to laughter. No case so much illustrates Swift's essential irreligion; since, if he had shared in ordinary human feelings on such subjects, not only he could not have been surprised at his own exclusion from the bench of bishops, *after* such ribaldries, but originally he would have abstained from them as inevitable bars to clerical promotion, even upon principles of public decorum.

As to the *style* of Swift, Mr Schlosser shows himself without sensibility in his objections, as the hackneyed English reader shows himself without philosophic knowledge of style in his applause. Schlosser thinks the style of Gulliver "somewhat dull." This shows Schlosser's presumption in speaking upon a point where he wanted, first, original delicacy of tact; and, secondly, familiar knowledge of English. Gulliver's style is *purposely* touched slightly with that dulness of circumstantiality which besets the excellent, but somewhat dull race of men, old sea-captains. Yet it wears only an aerial tint of dulness; the felicity of this colouring in Swift's management is, that it never goes the length of actually wearying, but only of giving a comic air of downright Wapping and Rotherhithe verisimilitude. All men grow dull, and ought to be dull, that live under a solemn sense of eternal danger, one inch only of plank (often worm-eaten) between themselves and eternity; and also that see for ever one wilderness of waters—sublime, but (like the wilderness on shore) monotonous. All sublime people, being monotonous, have a tendency to be dull, and sublime things also. Milton and Æschylus, the sublimest of men, are crossed at times by a shade of dulness. So is Bilidulgerid, so is the Sahara, so is the sea. Dulness is their weak side. But as to a sea-captain, a regular nor'-nor'-wester, and sou'-sou'-easter, he ought to be kicked out of the room if he is *not* dull. It is not "ship-shape," or barely tolerable, that he should be otherwise. Yet, after all, considering what I have stated about Captain Gulliver's nine voyages crowded into one pocket volume, he cannot really have much abused his professional license for being dull. Indeed, one has to look out an excuse for his being so little dull; which excuse is found in the fact that he had studied three years at a learned university. Captain Gulliver, though a sailor, I would have you to know, was a gownsman of Cambridge: so says Swift, who knew more about the captain than anybody now-a-days.

Now, on the other hand, you, commonplace reader, that (as an old tradition) believe Swift's style to be a model of excellence, hereafter I shall say a word to you, drawn from deeper principles. At present I content myself with these three propositions, which overthrow if you can:—

1. That the merit, which justly you ascribe to Swift, is *vernacularity;* and nothing better or finer; he never forgets his mother-tongue in exotic forms, unless we may call Irish exotic; for some Hibernicisms he certainly has. This merit, however, is exhibited—not, as *you* fancy, in a graceful artlessness, but in a coarse inartificiality. To be artless, and to be inartificial, are very different things; as different as being natural and being gross; as different as being simple and being homely.

2. That whatever, meantime, be the particular sort of excellence, or the value of the excellence, in the style of Swift, he had it in common with multitudes beside of that age. Defoe wrote a style for all the world the same as to kind and degree of excellence, only pure from Hibernicisms. So did every honest skipper (Dampier was something more) who had occasion to record his voyages in this world of storms. So did many a hundred of religious writers. And what wonder should there be in this, when the main qualification for such a style was plain good sense, natural feeling, unpretendingness, some little scholarly practice in putting together the clockwork of sentences, so as to avoid mechanical awkwardness of construction; but above all the advantage of a *subject,* such in its nature as instinctively to reject ornament, lest it should draw off attention from itself? Such subjects are common; but grand impassioned subjects insist upon a different treatment; and *there* it is that the true difficulties of style commence; and there it is that your worshipful Master Jonathan would have broke down irrecoverably.

3. [Which partly is suggested by the last remark.] That nearly all the blockheads with whom I have at any

time had the pleasure of conversing upon the subject of style (and pardon me for saying that men of the most sense are apt, upon two subjects—viz., poetry and style—to talk *most* like blockheads), have invariably regarded Swift's style not as if *relatively* good [*i. e.*, *given* a proper subject], but as if *absolutely* good—good unconditionally, no matter what the subject. Now, my friend, suppose the case, that the Dean had been required to write a pendant for Sir Walter Raleigh's immortal apostrophe to Death, or to many passages that I could select in Sir Thomas Brown's "Religio Medici," and his "Urn-burial," or to Jeremy Taylor's inaugural sections of his "Holy Living and Dying," do you know what would have happened? Are you aware what sort of ridiculous figure your poor bald Jonathan would have cut? About the same that would be cut by a forlorn scullion from a greasy eating-house at Rotterdam, if suddenly called away in vision to act as seneschal to the festival of Belshazzar the king, before a thousand of his lords.

Schlosser, after saying anything right and true (and he really did say the true thing about Swift's *essential* irreligion), usually becomes exhausted, like a boa-constrictor after eating his half-yearly dinner. The boa gathers himself up, it is to be hoped, for a long fit of dyspepsy, in which the horns and hoofs that he has swallowed may chance to avenge the poor goat that owned them. Schlosser, on the other hand, retires into a corner, for the purpose of obstinately talking nonsense, until the gong sounds again for a slight refection of sense. Accordingly he likens Swift, before he has done with him, to whom? I might safely allow the reader three years for guessing, if the greatest of wagers were depending between us. He likens him to Kotzebue, in the first place. How faithful the resemblance! How exactly Swift reminds you of Count Benyowski in Siberia, and of Mrs Haller mopping her eyes in the "Stranger!" One really is puzzled to say, according to the negro's distinction, whether Mrs Haller is more like the Dean of St Patrick's, or the Dean more like Mrs Haller. Anyhow, the likeness is prodigious, if it is not quite reciprocal. The other *terminus* of the comparison is Wieland. Now there *is* some shadow of a resemblance there. For Wieland had a touch of the comico-cynical in his nature; and it is notorious that he was often called the German Voltaire, which argues some tiger-monkey grin that traversed his features at intervals. Wieland's malice, however, was far more playful and genial than Swift's; something of this is shown in his romance of "Idris," and oftentimes in his prose. But what the world knows Wieland by is his "Oberon." Now in this gay, musical romance of Sir Huon and his enchanted horn, with its gleams of voluptuousness, is there a possibility that any suggestion of a scowling face like Swift's should cross the festal scenes?

From Swift the scene changes to Addison and Steele. Steele is of less importance; for, though a man of greater intellectual activity* than Addison, he had immeasurably

* "*Activity.*"—It is some sign of this, as well as of the more thoroughly English taste in literature which distinguished Steele, that hardly twice throughout the "Spectator" is Shakspere quoted or alluded to by Addison. Even those quotations he had from the theatre, or the breath of popular talk. Generally, if you see a line from Shakspere, it is safe to bet largely that the paper is Steele's; sometimes, indeed, of casual contributors; but, almost to a certainty, *not* a paper of Addison's. Another mark of Steele's superiority in vigour of intellect is, that much oftener in *him* than in other contributors strong thoughts came forward; harsh and disproportioned, perhaps to the case, and never harmoniously developed with the genial grace of Addison, but original, and pregnant with promise and suggestion.

less of genius. But, so far as concerns Addison, I am happy to support the character of Schlosser for consistency, by assuring the reader that, of all the monstrosities uttered by man upon Addison, and of all the monstrosities uttered by Schlosser upon man, a thing which he says about Addison is the worst. But this I reserve for a climax ahead. Schlosser really puts his best leg foremost at starting, and one thinks he's going to mend; for he catches a truth—viz., the following—that all the brilliancies of the Queen Anne period (which so many inconsiderate people have called the Augustan age of our literature) "point to this: that the reading public wished to be entertained, not roused to think; to be gently moved, not deeply excited." Undoubtedly what strikes a man in Addison, or *will* strike him when indicated, is the coyness and timidity, almost the girlish shame, which he betrays in the presence of all the elementary majesties belonging to impassioned or idealised human nature. Like one bred in crowded cities, when first left alone in forests or amongst mountains, he is frightened at their silence, their solitude, their magnitude of form, or their frowning glooms. It has been remarked by others, that Addison and his companions never rise to the idea of addressing the "nation" or the "people;" it is always the "town." Even their audience was conceived of by *them* under a miniature form. Yet for this they had some excuse in the state of facts. An author would like at this moment to assume that Europe and Asia were listening to him; and as some few copies of his book do really go to Paris and Naples, some to Calcutta, there is a sort of legal fiction that such an assumption is steadily taking root. Yet, unhappily, that ugly barrier of languages interferes. Schamyl, the Circassian chief, though much of a savage, is not so wanting in taste and discernment as to be backward in reading any book of yours or mine. Doubtless he yearns to read it. But then, you see, that infernal *Tchirkass* language steps between our book, the darling, and *him*, the discerning reader. Now just such a barrier existed for the "Spectator" in the travelling arrangements of England. The very few old heavies that had begun to creep along three or four main roads, depended so much on wind and weather, their chances of foundering were so uncalculated, their periods of revolution were so cometary and uncertain, that no body of scientific observations had yet been collected to warrant a man in risking by *them* a heavy bale of goods; and, on the whole, even for York, Norwich, or Winchester, a consignment of "*Specs*" was not quite a safe spec. Still, I could have told the Spectator who was anxious to make money, where he might have been sure of a distant sale, though returns would have been slow —viz., at Oxford and Cambridge. We know from Milton that old Hobson delivered his parcels pretty regularly eighty years before 1710. And, one generation before *that*, it is plain, by the interesting (though somewhat Jacobinical) letters of Joseph Mede,* the commenter on the Apocalypse, that news and politics of one kind or other (and scandal of *every* kind) found out for themselves a sort of contraband lungs to breathe through between London and Cambridge; not quite so regular as the tides of ebb and flood, but better than nothing. If you consigned a packet into the proper hands on the 1st of May, "as sure as death" (to speak *Scotticè*), it would be delivered within sixty miles of the capital before midsummer. Still there were delays; and these forced a man

* "*Letters of Joseph Mede.*"—Published more than thirty years ago by Sir Henry Ellis.

into carving his world out of London. That excuses the word *town*.

Inexcusable, however, were many other forms of expression in those days, which argued cowardly feelings. One would like to see a searching investigation into the state of society in Anne's days—its extreme artificiality, its sheepish reserve upon all the impassioned grandeurs, its shameless outrages upon all the decencies, of human nature. Certain it is, that Addison (because everybody) was in that meanest of conditions which blushes at any expression of sympathy with the lovely, the noble, or the impassioned. The wretches were ashamed of their own nature, and perhaps with reason; for in their own denaturalised hearts they read only a degraded nature. Addison, in particular, shrank from every bold and every profound expression as from an offence against good taste. He durst not for his life have used the word "passion," except in the vulgar sense of an angry paroxysm. He durst as soon have danced a hornpipe on the top of the "Monument," as have talked of a "rapturous emotion." What *would* he have said? Why, "sentiments that were of a nature to prove agreeable after an unusual rate." In their odious verses, the creatures of that age talk of love as something that "burns" them. You suppose at first that they are discoursing of tallow candles, though you cannot imagine by what impertinence they address *you*, that are no tallow-chandler, upon such painful subjects. And, when they apostrophise the woman of their heart (for you are to understand that they pretend to such an organ), they beseech her to "ease their pain." Can human meanness descend lower? As if the man, being ill from pleurisy, therefore had a right to take a lady for one of the dressers in a hospital, whose duty it would be to fix a burgundy-pitch plaster between his shoulders. Then to read of their Phillises and Strephons, and Chloes and Corydons—names that proclaim the fantasticalness of the life with which they are poetically associated—it throws me into such convulsions of rage, that I move to the window, and (without thinking what I am about) throw it up, calling, "*Police! police!*" What's *that* for? What can the police do in the business? Why, certainly nothing. What I meant in my dream was, perhaps [but one forgets *what* one meant upon recovering one's temper], that the police should take Strephon and Corydon into custody, whom I fancied at the other end of the room. And really the justifiable fury that arises upon recalling such abominable attempts at bucolic sentiments in such abominable language, sometimes transports me into a luxurious vision sinking back through one hundred and thirty years, in which I see Addison, Phillips (both John and Ambrose), Tickell, Fickell, Budgell, and Cudgell, with many others beside, all cudgelled in a round-robin, none claiming precedency of another, none able to shrink from his own dividend, until a voice seems to recall me to milder thoughts, by saying, "But surely, my friend, you never could wish to see Addison cudgelled? Let Strephon and Corydon be cudgelled without end, if the police can show any warrant for doing it. But Addison was a man of great genius." True, he was so. I recollect it suddenly, and will back out of any angry things that I have been misled into saying by Schlosser, who, by the by, was right, after all, for a wonder.

Now then I will turn my whole fury in vengeance upon Schlosser. And looking round for a stone to throw at him, I observe this: Addison could not be so entirely careless of exciting the public to think and feel as Schlosser pretends, when he took so much pains to inoculate that public with a sense of the Miltonic grandeur. The "Paradise Lost" had then been published barely forty years, which was nothing in an age without reviews or any other organs of literary advertisement; and though no Addison could eventually promote, for the instant he quickened, the circulation. If I recollect, Tonson's accurate revision of the text followed immediately upon Addison's papers. And it is certain that Addison* must have diffused the knowledge of Milton upon the Continent, from signs that soon followed. But does not this prove that I myself have been in the wrong as well as Schlosser? No; that's impossible. Schlosser is always in the wrong; but it's the next thing to an impossibility that I should be detected in an error: philosophically speaking, it is supposed to involve a contradiction. "But surely I said the very same thing as Schlosser, by assenting to what he said." Maybe I did; but then I have time to make a distinction, because my article is not yet finished; we are only at the beginning; whereas Schlosser can't make any distinction now, because his book is printed; and his list of *errata* (which is shocking, though he does not confess to the thousandth part) is actually published and finished. My distinction is, that, though Addison generally hated the impassioned, and shrank from it as from a fearful thing, yet this was when it combined with forms of life and fleshly realities (as in dramatic works), but not when it combined with elder forms of eternal abstractions. Hence he did not

* It is an idea of many people, and erroneously sanctioned by Wordsworth, that Lord Somers gave a powerful lift to the "Paradise Lost." He was a subscriber to the sixth edition, the first that had plates; but this was some years before the Revolution of 1688, and when he was simply *Mr* Somers, a barrister, with no effectual power of *literary* patronage.

read, and did not like, Shakspere; the music was here too rapid and life-like: but he sympathised profoundly with the solemn cathedral-chanting of Milton. An appeal to his sympathies which exacted quick changes in those sympathies he could not meet, but a more stationary key of solemnity he *could.* Indeed, this difference is illustrated daily. A long list can be cited of passages in Shakspere which have been solemnly denounced by many eminent men (all blockheads) as ridiculous: and if a man *does* find a passage in a tragedy which displeases him, it is sure to seem ludicrous. Witness the indecent exposures of themselves made by Voltaire, La Harpe, and many billions beside of bilious people. Whereas, of all the shameful people (equally billions and not less bilious) that have presumed to quarrel with Milton, not one has thought him ludicrous, but only dull and somnolent. In "Lear" and in "Hamlet," as in a human face agitated by passion, are many things that tremble on the brink of the ludicrous to an observer endowed with small range of sympathy or intellect. But no man ever found the starry heavens ludicrous, though many find them dull, and prefer, for a near view, a decanter of brandy. So, in the solemn wheelings of the Miltonic movement, Addison could find a sincere delight. But the sublimities of earthly misery and of human frenzy were for him a book sealed. Beside all which, Milton renewed the types of Grecian beauty as to *form;* whilst Shakspere, without designing at all to contradict these types, did so in effect by his fidelity to a new nature, radiating from a Gothic centre.

In the midst, however, of much just feeling, which one could only wish a little deeper, in the Addisonian papers on "Paradise Lost," there are some gross blunders of criticism, as there are in Dr Johnson, and from the self-same cause—an understanding suddenly palsied from defective passion. A feeble capacity of passion must, upon a question of passion, constitute a feeble range of intellect. But, after all, the worst thing uttered by Addison in these papers is not *against* Milton, but meant to be complimentary. Towards enhancing the splendour of the great poem, he tells us that it is a Grecian palace as to amplitude, symmetry, and architectural skill: but, being in the English language, it is to be regarded as if built in brick; whereas, had it been so happy as to be written in Greek, then it would have been a palace built in Parian marble. Indeed? that's smart—"that's handsome, I calculate!" Yet, before a man undertakes to sell his mother-tongue as old pewter trucked against gold, he should be quite sure of his own metallurgic skill; because else the gold that he buys may happen to be copper, and the pewter that he sells to be silver. Are you quite sure, my Addison, that you have understood the powers of this language which you toss away so lightly as an old tea-kettle? Is it a ruled case that you have exhausted its resources? Nobody doubts your grace in a certain line of composition; but it is only one line among many, and it is far from being amongst the highest. It is dangerous, without examination, to sell even old kettles; misers conceal old stockings filled with guineas in old tea-kettles: and we all know that Aladdin's servant, by exchanging an old lamp for a new one, caused an Iliad of calamities: his master's palace jumped from Bagdad to some place on the road to Ashantee; Mrs Aladdin and the piccaninnies were carried off as inside passengers; and Aladdin himself only escaped being lagged for a rogue and a conjurer by a flying jump after his palace. Now, mark the folly of man. Most of the people I am going to mention subscribed generally to the supreme excellence of

Milton, but each wished for a little change to be made, which, and which only, was wanted to perfection. Dr Johnson, though he pretended to be satisfied with the "Paradise Lost," even in what he regarded as the undress of blank verse, still secretly wished it in rhyme. That's No. 1. Addison, though quite content with it in English, still could have wished it in Greek. That's No. 2. Bentley, though admiring the blind old poet in the highest degree, still observed, smilingly, that after all he *was* blind. He, therefore, Slashing Dick,* could have wished that the great man had always been surrounded by honest people; but, as that was not to be, he could have wished that his amanuensis had been hanged; yet, as that also had become impossible, he could wish to do execution upon him in effigy, by sinking, burning, and destroying his handiwork; upon which basis of posthumous justice he proceeded to amputate all the finest passages in the poem. Slashing Dick was No. 3. Payne Knight, who in his own person had rendered services to literature, was a severer man even than Slashing Dick. He professed to look upon the first book of "Paradise Lost" as the finest thing that earth had to show; but, for that very reason, he could have wished, by your leave, to see the other eleven books sawed off, and sent overboard; because, though tolerable perhaps in another situation, they really were a national disgrace when standing behind that unrivalled portico of Book I. There goes No. 4. Then came a fellow, whose name was either not on his title-page, or I have forgotten

* *Slashing* was the characteristic epithet by which Pope described Bentley, in allusion, generally, to Bentley's bold style of practice in critical correction, but specially to his furious ravages up and down the "Paradise Lost," on the plea that Milton's amanuensis, whosoever he might be, had taken a base advantage of the great poet's blindness.

it, that pronounced the poem to be laudable, and full of good materials; but still he could have wished that the materials had been put together in a more workmanlike manner; which kind office he set about himself. He made a general clearance of all lumber; the expression of every thought he entirely re-cast; and he fitted up the metre with beautiful patent rhymes—not, I believe, out of any consideration for Dr Johnson's comfort, but on principles of mere abstract decency; as it was, the poem seemed naked, and yet was not ashamed. There went No. 5. *Him* succeeded a droller fellow than any of the rest. A French bookseller had caused a prose French translation to be made of the "Paradise Lost," without particularly noticing its English origin, or at least not in the title-page. Our friend No. 6, getting hold of this as an original French romance, translated it back into English prose, as a satisfactory novel for the season. His little mistake was at length discovered, and communicated to him with shouts of laughter; on which, after considerable kicking and plunging (for a man cannot but turn restive when he finds that he has not only got the wrong sow by the ear, but actually sold the sow to a bookseller), the poor translator was tamed into sulkiness; in which state he observed that he could have wished his own work, being evidently so much superior to the earliest form of the romance, might be admitted by the courtesy of England to take the precedency as the original "Paradise Lost," and to supersede the very rude performance of "Milton, Mr John." *

Schlosser makes the astounding assertion, that a compli-

* "*Milton, Mr John:*"—Dr Johnson expressed his wrath, in an amusing way, at some bookseller's hack, who, when employed to make an index, introduced Milton's name among the M's, and by way of being particularly civil, as "Milton, Mr John."

ment of Boileau to Addison, and a pure compliment of ceremony upon Addison's early Latin verses, was *(credite posteri!)* the making of Addison in England. Understand, Schlosser, that Addison's Latin verses were never heard of by England, until long after his English prose had fixed the public attention upon him; his Latin reputation, so far from being the foundation upon which he built, was a slight reaction from his English* reputation: and, secondly, understand that Boileau had at no time any such authority in England as to *make* anybody's reputation; he had first of all to make his own. A sure proof of this is, that Boileau's name was first published in London by Prior's burlesque of what the Frenchman had called an ode. This gasconading ode celebrated the passage of the Rhine in 1672, and the capture of a famous fortress ("*le fameux fort de Skink*") by Louis XIV., known to London at the time of Prior's parody by the name of "Louis Baboon."† *That* was not likely to recommend Master Boileau to any of the allies against the said Baboon, had it ever been heard of out of France. Nor was it likely to make him popular in England, that his name was first mentioned amidst shouts of laughter and mockery. It is another argument of the slight notoriety possessed by Boileau in England, that no attempt was ever made to translate even his satires, epistles, or "Lutrin," except by booksellers' hacks; and

* In Oxford, where naturally an academic reputation forestalls for any scholarlike student his more national reputation, some of Addison's Latin verses were probably the ground of his first premature notoriety. But in London, I believe that Addison was first made known by his "Blenheim" in 1704; most assuredly not by any academic exercise whatever.

† "*Louis Baboon*:"—As people read nothing in these days that is more than a month old, I am daily admonished that allusions the most obvious to anything in the rear of our own time need explanation. *Louis Baboon* is Swift's allegorico-jocular name for *Louis Bourbon*—*i. e.*, Louis XIV.

that no such version ever took the slightest root amongst ourselves, spite of Skink, from Addison's day down to our own. Boileau was essentially, and in two senses—viz., both as to mind and as to influence—*un homme borné*.

Addison's "Blenheim" is poor enough; one might think it a translation from some German original of those times. Gottsched's aunt, or Bodmer's wet-nurse, might have written it; but still no fibs even as to "Blenheim." His "enemies" did not say this thing against "Blenheim" "aloud," nor his friends that thing against it "softly." And why? Because at that time (1704–5) he had made no particular enemies, nor any particular friends; unless by friends you mean his Whig patrons, and by enemies his creditors.

As to "Cato," Schlosser, as usual, wanders in the shadow of ancient night. The English "people," it seems, so "extravagantly applauded" this wretched drama, that you might suppose them to have "altogether changed their nature," and to have forgotten Shakspere. That man must have forgotten Shakspere, indeed, and from *ramollissement* of the brain, who could admire "Cato." "But," says Schlosser, "it was only a 'fashion;' and the English soon repented." The English could not repent of a crime which they had never committed. Cato was not popular for a moment, nor tolerated for a moment, upon any literary ground, or as a work of art. It was an apple of temptation and strife thrown by the goddess of faction between two infuriated parties. "Cato," coming from a man without parliamentary connections, would have dropped lifeless to the ground. The Whigs have always affected a special love and favour for popular counsels: they have never ceased to give themselves the best of characters as regards public freedom. The Tories, as contradistinguished from the Jacobites, knowing that without *their* aid, the Revolution could not have been carried, most justly contended that the national liberties had been at least as much indebted to themselves. When, therefore, the Whigs put forth *their* man Cato to mouth speeches about liberty, as exclusively *their* pet, and about patriotism and all that sort of thing, saying insultingly to the Tories, "How do you like *that?* Does *that* sting?" "Sting, indeed!" replied the Tories; "not at all; it's quite refreshing to us, that the Whigs have not utterly disowned such sentiments, which, by their public acts, we really thought they *had.*" And, accordingly, as the popular anecdote tells us, a Tory leader, Lord Bolingbroke, sent for Booth, who performed Cato, and presented him *(populo spectante)* with fifty guineas "for defending so well the cause of the people against a perpetual dictator." In which words, observe, Lord Bolingbroke at once asserted the cause of his own party, and launched a sarcasm against a great individual opponent—viz., Marlborough. Now, Mr Schlosser, I have mended your harness: all right ahead: so drive on once more.

But, oh Castor and Pollux, whither—in what direction is it that the man is driving us? Positively, Schlosser, you must stop and let *me* get out. I'll go no further with such a drunken coachman. Many another absurd thing I was going to have noticed, such as his utter perversion of what Mandeville said about Addison (viz., by suppressing one word, and misapprehending all the rest). Such, again, as his point-blank misstatement of Addison's infirmity in his official character, which was *not* that "he could not prepare despatches in a good style," but diametrically the opposite case: that he insisted—so microscopically insisted on scruples of diction, that a serious retardation was threatened to the course of public business. But all these things are as nothing to what Schlosser says elsewhere. He actually describes Addison, on the whole, as a "dull prosaist," and the patron of pedantry! Addison, the man of all that ever lived most hostile even to what was good in pedantry, to its tendencies towards the profound in erudition, to its minute precision and the non-popular; Addison, the champion of all that is easy, natural, superficial—Addison a pedant, and a patron of pedantry!

Pope, by far the most important writer, English or continental, of his own age, is treated with more extensive ignorance by Mr Schlosser than any other, and (excepting Addison) with more ambitious injustice. A false abstract is given, or a false impression, of any one amongst his brilliant works, that is noticed at all; and a false sneer, a sneer irrelevant to the case, at any work dismissed by name as unworthy of notice. The three works selected as the gems of Pope's collection are, the "Essay on Criticism," the "Rape of the Lock," and the "Essay on Man." On the first, which (with Dr Johnson's leave) is the feeblest and least interesting of Pope's writings, being substantially a mere versification, like a metrical multiplication-table, of commonplaces the most mouldy with which criticism has baited its rat-traps; since nothing is said worth answering, it is sufficient to answer nothing. The "Rape of the Lock" is treated with the same delicate sensibility that we might have looked for in Brennus, if consulted on the picturesque, or in Attila the Hun, if adjured to decide æsthetically between two rival cameos. Attila is said (though no doubt falsely) to have described himself as not properly a man so much as the divine wrath incarnate. This would be fine in a melodrama, with Bengal lights burning on the stage. But, if ever he said such a naughty thing, he forgot to tell us what it was that had made him angry. By what *title* did *he* come into alliance with the divine wrath, which was not likely to consult a savage? And why did his wrath hurry, by forced marches, to the Adriatic? Now so much do people differ in opinion, that, to me, who look at him through a telescope from an eminence, fourteen centuries distant, he takes the shape rather of a Mahratta trooper painfully gathering *chout*, or a Scottish cateran levying black-mail, or a decent tax-gatherer with an ink-horn at his button-hole, and supported by a select party of constabulary friends. The very natural instinct which Attila always showed for following the trail of the wealthiest footsteps, seems to argue a most commercial coolness in the dispensation of his wrath. Mr Schlosser burns with the wrath of Attila against all aristocracies, and especially that of England. He governs his fury, also, with an Attila discretion in many cases; but not here. Imagine this Hun coming down, sword in hand, upon Pope and his Rosicrucian light troops, levying *chout* upon Sir Plume, and fluttering the dove-cot of the Sylphs. Pope's "duty it was," says this demoniac, to "scourge the follies of good society," and also "to break with the aristocracy." No, surely? something short of a total rupture would have satisfied the claims of duty? Possibly; but it would not have satisfied Schlosser. And Pope's guilt consists in having made his poem an idyl or succession of pictures representing the gayer aspects of society as it really was, and supported by a comic interest of the mock-heroic derived from a playful machinery, instead of converting it into a bloody satire. Pope, however, did not shrink from such assaults on the aristocracy, if these made any part of his duties. Such assaults he did actually make four times over, and twice at least* too often for his own peace, and

* "*Twice at least:*"—Viz., upon Aaron Hill, and upon the Duke of Chandos. In both cases the aggrieved parties sharpened the edge of the

perhaps for his credit at this day. It is useless, however, to talk of the poem as a work of art, with one who sees none of its exquisite graces, and can imagine his countryman Zachariä equal to a competition with Pope. But this it may be right to add, that the "Rape of the Lock" was *not* borrowed from the "Lutrin" of Boileau. That was impossible. Neither was it suggested by the "Lutrin." The story in Herodotus of the wars between cranes and pigmies, or the "Batrachomyomachia" (so absurdly ascribed to Homer), was *more* likely, though very unlikely, to have suggested the idea. Both these there is proof that Pope had read: there is none that he had read the "Lutrin;" nor did he read French with ease to himself. The "Lutrin," meantime, is as much below the "Rape of the Lock" in brilliancy of treatment, and in the festive gaiety of its incidents, as it is dissimilar in plan and in the quality of its pictures.

The "Essay on Man" is a more thorny subject. When a writer finds himself attacked and defended from all quarters, and on all varieties of principle, he is bewildered. Friends are as dangerous as enemies. He must not defy a bristling enemy, if he cares for repose; he must not disown a zealous defender, though defending him perhaps on a principle potentially ruinous, and making concessions on his own behalf abominable to himself; he must not explain away ugly phrases in one direction, or perhaps he is recanting the very words of his "guide, philosopher, and

---

unprovoked assault by the dignity of their own behaviour, by their command of temper, and by their manly disdain of all attempts to retaliate, by undervaluing their splendid assailant. Evil is the day for a conscientious man, when his sole resource for self-defence lies in a falsehood. And such, unhappily, was Pope's situation. His assaults upon Lady M. W. Montagu, and upon the two Duchesses of Marlborough, stand upon another basis.

friend;" he must not explain them away in another direction, or he runs full tilt into the wrath of mother Church —who will soon bring him to his senses by penance and discipline. Long Lents, and no lampreys allowed, would soon cauferise the proud flesh of heretical ethics. Pope did wisely, situated as he was, in a decorous nation, and closely connected, upon motives of honourable fidelity under political suffering, with the Roman Catholics, to say little in his own defence. That defence, and any reversionary cudgelling which it might entail upon the Quixote undertaker, he left—meekly but also slyly, humbly but yet cunningly—to those whom he professed to regard as greater philosophers than himself. All parties found their account in the affair. Pope slept in peace; several pugnacious gentlemen up and down Europe expectorated much fiery wrath in dusting each other's jackets; and Warburton, the attorney, ultimately earned his bishoprick in the service of whitewashing a writer, who was aghast at finding himself first trampled on as a deist, and then enthroned as a defender of the faith. Meantime, Mr Schlosser misinterprets Pope's courtesy, when he supposes his acknowledgments to Lord Bolingbroke sincere in their whole extent.

Of Pope's "Homer" Schlosser thinks fit to say, amongst other evil things, which it really *does* deserve (though hardly in comparison with the German hexametrical "Homer" of the ear-splitting Voss), "that Pope pocketed the subscription of the 'Odyssey,' and left the work to be done by his understrappers." Don't tell fibs, Schlosser. Never do *that* any more. True it is, and disgraceful enough in itself without lying, that Pope (like modern contractors for a railway or a loan) let off to sub-contractors several portions of the undertaking. He was perhaps not illiberal in the terms of his contracts. At least I know of people now-a-days (much better artists) that would execute such contracts, and enter into any penalties for keeping time, at thirty per cent. less. But *navvies* and bill-brokers, that are in excess now, then were scarce. Still the affair, though not mercenary, was illiberal in a higher sense of art; and no anecdote shows more pointedly Pope's sense of the mechanic fashion, in which his own previous share of the Homeric labour had been executed. It was disgraceful enough, and needs no exaggeration. Let it, therefore, be reported truly: Pope personally translated one-half of the "Odyssey"—a dozen books he turned out of his own oven; and, if you add the "Batrachomyomachia," his dozen was a baker's dozen. The journeymen did the other twelve; were regularly paid; regularly turned off when the job was out of hand; and never once had to "strike for wages." How much beer was allowed, I cannot say. This is the truth of the matter. So no more fibbing, Schlosser, if you please.

But there remains behind all these labours of Pope the "Dunciad," which is by far his greatest. I shall not, within narrow bounds, enter upon a theme so exacting; for in this instance I should have to fight not against Schlosser only, but against Dr Johnson, who has thoroughly misrepresented the nature of the "Dunciad," and consequently could not measure its merits. Neither he, nor Schlosser, in fact, ever read more than a few passages of this admirable poem. But the villany is too great for a brief exposure. One thing only I will notice of Schlosser's misrepresentations. He asserts (not when directly speaking of Pope, but afterwards, under the nead of Voltaire) that the French author's trivial and random "Temple de Gout" "shows the superiority in this species of poetry to have been greatly on the side of the Frenchman." Let us hear a reason, though but a Schlosser reason, for this opinion. Know, then, all men whom it concerns, that "the Englishman's satire only hit such people as would never have been known without his mention of them, whilst Voltaire selected those who were *still* (meaning even in Voltaire's day) called great, and their respective schools." Pope's men, it seems, never *had* been famous —Voltaire's might possibly cease to be so, but as yet they had *not* ceased; as yet they commanded interest. Now mark how I will put three bullets into that plank, riddle it so that the leak shall not be stopped by all the old hats in Heidelberg, and Schlosser will have to swim for his life. First, he is forgetting that, by his own previous confession, Voltaire, not less than Pope, had "immortalised a great many *insignificant* persons;" consequently, had it been any fault to do so, each alike was caught in that fault; and insignificant as the people might be, if they *could* be "immortalised," then we have Schlosser himself confessing to the possibility that poetic emblazonries might create a secondary interest where originally there had been none: a concession which is abundantly sufficient for the justification of Pope. Secondly, the question of merit does not graduate itself by the object of the archer, but by the style of his archery. Not the choice of victims, but the execution done is what counts. Even for continued failures it would plead advantageously, much more for continued and brilliant successes, that Pope fired at an object offering no sufficient breadth of mark. Thirdly, it is the grossest of blunders to say that Pope's objects of satire were obscure by comparison with Voltaire's. Grant that the Frenchman's example of a scholar—viz., the French Salmasius—was commandingly impressive. But so was the Englishman's scholar—viz., the English Bentley. Each was absolutely without a rival in his own day. Meantime, the day of Bentley was the very day of Pope. Pope's man had not even *begun* to fade; whereas the day of Salmasius, as respected Voltaire, had gone by for more than half-a-century. As to Dacier, whom Schlosser cites, *which* Dacier? "which king Bezonian?" The husband was a good* scholar; but madame was a poor sneaking fellow, fit only for the usher of a boarding-school. All this, however, argues Schlosser's twofold ignorance—first, of English authors; secondly, of the "Dunciad;"—else he would have known that even Dennis, mad John Dennis, was a much cleverer man than most of those alluded to by Voltaire. Cibber, though slightly a coxcomb, was born a brilliant man. Aaron Hill was so lustrous, that even Pope's venom (and by Pope's own confession) fell off spontaneously from *him*, like rain from oily plumage, leaving him to "mount far upwards with the swans of Thames;" and, finally, let it not be forgotten, that Samuel Clark, for one; Burnet, of the Charterhouse,† for a second; and Sir Isaac Newton, for a third, did not wholly escape Pope's knout. Now, if *that*

---

* See his edition of "Horace" in nine volumes, from which any man may learn, and be thankful.

† "*Burnet of the Charterhouse:*"—Let not the reader confound this Burnet with Gilbert Burnet, the Bishop of Salisbury. The latter was a gossiper, a slanderer, and, by the Duchess of Portsmouth's report, so notorious a falsifier of facts, that to repeat a story on *his* authority was—to insure its scoffing rejection by the whole court. Such was his character in that section of Europe (viz., the Court of Whitehall in the days of Charles II.) where he was most familiarly and experimentally known. That one of his sermons was burned by the hangman under orders from the House of Commons, is the sole consolatory fact in his most worldly career. Would there have been much harm in tying his lordship to the sermon? But the other Burnet, though too early for a sound Cosmogony (anarchon ara kai ateleutaion to Pan), was amongst the elect of earth by his eloquence.

rather impeaches the equity, and sometimes the judgment, of Pope, at least it contributes to show the groundlessness of Schlosser's objection — that the population of the "Dunciad," the characters that filled its stage, were inconsiderable.

FOX AND BURKE.

It is, or it *would* be, if Mr Schlosser were himself more interesting, a luxury to pursue his ignorance as to facts, and the craziness of his judgment as to the valuation of minds, throughout his comparison of Burke with Fox. The force of antithesis brings out into a feeble life of meaning what, in its own insulation, had been languishing mortally into nonsense. The darkness of Schlosser's "Burke" becomes *visible* darkness under the glimmering that steals over it from the desperate commonplaces of his "Fox." Fox is painted exactly as he *would* have been painted fifty years ago by any pet subaltern of the Whig Club, enjoying free pasture in Devonshire House. The practised reader knows well what is coming. Fox is "formed after the model of the ancients"—Fox is "simple"—Fox is "natural"—Fox is "chaste"—Fox is "forcible." Why, yes, in a sense, Fox is even "forcible:" but then, to feel that he was so, you must have *heard* him; whereas, for fifty-and-one years he has been silent. We of 1858, that can only *read* him, hearing Fox described as *forcible*, are disposed to recollect Shakspere's Mr Feeble amongst Falstaff's recruits, who also is described as *forcible*—viz., as the "most forcible Feeble." And, perhaps, a better description could not be devised for Fox himself —so feeble was he in matter, so forcible in manner; so powerful for instant effect, so impotent for posterity. In the Pythian fury of his gestures—in his screaming voice (for Fox's voice was shrill as a woman's)—in his directness of purpose, Fox would now remind you of some demon steam-engine on a railroad, some Fire-king or Salmoneus, that had counterfeited Jove's thunderbolts; hissing, bubbling, snorting, fuming; demoniac gas, you think—gas from Acheron must feed that dreadful system of convulsions. But pump out the imaginary gas, and, behold! it is ditch-water. Fox, as Mr Schlosser rightly thinks, was all of a piece—simple in his manners, simple in his style, simple in his thoughts. No waters in *him* turbid with new crystallisations; everywhere the eye could see to the bottom. No music in *him* dark with Cassandra meanings. Fox, indeed, disturb decent gentlemen by "allusions to all the sciences, from the integral calculus and metaphysics down to navigation!" Fox would have seen you hanged first. Burke, on the other hand, did all that, and other wickedness besides, which fills an 8vo page in Schlosser; and Schlosser crowns his enormities by charging him, the said Burke (p. 99), with "*wearisome tediousness.*" Among my own acquaintances are several old women, who think on this point precisely as Schlosser thinks; and they go further, for they even charge Burke with "tedious wearisomeness." Oh, sorrowful wo, and also woful sorrow, when an Edmund Burke arises, like a *cheeta* or hunting-leopard coupled in a tiger-chase with a German poodle. To think, in any Christian spirit, of the jungle—barely to contemplate, in a temper of merciful humanity, the incomprehensible cane-thickets, dark and bristly, into which that bloody *cheeta* will drag that unoffending poodle!

But surely the least philosophic of readers, who hates philosophy "worse than toad or asp," must yet be aware that, where new growths are not germinating, it is no sort of praise to be free from the throes of growth. Where expansion is hopeless, it is little glory to have escaped distortion. Nor is it any blame that the rich fermentation of grapes should disturb the transparency of their golden fluids. Fox had nothing new to tell us, nor did he hold a position amongst men that required, or would even have allowed, him to tell anything new. He was helmsman to a party; what he had to do, though seeming to *give* orders, was simply to repeat *their* orders. "Port your helm," said the party; "Port it is," replied the helmsman. But Burke was no steersman; he was the Orpheus that sailed with the Argonauts; he was their *seer*, seeing more in his visions than was always intelligible even to himself; he was their watcher through the starry hours; he was their astrological interpreter. Who complains of a prophet for being a little darker of speech than a post-office directory? or of him that reads the stars for being sometimes perplexed?

Yet, even as to facts, Schlosser is always blundering. Post-office directories would be of no use to *him*, nor link-boys, nor blazing tar-barrels. He wanders in a fog such as sits upon the banks of Cocytus, fancying that Burke in his lifetime was *popular*, perhaps too popular. Of course, it is so natural to be popular by means of "*wearisome tediousness*," that Schlosser, above all people, ought to credit such a tale. Burke has been dead just sixty-one years come next autumn. I remember the time from this accident, that my own nearest relative stepped, on a golden day of 1797, into that same suite of rooms at Bath (North Parade) from which, three hours before, the great man had been carried out to die at Beaconsfield. It is, therefore, you see, threescore years and one. Now, ever since then, his *collective* works have been growing in bulk by the incorporation of juvenile essays (such as his "European Settlements," his "Essay on the Sublime," on

"Lord Bolingbroke," &c.), or (as more recently) by the posthumous publication of his MSS.;* and yet, ever since then, in spite of growing age and growing bulk, are becoming more in demand. At this time, half-a-century after his last sigh, Burke *is* popular; a thing, let me tell

---

* "*Of his MSS.:*"—And, if all that I have heard be true, much has somebody to answer for, that so little has been yet published. The two executors of Burke were, Dr Lawrence of Doctors' Commons, a well-known M.P. in forgotten days, and Windham, a man too like Burke in compass and elasticity of mind ever to be spoken of in connection with forgotten things. Which of them was to blame I know not. But Mr R. Sharpe, M.P. for I know not what borough, told the following story. Let me pause at this name. R., as the reader will rightly suppose, represented the Christian name which his godfathers and his godmothers had indorsed upon him at the baptismal font. Originally this R. had represented *Richard:* but when Richard had swelled into portly proportions, had become an adult, and taken his seat in the House of Commons, the Pagan public of London raised him to the rank of *River;* and thenceforwards R. S. stood for "*River* Sharpe"—this honorary augmentation of old hereditary name being understood to indicate the απεραντολογια (or world-without-ending-ness of his eternal talk); in prophetic anticipation of which the poet Horace is supposed to have composed his two famous lines†—

> "Rusticus expectat dum defluat amnis at ille
> Labitur et labetur in omne volubilis œvum."

This Mr R. Sharpe, by the way, was a man of multitudinous dodges. He could (and he did, if you look into the parliamentary mirrors of those days) make a very neat speech upon occasion, and when time was plentiful, else he was generally hurried by business; for he was a London merchant (in the English sense, observe—not the Scottish), exporting, therefore, to every latitude in countless longitudes; so that his own mer-

---

† "*Famous lines:*"—Of which the following translation was executed, the first line by the late Mr William Cobbett (who hated Sharpe), and the last by Dryden:—

> "Chaw-bacon loiters till the stream be gone;
> Which flows—and, as it flows, for ever shall flow on."

But naturalists object (to Horace more properly than to Mr Cobbett) that of all men Chaw-bacon, as a rusticus familiar with all features of the *rus*, is least likely to make such a mistake as that of waiting for a river to run down. A *cit*, a townsman bred and born, is what Horace must have meant.

you, Schlosser, which never happened before, in island or in continent, amongst Christians or Pagans, to a writer steeped to his lips in *personal* politics. What a tilth of intellectual lava must that man have interfused amongst the refuse and scoria of such mouldering party rubbish, to

---

cantile letters exhausted his whole power of franking. This made him wear a selfish expression of countenance to that army of letter-writing ladies in whose eyes the final cause of an M.P. was, that he might give franks to his female acquaintances—a matter of some importance when a double letter usually cost you a pretty half-crown, which, and not five shillings, is what the French always mean by an *écu*. Mr Sharpe was chivalrous, nevertheless, and conceived himself a master in the most insinuating modes of deferential gallantry. But his seat in Parliament cost him exactly a thousand pounds sterling per annum. This sum he had to fetch back by franking, which lucrative privilege he applied naturally to all the heaviest despatches of his own firm. And under such circumstances, where each civility to his fair friends could be put into the scales and weighed in his counting-house, reasonably he neither stood nor understood any "nonsense." *Usque ad aras*—*i. e.*, so far as the ledger permitted—he wished to conduct himself towards women *en grand seigneur*, or even *en prince*. But to waste a frank upon *their* "nonsense"—a frank that paid all expenses from the Cornish Scillys northwards to John Groat, Esq., in Caithness—was the high road to bankruptcy. Consequently Mr Sharpe was less popular than else he might have been, with so abundant a treasure of anecdotes, of gossip, and (amongst select friends) of high-flavoured scandal. Him, the said Sharpe, I heard more than once at Wordsworth's say, that one or both of the executors had offered to *him* (the river) a huge travelling trunk, perhaps an imperial or a Salisbury boot (equal to the wardrobe of a family), filled with Burke's MSS., on the simple condition of editing them, with annotations. An Oxford man, and also the celebrated Mr Christian Curwen, then member for Cumberland, made, in my hearing, the same report. The Oxford man, in particular, being questioned as to the probable amount of MS., lamented that the gods had not made him an exciseman, with the gift of gauging barrels and other repositories; that he could not speak upon oath to the cubical contents; but this he could say, that having stripped up his coat-sleeve, he had endeavoured, by such poor machinery as nature had allowed him, to take the soundings of the trunk, but apparently there were none; with his middle finger he could find no bottom, for it was stopped by a dense stratum of MS.; below which, you know, other strata might lie *ad infinitum*. For anything proved to the contrary, the trunk might be bottomless.

force up a new verdure and laughing harvests, annually increasing for new generations! Popular he *is* now, but popular he was not in his own generation. And how could Schlosser have the face to say that he was? Did he never hear the notorious anecdote, that at one period Burke obtained the sobriquet of "dinner-bell?" And why? Not as one who invited men to a banquet by his gorgeous eloquence, but as one that gave a signal to shoals in the House of Commons for seeking refuge in a *literal* dinner from the oppression of his philosophy. This was, perhaps, in part a scoff of his opponents.* Yet there must have been some foundation for the scoff, since, at an earlier stage of Burke's career, Goldsmith had independently said, that this great orator

> "Went on refining,
> And thought of convincing, whilst *they* thought of *dining*."

I blame neither party. It ought not to be expected of any *popular* body that it should be patient of abstractions amongst the intensities of party strife, and the immediate necessities of voting. No deliberative body would less have tolerated such philosophic exorbitations from public business than the *agora* of Athens or the Roman Senate. So far the error was in Burke, not in the House of Commons. Yet also, on the other side, it must be remembered, that an intellect of Burke's, combining power and enormous compass, could not, from necessity of nature, abstain from such speculations. For a man to reach a remote

* I do not believe that at any time he was so designated, unless playfully and in special coteries. That the young, who were wearied, that the intensely practical, who distrusted him as a speculator, that the man of business, *natus rebus agendis*, who viewed him as a trespasser on the disposable time of the House, should combine intermittingly in giving expression to their feelings is conceivable, or even probable. The rest is exaggeration.

posterity, it is sometimes necessary that he should throw his voice over to them in a vast arch—it must sweep a parabola; which, therefore, rises high above the heads of those that stand next to him, and is heard by the by-standers but indistinctly, like bees swarming in the upper air before they settle on the spot fit for hiving.

See, therefore, the immeasurableness of misconception. Of all public men that stand confessedly in the first rank as to splendour of intellect, Burke was the *least* popular at the time when our blind friend Schlosser assumes him to have run off with the lion's share of popularity. Fox, on the other hand, as the leader of opposition, was at that time a household term of love or reproach from one end of the island to the other. To the very children playing in the streets, Pitt and Fox, throughout Burke's generation, were pretty nearly as broad distinctions, and as much a war-cry, as English and French, Roman and Punic. Now, however, all this is altered. As regards the relations between the two Whigs whom Schlosser so steadfastly delighteth to misrepresent,

> "Now is the winter of our discontent
> Made glorious summer"

as respects that intellectual potentate, Edmund Burke, the man whose true mode of power has never yet been truly investigated; whilst Charles Fox is known only as an echo is known; and, for any real *effect* of intellect upon this generation, for anything but the "whistling of a name," the Fox of 1780–1807 sleeps where the carols of the larks are sleeping that gladdened the spring-tides of those years —sleeps with the roses that glorified the beauty of their summers.*

* A man in Fox's situation is sure, whilst living, to draw after him trains of sycophants; and it is the evil necessity of newspapers the most

JUNIUS.

Schlossser talks of Junius, who is to him, as to many people, more than entirely the enigma of an enigma, a vapoury likeness of Hermes Trismegistus, or a dark shadow of the mediæval Prester John. Not only are most people unable to solve the enigma, but they have no idea of what it is that they are required to solve. Schlosser is in that predicament. I have to inform Schlosser that there are three separate questions about Junius, of which he has evidently never heard, and cannot, therefore, have many chances to spare for settling them. The three questions are these:—A. Who *was* Junius? B. What was it that armed Junius with a power over the public mind so unaccountable at this day. C. Why, having actually exercised such a power, and gained under his mask far more than he ever hoped to gain, did this Junius not come forward *in his own person*, when all the legal danger had long passed away, to claim a distinction that for *him* (among

---

independent that they *must* swell the mob of sycophants. The public compels them to exaggerate the true proportions of such people, as we see or hear every hour in our own day. Those who for the moment modify, or *may* modify, the national condition, become preposterous idols in the eyes of the gaping public; but with the sad necessity of being too utterly trodden under foot after they are shelved, unless they live in men's memory by something better than speeches in Parliament. Having the usual fate, Fox was complimented, *whilst living*, on his knowledge of Homeric Greek, which was a jest: he knew neither more nor less of Homer and his Ionic Greek than most English gentlemen of his rank; quite enough, that is, to read the "Iliad" with unaffected pleasure, far too little to revise the text of any ten lines without making himself ridiculous. The excessive slenderness of his general literature, English and French, may be seen in the letters published by his secretary, Trotter. But his fragment of a history, published by Lord Holland at two guineas, and currently sold for two shillings (not two *pence*, or else I have been defrauded of one shilling and tenpence), most of all proclaims the tenuity of his knowledge. He looks upon Malcolm Laing as a huge oracle; and having read even less than Hume—a thing not very easy—with great *naïveté*, cannot guess where Hume picked up his facts.

the vainest of men) must have been more precious than his heart's blood? The two questions B and C I have examined in past times, and I will not here repeat my conclusions further than to say, with respect to the last, that the reason for the author not claiming his own property was this—because he *dared* not; because, for that man who *was* Junius, it would have been mere *infamy* to avow himself as Junius; because it would have revealed a crime, and would have published a crime in his own earlier life, for which many a man is transported in our days, and for less than which many a man has been, in neighbouring lands, hanged, broken on the wheel, burned, gibbeted, or impaled. To say that he watched and listened at his master's key-holes, is nothing. It was not key-holes only that he made free with, but keys; he tampered with his master's seals; he committed larcenies—not like a brave man risking his life on the highway, but petty larcenies—larcenies in a dwelling-house—larcenies under the opportunities of a confidential situation—crimes which formerly, in the days of Junius, our bloody code never pardoned in villains of low degree. Junius was in the situation of Lord Byron's Lara, or—because Lara is a foul plagiarism—of Harriet Lee's Kruitzner. All the world over, *or nearly*, Lara moved in freedom as a nobleman, haughtily and irreproachably. But one spot there was on earth in which he durst not for his life show himself—one spot in which instantly he would be challenged as a criminal—nay, whisper it not, ye forests and rivers! challenged as a vile midnight thief. But this man, because he had money, friends, and talents, instead of going to prison, took himself off for a jaunt to the Continent. From the Continent, in full security, and in possession of the *otium cum dignitate*, he negotiated with the government, whom he had alarmed by publishing the secrets which he had stolen. He succeeded. He sold himself to great advantage. Bought and sold he was; and of course it is understood that if you buy a knave, and expressly in consideration of his knaveries, you secretly undertake, even without a special contract, not to hang him. "Honour bright!" Lord Barrington might certainly have indicted Junius at the Old Bailey, and had a reason for wishing to do so: but George III., who was a party to the negotiation, and all his ministers, would have said, with fits of laughter, "Oh, come now, my lord, you must *not* do that. For since we have bargained for a price to send him out as a member of council to Bengal, you see clearly that we could not possibly hang him *before* we had fulfilled our bargain. Then it is true we might hang him after he comes back; but since the man (being a clever man) has a fair chance in the interim of rising to be Governor-General, we put it to your candour, Lord Barrington, whether it would be for the public service to hang his excellency?" In fact, Sir Philip might very probably have been Governor-General, had his vile temper not overmastered him. Had he not quarrelled so viciously with Mr Hastings, it is ten to one that he might, by playing his cards well, have succeeded him. As it was, after enjoying an enormous salary, he returned to England, not Governor-General certainly, but still in no fear of being hanged. Instead of hanging him, on second thoughts, government gave him a red riband. He represented a borough in Parliament; he was an authority upon Indian affairs; he was caressed by the Whig party; he sat at good men's tables. He gave for toasts—*Joseph Surface* sentiments at dinner-parties—"The man that betrays" [something or other]—"The man that sneaks into" [other men's portfolios, perhaps]—"is". ay, *what* is he? Why, he is perhaps a Knight of the Bath, has a sumptuous mansion in St James's Square, dies full of years and honour, has a pompous funeral, and fears only some such epitaph as this—"Here lies, in a red riband, the man who built a great prosperity on the basis of an unparalleled knavery." I complain heavily of Mr Taylor, the very able unmasker of Junius, for blinking the whole questions B and C. He it is that has settled the question A, so that it will never be re-opened by a man of sense. A man who doubts, after *really* reading Mr Taylor's work, is not only a blockhead, but an irreclaimable blockhead. It is true that several men, among them Lord Brougham, whom Schlosser (though hating him, and kicking him) cites, still profess, or are *said to profess*, scepticism. But the reason is evident: they have not *read* the book, they have only heard of it. They are unacquainted with the strongest arguments, and even with the nature of the evidence.* Lord Brougham, indeed, is generally reputed to have reviewed

---

* Even in Dr Francis's "Translation of Select Speeches from Demosthenes," which Lord Brougham would be likely to consult in his own labours on that theme, there may be traced several peculiarities of diction that startle us in Junius. Sir Philip had them from his father, Dr Francis. And Lord Brougham ought not to have overlooked them. The same thing may be seen, as was pointed out by Mr Taylor, in the notes to Dr Francis's translation of "Horace." These points, though not *independently* of conclusive importance, become far more so in combination with others. The reply made to me once by a publisher of some eminence upon this question is remarkable, and worth repeating. "I feel," he said, "the impregnability of the case made out for Sir Philip Francis by Mr Taylor. But the misfortune is, that I have seen so many previous impregnable cases made out for other claimants." Ay, that *would* be unfortunate. But the misfortune for this repartee was, that I, for whose use it was intended, not being in the predicament of a *stranger* to the dispute, having seen every page of the pleadings, knew all (except Mr Taylor's) to be false in their statements of fact; after which, that their arguments should be ingenious or subtle, signified nothing.

Mr Taylor's book. *That* may be; it is probable enough. What I am denying is not at all that Lord Brougham *reviewed* Mr Taylor, but that Lord Brougham *read* Mr Taylor. And there is not much wonder in *that*, when we see professed writers on the subject, bulky writers, writers of answers and refutations, dispensing with the whole of Mr Taylor's book, single paragraphs of which would have forced them to cancel the sum total of their own. The possibility of scepticism, after really *reading* Mr Taylor's book, would be the strongest exemplification upon record of Sancho's proverbial reproach, that some men "want better bread than is made of wheat"—would be the old case renewed from the scholastic grumblers, "that some men do not know when they are answered." They have got their *quietus*, and they still continue to "maunder" on with objections long since disposed of. In fact, it is not too strong a thing to say—and Chief-Justice Dallas *did* say something like it—that if Mr Taylor is not right, if Sir Philip Francis is *not* Junius, then was no man ever yet hanged on sufficient evidence. Even confession is no absolute proof. Even confessing to a crime, the man may be mad, or a knavish simulator. Well, at least seeing is believing: if the court sees a man commit an assault, will not *that* suffice? Not at all: ocular delusions on the largest scale are common. What's a court? Lawyers have no better eyes than other people. Their physics are often out of repair; and whole cities have been known to see things that could have no existence. Now, all other evidence is held to be short of this blank seeing or blank confessing. But I am not at all sure of *that*. Circumstantial evidence, that multiplies indefinitely its points of *internexus*, its nodes of intersection, with known admitted facts, is more impressive than any possible direct testimony. If you detect a fellow with a large sheet of lead, that by many (to wit, seventy) salient angles—that by tedious (to wit, sixty-nine) re-entrant angles—fits into and owns its sisterly relationship to all that is left of the lead upon your roof, this tight fit will weigh more with a jury than even if my Lord Chief-Justice should jump into the witness-box, swearing that with judicial eyes he saw the vagabond cutting the lead whilst he himself sat at breakfast; or even than if that very vagabond should protest before this honourable court that he *did* cut the lead, in order that he (the said vagabond) might have hot rolls and coffee as well as my lord, the witness. If Mr Taylor's body of evidence does *not* hold water, then is there no evidence extant upon any question, judicial or not judicial, that *will*.

But I blame Mr Taylor heavily for throwing away the whole argument deducible from B and C; not as any debt that rested particularly upon *him* to public justice; but as a debt to the integrity of his own book. That book is now a fragment; admirable as regards A; but (by omitting B and C) not sweeping the whole area of the problem. There yet remains, therefore, the dissatisfaction which is always likely to arise—not from the smallest *allegatio falsi*, but from the large *suppressio veri*. B, which, on any other solution than the one I have proposed, is perfectly unintelligible, now becomes plain enough. To imagine a heavy, coarse, hard-working government, seriously affected by such a bauble as *they* would consider performances on the tight-rope of style, is mere midsummer madness. "Hold your absurd tongue," would any of the ministers have said to a friend descanting on Junius as a powerful artist of style; "do you dream, dotard, that this baby's rattle is the thing that keeps us from sleeping? Our eyes are fixed on something else: that fellow, whoever he is, knows what he ought *not* to know; he has had his hand in some of our pockets: he's a good locksmith, is that Junius; and before he reaches Tyburn, who knows what amount of mischief he may do to self and partners?" The rumour that ministers were themselves alarmed (which was the naked truth) travelled downwards; but the *why* did not travel; and the innumerable blockheads of lower circles, not understanding the real cause of fear, sought a false one in the supposed thunderbolts of the rhetoric. Opera-house thunderbolts they were: and strange it is, that grave men should fancy newspapers, teeming (as they have always done) with *Publicolas*, with *Catos*, with *Algernon Sydneys*, able by such trivial small-shot to gain a moment's attention from the potentates of Downing Street. Those who have despatches to write, councils to attend, and votes of the Commons to manage, think little of Junius Brutus. A Junius Brutus, that dares not sign by his own honest name, is presumably skulking from his creditors. A Timoleon who hints at assassination in a newspaper, one may take it for granted, is a manufacturer of begging letters. And it is a conceivable case that a twenty-pound note, enclosed to Timoleon's address through the newspaper office, might go far to soothe that great patriot's feelings, and even to turn aside his avenging dagger. These sort of people were not the sort to frighten a British Ministry. One laughs at the probable conversation between an old hunting squire coming up to comfort the First Lord of the Treasury, on the rumour that he was panicstruck. "What, surely, my dear old friend, you're no afraid of Timoleon?"—First Lord. "Yes, I am."—C. Gent. "What, afraid of an anonymous fellow in the papers?"—F. L. "Yes, dreadfully."—C. Gent. "Why, I always understood that these people were a sort of shams—living in Grub Street—or where was it that Pope used to tell us they lived? Surely you're not afraid of Timoleon, because some people think he's a patriot?"—F. L. "No, not at all; but I am afraid because some people think he's a housebreaker!" In that character only could Timoleon become formidable to a Cabinet Minister; and in some such character must our friend, Junius Brutus, have made himself alarming to government. From the moment that B is properly explained, it throws light upon C. The government was alarmed—not at such moonshine as patriotism, not at such a soap-bubble as rhetoric, but because treachery was lurking amongst their own households; and, if the thing went on, the consequences might be appalling. But this domestic treachery, which accounts for B, accounts at the same time for C. The very same treachery that frightened its objects at the time by the consequences it might breed, would frighten its author afterwards from claiming its literary honours by the remembrances it might awaken. The mysterious disclosures of official secrets, which had once roused so much consternation within a limited circle, and (like the French affair of the diamond necklace) had sunk into neglect only when all clue seemed lost for *perfectly* unravelling it, would revive in all its mystical interest when a discovery came before the public—viz., a claim on the part of Francis to have written the famous letters, which must at the same time point a strong light upon the true origin of the treacherous disclosures made in those letters. Some astonishment had always existed as to Francis—how he rose so suddenly into rank and station: some astonishment had always existed as to Junius, how he should so suddenly have fallen asleep as a writer in the journals. The coincidence of this sudden and unaccountable silence with that sudden and unaccountable Indian appointment of Francis; the extraordinary familiarity of Junius, which had *not altogether escaped notice*, with the secrets of one particular office—viz., the War Office; the sudden recollection, sure to flash upon all who remembered Francis, if again he should become revived into suspicion, that he had held a situation of trust in that particular War Office; all these little recollections would begin to take up their places in a connected story: *this* and *that*, laid together, *that* and *this*, spelled into most significant words, would become clear as daylight; and to the keen eyes of still surviving enemies—Horne Tooke, "little Chamier," Ellis, to the English houses of Fitzroy and Russell, to the Scottish houses of Murray and Wedderburne—the whole progress and catastrophe of the scoundrelism, the perfidy and the profits of the perfidy, would soon become as intelligible as any tale of midnight burglary from without, in concert with a wicked butler within, that was ever sifted by judge and jury at the Old Bailey, or critically reviewed by Mr John Ketch at Tyburn.

Francis was the man. Francis was the wicked butler within, whom Pharaoh ought to have hanged, but whom he clothed in royal apparel, and mounted upon a horse that carried him to a curule chair of honour. So far his burglary prospered. But, as generally happens in such cases, this prosperous crime subsequently became the killing curse of long years to Francis. By a just retribution, the success of Junius, in two senses so monstrously exaggerated—exaggerated by a romantic over-estimate of its intellectual power through an error of the public, not admitted to the secret, and equally exaggerated as to its political power by the government, in the hush-money for its future suppression—became the self-avenger to the successful criminal. This criminal was one who, with a childish eagerness, thirsted for literary distinction above all other distinction, as for the *amreeta* cup of immortality. And, behold! there the brilliant bauble lay, glittering in the sands of a solitude, unclaimed by any man; disputed with him (if he chose to claim it) by nobody; and yet for his life he durst not touch it. Sir Philip stood—he knew that he stood—in the situation of a murderer who has dropped an inestimable jewel upon the murdered body in the death-struggle with his victim. The jewel is his! Nobody will deny it. He may have it for asking. But to ask is—to die; to die the death of a felon. "Oh yes!" would be the answer, "here's your jewel, wrapped up safely in tissue paper. But here's another lot that goes along with it—no bidder can take them apart—viz., a halter, also wrapped up in tissue paper." Francis, in relation to Junius, was in that exact predicament. "You, then, are Junius? You are that famous man who has been missing since 1772? And you can prove it? God bless me! sir, what a long time you've been sleeping: everybody's gone to bed from that generation. But let us have a look at you, before you move off to prison. I like to look at clever men; particularly men that are *too* clever; and you, my dear sir, are too clever by half. I regard you as the brightest specimen of the swell-mob, and in fact as the very ablest scoundrel that at this hour rests in Europe unhanged!"—Francis died, and made no sign. Peace of mind he had parted with for a peacock's feather; which feather, living or dying, he durst not mount in the plumage of his cap.

PROTESTANTISM.*

THE work whose substance and theme are thus briefly abstracted is at this moment (1847) making a noise in the world. It is ascribed by report to two bishops—not jointly, but alternatively—in the sense that, if one did *not* write the book, the other *did*. The Bishops of Oxford and St David's, Wilberforce and Thirlwall, are the two pointed at by the popular finger; and, in some quarters, a third is suggested—viz., Stanley, Bishop of Norwich. The betting, however, is altogether in favour of Oxford. So runs the current of *public* gossip. But the public is a bad guesser, "stiff in opinion," and almost "always in the wrong." Now let *me* guess. When I had read for ten minutes, I offered a bet of seven to one (no takers) that the author's name began with H. Not out of any love for that amphibious letter; on the contrary, being myself what Professor Wilson calls a *hedonist*, or philosophical voluptuary, murmuring, with good reason, if a rose leaf lies doubled below me, naturally I murmur at a letter that

* This little paper, founded on a "Vindication of Protestant Principles"—by Phileleutherus Anglicanus—might perhaps sufficiently justify itself by the importance of the principles discussed, if it replied to a mere imaginary antagonist. But this was not so. "The Vindication" was a real book, and, as a startling phenomenon, made a sudden and deep impression.

puts one to the expense of an aspiration, forcing into the lungs an extra charge of raw air on frosty mornings. But truth is truth, in spite of frosty air. And yet, upon further reading, doubts gathered upon my mind. The H. that I mean is an Englishman; now it happens that here and there a word, or some peculiarity in using a word, indicates, in this author, a Scotchman; for instance, the expletive "just," which so much infests Scottish phraseology, written or spoken, at page 1; elsewhere the word "*shortcomings*," which, being horridly tabernacular, and such that no gentleman could allow himself to touch it without gloves, it is to be wished that our Scottish brethren would resign, together with "*backslidings*," to the use of field-preachers. But worse, by a great deal, and not even intelligible in England, is the word *thereafter*, used as an adverb of time; *i.e.*, as the correlative of *hereafter*. *Thereafter*, in pure vernacular English, bears a totally different sense. In "Paradise Lost," for instance, having heard the character of a particular angel, you are told that he spoke *thereafter*; *i. e.*, spoke agreeably to that character. "How a score of sheep, Master Shallow?" The answer is, "*Thereafter* as they be." Again, "Thereafter as a man sows shall he reap"—*i. e.*, conformably or answerably to what he sows. The objections are overwhelming to the Scottish use of the word; first, because already in Scotland it is a barbarism transplanted from the filthy vocabulary of attorneys, locally called *writers*; secondly, because in England it is not even intelligible, and, what is worse still, sure to be *mis*-intelligible. And yet, after all, these exotic forms may be a mere blind. The writer is, perhaps, purposely leading us astray with his "*thereafters*" and his horrid "*shortcomings*." Or, because London newspapers and Acts of Parliament are beginning to be more and more polluted with these barbarisms, he may even have caught them unconsciously. And, on looking again at one case of "*thereafter*"—viz., at page 79—it seems impossible to determine whether he uses it in the classical English sense, or in the sense of leguleian barbarism.

This question of authorship, meantime, may seem to the reader of little moment. Far from it! The weightier part of the interest depends upon that very point. If the author really *is* a bishop, or supposing the public rumour so far correct as that he is a man of distinction in the English Church, then, and by that simple fact, this book, or this pamphlet, interesting at any rate for itself, becomes separately interesting through its authorship, so as to be the most remarkable phenomenon of the day; and why? Because the most remarkable expression of a movement, accomplished and proceeding in a quarter that, if any on this earth, might be thought sacred from change. Oh, fearful are the motions of time, when suddenly lighted up to a retrospect of thirty years! Pathetic are the ruins of time in its slowest advance! Solemn are the prospects, so new and so incredible, which time unfolds at every turn of its wheeling flight! Is it come to this? Could any man, one generation back, have anticipated that an English dignitary, and speaking on a very delicate religious question, should deliberately appeal to a writer confessedly infidel, and proud of being an infidel, as a "triumphant" settler of Christian scruples? But if the infidel is right—a point which I do not here discuss; but if the infidel is a man of genius—a point which I do not deny—was it not open to cite him, even though the citer were a bishop? Why, yes—uneasily one answers, *yes;* but still the case records a strange alteration; and still one could have wished to hear such a doctrine, which ascribes human infirmity (nay, human criminality) to *every* book of the Bible, uttered by anybody rather than by a father of the church, and guaranteed by anybody rather than by an infidel in triumph. A boy may fire his pistol unnoticed; but a sentinel, mounting guard in the dark, must remember the trepidation that will follow any shot from *him*, and the certainty that it will cause all the stations within hearing to get under arms immediately. Yet why, if this bold opinion *does* come from a prelate, he being but one man, should it carry so alarming a sound? Is the whole bench of bishops bound and compromised by the audacity of any one amongst its members? Certainly not. But yet such an act, though it should be that of a rash precursor, marks the universal change of position; there is ever some sympathy between the van and the rear of the same body at the same time; and the boldest could not have dared to go ahead so rashly, if the rearmost was not known to be pressing forward to his support far more closely than thirty years ago he could have done. There have been, it is true, heterodox professors of divinity and freethinking bishops before now. England can show a considerable list of such people—even Rome has a smaller list. Rome, that weeds all libraries, and is continually burning books, in effigy, by means of her vast *Index Expurgatorius*,* which index, continually, she is enlarging by successive supple-

---

* "*Index Expurgatorius:*"—A question of some interest arises upon the casuistical construction of this index. We that are not by name included—may we consider ourselves indirectly licensed? Silence, I should hope, gives consent. And if it wasn't that the present Pope, being a horrid Radical, would be sure to blackball *me* as an honest Tory, I would send him a copy of my *Opera Omnia*, requesting his Holiness to say, by return of post, whether I ranked amongst the chaff winnowed by St Peter's flail, or had his gracious permission to hold myself amongst the pure wheat gathered into the Vatican garner.

ments, needs also an *Index Expurgatorius* for the catalogue of her prelates. Weeds there are in the very flower-garden and conservatory of the church. Fathers of the church are no more to be relied on, as safe authorities, than we rascally lay authors, that notoriously will say anything. And it is a striking proof of this amongst our English bishops, that the very man who, in the last generation, most of all won the public esteem as the champion of the Bible against Tom Paine, was privately known amongst us connoisseurs in heresy (that are always prying into ugly secrets) to be the least orthodox thinker, one or other, amongst the whole brigade of eighteen thousand contemporary clerks who had subscribed the Thirty-nine Articles. Saving your presence, reader, his lordship was no better than a bigoted Socinian, which, in a petty diocese that he never visited, and amongst South Welshmen, that are all incorrigible Methodists, mattered little, but would have been awkward had he come to be Archbishop of York; and that he did *not*, turned upon the accident of a few weeks too soon, by which the Fates cut short the thread of the Whig Ministry in 1807. Certainly for a Romish or an English bishop to be a Socinian is *un peu fort*. But I contend that it is quite possible to be far less heretical, and yet dangerously bold; yes, upon the free and spacious latitudes purposely left open by the English Thirty-nine Articles (ay, or by *any* Protestant Confession), to plant novelties not less startling to religious ears than Socinianism itself. Besides (which adds to the shock), the dignitary now before us, whether bishop or no bishop, does not write in the tone of a conscious heretic; or, like Archdeacon Blackburne* of old, in a spirit of hostility to

* "*Archdeacon Blackburne:*"—He was the author of "The Confessional," which at one time made a memorable ferment amongst all those

his own fellow-churchmen; but, on the contrary, in the tone of one relying upon support from his clerical brethren, he stands forward as expositor and champion of views now prevailing amongst the *elite* of the English Church. So construed, the book is, indeed, a most extraordinary one, and exposes a record that almost shocks one of the strides made in religious speculation. Opinions change slowly and stealthily. The steps of the changes are generally continuous; but sometimes it happens that the notice of such steps, the publication of such changes, is *not* continuous, that it comes upon us *per saltum*, and consequently with the stunning effect of an apparent treachery. Every thoughtful man raises his hands with an involuntary gesture of awe at the revolutions of so revolutionary an age, when thus summoned to the spectacle of an English prelate serving a piece of artillery against what once were fancied to be main outworks of religion, and at a station sometimes considerably in advance of any station ever occupied by Voltaire.*

It is this audacity of speculation, I apprehend, this *étalage* of bold results, rather than any success in their development, which has fixed the public attention. Develop-

---

who loved as sons, or who hated as Nonconformists, the English Establishment. This was his most popular work, but he wrote many others in the same temper, that fill six or seven octavos. I fear that it may be a duty to read him; and if it is, then I think of his seven octavos with holy horror.

* "*Voltaire:*"—Let not the reader misunderstand me; I do not mean that the clerical writer now before us (bishop or not bishop) is more hostile to religion than Voltaire, or is hostile at all. On the contrary, he is, perhaps, profoundly religious, and he writes with neither levity nor insincerity. But this conscientious spirit, and this piety, do but the more call into relief the audacity of his freethinking—do but the more forcibly illustrate the prodigious changes in the spirit of religious philosophy wrought by time, and by the contagion from secular revolutions.

ment, indeed, applied to philosophic problems, or research applied to questions of erudition, was hardly possible within so small a compass as one hundred and seventeen pages, for *that* is the extent of the work, except as regards the notes, which amount to seventy-four pages more. Such brevity, on such a subject, is unseasonable, and almost culpable. On such a subject as the Philosophy of Protestantism—"*satius erat silere, quam parcius dicere.*" Better were absolute silence, more respectful as regards the theme, less tantalising as regards the reader, than a style of discussion so fragmentary and so rapid.

But, before we go farther, what are we to call this bold man? One must have some name for a man that one is reviewing; and, as he comes abroad *incognito*, it is difficult to say what name *could* have any propriety. Let me consider: there are three bishops in the field, Mr H., and the Scotchman—that makes five. But every one of these, you say, is represented equally by the name in the title—"Phileleutherus Anglicanus." True, but *that's* as long as a team of horses. If it had but *Esquire* at the end, it would measure against a Latin Hexameter verse. I'm afraid that we must come at last to *Phil.* I've been seeking to avoid it, for it's painful to say "Jack" or "Dick" either *to* or *of* an ecclesiastical great gun. But if such big-wigs *will* come abroad in disguise, and with names as long as Fielding's Hononchrononthononthologus, they must submit to be hustled by pickpockets and critics, and to have *their* names docked as well as profane authors.

Phil., then, be it—that's settled. Now, let us inquire what it is that *Phil.* has deen saying, to cause such a sensation amongst the Gnostics. And, to begin at the beginning, what is *Phil's.* capital object? *Phil.* shall state it himself—these are his opening words:—"In the following pages we propose to vindicate the fundamental and inherent *principles* of Protestantism." Good; but what *are* the fundamental principles of Protestantism? "They are," says *Phil.*, "the sole sufficiency of Scripture,* the right of private judgment in its interpretation, and the authority of individual conscience in matters of religion." Errors of logic show themselves more often in a man's terminology, and his antitheses, and his subdivisions, than anywhere else. *Phil.* goes on to make this distinction, which brings out his imperfect conception. "We," says he (and, by the way, if *Phil.* is *we*, then it must be my duty to call him *they*)—"we do not propose to defend the varieties of *doctrine* held by the different communities of Protestants." Why, no; that would be a sad task for the most skilful of funambulists or theological tumblers, seeing that many of these varieties stand related to each other as categorical affirmative and categorical negative: it's heavy work to make *yes* and *no* pull together in the same proposition. But this, fortunately for himself, *Phil.* declines. You are to understand that he will not undertake the defence of Protestantism in its *doctrines*, but only in its *principles*. That won't do; that antithesis is as hollow as a drum;

* "*Sole sufficiency of Scripture:*"—This is much too elliptical a way of expressing the Protestant meaning. Sufficiency for *what?* "Sufficiency for salvation" is the phrase of many, and I think elsewhere of *Phil.* But *that* is objectionable on more grounds than one; it is redundant, and it is aberrant from the true point contemplated. *Sufficiency for itself, without alien helps,* is the thing contemplated. The Greek *autarkeia* (αὐταρκεια), self-sufficiency, or, because that phrase, in English, has received a deflection towards a bad meaning, the word *self-sufficingness* might answer; sufficiency for the exposition of its own most secret meaning, out of fountains within itself; needing, therefore, neither the supplementary aids of tradition, on the one hand, nor the complementary aids on the other (in the event of unprovided cases, or of dilemmas arising) from the infallibility of a *living* expounder.

and, if the objection were verbal only, I would not make it. But the contradistinction fails to convey the real meaning. It is not that he has falsely expressed his meaning, but that he has falsely developed that meaning to his own consciousness. Not the word only is wrong; but the wrong word is put forward for the sake of hiding the imperfect idea. What he calls *principles* might almost as well be called *doctrines;* and what he calls *doctrines* as well be called *principles.* But of these terms, apart from the rectifications suggested by the context, no man could collect his drift, which is simply this. Protestantism, we must recollect, is not an absolute and self-dependent idea; it stands in relation to something antecedent, against which it protests—viz., Papal Rome. And under what phasis does it protest against Rome? Not against the Christianity of Rome, because every Protestant Church, though disapproving a great deal of *that,* disapproves also a great deal in its own sister churches of the protesting household; and because every Protestant Church holds a great deal of Christian truth, in common with Rome. But what furnishes the matter of protest is—the *deduction of the title* upon which Rome plants the right to be a church at all. This deduction is so managed by Rome as to make herself, not merely a true church (which many Protestants grant), but the exclusive church. Now, what *Phil.* in effect undertakes to defend is not principles by preference to doctrines (for they are pretty nearly the same thing), but the question of title to teach at all, in preference to the question of what is the thing taught. *There* is the distinction, as I apprehend it. All these terms—"principle," "doctrine," "system," "theory," "hypothesis"—are used nearly always most licentiously, and as arbitrarily as a Newmarket jockey selects the colours for his riding-dress. It is true that one shadow of justification offers itself for *Phil.'s* distinction. All principles are doctrines, but all doctrines are not principles. Which, then, in particular? Why, those properly are principles which contain the *principia*, the beginnings, or starting-points of evolution, out of which any system of truth is developed. Now, it may seem that the very starting-point of our Protestant pretensions is, first of all, to argue our *title* or right to be a church *sui juris;* apparently we must begin by making good our *locus standi*, before we can be heard upon our doctrines. And upon this mode of approach, the pleadings about the *title*, or right to teach at all, taking precedency of the pleadings about the particular things taught, would be the *principia*, or beginnings of the whole process, and so far would be entitled by preference to the name of *principles*. But such a mode of approach is merely an accident, and contingent upon our being engaged in a polemical discussion of Protestantism in relation to Popery. *That*, however, is a pure matter of choice; Protestantism may be discussed, as though Rome were not, in relation to its own absolute merits; and this treatment is the logical treatment, applying itself to what is permanent in the *nature* of the object; whereas the other treatment applies itself to what is casual and vanishing in the *history* (or the origin) of Protestantism. For, after all, it would be no great triumph to Protestantism that she should prove her birthright to revolve as a *primary* planet in the Christian system; that she had the same original right as Rome to wheel about the great central orb, undegraded to the rank of satellite or secondary projection—if, in the meantime, telescopes should reveal the fact that she was pretty nearly a sandy desert. *What* a church teaches is true or not true, without reference to her independent right of teaching; and eventually, when the irritations of earthly feuds and political schisms shall be tranquillised by time, the philosophy of this whole question will take an inverse order. The credentials of a church will not be put in first, and the quality of her doctrine discussed as a secondary question. On the contrary, her credentials will be sought *in* her doctrine. The protesting church will say, I have the *right* to stand separate, because I *do* stand; and from my holy teaching I deduce my title to teach. *Jus est ibi summum docendi, ubi est fons purissimus doctrinæ.* That inversion of the Protestant plea with Rome is even now valid with many; and, when it becomes universally current, then the *principles*, or great beginnings of the controversy, will be transplanted from the centre, where *Phil.* places them, to that very *locus* which he neglects. One church may say—My doctrine must be holy, because it is admitted that I have the authentic commission from Heaven to teach. But equally another church may say—My commission to teach must be conceded, because my teaching is holy. The first deduces the purity of her doctrine from her divine commission to teach. But the second, with logic as forcible, deduces her divine commission to teach from the purity of her doctrine.

There is another expression of *Phil.'s* to which I object. He describes the doctrines held by all the separate Protestant churches as doctrines of Protestantism. I would not delay either *Phil.* or myself for the sake of a trifle; but an impossibility is *not* a trifle. If from orthodox Turkey* you pass to heretic Persia, if from the rigour of the

* "*Orthodox Turkey:*"—At Mecca, or more probably throughout the Mussulman world, the Ottoman Sultan is regarded as the true filial champion *ed deen* [*i. e.*, of the faith]. He is the *right*-hand pillar; whereas the Shah of Persia is a heterodox believer, and therefore an unsound pillar. But it illustrates powerfully the non-spirituality of this religion (though pirated chiefly from the Bible), that this great schism

Sonnees (orthodox Mussulmans) to the laxity of the *Sheeahs* (Mahometan heretics), you could not, in explaining those schisms, go on to say, "And these are the doctrines *of* Islamism;" for they destroy each other. Both are supported by earthly powers; but only one could be supported by a central organ of Islamism, if such there were. So of Calvinism and Arminianism; you cannot call them doctrines *of* Protestantism, as if growing out of some reconciling Protestant principles; one of the two, though not manifested to human eyes in its falsehood, must secretly be false; and a falsehood cannot be a doctrine of Protestantism. It is more accurate to say that the separate creeds of Turkey and Persia are *within* Mahometanism; such—viz., as that neither excludes a man from the name of Mussulman; and, again, that Calvinism and Arminianism are doctrines *within* the Protestant Church—as a church of general toleration for all religious doctrines not *demonstrably* hostile to any cardinal truth of Christianity.

Phil., then, we all understand, is not going to traverse the vast field of Protestant opinions as they are distributed through our many sects; *that* would be endless; and he illustrates the mazy character of the wilderness over which these sects are wandering,

> "Ubi passim
> Palantes error recto de tramite pellit,"

by the four cases of—1. the Calvinist; 2. the Newmanite; 3. the Romanist;* 4. the Evangelical enthusiast—as holding

---

in Islamism does not turn upon any point of doctrine, but simply upon a most trivial question of historic fact—viz., who were *de jure* the immediate successors of Mahomet.

* "*The Romanist:*"—What, amongst Protestant sects? Ay, even so. It's *Phil.'s* mistake, not mine. He will endeavour to doctor the case, by pleading that he was speaking universally of Christian error; but the position of the clause forbids this plea. Not only in relation to what immediately precedes, the passage must be supposed to contemplate *Pro-*

systems of doctrine, "no one of which is capable of recommending itself to the favourable opinion of an impartial judge." Impartial! but what Christian *can* be impartial?

---

testant error; but the immediate inference from it—viz., that "the world may well be excused for doubting whether there is, after all, so much to be gained by that liberty of private judgment, which is the essential characteristic of Protestantism; whether it be not, after all, merely a liberty to fall into error," nails *Phil.* to that construction—argues too strongly that it is an oversight of indolence. *Phil.* was sleeping for the moment, which is excusable enough towards the end of a book, but hardly in section 1. P.S.—I have since observed (which *not* to have observed is excused, perhaps, by the too complex machinery of hooks and eyes between the text and the notes involving a double reference—first, to the section; second, to the particular clause of the section) that *Phil.* has not here committed an inadvertency; or, if he *has*, is determined to fight himself through his inadvertency, rather than break up his quaternion of cases. "In speaking of Romanism as arising from a misapplication of Protestant principles, we refer, not to those who were born, but to those who have become members of the Church of Rome." What is the name of those people? And where do they live? I have heard of many who think (and there *are* cases in which most of us, that meddle with philosophy, are apt to think) occasional principles of Protestantism available for the defence of certain Roman Catholic mysteries too indiscriminately assaulted by the Protestant zealot; but, with this exception, I am not aware of any parties professing to derive their Popish learnings *from* Protestantism; it is *in spite of* Protestantism, as seeming to *them* not strong enough, or through principles omitted by Protestantism, which therefore seems to *them* not careful enough or not impartial enough, that Protestants have lapsed to Popery. Protestants have certainly been known to become Papists, not through Popish arguments, but simply through their own Protestant books; yet never, that I heard of, through an *affirmative* process, as though any Protestant argument involved the rudiments of Popery, but by a *negative* process, as fancying the Protestant reasons, though lying in the right direction, not going far enough; or, again, though right partially, yet defective as a whole. *Phil.* therefore seems to me absolutely caught in a sort of *Furcæ Caudinæ*, unless he has a dodge in reserve to puzzle us all. In a different point, I, that hold myself a *doctor seraphicus*, and also *inexpugnabilis* upon quillets of logic, justify *Phil.*, whilst also I blame him. He defends himself rightly for distinguishing between the Romanist and Newmanite on the one hand, between the Calvinist and the Evangelican man on the other, though perhaps a young gentleman, commencing his studies on the *Organon*, will fancy that here he has *Phil.* in a trap; for these distinc-

To be free from all bias, and to begin his review of sects in that temper, he must begin by being an infidel. Vainly a man endeavours to reserve in a state of neutrality any preconceptions that he may have formed for himself, or prepossessions that he may have inherited from "mamma;" he cannot do it any more than he can dismiss his own shadow. Every man that lives, has (or has had) a *mamma*, who has made it impossible for him to be neutral in religious beliefs. And it is strange to contemplate the weakness of strong minds in fancying that they can. Calvin, whilst amiably engaged in hunting Servetus to death, and writing daily letters to his friends, in which he expresses his hope that the executive power would not think of burning the poor man, since really justice would be quite satisfied by cutting his head off, meets with some correspondents who conceive (idiots that they were!) even that little amputation not absolutely indispensable. But Calvin soon settles *their* scruples. You don't perceive, he tells them, what this man has been about. When a writer attacks Popery, it's very wrong in the Papists to cut his head off; and why? Because he has

tions, he will say, do not entirely exclude each other as they ought to do. The class calling itself Evangelical, for instance, may also be Calvinistic; the Newmanite is not, *therefore*, anti-Romish. True, says *Phil.;* I am quite aware of it. But to be aware of an objection is not to answer it. The fact seems to be, that the actual combinations of life, not conforming to the truth of abstractions, compel us to seeming breaches of logic. It would be right practically to distinguish the Radical from the Whig; and yet it might shock *Duns* or *Lombardus*, the *magister sententiarum*, when he came to understand that partially the principles of Radicals and Whigs coincide. But, for all that, the logic which distinguishes them is right; and the apparent error must be sought in the fact, that all cases (political or religious) being cases of life, are *concretes*, which never conform to the exquisite truth of abstractions. Practically, the Radical *is* opposed to the Whig, though casually the two are continually in conjunction; for, as *acting* partisans, they work *from* different centres, and finally, *for* different results.

only been attacking error. But here lies the difference in this case; Servetus had been attacking the TRUTH. Do you see the distinction, my friends? Consider it, and I am sure you will be sensible that this quite alters the case. It is shocking, it is perfectly ridiculous, that the Bishop of Rome should touch a hair of any man's head for contradicting *him;* and why? Because, do you see, *he* is wrong. On the other hand, it is evidently agreeable to philosophy, that I, John Calvin, should shave off the hair, and, indeed, the head itself (as I heartily hope* will be done in this present case), of any man presumptuous enough

* The reader may imagine that, in thus abstracting Calvin's epistolary sentiments, I am a little improving them. Certainly they would bear improvement, but that is not my business. What the reader sees here is but the result of bringing scattered passages into closer juxtaposition, whilst, as to the strongest (viz., the most sanguinary) sentiments here ascribed to him, it will be a sufficient evidence of my fidelity to the literal truth, if I cite three separate sentences. Writing to Farrel, he says, "*Spero* capitale saltem fore judicium." Sentence of the court, he *hopes,* will, at any rate, reach the life of Servetus. Die he must, and die he shall. But why should he die a cruel death? "Pœnæ vero atrocitatem remitti cupio." To the same purpose, when writing to Sultzer, he expresses his satisfaction in being able to assure him that a principal civic officer of Geneva was, in this case, entirely upright, and animated by the most virtuous sentiments. Indeed! what an interesting character! and in what way now might this good man show this beautiful tenderness of conscience? Why, by a fixed resolve that Servetus should not in any case escape the catastrophe which I, John Calvin, am longing for ("ut saltem exitum, *quem optamus,* non fugiat"). Finally, writing to the same Sultzer, he remarks that—when we see the Papists such avenging champions of their own superstitious fables as not to falter in shedding innocent blood, "pudeat Christianos magistratus [as if the Roman Catholic magistrates were not Christians] in tuendâ *certâ* veritate nihil prorsus habere animi"—"Christian magistrates ought to be ashamed of themselves for manifesting no energy at all in the vindication of truth undeniable;" yet really, since these magistrates had at that time the full design, which design not many days after they executed, of maintaining truth by fire and faggot, one does not see the call upon them for blushes so very deep as Calvin requires. Hands so crimson with blood might compensate the absence of crimson cheeks.

to contradict *me;* but then, why? For a reason that makes all the difference in the world, and which, one would think, idiocy itself could not overlook—viz., that I, John Calvin, am right—right through three degrees of comparison—right, righter, or more right, rightest, or most right.

The self-sufficingness of the Bible, and the right of private judgment—here, then, are the two great characters in which Protestantism commences; these are the bulwarks behind which it intrenches itself against Rome. And it is remarkable that these two great preliminary laws, which soon diverge into fields so different, at the first are virtually one and the same law. The refusal of a Delphic oracle at Rome alien to the Bible, extrinsic to the Bible, and claiming the sole interpretation of the Bible; the refusal of an oracle that reduced the Bible to a hollow mask, underneath which fraudulently introducing itself any earthly voice could mimic a heavenly voice, was in effect to refuse the coercion of this false oracle over each man's conscientious judgment; to make the Bible independent of the Pope, was to make man independent of *all* religious controllers. The *self-sufficingness of Scripture*, its independency of any external interpreter, passed in one moment into the other great Protestant doctrine of *Toleration*. It was but the same triumphal monument under a new angle of sight, the golden and silver faces of the same heraldic shield. The very same act which denies the right of interpretation to a mysterious Papal phœnix, renewed from generation to generation, having the antiquity and the incomprehensible omniscience of the Simorg,* that ancient bird in Southey,

---

* "*The Simorg:*"—If the reader has not made the acquaintance of this mysterious bird, eldest of created things, it is time he should. The Simorg would help him out of all his troubles, if the reader could find him at home. Let him consult Southey's "Thalaba."

transferred this right of mere necessity to the individuals of the whole human race. For where else could it have been lodged? Any attempt in any other direction was but to restore the Papal power in a new impersonation. Every man, therefore, suddenly obtained the right of interpreting the Bible for himself. But the word "*right*" obtained a new sense. Every man has the right, protected by the Queen's Bench, of publishing an unlimited number of metaphysical systems; and, under favour of the same indulgent Bench, we all enjoy the unlimited right of laughing at him. But not the whole race of man has a right to *coerce*, in the exercise of his intellectual rights, the humblest of individuals. The rights of men are thus unspeakbly elevated; for, being now freed from all anxiety, being sacred as merely *legal* rights, they suddenly rise into a new mode of responsibility as *intellectual* rights. As a Protestant, every mature man, the very humblest and poorest, has the same dignified right over his own opinions and profession of faith that he has over his own hearth. But his hearth can rarely be abused; whereas his religious system, being a vast kingdom, opening by immeasurable gates upon worlds of light and worlds of darkness, now brings him within a new amenability—called upon to answer new impeachments, and to seek for new assistances. Formerly another was answerable for his belief; if that were wrong, it was no fault of his. Now he has new rights, but these have burdened him with new obligations. Now he is crowned with the glory and the palms of an intellectual creature, but he is alarmed by the certainty of corresponding struggles. Protestantism it is that has created him into this child and heir of liberty; Protestantism it is that has invested him with these unbounded privileges of private judgment, giving him in one moment the sublime powers of a Pope within one solitary conscience; but Protestantism it is that has introduced him to the most dreadful of responsibilities.

I repeat that the twin maxims, the columns of Hercules through which Protestantism entered the great sea of human activities, were originally but two aspects of one law: to deny the Papal control over men's conscience being to affirm man's self-control, was, therefore, to affirm man's universal right to toleration, which again implied a corresponding *duty* of toleration. Under this bi-fronted law, generated by Protestantism, but in its turn regulating Protestantism, *Phil.* undertakes to develop all the principles that belong to a Protestant church. The *seasonableness* of such an investigation—its critical application to an evil now spreading like a fever through Europe—he perceives fully, and in the following terms he expresses this perception:—

"That we stand on the brink of a great theological crisis, that the problem must soon be solved, how far orthodox Christianity is possible for those who are not behind their age in scholarship and science; this is a solemn fact, which may be ignored by the partisans of shortsighted bigotry, but which is felt by all, and confessed by most of those who are capable of appreciating its reality and importance. The deep sybilline vaticinations of Coleridge's philosophical mind, the practical working of Arnold's religious sentimentalism, and the open acknowledgment of many divines who are living examples of the spirit of the age, have all, in different ways, foretold the advent of a Church of the Future."

This is from the preface, p. ix., where the phrase, *Church of the Future*, points to the Prussian minister's (Bunsen's) *Kirche der Zukunft:* but in the body of the work, and not far from its close (p. 114), he recurs to this crisis, and more circumstantially.

Phil. embarrasses himself and his readers in this development of Protestant principles. His own view of the task before him requires that he should separate himself from the consideration of any particular church, and lay aside all partisanship, plausible or not plausible. It is his own overture that warrants us in expecting this. And yet, before we have travelled three measured inches, he is found entangling himself with Church of Englandism. Let me not be misunderstood, as though, borrowing a Bentham word, I were therefore a Jerry Benthamite: I, that may describe myself generally as *Philo-Phil.*, am not less a son of the "Reformed Anglican Church" than *Phil.* Consequently, it is not likely that, in any vindication of that church, simply *as* such, and separately for itself, I should be the man to find grounds of exception. Loving most of what *Phil.* loves, loving *Phil.* himself, and hating (I grieve to say), with a theological hatred, whatever *Phil.* hates, why should I demur at this particular point to a course of argument that travels in the line of my own partialities? And yet I *do* demur. Having been promised a philosophic defence of the principles concerned in the great European schism of the sixteenth century, suddenly we find ourselves collapsing from that altitude of speculation into a defence of one individual church. Nobody would complain of *Phil.*, if, *after* having deduced philosophically the principles upon which all Protestant separation from Rome should revolve, he had gone forward to show, that in some one of the Protestant churches, more than in others, these principles had been asserted with peculiar strength, or carried through with special consistency, or associated pre-eminently with the other graces of a Christian church, such as a ritual more impressive to the heart of man—where lies the defence for the sublime Anglican Liturgy; or a polity more symmetrical with the structure of English society—where lies the defence of Episcopacy. Once having unfolded from philosophic grounds the primary conditions of a pure scriptural church, *Phil.* might then, without blame, have turned sharp round upon us, saying, such being the conditions under which the great idea of a true Christian church must be *constructed,* I now go on to show that the Church of England has conformed to those conditions more faithfully than any other. But to entangle the pure outlines of the idealising mind with the practical forms of any militant church, embarrassed (as we know all churches to have been) by pre-occupations of judgment, derived from feuds too local and interests too political—moving, also (as we know all churches to have moved), in a spirit of compromise, occasionally from mere necessities of position; this is in the result to injure the object of the writer doubly: first, as leaving an impression of partisanship: the reader is mistrustful from the first, as against a judge that in reality is an advocate; second, without reference to the effect upon the reader, directly to *Phil.* it is injurious, by fettering the freedom of his speculations; or, if leaving their freedom undisturbed, by narrowing their compass.

And if *Phil.*, as to the general movement of his Protestant pleadings, modulates too little in the transcendental key, sometimes he does so too much. For instance, at p. 69, sec. 35, we find him half calling upon Protestantism to account for her belief in God. How then? Is this belief special to Protestants? Are Roman Catholics, are those of the Greek, the Armenian, and other Christian churches, atheistically given? We used to be told that there is no royal road to geometry. I don't know whether there is or not; but I am sure there is no Protestant by-road, no Reformation short-cut, to the demonstration of Deity. It is true that *Phil.* exonerates his philosophic scholar, when throwing himself in Protestant freedom upon pure intellectual aids, from the vain labour of such an effort. He consigns him, however philosophic, to the evidence of "inevitable assumptions, upon axiomatic postulates, which the reflecting mind is compelled to accept, and which no more admit of doubt and cavil than of establishment by formal proof." I am not sure whether I understand *Phil.* in this section. Apparently he is glancing at Kant. Kant was the first person, and perhaps the last, that ever undertook formally to demonstrate the indemonstrability of God. He showed that the three great arguments for the existence of the Deity were virtually one, inasmuch as the two weaker borrowed their value and *vis apodeictica* from the more rigorous metaphysical argument. The physico-theological argument he forced to back, as it were, into the cosmological, and *that* into the ontological. After this reluctant *regressus* of the three into one, shutting up like a spy-glass, which (with the iron hand of Hercules forcing Cerberus up to daylight) the stern man of Königsberg resolutely dragged to the front of the arena, nothing remained, now that he had this pet scholastic argument driven up into a corner, than to break its neck—which he did. Kant took the conceit out of all the three arguments; but, if this is what *Phil.* alludes to, he should have added, that these three, after all, were only the arguments of speculating or *theoretic* reason. To this faculty Kant peremptorily denied the power of demonstrating the Deity; but then that same *apodeixis*, which he had thus inexorably torn from reason under one manifestation, Kant himself restored to the reason in another (the *praktische vernunft*). God he asserts to be a postulate of the human reason, as speaking through the conscience and will, not proved *ostensively*, but indirectly proved as being *wanted* indispensably, and presupposed in other necessities of our human nature. This, probably, is what *Phil.* means by his shorthand expression of "axiomatic postulates." But then it should not have been said that the case does not "admit of formal proof," since the proof is as "formal" and rigorous by this new method of Kant as by the old obsolete methods of Sam. Clarke and the schoolmen.*

But it is not the too high or the too low—the too much or the too little—of what one might call by analogy the *transcendental* course, which I charge upon *Phil.* It is, that he is too desultory—too eclectic. And the secret purpose, which seems to me predominant throughout his work, is, not so much the defence of Protestantism, or even of the Anglican Church, as a report of the latest novelties that have found a roosting-place in the English Church, amongst the most temperate of those churchmen who keep pace with modern philosophy; in short, it is a selection from the classical doctrines of religion, exhibited under their newest revision; or, generally, it is an attempt to show, from what is going on amongst the most moving orders in the English Church, how far it is possible that strict orthodoxy should bend, on the one side, to new impulses, derived from an advancing philosophy, and yet, on the other side, should reconcile itself, both verbally and in spirit, with ancient standards. But if *Phil.* is eclectic, then *I* will be eclectic; if *Phil.* has a right to be desultory, then *I* have a right. *Phil.* is my leader. I can't in reason be expected to be better than *he* is. If I'm wrong, *Phil.* ought to set me a better example. And here, before this

* The method of Des Cartes was altogether separate and peculiar to himself; it is a mere conjurer's juggle; and yet, what is strange, like some other audacious sophisms, it is capable of being so stated as most of all to baffle the subtle dialectician; and Kant himself, though not cheated, was never so much perplexed in his life as in the effort to make its hollowness apparent.

honourable audience of the public, I charge all my errors (whatever they may be, past or coming) upon *Phil.*'s misconduct.

Having thus established my patent of vagrancy, and my license for picking and choosing, I choose out these three articles to toy with:—first, Bibliolatry; second, Development applied to the Bible and Christianity; third, Philology, as the particular resource against false philosophy, relied on by *Phil.*

Bibliolatry.—We Protestants charge upon the Ponteficii, as the more learned of our fathers always called the Roman Catholics, *Mariolatry;* they pay undue honours, say we, to the Virgin. They, in return, charge upon us *Bibliolatry,* or a superstitious allegiance—an idolatrous homage—to the words, to the syllables, and to the very punctuation of the Bible. They, according to *us,* deify a woman; and we, according to *them,* deify an arrangement of printer's types. As to *their* error, we need not mind *that:* let us attend to our own. And to this extent it is evident at a glance that Bibliolatrists *must* be wrong—viz., because as a pun vanishes on being translated into another language, even so would, and must melt away, like ice in a hot-house, a large majority of those conceits which every Christian nation is apt to ground upon the verbal text of the Scriptures in its own separate vernacular version. But once aware that much of their Bibliolatry depends upon ignorance of Hebrew and Greek, and often depends upon peculiarity of idiom or structures in modern tongues, cautious people begin to suspect the whole. Here arises a very interesting, startling, and perplexing situation for all who venerate the Bible; one which must always have existed for prying, inquisitive people, but which has been incalculably sharpened for the apprehension of these days by the extraordinary advances made and being made in Oriental and Greek philology. It is a situation of public scandal even to the deep reverencers of the Bible; but a situation of much more than scandal, of real grief, to the profound and sincere amongst religious people. On the one hand, viewing the Bible as the Word of God, and not merely so in the sense of its containing most salutary counsels, but, in the highest sense, of its containing a revelation of the most awful secrets, they cannot for a moment listen to the pretence that the Bible has benefited by God's inspiration only as other good books may be said to have done. They are confident that, in a much higher sense, and in a sense incommunicable to other books, it is inspired. Yet, on the other hand, as they will not tell lies, or countenance lies, even in what seems the service of religion, they cannot hide from themselves that the materials of this imperishable book are perishable, frail, liable to crumble, and actually *have* crumbled to some extent, in various instances. There is, therefore, lying broadly before us, something like what Kant called an antinomy—a case where two laws equally binding on the mind are, or seemed to be, in collision. Such cases occur in morals—cases which are carried out of the general rule, and the jurisdiction of that rule, by peculiar deflections; and from the word *case* we derive the word *casuistry*, as a general science dealing with such anomalous cases. There is a casuistry, also, for the speculative understanding, as well as for the moral (which in Kant's terminology is the *practical)* understanding. And this question, as to the inspiration of the Bible, with its apparent conflict of forces, repelling it and yet affirming it, is one of its most perplexing and most momentous problems.

My own solution of the problem would reconcile all that

is urged against an inspiration with all that the internal necessity of the case would plead in behalf of an inspiration. So would *Phil.'s.* His distinction, like mine, would substantially come down to this—that the grandeur and extent of religious truth is not of a nature to be affected by verbal changes such as *can* be made by time, or accident, or without treacherous design. It is like lightning, which could not be mutilated, or truncated, or polluted. But it may be well to rehearse a little more in detail, both *Phil.'s* view and my own. Let my principal go first; make way, I desire, for my leader: let this honourable man *Phil.*, whom I, *Philo-Phil.*, now take by the right hand, and solemnly present to the public—let this Daniel who has come to judgment have precedency, as, in all reason, it is my duty to see that he has.

Whilst rejecting altogether any inspiration as attaching to the separate words and phrases of the Scriptures, *Phil.* insists upon such an inspiration as attaching to the spiritual truths and doctrines delivered in these Scriptures. And he places this theory in a striking light, equally for what it affirms and for what it denies, by these two arguments—first (in affirmation of the real spiritual inspiration), that a series of more than thirty writers, speaking in succession along a vast line of time, and absolutely without means of concert, yet all combine unconsciously to one end—lock like parts of a great machine into one system—conspire to the unity of a very elaborate scheme, without being at all aware of what was to come after. Here, for instance, is one, living nearly one thousand six hundred years before the last in the series, who lays a foundation (in reference to man's ruin, to God's promises and plan for human restoration), which is built upon and carried forward by all, without exception, that follow. Here come a multitude that prepare each for his successor—that unconsciously integrate each other—that, finally, when reviewed, make up a total drama, of which each writer's separate share would have been utterly imperfect without corresponding parts that he could not have foreseen. At length all is finished. A profound piece of music, a vast oratorio, perfect and of elaborate unity, has resulted from a long succession of strains, each for itself fragmentary. On such a final creation resulting from such a distraction of parts, it is indispensable to suppose an overruling inspiration, in order at all to account for the final result of a most elaborate harmony. Besides, which would argue some inconceivable magic, if we did not assume a providential inspiration watching over the coherencies, tendencies, and intertesselations (to use a learned word) of the whole—it happens that, in many instances, typical things are recorded—things ceremonial, that could have no meaning to the person recording—prospective words, that were reported and transmitted in a spirit of confiding faith, but that could have little meaning to the reporting parties for many hundreds of years. Briefly, a great mysterious *word* is spelt as it were by the whole sum of the scriptural books—every separate book forming a letter or syllable in that secret and that unfinished word, as it was for so many ages. This co-operation of ages, not able to communicate or concert arrangements with each other, is neither more nor less an argument of an overruling inspiration, than if the separation of the contributing parties were by space, and not by time. As if, for example, every island at the same moment were to send its contribution, without previous concert, to a sentence or chapter of a book; in which case the result, if full of meaning, much more if full of awful and profound meaning, could not be explained rationally without the assumption of a supernatural overruling of these unconscious co-operators to a common result. So far on behalf of inspiration. Yet, on the other hand, as an argument in denial of any blind mechanic inspiration cleaving to words and syllables, *Phil.* notices this consequence as resulting from such an assumption—viz., that if you adopt any one gospel, St John's suppose, or any one narrative of a particular transaction, as inspired in this minute and pedantic sense, then for every other report, which, adhering to the spiritual *value* of the circumstances, and virtually the same, should differ in the least of the details, there would instantly arise a solemn degradation. All parts of Scripture, in fact, would thus be made active and operative in degrading each other.

Such is *Phil.'s* way of explaining θεοπνευστια* *(theopneustia)*, or divine prompting, so as to reconcile the doctrine affirming a *virtual* inspiration, an inspiration as to the truths revealed, with a peremptory denial of any inspiration at all, as to the mere verbal vehicle of those revelations. He is evidently as sincere in regard to the inspiration which he upholds, as in regard to that which he denies. *Phil.* is honest, and *Phil.* is able. Now comes *my* turn. I rise to support my leader, and shall attempt to wrench this notion of a verbal inspiration from the hands of its champions by a *reductio ad absurdum*—viz., by showing the

* "Θεοπνευστια:"—I must point out to *Phil.* an oversight of his as to this word at page 45; he there describes the doctrine of *theopneustia* as being that of "plenary and *verbal* inspiration." But this he cannot mean, for obviously this word *theopneustia* comprehends equally the verbal inspiration which he is denouncing, and the inspiration of power or spiritual virtue which he is substituting. Neither *Phil.*, nor any one of his school, is to be understood as rejecting *theopneustia*, but as rejecting that particular mode of *theopneustia* which appeals to the eye by mouldering symbols, in favour of that other mode which appeals to the heart by incorruptible radiations of inner truth.

monstrous consequences to which it leads—which form of logic *Phil.* also has employed; but mine is different, and more elaborate. Yet, first of all, let me frankly confess to the reader, that some people allege a point-blank assertion by Scripture itself of its own verbal inspiration; which assertion, if it really *had* any existence, would summarily put down all cavils of human dialectics. *That* makes it necessary to review this assertion. This famous passage of Scripture, this *locus classicus*, or prerogative text, pleaded for the *verbatim et literatim* inspiration of the Bible, is the following; and I will so exhibit its very words as that the reader, even if no Grecian, may understand the point in litigation. The passage is this: Πασα γραφη θεοπνευστος και ὠφελιμος, &c., taken from St Paul (2 Tim. iii. 16). Let us construe it literally, expressing the Greek by Latin characters: *Pasa graphé*, all written lore (or every writing)—*theopneustos*, God-breathed, or God-prompted—*kai*, and (or also) —*ophelimos*, serviceable—*pros*, towards—*didaskalian*, doctrinal truth. Now this sentence, when thus rendered into English according to the rigour of the Grecian letter, wants something to complete its sense—it wants an *is*. There is a subject, as the logicians say, and there is a predicate (or something affirmed of that subject), but there is no *copula* to connect them—we miss the *is*. This omission is common in Greek, but cannot be allowed in English. The *is* must be supplied; but *where* must it be supplied? That's the very question, for there is a choice between two places; and, according to the choice, will the word *theopneustos* become part of the subject or part of the predicate, which will make a world of difference. Let us try it both ways:—

1. All writing inspired by God (*i. e.*, being inspired by God, supposing it inspired, which makes *theopneustos* part of the subject) IS also profitable for teaching, &c.

2. All writing IS inspired by God, and profitable, &c. (which makes *theopneustos* part of the predicate.)

Now, in this last way of construing the text, which is the way adopted by our authorised version, one objection strikes everybody at a glance—viz., that St Paul could not possibly mean to say of all writing, indiscriminately, that it was divinely inspired, this being so revoltingly opposed to the truth. It follows, therefore, that, on this way of interpolating the *is*, we must understand the Apostle to use the word *graphé*, writing, in a restricted sense, not for writing generally, but for sacred writing, or (as our English phrase runs) "*Holy Writ;*" upon which will arise three separate demurs: First, one already stated by *Phil.*—viz., that when *graphé* is used in this sense, it is accompanied by the article; the phrase is either ἡ γραφη, "the writing," or else (as in St Luke) αι γραφαι, "the writings," just as in English it is said, "the Scripture," or "the Scriptures." Secondly, that, according to the Greek usage, this would not be the natural place for introducing the *is*. Thirdly—which disarms the whole objection from this text, *howsoever* construed—that, after all, it leaves the dispute with the bibliolaters wholly untouched. We also, the anti-bibliolaters, say that all Scripture is inspired, though we may not therefore suppose the apostle to be here insisting on that doctrine. But no matter whether he is or not, in relation to this dispute. Both parties are contending for the inspiration—so far they are agreed; the question between them arises upon quite another point—viz., as to the *mode* of that inspiration, whether incarnating its golden light in the corruptibilities of perishing syllables, or in the sanctities of indefeasible, word-transcending ideas. Now, upon that question, the apostolic words, torture them how you please, say nothing at all.

There is, then, no such dogma (or, to speak *Germanicè*, no such *macht-spruch*) in behalf of verbal inspiration as has been ascribed to St Paul; and I pass to my own argument against it. This argument turns upon the self-confounding tendency of the common form ascribed to θεοπνευστια, or divine inspiration. When translated from its true and lofty sense of an inspiration—brooding, with outstretched wings, over the mighty abyss of *secret* truth—to the vulgar sense of an inspiration, burrowing, like a rabbit or a worm, in grammatical quillets and syllables, mark how it comes down to nothing at all; mark how a stream, pretending to derive itself from a heavenly fountain, is finally lost and confounded in a morass of human perplexities.

First of all, at starting, we have the inspiration (No. 1) to the original composers of the sacred books. *That* I grant, though distinguishing as to its nature.

Next, we want another inspiration (No. 2) for the countless *translators* of the Bible. Of what use is it to a German, to a Swiss, or to a Scotsman, that, three thousand years (plus two hundred) before the Reformation, the author of the Pentateuch was kept from erring by a divine restraint over his words, if the authors of this Reformation—Luther, suppose, Zwingle, John Knox—either making translations themselves, or *relying* upon translations made by others under no such verbal restraint, have been left free to bias his mind, pretty nearly as much as if the original Hebrew writer had been resigned to his own human discretion?

Thirdly, even if we adopt the inspiration No. 2, *that* will not avail us; because many *different* translators exist. Does the very earliest translation of the Law and the Prophets—viz., the Greek translation of the Septuagint—always agree verbally with the Hebrew? Or the Samaritan Pentateuch always with the Hebrew? Or do the earliest Latin versions of the entire Bible agree *verbally* with modern Latin versions? Jerome's Latin version, for instance, memorable as being that adopted by the Romish Church, and known under the name of the *Vulgate*, does it agree verbally with the Latin versions of the Bible or parts of the Bible made since the Reformation? In the English, again, if we begin with the translatior still sleeping in MS., made five centuries ago—in fact, about Chaucer's time—and passing from that to the first *printed* translation (which was, I think, Coverdale's, in 1535), if we thence travel down to our own day, so as to include all that have confined themselves to separate versions of some one book, or even of some one cardinal text, countless are the versions that differ—and to the idolater of words, *all* differences are important. Here, then, on that doctrine of inspiration which ascribes so much to the power of *verbal* accuracy, we shall want a third inspiration (No. 3) for the guidance of each separate Christian applying himself to the Scriptures in his mother tongue. The man who seeks to benefit by inspiration in his choice of a translator will have to select from a multitude, since nobody contends that the truth is uniformly exhibited throughout any one version, but grants that it is dispersed in fractions through a multitude.

Fourthly, as these differences of version arise often under the *same* reading of the original text; but as, in the meantime, there are many *different* readings, here a fourth source of possible error calls for a fourth inspiration overruling us to the proper choice amongst various readings. What may be called a "textual" inspiration for *selecting* the right reading is requisite for the very same reason, neither more nor less, which supposes any verbal inspiration originally requisite for *constituting* a right reading. It matters not in which stage of the Bible's progress the error commences; first stage and last stage are all alike in the sight of God. There was, reader, as perhaps you know, about six-score years ago, another *Phil.*, not the same as this *Phil.* now before us (who would be quite vexed if you fancied him as old as all *that* comes to—oh dear, no! he's not near as old)—well, that earlier *Phil.* was Bentley, who wrote (under the name of *Phileleutherus Lipsiensis*) a pamphlet connected with this very subject, partly against an English infidel of that day. In that pamphlet, *Phil.* the first pauses to consider and value this very objection from textual variation to the validity of Scripture; for the infidel (as is usual with infidels) being no great scholar, had argued as though it were impossible to urge anything whatever for the Word of God, since so vast a variety in the readings rendered it impossible to know what *was* the Word of God. Bentley, though rather rough, from having too often to deal with shallow coxcombs, was really and unaffectedly a pious man. He was shocked at this argument, and set himself seriously to consider it. Now, as all the various readings were Greek, and as Bentley happened to be the first of Grecians, his deliberate review of this argument is entitled to great attention. There were, at that moment when Bentley spoke, something more (as I recollect) than ten thousand varieties of reading in the text of the New Testament; so many had been collected in the early part of Queen Anne's reign by Wetstein, the Dutchman, who was then at the head of the collators. Mill, the Englishman, was at that very time making further collations. How many he added, I cannot tell without consulting books—a thing which I very seldom do. But since that day, and long after Bentley and

Mill were in their graves, Griesbach, the German, rose to the top of the tree, by towering above them all in the accuracy of his collations. Yet, as the harvest comes before the gleanings, we may be sure that Wetstein's barn housed the very wealth of all this variety. Of this it was, then, that Bentley spoke. And what *was* it that he spoke? Why, he, the great scholar, pronounced, as with the authority of a Chancery decree, that the vast majority of various readings made no difference at all in the sense. In the *sense*, observe; but many things *might* make a difference in the sense, which would still leave the doctrine undisturbed. For instance, in the passage about a camel going through the eye of a needle, it will make a difference in the sense, and a very noticeable difference, whether you read in the Greek word for *camel* the oriental animal of that name, or a ship's cable, sometimes so called; but no difference at all arises in the spiritual doctrine. Or, illustrating the case out of Shakspere, it makes no difference as to the result, whether you read in Hamlet "to take arms against a *sea* of troubles," or (as has been suggested) "against a *siege* of troubles;" but it makes a difference as to the integrity of the image.* What has a sea to do with

* "*Integrity of the image:*"—One of the best notes ever written by Warburton was in justification of the old reading, *sea*. It was true, that against a *sea* it would be idle to take *arms*. We, that have lived since Warburton's day, have learned, by the solemn example of Mrs Partington (which, it is to be hoped, none of us will ever forget), how useless, how vain it is to take up a mop against the Atlantic Ocean. Can it be said that Mrs Partington lived in vain, if she demonstrated this relation between mops and the Atlantic? Great is the mop, great is Mrs Partington, but greater is the Atlantic. Yet, though all arms must be idle against the sea considered literally, and *κατα την φαντασιαν* under that image, Warburton contended justly that all images, much employed, *evanesce* into the ideas which they represent. A *sea* of troubles comes to mean only a *multitude* of troubles. No image of the sea is suggested; and arms, incongruous in relation to the literal

arms? What has a camel,* the quadruped, to do with a needle? A prodigious minority, therefore, there is of such various readings as slightly affect the *sense;* but this minority becomes next to nothing, when we inquire for such as affect any *doctrine.* This was Bentley's opinion upon the possible disturbance offered to the Christian by various readings in the New Testament. You thought that the carelessness, or, at times, even the treachery of men, through so many centuries, must have ended in corrupting the original truth; yet, after all, you see the light burns as brightly and steadily as ever. We, now, that are not bibliolatrists, no more believe that, from the disturbance of a few words here and there, any evangelical truth can have suffered a wound or mutilation, than we believe that the burning of a wood, or even of a forest, which happens in our vast American possessions, sometimes from natural causes (lightning, or spontaneous combustion), sometimes from an Indian's carelessness in lighting his culinary fires, sometimes from an Englishman's carelessness, when throwing away into a drift of dry leaves the fuming reliques of his cigar, can seriously have injured botany. But for *him,* who conceives an inviolable sanctity to have

---

sea, is not so in relation to a multitude; besides, that the image *arms* itself evanesces for the same reason into *resistance.* For this one note, which I cite from boyish remembrance, I have always admired the subtlety of Warburton.

* Meantime, though using this case as an illustration, I believe that *camel* is, after all, the true translation; first, on account of the undoubted proverb in the East about the *elephant* going through the needle's eye; the relation is that of *contrast* as to magnitude; and the same relation holds as to the camel and the needle's eye; secondly, because the proper word for a cable, it has been alleged, is not "camelus," but "camilus." What has an elephant to do with a needle? Why, he has this to do: the needle's eye, under its narrow function, takes charge of physical magnitude in one extreme—the elephant of the same idea in another extreme.

settled upon each word and particle of the original record, there *should* have been strictly required an inspiration (No. 5) to prevent the possibility of various readings arising. It is too late, however, to pray for *that;* the various readings *have* arisen; here they are, thirty thousand in amount; and what's to be done now? The only resource for the bibliolatrist is—to invoke a new inspiration for helping him out of his difficulty, by guiding his choice. We, anti-bibliolaters are not so foolish as to believe that God, having once sent a deep message of truth to man, would suffer it to lie at the mercy of a careless or a wicked copyist. Treasures so vast would not be left at the mercy of accidents so vile. Very little more than two hundred years ago, a London compositor, not wicked at all, but simply drunk, in printing Deuteronomy, left out the most critical of words; the seventh commandment he exhibited thus—"Thou *shalt* commit adultery;" in which form the sheet was struck off. And though in those days no practical mischief could arise from this singular *erratum,* which English Griesbachs will hardly enter upon the roll of various readings, yet, harmless as it was, it met with punishment. "Scandalous!" said Laud; "shocking! to tell men in the seventeenth century, as a biblical rule, that they positively must commit adultery!" The brother compositors of this drunken biblical reviser, being too honourable to betray the individual delinquent, the Star-Chamber fined the whole "chapel." A black Monday *that* must have been for the self-accusing compositors. Now, the copyists of MSS. were as certain to be sometimes drunk as this compositor—famous by his act, utterly forgotten in his person—whose crime is remembered, the record of whose name has perished. We therefore hold that it never was in the power, or placed within the discretion, of any copyist, whether writer or printer, to injure the sacred oracles. But the bibliolatrist cannot say *that*; because, if he does, then he is formally unsaying the very principle which is meant by bibliolatry. He therefore must require another supplementary inspiration—viz., No. 5, if I count right, to direct him in his choice of the true reading amongst so many as continually offer themselves.*

Fifthly, as all words cover ideas, and many a word covers a choice of ideas, and very many ideas split into a variety of modifications, we shall, even after a fifth inspiration has qualified us for selecting the true reading, still be at a loss how, with regard to this right reading, to select the right acceptation. So *there*, at that fifth stage, in rushes the total deluge of human theological controversies. One church, or one sect, insists upon one sense; second church or second sect, "to the end of time,"

* I recollect no variation in the text of Scripture which makes any startling change, even to the amount of an eddy in its own circumjacent waters, except that famous passage about the three witnesses—"*There are three that bare record in heaven*," &c. This has been denounced with perfect fury as an interpolation; and it is impossible to sum up the quart bottles of ink, black and blue, that have been shed in the dreadful skirmish. Porson even, the all-accomplished Grecian, in his letters to Archdeacon Travis, took a conspicuous part in the controversy. His wish was, that men should think of him as a second Bentley tilting against Phalaris; and he stung like a hornet. To be a Cambridge man in those days was to be a hater of all Establishments in England; things and persons were hated alike. It may chance that on this subject Master Porson will get stung through his coffin, before he is many years deader. However, if this particular variation troubles the waters just around itself (for it would desolate a Popish village to withdraw its local saint), yet carrying one's eye from this Epistle to the whole domains of the New Testament—yet, looking away from that defrauded village to universal Christendom, we must exclaim—What does one miss? Surely Christendom is not disturbed because a village suffers wrong; the sea is not roused because an eddy in a corner is boiling; the doctrine of the Trinity is not in danger because Mr Porson is in a passion.

insists upon another. Babel is upon us; and, to get rid of Babel, we shall need a sixth inspiration. No. 6 is clamorously called for.*

But we all know, each knows by his own experience, that No. 6 is not forthcoming; and in the absence of *that*, what avail for *us* the others? "Man overboard!" is the cry upon deck; but what avails it for the poor drowning creature that a rope being thrown to him is thoroughly secured at one end to the ship, if the other end floats wide of his grasp? We are in prison: we descend from our prison-roof, that seems high as the clouds, by knotting together all the prison bedclothes, and all the aids from friends outside. But all is too short: after swarming down the line, in middle air, we find ourselves hanging:

* One does not wish to be tedious; or, if one *has* a gift in that way, naturally one does not wish to bestow it *all* upon a stranger, as "the reader" usually is, but to reserve part for the fireside, and the use of one's most beloved friends; else I could torment the reader by a long succession of numbers. But one more of the series—viz., No. 7, as a parting *gage d'amitié*—he must positively permit me to drop into his pocket. Supposing, then, that No. 6 were surmounted, and that, supernaturally, you knew the value to a hair's-breadth of every separate word (or, perhaps, composite phrase made up from a constellation of words), still you are lost again; for oftentimes, and especially in St Paul, the words may be known, their sense may be known, but their *logical relation* is still doubtful. The word X and the word Y are separately clear; but has Y the dependency of a consequence upon X, or no dependency at all? Does Y modify X, or not? Is the clause which stands eleventh in the series a direct prolongation of that which stands tenth? or is the tenth wholly independent and insulated? or does it occupy the place of a parenthesis, so as to modify the ninth clause? People that have practised composition with a vigilant eye know also, by thousands of cases, how infinite is the disturbance caused in the logic of a thought by the mere position of a word as despicable as the word *even*. A mote, that is itself invisible, shall darken the august faculty of sight in a human eye—the heavens shall be hidden by a wretched atom that dares not show itself—and the station of a syllable shall cloud the judgment of a council. Nay, even an ambiguous emphasis falling to the right-hand word or the left-hand word shall confound a system.

sixty feet of line are still wanting. To reascend—*that* is impossible: to drop boldly—alas! *that* is to die.

Meantime, what need of this eternal machinery, that eternally is breaking like ropes of sand? Or of this earth resting on an elephant, that rests on a tortoise, that, when all is done, must still consent to rest on the common atmosphere of God? These chains of inspiration are needless. The great ideas of the Bible protect themselves. The heavenly truths, by their own imperishableness, defeat the mortality of languages with which for a moment they are associated. Is the lightning dimmed or emasculated, because for thousands of years it has blended with the tarnish of earth and the steams of earthly graves? Or light, which so long has travelled in the chambers of our sickly air, and searched the haunts of impurity—is that less pure than it was in the first chapter of Genesis? Or that more holy light of truth—the truth, suppose, written from his creation upon the tablets of man's heart—which truth never was imprisoned in any Hebrew or Greek, but has ranged for ever through courts and camps, deserts and cities, the original lesson of justice to man—of piety to God, has that become tainted by intercourse with flesh? or has it become hard to decipher, because the very heart, that human heart where it is inscribed, is so often blotted with falsehoods? You are aware, perhaps, reader, that in the Mediterranean Sea, off the coast of Asia Minor (and, indeed, elsewhere), through the very middle of the salt-sea billows, rises up, in silvery brightness, an aspiring column of *fresh* water.* In the desert of the sea are found foun-

* See Mr Yates's "Annotations upon Fellowes's Researches in Anatolia," as *one* authority for this singular phenomenon, which has since been noticed in the Persian Gulf. This most interesting phenomenon was witnessed by the Generals Outram and Havelock, in company with most of their army, on the expedition against Persia, within the last

tains—sister fountains to those of Ishmael and Isaac in the Arabian sands! Are these fountains poisoned for the poor victim of fever, because they have to travel through a contagion of waters not potable? Oh no! They bound upwards like arrows, cleaving the seas above with as much projectile force as the glittering waterworks of Versailles cleave the air, and rising as sweet to the lip as ever mountain torrent that comforted the hunted fawn.

It is impossible to suppose that any truth, launched by God upon the agitations of things so unsettled as languages, *can* perish. The very frailty of languages is the strongest proof of this; because it is impossible to suppose that anything so great can have been committed to the fidelity of anything so treacherous. There is laughter in heaven when it is told of man, that he fancies his earthly jargons, which, to heavenly ears, must sound like the chucklings of poultry, equal to the task of hiding or distorting any light of revelation. Had *words* possessed any authority or restraint over scriptural truth, a much worse danger would have threatened it than any malice in the human will, suborning false copyists, or surreptitiously favouring depraved copies. Even a general conspiracy of the human race for such a purpose would avail against the Bible only as a general conspiracy to commit suicide might avail against the drama of God's providence. Either conspiracy would first become dangerous when either became possible. But a real danger seems to lie in the insensible corruption going on for ever within all languages, by

twelve months [February, 1858]. In fact, if a fountain bursts out with the sudden impetus of a fiery projectile, forced upwards by earthquake, which may happen on the barren floor of the ocean as probably as in many other situations, then, supposing the column of water above not too dense, the fountain of fresh water will naturally cleave the marine water like an arrow.

means of which they are eternally dying away from their own vital powers; and that is a danger which is travelling fast after all the wisdom and the wit, the eloquence and the poetry of this earth, like a mountainous wave, and will finally overtake them—their very vehicles being lost and confounded to human sensibilities. But such a wave will break harmlessly against scriptural truth; and not merely because that truth will for ever evade such a shock by its eternal transfer from language to language—from languages dying out to languages in vernal bloom—but also because, if it could *not* evade the shock, supreme truth would surmount it for a profounder reason. A danger analogous to this once existed in a different form. The languages into which the New Testament was first translated offered an apparent obstacle to the translation that seemed insurmountable. The Latin, for instance, did not present the spiritual words which such a translation demanded; and how *should* it, when the corresponding ideas had no existence amongst the Romans? Yet, if not spiritual, the language of Rome was intellectual; it was the language of a cultivated and noble race. But what shall be done if the New Testament seeks to drive a tunnel through a rude forest race, having an undeveloped language, and understanding nothing but war? Four centuries after Christ, such a case did actually occur: the Gothic Bishop Ulphilas set about translating the Gospels for his countrymen. He had no words for expressing spiritual relations or spiritual operations. The new nomenclature of moral graces, humility, resignation, the spirit of forgiveness, &c., hitherto unrecognised for virtues amongst men, having first of all been shown as blossoms and flowers, and distinguished from weeds, by Christian gardening, had to be reproduced in the Gothic language, with apparently no means whatever of effecting it. In this earliest of what we may call ancestral translations (for the Goths were of our own blood), and, therefore, by many degrees, this most interesting of translations for *us*, may be seen to this day, when nearly fifteen centuries have passed, *how* the good bishop succeeded, to what extent he succeeded, and by what means. I shall take a separate opportunity for investigating that problem; but at present I will content myself with noticing a remarkable principle which applies to the case, and illustrating it by a remarkable anecdote. The principle is this—that in the grander parts of knowledge, which do not deal much with petty details, nearly all the *building* or constructive ideas (those ideas which build up the system of that particular knowledge) lie involved within each other; so that any one of the series, being awakened in the mind, is sufficient (given a multitude of minds) to lead backwards or forwards, analytically or synthetically, into many of the rest. That is the principle;* and the story which illustrates it is this:—A great

* *That is the principle:*"—I am afraid, on reviewing this passage, that the reader may still say, "*What* is the principle?" I will add, therefore, the shortest explanation of my meaning. If into any Pagan language you had occasion to translate the word *love*, or *purity*, or *penitence*, &c., you could not do it. The Greek language itself perhaps the finest (all things weighed and valued) that man has employed, could not do it. The *scale* was not so pitched as to make the transfer possible. It was to execute organ music on a guitar. And, hereafter, I will endeavour to show how scandalous an error has been committed on this subject, not by scholars only, but by religious philosophers. The relation of Christian ethics (which word ethics, however, is itself most insufficient) to natural or universal ethics is a field yet uncultured by a rational thought. The first word of sense has yet to be spoken. There lies the difficulty; and the principle which meets it is this, that what any one idea could never effect for itself (insulated, it must remain an unknown quality for ever), the total system of the ideas developed from its centre would effect for each separately. To know the part, you must first know the whole, or know it, at least, by some outline. The idea of *purity*, for instance, in its Christian altitude, would be utterly incomprehensible,

work of Apollonius, the sublime geometer, was supposed in part to have perished: seven of the eight books remained in the original Greek; but the eighth was missing. The Greek, after much search, was not recovered; but at length there was found (in the Bodleian, I think) an Arabic translation of it. An English mathematician (Halley), knowing not one word of Arabic, determined (without waiting for that Arabic key) to pick the lock of this MS. And he did so. Through strength of preconception, derived equally from his knowledge of the general subject, and from his knowledge of this particular work in its earlier sections, using also to some extent the subtle art of the decipherer,* now become so powerful an instrument of analysis, he translated the whole Arabic MS. He printed it—he pub-

---

and, besides, could not sustain itself for a moment if by any glimpse it were approached. But when a *ruin* was unfolded that had affected the human race, and many things heretofore unobserved, *because uncombined*, were gathered into a unity of evidence to that ruin, spread through innumerable channels, the great altitude would begin dimly to reveal itself by means of the mighty depth in correspondence. One deep calleth to another. One after one the powers lodged in the awful succession of uncoverings would react upon each other; and thus the feeblest language would be as capable of receiving and reflecting the system of truths (because the system is an arch that supports itself) as the richest and noblest; and for the same reason that makes geometry careless of language. The vilest jargon that ever was used by a shivering savage of Terra del Fuego is as capable of dealing with the sublime and eternal affections of space and quantity, with up and down, with more and less, with circle and radius, angle and tangent, as is the golden language of Athens.

* "*Art of the decipherer:*"—An art which, in the seventeenth century, had been greatly improved by Wallis, Savilian professor of geometry at Oxford, the improver of analytic mathematics, and the great historian of algebra. Algebra it was that suggested to him his exquisite deciphering skill, and the Parliamentary War it was that furnished him with a sufficient field of practice. The king's private cabinet of papers, all written in cipher, and captured in the royal coach on the decisive day of Naseby (June, 1645), was (I believe) deciphered by Wallis, *proprio marte;* that is to say, without assistance.

lished it. He tore the hidden truth—he extorted it from the darkness of a perfectly unknown language—he would not suffer the Arabic to hide a treasure from man. And the book remains a monument to this day, that a system of ideas, having internal coherency and interdependency, is vainly hidden under a mask of words; that it may be illuminated and restored chiefly through the reciprocal involutions of the hidden ideas themselves. The same principle applies, and *à fortiori* applies, to religious truth, as one which lies far deeper than geometry in the spirit of man, one to which the inner attestation is profounder, and to which the key-notes of Scripture (once awakened on the great organ of the human heart) are sure to call up corresponding echoes. It is not in the power of language to arrest or to defeat this mode of truth; because, when once the fundamental base is furnished by revelation, the human heart itself is able to co-operate in developing the great harmonies of the system, without aid from language, and in defiance of language—without aid from human learning, and in defiance of human learning, by a machinery of spiritual counterpoint.

Finally, there is another security against the suppression or distortion of any great biblical truth by false readings, which I will state in the briefest terms. The reader is aware of the boyish sport sometimes called "drake-stone:" a flattish stone is thrown by a little dexterity so as to graze the surface of a river, but so, also as in grazing it to dip slightly below the surface, to rise again from this dip, again to dip, again to rise, and so on alternately dipping and rising *à plusieurs reprises*. In the same way, with the same effect of alternate resurrections, all scriptural truths reverberate and diffuse themselves along the pages of the Bible; none is confined to one text, or to one mode of enunciation; all parts of the scheme are eternally chasing each other, like the parts of a fugue; they hide themselves in one chapter, only to restore themselves in another; they diverge, only to recombine; and under such a vast variety of expressions, that even in that way, supposing language to have powers over religious truth—which it never had, or can have—any abuse of such a power would be thoroughly neutralised. The case resembles the diffusion of vegetable seeds through the air and through the waters; draw a *cordon sanitaire* against dandelion or thistledown, and see if the armies of earth would suffice to interrupt this process of radiation, which yet is but the distribution of weeds. Suppose, for instance, the text about the *three heavenly witnesses* to have been eliminated finally as an interpolation. The first thought is—*there* goes to wreck a great doctrine! Not at all. That text occupied but a corner of the garden. The truth, and the secret implications of the truth, have escaped at a thousand points in vast arches above our heads, rising high above the garden wall, and have sown the earth with memorials of the mystery which they envelop.

The final inference is this—that scriptural truth is endowed with a self-conservative and a self-restorative virtue; it needs no long successions of verbal protection by inspiration; it is self-protected; first, internally, by the complex power which belongs to the Christian *system* of involving its own integrations, in the same way as a musical chord involves its own successions of sound, and its own technical *resolutions;* secondly, in an external and obvious way, it is protected by its prodigious iteration, and secret *presupposal* in all varieties of form. Consequently, as the peril connected with language is thus effectually neutralised, the call for any verbal inspiration (which, on separate grounds, appears to be self-confounding) shows itself now, in a *second* form, to be a gratuitous and superfluous delusion, since, in effect, it is a call for protection against a danger which cannot have any existence.

There is another variety of bibliolatry arising in a different way—not upon errors of language incident to human infirmity, but upon deliberate errors indispensable to divine purposes. The case is one which has been considered with far too little attention, else it could never have been thought strange that Christ should comply in things indifferent with popular errors. A few words will put the reader in possession of my view. Speaking of the Bible, *Phil.* says, "We admit that its separate parts are the work of frail and fallible human beings. We do not seek to build upon it systems of cosmogony, chronology, astronomy, and natural history. We know no reason of internal or external probability which should induce us to believe that such matters could ever have been the subjects of direct revelation." Is *that* all? There is no reason, certainly, for expectations so unreflecting; but is there no adamantine reason against them? It is no business of the Bible, we are told, to teach science. Certainly not; but that is far too little. It is an obligation resting upon the Bible, if it is to be consistent with itself, that it should *refuse* to teach science; and, if the Bible ever *had* taught any one art, science, or process of life, capital doubts would have clouded our confidence in the authority of the book. By what caprice, it would have been asked, is a divine mission abandoned suddenly for a human mission? By what caprice is this one science taught, and others not? Or these two, suppose, and not all? But an objection even deadlier would have followed. It is clear as is the purpose of daylight, that the whole body of the arts and sciences composes one vast machinery for the irritation and development of the human intellect. For this end they exist. To see God, therefore, descending into the arena of science, and contending, as it were, for his own prizes, by teaching science in the Bible, would be to see him intercepting from their self-evident destination (viz., man's intellectual benefit) his own problems by solving them himself. No spectacle could more dishonour the divine idea—could more injure man under the mask of aiding him. *The Bible must not teach anything that man can teach himself.* Does a doctrine require a revelation?—then nobody but God *can* teach it. Does it require none?—then, in whatever case God has qualified man to do a thing for himself, he has in that very qualification silently laid an injunction upon man to do it. But it is fancied that a divine teacher, without descending to the unworthy office of teaching science, might yet have kept his own lanquage free from all collusion with human error. Hence, for instance, it has been argued that any language in the Bible implying the earth to be stationary, and central to our system, could not express a mere compliance with the popular errors of the time, but must be taken to indicate the absolute truth. And so grew the anti-Galilean fanatics. Out of similar notions have risen the absurdities of a polemic Bible chronology, &c.* Meantime, if

* The Bible cosmology stands upon another footing. *That* is not gathered from a casual expression, shaped to meet popular comprehension, but is delivered directly, formally, and elaborately, as a natural preface to the history of man and his habitation. Here, accordingly, there should be no call for accommodation to vulgar ignorance, because the ignorant populace starts with no creed or preconceptions, false or true. In fact, what most disturbs the grandeur and solemnity of the Mosaical cosmogony is the perverseness of the bibliolater. He, finding the English word *day* employed in the measurement of the intervals, takes it for granted that this must mean a *nychthemeron* of twenty-four hours; imports, therefore, into

a man sets himself steadily to contemplate the consequences which must inevitably have followed any deviation from the customary erroneous phraseology of the people, he will see the utter impossibility that a teacher (pleading a heavenly mission) could allow himself to deviate by one hair's-breadth (and why should he wish to deviate?) from the ordinary language of the times. To have uttered one syllable, for instance, that implied motion in the earth, would have issued into the following ruins:—First, it would have tainted the teacher with the reputation of lunacy. Secondly, it would have placed him in this inextricable dilemma. On the one hand, to answer the questions prompted by his own perplexing language, would have opened upon him, as a necessity, one stage after another of scientific cross-examination, until his spiritual mission would have been forcibly swallowed up in the mission of natural philosopher; but, on the other hand, to pause resolutely at any one stage of this public examination, and to refuse all further advance, would be, in the popular opinion, to retreat as a baffled disputant from insane paradoxes which it had not been found pos-

---

the biblical text this conceit; fights for this conceit as for a revelation from heaven; and thus disfigures the great inaugural chapter of human history with this feature of a fairy tale. But this word, which so ignorantly he presumes to be an ordinary human day, bears that meaning biblically only in common historical transactions between man and man—never once in the great prophetic writings, where God comes forward as himself the principal agent. It then means always a vast and mysterious duration—undetermined, even to this hour. The *heptameron*, or seven days' work of Creation and Rest, is not a week, but a shadowy adumbration of a week, comprising perhaps millions of years. Let me ask this question—In Daniel, whether considered (as in past ages he was) a prophet, or (as in this generation he is, even by pious men like Dr Arnold of Rugby) simply a writer of history, and posterior to the events contemplated—has any man been foolish enough to regard his 1260 *days* as literally such—viz., as no more than 180 weeks?

sible to support. One step taken in that direction was fatal, whether the great heavenly envoy retreated from his own words to leave behind the impression that he was defeated as a rash speculator, or stood to these words, and thus fatally entangled himself in the inexhaustible succession of explanations and justifications. In either event the spiritual mission was at an end: it would have perished in shouts of derision, from which there could have been no retreat, and no retrieval of character. The greatest of astronomers, rather than seem ostentatious or unseasonably learned, will stoop to the popular phrase of the sun's rising, or the sun's motion in the ecliptic. But God, for a purpose commensurate with man's eternal welfare, is by these critics supposed incapable of the same petty abstinence.

A similar line of argument applies to all the compliances of Christ with the Jewish prejudices (partly imported from the Euphrates) as to demonology, witchcraft, &c. By the way, in this last word "witchcraft," and the too memorable histories connected with it, lies a perfect mine of bibliolatrous madness. As it illustrates the folly and the wickedness of the bibliolaters, let us pause upon it.

The word *witch*, these bibliolaters take it for granted, must mean exactly what the original Hebrew means, or the Greek word chosen by the LXX.; so much, and neither more nor less. That is, from total ignorance of the machinery by which language moves, they fancy that every idea and word which exists, or has existed, for any nation, ancient or modern, must have a direct interchangeable equivalent in all other languages; and that, if the dictionaries do not show it, *that* must be because the dictionaries are bad. Will these worthy people have the goodness, then, to translate *coquette* into Hebrew, and *post-office* into

Greek? The fact is, that all languages, and in the ratio of their development, offer ideas absolutely separate and exclusive to themselves. In the highly-cultured languages of England, France, and Germany, are words, by thousands, which are strictly untranslatable. They may be approached, but cannot be reflected as from a mirror. To take an image from the language of eclipses, the correspondence between the disk of the original word and its translated representative is, in thousands of instances, not *annular;* the centres do not coincide; the words overlap; and this arises from the varying modes in which different nations *combine* ideas. The French word shall combine the elements, *l, m, n, o*—the nearest English word, perhaps, *m, n, o, p*—by one element richer, by one element poorer. For instance, in all words applied to the *nuances* of manners, and generally to *social* differences, how prodigious is the wealth of the French language! How merely untranslatable for all Europe! In the language of high passion, how bare and beggarly is the French! how incapable of rendering Shakspere! I suppose, my bibliolater, you have not yet finished your Hebrew or Arabic translation of *coquette.** Well, you shall be excused from *that,* if you will only translate it into English. You cannot: you are obliged to keep the French word; and yet you take for granted, without inquiry, that in the word "witchcraft," and in the word "witch," applied to the sorceress of Endor, our authorised English Bible of King James's day must be correct. And your wicked bibliolatrous ancestors proceeded on that idea throughout Christendom to murder harmless, friendless, and oftentimes crazy old women.

---

* "*Coquette:*"—Virgil comes near to one phasis of this idea—Malo me Galatea petit lasciva puella, et fugit ad salices, *et se cupit ante videri.* *Lasciva* is merely *frolicsome:* in the last line appears the coquette.

Meantime the witch of Endor in no respect resembled our modern domestic witch.* There was as much difference as between a Roman Proconsul, surrounded with eagle-bearers, and a commercial Consul's clerk, with a pen behind his ear. Apparently she was not so much a Medea

* "*The domestic witch:*"—It is the common notion that the superstition of the *evil eye*, so widely diffused in southern lands, and in some, as Portugal, for example, not a slumbering, but a fiercely operative superstition, is unknown in England and other northern latitudes. On the contrary, to my thinking, the regular old vulgar witch of England and Scotland was but an impersonatrix of the very same superstition. Virgil expresses this mode of sorcery to the letter, when his shepherd says—

"Nescio quis teneros *oculus* mihi fascinat agnos."

Precisely in that way it was that the British witch operated. She, *by her eye*, was supposed to blight the natural powers of growth and fertility. By the way, I ought to mention, as a case parallel to that of the Bible's recognising witchcraft, and of enlightened nations continuing to punish it, that St Paul himself, in an equal degree, recognises the *evil eye;* that is, he uses the idea (though certainly not meaning to accredit such an idea), as one that briefly and energetically conveyed his meaning to those whom he was addressing. "Oh, foolish Galatians, who hath bewitched you?" That is, literally, who has fascinated your senses by the evil eye? For the Greek is, *tis umas ebaskanen?* Now the word *ebaskanen* is a past tense of the verb *baskaino*, which was the technical term for the action of the evil eye. Without having written a treatise on the Æolic digamma, probably the reader is aware that F is V, and that, in many languages, B and V are interchangeable letters through thousands of words, as the Italian *tavola*, from the Latin *tabula*, diavolo, from the Greek *diabolos*, &c. Under that little process it was that the Greek *baskaino* transmigrated into the Latin *fascino;* so that St Paul's word, in speaking to the Galatians, is the very same word as Virgil's, in speaking of the shepherd's flock as charmed by the evil eye. For first of all, St Paul's word *Baskaino* was undoubtedly pronounced *Vaskaino;* just as *Sebastopol* is orientally pronounced Sevastopol, and as *Sebastos*, which is the Greek equivalent for the Roman *Augustus*, was always pronounced Sevastos. By this process, the Grecian word *Baskaino* became *Vaskaino*, and then, with hardly any change, the Latin *Fascino* pronounced "Fas*k*ino." For the Roman "*c*" had in *all* situations the force of "*k*." Thus Cæsar was always Keysar (therefore in Greek Καισαρ); and our wicked friend Cicero was always *Kikero* (in Greek therefore Κικερων). Except for the accent on the first syllable of Fascino, the Greek and the Roman word were therefore identical to the ear, though slightly different to the eye.

as an Erichtho. (See the *Pharsalia.*) She was an *Evocatrix*, or female necromancer, evoking phantoms that stood in some unknown relation to dead men; and then by some artifice (it has been supposed) of ventriloquism,* causing these phantoms to deliver oracular answers upon great political questions. Oh, that one had lived in the times of those New England wretches that desolated whole districts and terrified vast provinces by their judicial murders of witches, under plea of a bibliolatrous warrant; until at last the fiery furnace, which they had heated for women and children, shot forth flames that, like those of Nebuchadnezzar's furnace, seizing upon the very agents of his cruelty, began to reach the murderous judges themselves and the denouncers! Oh, glory of retribution to see the wicked judge of New England roasted in the fire which himself had kindled—to see the cruel bibliolater, in Hamlet's words, "hoist by his own petard."

Yet, after all, are there not express directions in Scripture to exterminate witches from the land? Certainly; but *that* does not argue any scriptural recognition of witchcraft as a possible offence. An imaginary crime may imply a criminal intention that is *not* imaginary; but also, which much more directly concerns the interests of a state, a criminal purpose, that rests upon a pure delusion, may work by means that are felonious for ends that are fatal. At this moment, we English and the Spaniards have laws, and severe ones, against witchcraft—viz., in the West Indies; and indispensable it is that we should. The Obeah man from Africa can do no mischief to one of *us*. The proud and enlightened white man despises his arts; and

---

* I am not referring to German infidels. Very pious commentators have connected her with the *engastrimuthoi* (εγγαστριμυθοι), or ventriloquists.

for *him*, therefore, these arts have no existence, for they work only through strong preconceptions of their reality, and through trembling faith in their efficacy. But by that very agency they are all-sufficient for the ruin of the poor credulous negro; he is mastered by original faith, and has perished by a languishing decay thousands of times under the knowledge that *Obi* had been set for him. Justly, therefore, do our colonial courts punish the Obeah sorcerer, who (though an impostor) is not the less a murderer. Now the Hebrew witchcraft was probably even worse; equally resting on delusions, equally nevertheless it worked for unlawful ends, and (which chiefly made it an object of divine wrath) it worked *through* idolatrous agencies. All the spells, the rites, the invocations were doubtless Pagan. The witchcraft of Judea therefore must have kept up that connection with idolatry which it was the unceasing effort of the Hebrew polity to exterminate from the land. Consequently, the Hebrew commonwealth might, as consistently as our own in Trinidad and Jamaica, denounce and punish witchcraft without liability to the inference that it therefore recognised the pretensions of witches as real, in the sense of working their bad ends by the means which they alleged. Their magic was causatively of no virtue at all; but, being believed in like the equally false but equally operative belief of the African negro in *Obi*, it became, through and by that potent belief, the occasional means of exciting the imagination of its victims; after which the consequences were the same as if the magic had acted physically according to its pretences.*

* Does that argument not cover "the New England wretches," so unreservedly denounced in a preceding paragraph?—American Ed. *Answer from this side of the Atlantic.*—No, surely the difference is vast between the two cases. The persons denounced and arrested in New England

2. *Development*, as applicable to Christianity, is a doctrine of the very days that are passing over our heads, and due to Mr Newman, originally the ablest son of Puseyism, but now a powerful architect of religious philosophy on his own account. I should have described him more briefly as a "master-builder," had my ear been able to endure a sentence ending with two consecutive trochees, and each of those trochees ending with the same syllable *er*. Ah, reader! I would the gods had made thee rhythmical, that thou mightest comprehend the thousandth part of my labours in the evasion of cacophony. *Phil.* has a general dislike to the Puseyites, though he is too learned to be ignorant (as are often the Low-Church, or Evangelical, party in England), that, in many of their supposed innovations, the Puseyites were really only restoring what the torpor of the eighteenth century had suffered to go into disuse. They were *reforming* the Church in the sense sometimes belonging to the particle *re*—viz., *retroforming*

---

were entirely passive; or were so generally; they did nothing at all—they were not seeking to injure others. But the Obeah man never moved except for evil purposes; either as an agent in the service of some other man's malice, or in the service of his own rapacity—as an extortioner relying upon the mystic terrors of his negro victims. Let the reader consult Bryan Edwards in his "West Indies"—a well-known book of 60 years back. Or, as I now dimly remember, in Miss Edgeworth's earliest novel of "Belinda," he will find a lively sketch embodying most of the features characterising the African form of magic; that is, the special magic of Obi (which, by the way, was popularised in London and Liverpool some 50 years back by the picturesque drama of "Obi, or Three-fingered Jack"). But for a larger view of African magic, not limited to the Koromantyn form of *Obi*, I would refer the reader to some interesting disclosures (founded on personal experience) in the "African Memoranda" of Captain Beavor. The book belongs to the last generation, and must be more than 40 years old. The author was a Post-captain in our navy; and I may mention incidentally that he was greatly admired by Coleridge and Wordsworth for the meditative and philosophic style of mind exhibited in his book.

it, moulding it back into compliance with its original form and model. It is true that this effort for quickening the Church, and for adorning her exterior service, moved under the impulse of too undisguised a sympathy with Papal Rome. But there is no great reason to mind *that* in our age and our country. Protestant zealotry may be safely relied on in this island as a match for Popish bigotry. There will be no love lost between them—be assured of *that*—and justice will be done to both, though neither should do it to her rival; for philosophy, which has so long sought only amusement in either, is in these latter days of growing profundity applying herself steadily to the profound truths which dimly are descried lurking in both. It is these which Mr Newman is likely to illuminate, and not the faded forms of an obsolete ceremonial that cannot now be restored effectually, were it even important that they should. Strange it is, however, that he should open his career by offering to Rome, as a mode of homage, this doctrine of development, which is the direct inversion of her own. Rome founds herself upon the idea, that to *her*, by tradition and exclusive privilege, was communicated, once for all, the whole truth from the beginning. Mr Newman lays his corner-stone in the very opposite idea of a gradual development given to Christianity by the motion of time, by experience, by expanding occasions, and by the progress of civilisation. Is Newmanism likely to prosper? Let me tell a little anecdote. Twenty years ago, roaming one day (as so often I did) with our immortal Wordsworth, I took the liberty of telling him, at a point of our walk, where nobody could possibly overhear me, unless it were old Father Helvellyn, that I feared his theological principles were not quite so sound as his friends would wish. They wanted tinkering a little. But what was worse,

I did not see how they *could* be tinkered in the particular case which prompted my remark; for in that place, to tinker, or in any respect to alter, was to destroy. It was a passage in the "Excursion," where the Solitary had described the baptismal rite as washing away the taint of original sin, and, in fact, working the effect which is called technically *regeneration*. In the "Excursion" this view was advanced, not as the poet's separate opinion, but as the avowed doctrine of the English Church, to which church Wordsworth and myself yielded gladly a filial reverence. But *was* this the doctrine of the English Church? *That* I doubted; and judging by my own casual experience, I fancied that a considerable majority in the church gave an interpretation to this sacrament differing by much from that in the "Excursion." Wordsworth was startled and disturbed at hearing it whispered even before Helvellyn, who is old enough to keep a secret, that his theology might possibly limp a little. I, on *my* part, was not sure that it *did*, but I feared so; and, as there was no chance that I should be murdered for speaking freely (though the place was lonely, and the evening getting dusky, and W. W. had a natural resemblance to Mrs Ratcliffe's Schedoni and other assassins roaming through prose and verse), I stood to my disagreeable communication with the courage of a martyr. The question between us being one of mere fact (not what *ought* to be the doctrine, but what *was* the doctrine of our English Church at that time), there was no opening for much discussion; and, on Wordsworth's suggestion, it was agreed to refer the point to his learned brother, Dr Christopher Wordsworth, just then meditating a visit to his native lakes. That visit in a short time "came off;" and then, without delay, our dispute "came on" for judgment. I had no bets upon the issue—one can't bet with Wordsworth—and I don't know that I should have ventured to back myself in a case of that nature. However, I felt a slight anxiety on the subject, which was very soon and kindly removed by Dr Wordsworth's deciding, "sans phrase," that I, the original mover of the strife, was wrong; wrong as wrong could be; without an opening in fact to any possibility of being *more* wrong. To this decision I bowed at once, on a principle of courtesy. One ought always to presume a man right within his own *profession*, even if privately one should think him wrong. But I could not think *that* of Dr Wordsworth. He was a D.D.; he was head of Trinity College, which has *my* entire permission to hold its head up amongst twenty colleges, as the leading one in Cambridge (provided it can also obtain St John's permission), "and which," says *Phil.*, "has done more than any other foundation in Europe for the enlightenment of the world, and for the overthrow of literary, philosophical, and religious superstitions." I quarrel not with this bold appreciation, remembering reverentially that Isaac Barrow, that Isaac Newton, that Richard Bentley belonged to Trinity, but I wish to understand it. The total pretensions of the college can be known only to its members; and therefore *Phil.* should have explained himself more fully. He *can* do so, for *Phil.* is certainly a Trinity man. If the police are in search of him, beyond a doubt they'll hear of him at Trinity. Suddenly it strikes me as a dream that Lord Bacon also belonged to this college. As to Dr Wordsworth, he was, or had been, an examining chaplain to the Archbishop of Canterbury. Now to suppose Lambeth in fault on such a question, is equivalent to the old Roman formula of *Solem dicere falsum.* What other court of appeal was known to man? So I submitted as cheerfully as if the learned doctor, instead of kicking me out of court, had been handing me in. Yet, for all that, as I returned musing past Rydal Water, I could not help muttering to myself—Ay, now, what rebellious thought was it that I muttered? You fancy, reader, that perhaps I said, "But yet, doctor, in spite of your wig, I am in the right." No; you're quite wrong; I said nothing of the sort. What I *did* mutter was this:—"The prevailing doctrine of the church must be what Dr Wordsworth says—viz., that baptism *is* regeneration—he cannot be mistaken as to *that*—and I have been misled by the unfair proportion of evangelical people, bishops, and others, whom accident has thrown in my way at Barley Wood (Hannah More's). These, doubtless, form a minority in the church; and yet, from the strength of their opinions, from their being a moving party, as also from their being a growing party, I prophesy this issue, that many years will not pass before this very question, now slumbering, will rouse a feud within the English Church. There is a quarrel brewing. Such feuds, long after they are ripe for explosion, sometimes slumber on, until accident kindles them into flame." That accident was furnished by the tracts of the Puseyites; and since then, according to the word which I spoke on Rydal Water, there has been open war raging upon this very point.

At present, with even more certainty, I prophesy that mere necessity, a necessity arising out of continual collisions with sceptical philosophy, will, in a few years, carry all churches enjoying a learned priesthood into the disputes connected with this doctrine of development. *Phil.* meantime is no friend to that Newmanian doctrine; and in sect. 31, p. 66, he thus describes it:—"According to these writers" (viz., the writers "who advocate the theory of development"), "the progressive and gradual development of religious truth, which appears to *us*" (*us*, in the mouth of an *anti-Newmanite*, meaning the *Old*-mannians) "to have been terminated by the final revelation of the Gospel, has been going on ever since the foundation of the church, is going on still, and must continue to advance. This theory presumes that the Bible does not contain a full and final exposition of a complete system of religion; that the church has developed from the Scriptures true doctrines not *explicitly* contained therein," &c. &c.

But, without meaning to undertake a defence of Mr Newman (whose book I am as yet too slenderly acquainted with), may I be allowed, at this point, to intercept a fallacious view of that doctrine, as though essentially it proclaimed some imperfection in Christianity. The imperfection is in us, the Christians, not in Christianity. The impression given by *Phil.* to the hasty reader is, that, according to Newmanism, the Scriptures make a good beginning, to which we ourselves are continually adding—furnish a foundation, on which we ourselves build the superstructure. Not so. In the course of a day or a year, the sun passes through a vast variety of positions, aspects, and corresponding powers, in relation to ourselves. Daily and annually he is *developed* to us—he runs a cycle of development. Yet, after all, this practical result does not argue any change or imperfection, growth or decay, in the sun. This great orb is stationary as regards his place, and unchanging as regards his power. It is the subjective change in ourselves that projects itself into this endless succession of *apparent* changes in the object. Not otherwise on the scheme of religious development; the Christian theory and system are perfect from the beginning. In itself, Christianity changes not, neither waxing nor waning; but the motions of time and the evolutions of experience continually uncover new parts of its *unchanging* disk. The orb *grows*, so far as practically we are speaking of our own benefit or our own perceptions; but absolutely, as regards itself in its essence, the orb, eternally the same, has simply more or fewer of its digits exposed. Christianity, perfect from the beginning, had in its earlier stages a curtain over much of its disk, which Time and Social Progress are continually withdrawing. This I say not as any deliberate judgment on development, but merely as a suspending, or *ad interim* idea, by way of barring too summary an interdict against the doctrine at this premature stage. *Phil.*, however, hardens his face against Newman and all his works. Him and them he defies; and would consign, perhaps secretly, to the care of a well-known (not new, but) old gentleman, if only he had any faith in that old gentleman's existence. On that point he is a fixed infidel, and quotes with applause the answer of Robinson, the once celebrated Baptist clergyman, who being asked if he believed in the devil, replied, "Oh no; *I*, for my part, believe in God—don't *you?*" as if each belief alternately involved a negation of the other.

Phil., therefore, as we have seen, in effect condemns development. But at p. 33, when as yet he is not thinking of Mr Newman, he says, "If knowledge is progressive, the *development* of Christian doctrine must be progressive likewise." I do not see the *must;* but I see the Newmanian cloven foot. As to the *must*, knowledge is certainly progressive; but the development of the multiplication table is not therefore progressive, nor of anything else that is finished from the beginning. My reason, however, for quoting the sentence, is because here we suddenly detect *Phil.* laying down in his own person that doctrine which in Mr Newman he had regarded as heterodox. *Phil.* is taken red-hand, as the English law expresses it, crimson with the blood of his offence; assuming, in fact, an original imperfection *quoad* the *scire,* though not *quoad* the *esse;* as to the "*exposition* of the system," though not as to the "*system*" itself of Christianity. Mr Newman, after all, asserts (I believe) only one mode of development as applicable to Christianity. *Phil.* having broke the ice, may now be willing to allow of two developments; whilst I, that am always for going to extremes, finding moderation to be the worst thing in this present world, should be disposed to assert three, viz.:—

First, the *Philological* development. And this is a point on which I, *Philo-Phil.* (or, as for brevity you may call me, *Phil-Phil.*), shall, without wishing to do so, vex *Phil.* It's shocking that one should vex the author of one's existence, which *Phil.* certainly is in relation to me, when considered as *Phil-Phil.;* for I, in my incarnation of *Phil-Phil.*, certainly could not have existed, had not *Phil.* pre-existed. Still it is past all denial, that, to a certain extent, the Scriptures must benefit, like any other book, by an increasing accuracy and compass of learning in the *exegesis* applied to them. But, if all the world denied this, *Phil.*, my parent, is the man that cannot; since he it is that relies upon philological knowledge as the one resource of Christian philosophy in all circumstances of difficulty for any of its interests, positive or negative. Philology, according to *Phil.*, is the sheet-anchor of Christianity. Already it is the author of a Christianity more in harmony with philosophy; and, as regards the future, *Phil.* it is that charges Philology with the whole service of divinity. Wherever anything, being right, needs to be defended—wherever anything, being amiss, needs to be improved—on Philology it is that the burden rests. Oh, what a life he will lead this poor Philology! Philology, with *Phil.*, is the great benefactress for the past, and the sole trustee for the future. Philology is the Mrs Partington that not only engages in single duel with the Atlantic Ocean, armed simply with her mop, but also undertakes to mop out the Atlantic from all trespass or intrusion through all time coming. Here, therefore, *Phil.* is caught in a fix, *habemus confitentem.* He denounces development when dealing with the Newmanites; he relies on it when vaunting the functions of Philology; and the only evasion for *him* would be to distinguish about the modes of development, were it not that, by insinuation, he has apparently denied all modes.

Secondly, there is the *Philosophic* development, from that constant reaction upon the Bible which is maintained by advancing knowledge. This is a mode of development continually going on, and reversing the steps of past human follies. In every age, man has imported his own crazes into the Bible, fancied that he saw them there, and then drawn sanctions to his wickedness or absurdity from what were nothing else than reflexes projected from his own monstrous errors, or, at best, puerile conceits of adventurous ignorance. Thus did the Papists draw a plenary justification of intolerance, or even of atrocious persecution, from the evangelical "*Compel them to come in!*" The right of unlimited coercion was read in those words. People, again, that were democratically given, or had a fancy for treason, heard a trumpet of insurrection in the words, "*To your tents, oh Israel!*" But far beyond these in multitude were those that drew from the Bible the most extravagant claims for kings and rulers. "Rebellion was as the sin of witchcraft." This was a jewel of a text:

it killed two birds with one stone—viz., simultaneously condemning all constitutional resistance, the most wise and indispensable, to the most profligate of kings, and also consecrating the filthiest of man's follies as to witchcraft. Broomsticks, as aerial horses, were proved out of it most clearly, and also the atrocity of representative government. What a little text to contain so much! Look into Algernon Sidney, or into Locke's controversy with Sir Robert Filmer's "Patriarcha,"* or into any books of those days on political principles, and it will be found that Scripture was so used as to form an absolute bar against human progress. All public benefits were, in the most *verbal* sense, made to be *precarious*, as depending upon prayers (*preces*—whence *precor*, and our own *precarious*) to those who had an interest in refusing them. All improvements were eleemosynary; for the initial step in all cases belonged to the crown; and except as bounty or lordly alms from the crown, no reform was possible. "The right divine of kings to govern wrong" was in those days what many a man would have died for—what many a man *did* die for; and all in pure simplicity of heart—faithful to the Bible, but to the Bible of misinterpretation. They obeyed (and most sincerely, because often to their own ruin) an order which they had misread. Their sincerity, the disinterestedness of their folly, is evident; and in that degree is evident the opening for Scripture development. Nobody could better obey Scripture as *they* had understood it. Change in the obedience there could be none for the better; it demanded only that there should be a change in the interpretation, and that change would be what is meant by a *development* of Scripture. Two cen-

* "*Filmer's Patriarcha:*"—I mention the *book* as the antagonist, and not the man, because (according to my impression) Sir Robert was dead when Locke was answering him.

turies of enormous progress in the relations between subjects and rulers have altered the whole reading. "*How readest thou?*" was the question of Christ himself; that is, in what meaning dost thou read the particular Scripture that applies to this case, so as to escape a superstitious obedience to its mere *letter*, which so often "killeth?" All the texts and all the cases remain at this hour just as they were for our ancestors; and our reverence for these texts is as absolute as theirs; but we, applying lights of experience which *they* had not, construe these texts by a different logic. *There* now is development applied to the Bible in one of its many *strata*—that particular *stratum* which connects itself most with civil polity. Again, what a development have we made of Christian truth, how differently do we now read our Bibles in relation to the poor tenants of dungeons that once were thought, even by Christian nations, to have no rights at all!—in relation to "all prisoners and captives;"* and in relation, above all, to slaves! The New Testament had said nothing *directly* upon the question of slavery; nay, by the misreader it was rather supposed *indirectly* to countenance that institution. But mark—it is Mahometanism, having little faith in its own *spiritual* power of rectification, that dares not confide in its children for developing anything, but must tie them up for every contingency by the *letter* of a rule. Christianity—how differently does *she* proceed! She throws herself broadly upon the pervading spirit which burns within her morals. "Let them alone," she says of nations; "leave them to themselves. I have put a new law into their hearts, and a new heart (a heart of flesh, where be-

* Words from one of the beautiful petitions in the Litany of the Anglican Church.

fore was a stony heart) into all my children; and if it is really there, and really cherished, that law, read by that heart, will tell them—will develop for them—what it is that they ought to do in every case as it arises, though never noticed in words, when once its consequences are comprehended." No need, therefore, for the New Testament *explicitly* to forbid slavery; silently and *implicitly* it is forbidden in many passages of the New Testament, and it is at war with the spirit of all. Besides, the religion which trusts to formal and literal rules breaks down the very moment that a new case arises not described in the rules. Such a case is virtually unprovided for, unless it answer circumstantially to a type laid down by anticipation in some great premonitory model of legislation; whereas every case, together with its moral relations, is expounded by a religion that speaks through a spiritual organ to an apprehension spiritually trained in man. Accordingly, we find that, when a new mode of intoxication is introduced, or a mode which, *not* being new, was unknown to Mahomet (or at least was overlooked by him), devout Mussulmans hold themselves absolved from the interdict of the Koran as to strong drink, on the ground that this interdict applied itself to the fermentations of grapes, and scandalously unaware, in its bee-like limitation of prophetic vision,* that such blessings would arise in the

* "*Bee-like limitation of prophetic vision:*"—Grosser ignorance than my own in most sections of natural history is not easily imagined. I retreat in panic from a cross-examination upon such themes by a child of five years. But, nevertheless, I am possessed of various odd fragments in this field of learning, mostly achieved by my own casual observation up and down innumerable solitary roamings. I am also possessed of one solitary zoological fact, borrowed, and not self-originated (which I fear may turn out to be a falsehood), as to the optics of the bee. I picked it up about fifty years ago in a most unlikely quarter—viz., the little work of a sentimentalist and a discounting poet—namely, Samuel Rogers—which is my chief rea-

Christian world, as brown stout and Bass's medicinal ale, which the Prophet himself might have found useful as a *viaticum*, on his *flight* to (or *from*, was it?) Medina.

And so it would have been with Christians, if the New Testament had contented itself with *literal* prohibitions of slavery, or of the commerce in slaves. Thousands of verbal variations would have been introduced, which no *letter* of the Scriptures could have been comprehensive enough to intercept. For instance, did servants, prædial and household, such as the Greeks termed Θητες [*Thetes*], fall within the description of Δουλοι (*i. e.*, slaves)? Were serfs, again, to be accounted slaves, or the bondsmen and *ascripti glebæ* of feudal Europe? At what point was the line to be drawn? or what was the essential and logical distinction by which Greek and Roman slavery determined its own more or less of assimilation to the modern negro slavery in the West Indies for the three-and-a-half last centuries, and (in the Spanish South American colonies) of the Indian slavery? Or again, speaking more frankly and nationally, of those amongst our own brothers and sisters, both in England and Scotland, that until very lately were born and bred subterraneously, and passed their whole lives subterraneously in mines or collieries, Scotch or English alike, and were by lawyers regarded as *ascripti metallo* borne upon the establishment as regular working tools, indorsed upon the machinery as so many spokes in a mighty wheel, shafts and tubes in the "plant" of the con-

---

son for viewing it sceptically. He, in his "Pleasures of Memory," asserts that the bee, too busy for star-gazing, sees only to the extent of half-an-inch beyond his own eye. I know people with a range of vision considerably less. Will the reader permit me to present him with this little contribution to his stores of zoological science, before it has time to explode (in the event of being unsound)? I expect no premium or *bonus*, by way of *commission* on fifty years' porterage.

cern, and liable to be pursued as fugitive slaves, in the case of their coming up to daylight, and walking off to some other district.* Would these poor Pariahs, Scotch

---

* These hideous abuses, which worked for generations through the silent aid of dense ignorance in some quarters, and of old traditional maxims in others, under the darkness of general credulity, and riveted locally by brazen impudence in lawyers, gave way (I believe), not to any express interference of the legislature [for in these monstrous inroads upon human rights the old proverbial saying was exemplified—*Out of sight, out of mind;* and no bastille can be so much out of sight as a mine or a colliery], but simply to the instincts of truth and knowledge slowly diffusing their contagious light. Latterly, indeed, the House of Commons interfered powerfully to protect *women* from working in mines, and the poor creatures most fervently returned thanks to the House—but, as I saw and said at the time, under the unfortunate misconception that the gracious and paternal senate would send a supplementary stream of gold and silver, in lieu of that particular stream which the honourable House had seen cause suddenly to freeze up for ever. Not that I would insinuate the reasonableness, or even the possibility, of Parliament's paying permanent wages to these poor mining women; but I *do* contend, that in the act of correcting a ruinous social evil, that never could have reached its climax unless under the criminal negligence of Parliament, naturally and justly the duty fell upon that purblind Parliament of awarding to these poor mining families such an indemnification, once for all, as might lighten and facilitate the harsh transition from double pay to single pay which the new law had suddenly exacted. As a sum to be paid by a mighty nation, it was nothing at all: as a sum to be received by a few hundreds of working households, at a moment of unavoidable hardship and unforeseen change, it would have been a serious and seasonable relief, acknowledged with gratitude. Meantime, I am not able to say whether *all* the evils of female participation in mining labour, as contemplated by the wisdom of Parliament, so fearfully disturbing the system of their natural household functions, and lowering so painfully the dignity of their sexual position, have even yet been purified. Mr Bald, a Scottish engineer, chiefly applying his science to collieries, describes a state of degradations as pressing upon the female co-operators in the system of some collieries, which is likely enough to prevail at this hour [February, 1858], inasmuch as the substitution of male labour would often prove too costly, besides that the special difficulty of the case would thus be aggravated: I speak of cases where the avenues of descent into the mine are too low to admit of horses; and the women, whom it is found necessary to substitute, being obliged to assume a cowering attitude, gradually subside into this unnatural posture (as a fixed memorial of their brutal degrada-

and English, have stood within the benefit of any scriptural privilege, had the New Testament legislated in their behalf, and contented itself with the mere verbal *letter* of their description as Δουλοι (slaves)? Ten thousand evasions, distinctions, and subdistinctions, would have neutralised the intended relief; and a verbal refinement would for ever have defeated a merely verbal concession. Endless would be the virtual restorations to slavery under a Mahometan appeal to the *letter* of the scriptural command: endless would be the defeats of these restorations under a Christian appeal to the pervading *spirit* of God's revealed command, and under an appeal to the direct voice of God, ventriloquising through the secret whispers of man's conscience. Meantime, this sort of development (it may be objected) is not so much a light which Scripture throws out upon human life, as inversely a light which human life and its eternal evolutions throw back upon Scripture. True: but then the very possibility of such developments for life, and for the deciphering intellect of man, was first of all opened by the spirit of Christianity. Christianity,

---

tion). The spine in these poor women, slaving on behalf of their children, becomes permanently horizontal, and at right angles to their legs. In process of time they lose the power of bending back into the perpendicular attitude conferred by nature as a symbolic privilege of grandeur upon the human race; at least if we believe the Roman poet, who tells us that *She* (meaning Nature)

> "Os homini sublime dedit, cœlumque tueri
> Jussit, et erectos ad sidera tollere vultus:"

i.e., to the race of man she gave an aspiring countenance, and laid her commands upon that race to fix his gaze upon the heavens overhead, and to lift up all faces erect and bold to the imperishable stars. But these faithful mothers, loyal to their duties in scorn of their own personal interests, oftentimes exulted in tossing away from them, as a worthless derelict, their womanly graces of figure and motion—dedicating and using up these graces as a fund for ransoming their daughters from all similar degradation in time to come.

for instance, brings to bear seasonably upon some opening, offered by a new phasis in the aspects of society, a new and kindling truth. This truth, caught up by some influential organ of social life, is prodigiously expanded by human experience; and subsequently, when travelling back to the Bible as an improved or illustrated text, is found to be made up in its details of many human developments. Does *that* argue any disparagement to Christianity, as though she contributed little, and man contributed much? On the contrary, man would have contributed nothing at all, but for that first elementary impulse by which Christianity awakened man's attention to the slumbering instincts of truth, started man's movement in the new direction, and moulded man's regenerated principles. To give one instance: Public charity, the charity that grows out of tender and apprehensive sympathy with human sufferings—when did it commence, and where? Who first thought of it as a paramount duty for all who had any available power—as an awful right, clamorously pleading its pangs night and day in the ear of God and man? What voice, melodious as the harps of Paradise—voice which "all the company of heaven" must have echoed with a choral antiphony, first of all insisted on cold and hunger as dreadful realities afflicting poor women and innocent children? It was the voice of one that sat upon a throne; and he was the first man, having power to realise his benign purposes, that read in the rubric of man's duties any call for such purposes. But why it was that he first read the secret writing which the whole pagan world, Rome, and insolent Greece, had so obstinately ignored, suddenly becomes clear as daylight, when we learn that he—the inaugurator of eleemosynary aid to the afflictions of man—was the first son of Christianity that sat upon a throne.

Yes, Constantine it was, earliest of Christian princes, that first* of all invested Pauperism with the majesty of an

---

* "*Constantine that first:*"—But let me warn the reader not to fancy that the public largesses of corn to the humbler citizens of Rome had intercepted the possibility of this precedency for Constantine by many generations before he was known, or even before Christianity was revealed. There was no vestige of charity in the Roman distributions of grain. These distributions moved upon the same impulse as the *sportulæ* of the great oligarchic houses, and the *donatives* of princely officers to their victorious soldiery upon great anniversaries, or upon accessions to the throne, or upon adoptions of successors, &c. All were political, oftentimes rolling through the narrowest grooves of intrigue; and so far from contemplating any collateral or secondary purpose of charity, that the most earnest inquiry on such occasions was—to find pretexts for excluding men from the benefit of the bounty. The primary thought was—who should *not* be admitted to participate in the dole. And at any rate none *were* admitted but citizens in the most rigorous and the narrowest sense. *Constantine* it was:—I do not certainly know that I have anywhere called the reader's attention to another great monument which connected the name of Constantine by a separate and hardly noticed tie with the propagation of Christianity. What name is it that, being still verdant and most interesting to all the nations of Christendom, serves as a daily memorial to refresh our reverence for the emperor Constantine? What but his immortal foundation of *Constantinople,* imposed upon the ruins of the elder city Byzantium, in the year of Christ 313, now therefore in the 1565th year of its age; which city of Constantinople is usually regarded, by those who have science comprehensive enough for valuing its various merits, as enjoying the most august site and circumstantial advantages, in reference to climate, commerce, navigation, sovereign policy, and centralisation, on this planet—with the doubtful reservation of one single South American station, viz., that of the Brazilian city Rio Janeiro (or, as we usually call it, Rio). Doubtless these magnificent natural endowments did much to influence the choice of Constantine; and yet I believe that no economic advantages, even though greater and more palpable, would have been sufficient to disengage his affections from a scene so consecrated by grand historical recollections as Rome, had not one overwhelming repulsion, ineradicably Roman, violently disenchanted him for ever. This turned upon religion. *Rome,* it was found, *could not be depaganised.* Too profound, too inveterately entangled with the very soil and deep substructions of Latium were the old traditional records, promises, auguries, and mysterious splendours of concentrated Heathenism *in,* and *on,* and nine times *round about,* and 50 fathoms *below,* and countless fathoms in upper air *above* this most memorable of capital cities.

organ amongst political forces, on the scriptural warrant that the poor should never cease out of the land—Constantine that conferred upon misery, as a mighty potentate dwelling for ever in the skirts of populous cities, the privilege of appearing by a representative and a spokesman in the council-chamber of the Empire.

Had, then, the Pagans of all generations before Con-

Jupiter Capitolinus, the Sybil's Books, which for Roman minds were authentic, the dread cloister of Vestal Virgins, Jupiter Stator, and the undeniable omen of the Twelve Vultures*—centuries of mysterious sympathy between dim records and dim inquiries, could no more be washed away from the credulous heart of the Roman *plebs*, than the predictions of Nostradamus from the expecting and listening faith of Catherine de' Medici and her superstitious court. In short, fifty baptisms could not have washed away the deep-seated scrofula of Paganism in Rome. Constantine therefore wisely drew away a select section of the population to the quiet waters of the Propontis *(the Sea of Marmŏra,* which oblige me by pronouncing as if an imperfect rhyme to *armoury,* not as if the *o* in the penult. were accented). And thus, by a double service to Christianity—viz., by a solemn institution of charitable contributions to the poor, as their absolute right under the Christian law, and by a wise shepherd's segregation of diseased members from his flock—he earned meritoriously, and did not win by luck, that fortunate destiny which has locked up his name into that of the regenerated Rome—the earliest Christian city—and the mother of the Second, or the Oriental Roman Empire.

---

* "*Omen of the twelve vultures:*"—The reader must not allow himself to be repelled from the plain historic truth by foolish reproaches of superstition or credulity. The fact of twelve vultures having appeared under ceremonial circumstances, at what may be considered the inauguration of Rome, and was so understood at the time, is as certain as any fact the best attested in the history of Rome. And as it repeatedly announced itself during the lapse of these twelve centuries, when as yet they were far from being completed, there cannot be a reasonable doubt that a most impressive coincidence did occur between the early prophesy and its extraordinary fulfilment. In a gross general statement, such as *can* be made in a single sentence, we may describe the duration of Rome, from Romulus to Christ, as 750 years, which leaves about 450 to be accounted for, in order to make up the tale of the twelve vultures. And pretty exactly that number of 450, plus 2 or 3 suppose, measures the interval between Christ and Augustulus.

stantine, or more strictly before the Christian era, no charity, no pity, neither money nor verbal sympathy at the service of despairing poverty? No, none at all. Supposing, for instance, any Gentile establishments to have existed up and down Greece, or Egypt, or the Grecianised regions of Asia Minor and Syria, at the Apostolic era, these would undoubtedly have been referred to by the apostles as furnishing models to emulate, or to copy with improvements, or utterly and earnestly to ignore, under terror of contagion from some of those fundamental errors in their plan theoretically, or in their administration practically, which might be counted on as pretty certain to pollute the executive details, however decent in their first originating purpose. Upon any one of some half-dozen motives, St Paul, in his boundless activity of inquiry and comparison, would have found cause to mention such institutions. And again, in the next generation, under the Emperor Trajan, Pliny would have had abundant ground for dwelling on this early *communism* and system of reciprocal charity established amongst the Christians, had he not recoiled from thus emblazoning the beneficence of an obnoxious sect, when conscious that no parallel public bounty could be pleaded as a set-off on the side of those who desired to persecute this new-born sect. There remains, moreover, a damnatory evidence on this point, much more unequivocal and direct, in the formal systems of ethics still surviving from the Pagan world under the noonday splendour of its civilisation: Aristotle's, for example, at the epoch of Alexander the Great; and Cicero's, at a corresponding period of refinement three centuries later in Rome. Now, in these elaborate systems, which have come down to us unmutilated, no traces are to be found of any recognised duty moving in the direction of public aid and relief to the sufferers from poverty. Our wicked friend Kikero,* for instance, who *was* so bad, but *wrote* so well, who *did* such naughty things, but *said* such pretty things, has himself noticed in one of his letters, with petrifying coolness, that he knew of destitute old women in Rome, who went without tasting food for one, two, or even three days. After making such a statement, did Kikero not tumble down-stairs, and break at least three of his legs, in his hurry to call a public meeting for the redressing of so cruel a grievance? Not he: the man continued to strut up and down his library, in a toga as big as the "Times" newspaper, singing out—

"Cedant arma togæ; concedat laurea laudi."

And, if Kikero noticed the case at all, it was only as a fact that might be interesting to natural philosophers, or to speculators on the theories of a *plenum* and a *vacuum*, or to Greek physicians investigating the powers of the human stomach, or to connoisseurs in old women. No drachma or denarius, be well assured, ever left the secret lockers or hidden fobs of this discreet barrister upon so blind a commission as that of carrying consolation to a superfluous old woman—not enjoying so much as the *jus suffragii*. By a thousand indirect notices, it might be shown

* It is interesting to observe, at this moment, how the proofs accumulate from the ends of the earth that the Roman C was always in value equal to K. The imperial name of Cæsar has survived in two separate functions. It is found as a family name rooted amongst oriental peoples, and is always Keyser. But also it has survived as an official title, indicating the sovereign ruler. At this moment, from Milan, under the shadow of the Alps, to Lucknow, under the shadow of the Himalayas, this immortal Roman name popularly expresses the office of the supreme magistrate. *Keyser* is the current titular designation of the king who till lately reigned over Oude; and *der Kayser*, on the fiction which made the Empire of Germany a true lineal successor to the Western Roman Empire, has always indicated the Emperor—once German, now simply Austrian.

that an act of charity would, in the eyes of Pagan moralists, have taken rank as an act of drunkenness.

Yes, the great planetary orb of charity in its most comprehensive range—not that charity only which interprets fo. the best all doubtful symptoms, not that charity only which "hopeth all things," and which, even to the relenting criminal, gives back an opening for recovering his lost position by showing that for *him* also there is shining in the distance a reversionary hope—but that charity also which brings aid that is effectual, and sympathy that is unaffected, to the households sitting in darkness—this great diffusive orb, and magnetic centre of every perfect social system, first wheeled into its place and functions on that day when Christianity shot above the horizon. But the idea, but the principle, but the great revolutionary fountain of benediction, was all that Christianity furnished, or needed to furnish. The executive arrangements, the endless machinery, for diffusing, regulating, multiplying, exalting this fountain—all this belongs no longer to the Bible, but to man. And why not? What blindness to imagine that revelation would have promoted its own purposes by exonerating man from *his* share in the total work. So far from *that*, thus and no otherwise it was—viz., by laying upon man a necessity for co-operating with heaven—that the compound object of this great revolution had any chance of being accomplished. It was as much the object of Christianity that he who exercised charity should be bettered, as he that benefited by charity—the agent equally with the object. Only in that way is Shakspere's fine anticipation realised of a two-fold harvest, and a ouble moral won; for the fountain itself

> "Is twice blessed:
> It blesseth him that gives, and him that takes."

But if Providence had reserved to itself the whole of the work—not merely the first suggestion of a new and divine magnetism for interlinking reciprocally all members of the human family, but had also appropriated the whole process of deducing and distributing into separate rills the irrigation of God's garden upon earth, in that act it would have defeated on the largest scale its own scheme of training for man; just as much as if (according to a former speculation of mine) God, by condescending to teach science in the Bible (astronomy suppose, chronology, or geology), had thus at one blow, besides defrauding the true and avowed mission of the Bible, self-counteractingly stepped in to solve his own problems, and thus had violently intercepted those very difficulties which had been strewed in man's path *seriatim*, and so as to advance by measured increments of difficulty, for the specific purpose of applying graduated irritations to the stimulation of man's intellect. Equally in the training of his moral habits, and in the development by successive steps of his intellect, man and the religion of man must move by co-operation; and it cannot be the policy or the true meaning of revelation to work towards any great purpose in man's destiny otherwise than through the co-agency of man's faculties, improved in the whole extent of their capacities. This case, therefore (of charity arising suddenly as a new command to man), teaches three great inferences:—

First, the power of a religion to stimulate vast developments in man, when itself stimulated by a social condition not sleeping and passive, but in a vigilant state of healthy activity.

Secondly, that if all continued cases of interchangeable development—that is, of the Bible downwards upon man, or reversely of man upwards upon the Bible and its interpretation—may be presumed to argue a concurrent action between Providence and man, it follows that the *human* element in the co-agency will always account for any admixture of evil or error, without impeaching in any degree the doctrine of a general overriding inspiration. For instance, I see little reason to doubt that economically the apostles had erred, and through their very simplicity of heart had erred, as to that joint-stock company which they, so ignorant of the world, had formed in an early stage of the infant church; and that Ananias and Sapphira had fallen victims to a perplexity and a collision between their engagements and their natural rights, such as overthrew their too delicate sensibilities. But, if this were really so, the human element carries away from the divine all taint of reproach. There lies one mode of benefit from this joint agency of man and Providence.*

Thirdly, we see here illustrated one amongst innumerable cases of development applicable to the Bible. And this power of development in general proves one other thing of the last importance to prove—viz., the power of Christianity to work in co-operation with time and social progress—to work variably, according to the endless variation of time and place. And this is the exact *shibboleth* of a spiritual religion.

For, in conclusion, here lies a consideration of deadliest importance. On reviewing the history of false religions,

* Coleridge, as may be seen in his "Notes on English Divines," though free in a remarkable degree, for one so cloudy in his speculative flights, from any spirit of licentious tampering with the text of the New Testament, or with its orthodox explanation, was yet deeply impressed with the belief that the apostles had gone far astray in their first provision for the pecuniary necessities of the infant Church; and he went so far as to think that they had even seriously crippled its movements, by accumulations of debt that might have been evaded.

and inquiring what it was that ruined them, or caused them to tremble, or to exhibit premonitory signs of coming declension, rarely or never amongst such causes has been found any open exhibition of violence. The gay mythologic religion of Greece melted away in silence; that of Egypt, more revolting to unfamiliarised sensibilities, more gloomy, and apparently reposing on some basis of more solemn and less allegoric reality, exhaled like a dream—*i. e.*, without violence, by *internal* decay. I mean, that no violence existed where the religion fell, and there *was* violence where it did *not*. For even the dreadful fanaticism of the early Mahometan sultans in Hindostan, before the accession of Baber and his Mogul successors from the house of Timour, failed to crush the monstrous idolatries of the Hindoos. All false religions have perished by their own hollowness, and by internal decay, under the searching trials applied by life and the changes of life, by social mechanism and the changes of social mechanism, which wait in ambush upon *every* mode of religion. False modes of religion could not respond to the demands exacted from them, or the questions emerging. One after one they have collapsed, as if by palsy, and have sunk away under new aspects of society and new necessities of man which they were not able to face. Commencing in one condition of society, in one set of feelings, and in one system of ideas, they sank instinctively under any great change in these elements, to which they had no natural power of plastic self-accommodation. A false religion furnished always a key to one subordinate lock; but a religion that is true will prove a master-key for all locks alike. This transcendental principle, through which Christianity transfers herself so readily from climate to climate,* from land to land, from century to century, from the simplicity of shepherds to the utmost refinement of philosophers, carries with it a corresponding necessity (corresponding, I mean, to such infinite flexibility) of an infinite development. The paganism of Rome, so flattering and so sustaining to the Roman nationality and pride, satisfied no spiritual necessity: dear to the Romans as citizens, it was at last killing to them as men.

---

* "*From climate to climate:*"—Sagacious Mahometans are often troubled and scandalised by the secret misgiving that, after all, their Prophet must have been an ignorant man. It is clear that the case of a cold climate had never occurred to him; and even a hot one was conceived by him under conditions too palpably limited. Many of the Bedouin Arabs complain of ablutions incompatible with their half-waterless position. Mahomet coming from the Hedjas, a rich tract, and through that benefit the fruitful mother of noble horses, knew no more of the arid deserts and Zaarrahs than do I. These oversights of its founder would have proved fatal to Islamism, had Islamism succeeded in producing a high civilisation.

THE PAGAN ORACLES.

It is remarkable—and, without a previous explanation, it might seem paradoxical to say it—that oftentimes, under a continual accession of light, important subjects grow more and more enigmatical. In times when nothing was explained, the student, torpid as his teacher, saw nothing which called for explanation—all appeared one monotonous blank. But no sooner had an early twilight begun to solicit the creative faculties of the eye, than many dusky objects, with outlines imperfectly defined, began to converge the eye, and to strengthen the nascent interest of the spectator. It is true that light, in its final plenitude, is calculated to disperse all darkness. But this effect belongs to its consummation. In its earlier and *struggling* states, light does but reveal darkness. It makes the darkness palpable and "visible."* Of which we may see a sen-

* Accordingly, some five-and-thirty years ago I attempted to show that Milton's famous expression in the "Paradise Lost," "*No light, but rather darkness visible*," was not (as critics imagined) a gigantic audacity, but a simple trait of description, faithful to the literal realities of a phenomenon (sullen light intermingled with massy darkness) which Milton had noticed with closer attention than the mob of careless observers. Equivalent to this is Milton's own expression, "*Teach light to counterfeit a gloom*," in "L'Penseroso."

sible illustration in a gloomy glass-house, where the sullen lustre from the furnace does but mass and accumulate the thick darkness in the rear upon which the moving figures are relieved. Or we may see an intellectual illustration in the mind of the savage, on whose blank surface there exists no doubt or perplexity at all, none of the pains connected with half-knowledge; he is conscious of no darkness. simply because for *him* there exists no visual ray of speculation—no vestige of prelusive light.

Similar, and continually more similar, has been the condition of ancient history. Once yielding a mere barren crop of facts and dates, slowly it has been kindling of late years into life and deep interest under superior treatment. And hitherto, as the light has advanced, *pari passu* have the masses of darkness strengthened. Every question solved has been the parent of three new questions unmasked. And the power of breathing life into dry bones has but seemed to multiply the skeletons and lifeless remains; for the very natural reason—that these dry bones formerly (whilst viewed as incapable of revivification) had seemed less numerous, because everywhere confounded to the eye with stocks and stones, so long as there was no motive of hope for marking the distinction between them.

Amongst all the illustrations which might illuminate this truth, none is so instructive as the large question of Pagan Oracles. Every part, indeed, of the Pagan religion—the course, geographically or ethnographically, of its traditions, the vast labyrinth of its mythology, the deductions of its contradictory genealogies, the disputed meaning of its many secret "mysteries" [τελεται—symbolic rites or initiations], all these have been submitted of late years to the scrutiny of glasses more powerful, applied under more combined arrangements, and directed according to new principles more comprehensively framed. I cannot in sincerity affirm—always with immediate advantage. But, even where the individual effort may have been a failure as regarded the immediate object, rarely, indeed, has it happened that much indirect illumination did not result—which, afterwards entering into combination with other scattered currents of light, has issued in discoveries of value; although, perhaps, any one contribution, taken separately, had been, and would have remained, inoperative. Much has been accomplished, chiefly of late years; and, confining our view to ancient history, almost exclusively amongst the Germans—by the Savignys, the Niebuhrs, the Ottfried Muellers. And, if that *much* has left still more to do, it has also brought the means of working upon a scale of accelerated speed.

The books now existing upon the ancient oracles—above all, upon the Greek oracles—amount to a small library. The facts have been collected from all quarters—examined, sifted, winnowed. Theories have been raised upon these facts under every angle of aspect; and yet, after all, I profess myself dissatisfied. Amongst much that is sagacious, I feel, and I resent with disgust, a taint of falsehood diffused over these recent speculations from vulgar and even counterfeit incredulity; the one gross vice of German philosophy, not less determinate or less misleading than that vice which heretofore, through many centuries, had impoverished this subject, and had sealed up its discussion under the anile superstition of the ecclesiastical fathers.

These fathers, both Greek and Latin, had the ill fortune to be extravagantly esteemed by the Church of Rome; whence, under a natural reaction, they were systematically depreciated by the great leaders of the Protestant Reformation. And yet hardly in a corresponding degree. For there was, after all, even among the reformers, a deep-seated prejudice in behalf of all that was "primitive" in Christianity; under which term, by some confusion of ideas, the *Patristic* literature benefited. Primitive Christianity was reasonably venerated, and on this argument—that for the first three centuries it was more demonstrably sincere. I do not think so much of that sincerity which affronted the fear of persecution; because, after all, the searching persecutions were rare and intermitting, and not, perhaps, in any case, so fiery as they have been represented. I think more of that gentle but insidious persecution which lay in the solicitations of besieging friends, and more still of the continual temptations which haunted the irresolute Christian in the fascinations of the public amusements. The theatre, the circus, and, far beyond both, the cruel amphitheatre, constituted, for the ancient world, a passionate enjoyment, that by many authors, and especially through one period of time, is described as going to the verge of frenzy. And we, in modern times, are far too little aware in what degree these great carnivals, together with another attraction of great cities, the pomps and festivals of the Pagan worship, broke the monotony of domestic life, which, for the old world, was even more oppressive than it is for us. In all principal cities, so as to be within the reach of almost all provincial inhabitants, there was a hippodrome, often uniting the functions of the circus and the amphitheatre; and there was a theatre. From all such pleasures the Christian was sternly excluded by his very profession of faith. From the festivals of the Pagan religion his exclusion was even more absolute; against *them* he was a sworn militant protester from the hour of his baptism. And when these modes of pleasurable relaxation had been subtracted from ancient life, what could remain? Even less, perhaps, than most readers have been led to consider. Because the ancients had no such power of extensive locomotion, of refreshment for their wearied minds, by travelling and change of scene, as we children of modern civilisation. No ships had then been fitted up for passengers, nor public carriages established, nor roads opened extensively, nor hotels so much as imagined hypothetically; because the relation of ξενια,* or the obligation to reciprocal hospitality, and partially the Roman relation of patron and client had stifled the first motions of enterprise in any such direction; in fact, no man travelled but the soldier and the man of political authority. Consequently, in sacrificing public amusements, the Christians sacrificed *all* pleasure whatsoever that was not rigorously domestic; whilst, in facing the contingencies of persecutions that might arise under the rapid succession of changing emperors, they faced a perpetual *anxiety* more trying to the fortitude than any fixed and measurable evil. Here, certainly, we have a guarantee for the deep faithfulness of

---

* "*Relation of Xenia*:"—A citizen of Rome, if likely to travel, established correspondents all over the Mediterranean; of course, therefore, at so splendid a city as Corinth. After *that*, the Corinthian correspondent, when drawn by business of any kind to Rome, went thither without anxiety—relying upon his privilege; and upon producing his *tessera*, or ticket of identification, he was immediately admitted to all the rights of hospitality; foremost amongst which ranked the advantage of good counsel against the risk of collision with the laws or usages of a strange city; and the further advantage of powerful aid in the case of having already incurred that risk. Inversely, the Roman enjoyed a parity of protection and hospitable entertainment on going to Corinth. And not unfrequently this reciprocal tie descended through several generations. The distant households drew upon each other *at sight*.

early Christians, such as never can exist for more mixed bodies of professors, subject to less searching trials.

Better the primitive Christians were perhaps (not individually better, but better on the total body), yet they were not in any intellectual sense wiser. Unquestionably the elder Christians participated in the local follies, prejudices, superstitions, of their several provinces and cities, except where any of these happened to be too conspicuously at war with the spirit of love or the spirit of purity which exhaled at every point from the Christian faith; and, in all intellectual features, as were the Christians generally, such were the fathers. Amongst the Greek fathers, one might be unusually learned, as Clement of Alexandria; and another might be reputed unusually eloquent, as Gregory Nazianzen, or Basil. Amongst the Latin fathers, one might be a man of admirable genius, as far beyond the poor, vaunted Rousseau in the impassioned grandeur of his thoughts, as he was in truth and purity of heart; I speak of St Augustine (more briefly known as St Austin), and many might be distinguished by various literary merits. But could these advantages anticipate a higher civilisation? Most unquestionably some of the fathers were the *élite* of their own age, but not in advance of their age. They, like all their contemporaries, were besieged by errors, ancient, inveterate, traditional; and accidentally, from one cause special to themselves, they were not merely liable to error, but usually prone to error. This cause lay in the *polemic* form which so often they found a necessity, or a convenience, or a temptation for assuming, as teachers or defenders of the truth.

He who reveals a body of awful truth to a candid and willing auditory, is content with the grand simplicities of truth in the quality of his proofs. And truth, where it happens to be of a high order, is generally its own witness to all who approach it in the spirit of child-like docility. But far different is the position of that teacher who addresses an audience composed in various proportions of sceptical inquirers, obstinate opponents, and malignant scoffers. Less than an apostle is unequal to the suppression of all human re-actions incident to wounded sensibilities. Scorn is too naturally met by retorted scorn; malignity in the Pagan, which characterised all the known cases of signal opposition to Christianity, could not but hurry many good men into a vindictive pursuit of victory. Generally, where truth is communicated *polemically* (that is, not as it exists in its own inner simplicity, but as it exists in external relation to error), the temptation is excessive to use those arguments which will tell at the moment upon the crowd of bystanders, by preference to those which will approve themselves ultimately to enlightened disciples. Hence it is, that, like the professional rhetoricians of Athens, not seldom the Christian fathers, when urgently pressed by an antagonist equally mendacious and ignorant, could not resist the human instinct for employing arguments such as would baffle and confound the unprincipled opponent, rather than such as would satisfy the earnest inquirer. If a man denied himself all specious arguments, and all artifices of dialectic subtlety, he must renounce the hopes of a *present* triumph; for the light of absolute truth on moral or on spiritual themes is too dazzling to be sustained by the diseased optics of those habituated to darkness. And hence I explain not only the many gross delusions of the fathers, their sophisms, their errors of fact and chronology, their attempts to build great truths upon fantastic etymologies, or upon popular conceits in science that have long since exploded, but also their occasional unchristian tempers. To contend with an unprincipled and malicious liar, such as Julian the Apostate, in its original sense the first deliberate *miscreant* or *conscious* misbeliever, offered a dreadful snare to any man's charity. And he must be a furious bigot who will justify the rancorous lampoons* of Gregory Nazianzen against his sovereign. Am I, then, angry on behalf of Julian? So far as *he* was interested, not for a moment would I have suspended the descending scourge. Cut him to the bone, I should have exclaimed at the time! Lay the knout into every "raw" that can be found! For I am of opinion that Julian's duplicity is not yet adequately understood. But what was right as regarded the claims of the criminal, was *not* right as regarded the duties of his opponent. Even in this mischievous renegade, trampling with his ourang-outang hoofs the holiest of truths, a Christian bishop ought still to have respected his emperor, through the brief period in which he *was* such, and to have commiserated his benighted brother, however wilfully astray, and however hatefully seeking to quench that light for other men, which, for his own misgiving heart (as might perhaps be demonstrated), he never *did* succeed in quenching. I do not wish to enlarge upon a theme both copious and easy. But here, and everywhere, speaking of the fathers as a body, I charge them with antichristian practices of a twofold order: sometimes as supporting their great cause in a spirit alien to its own, retorting in a temper not less uncharitable than that of their opponents; sometimes, again, as adopting

* "*Lampoons:*"—Too literally lampoons; for, as those meant personal invectives affixed to lamp-posts, where they could be read by everybody, so Gregory of Nazianzum himself entitled each of several successive libels on the Emperor Julian by the name of *stylites*, or libel affixed to a pillar of a public portico.

arguments that are unchristian in their ultimate grounds; resting upon errors the refutation of errors; upon superstitions the overthrow of superstitions; and drawing upon the armouries of darkness for weapons that, to be durable, ought to have been of celestial temper. Alternately, in short, the fathers trespass against those affections which furnish to Christianity its moving powers, and against those truths which furnish to Christianity its guiding lights. Indeed, Milton's memorable attempt to characterise the fathers as a body, contemptuous as it is, can hardly be challenged as overcharged.

Never in any instance were these aberrations of the fathers more vividly exemplified than in their theories upon the Pagan Oracles. On behalf of God, they were determined to be wiser than God; and, in demonstration of scriptural power, to advance doctrines which the Scriptures had nowhere warranted. At this point, however, I shall take a short course; and, to use a vulgar phrase, shall endeavour to "kill two birds with one stone." It happens that the earliest book in our modern European literature, which has subsequently obtained a station of authority on the subject of the ancient Oracles, applied itself entirely to the erroneous theory of the fathers. This is the celebrated *Antonii Van Dale* "*De Ethnicorum Oraculis Dissertationes*," which was published at Amsterdam *at least* as early as the year 1682; that is, one hundred and seventy-six years ago. And upon the same subject there has been no subsequent book which maintains an equal rank. Van Dale might have treated his theme simply with a view to the investigation of the truth, as some recent inquirers have preferred doing; and, in that case, the fathers would have been noticed only as incidental occasions might arise to bring forward their opinions—true or false. But to this author the errors of the fathers seemed capital; worthy, in fact, of forming his *principal* object; and, knowing their great authority in the Papal Church, he anticipated, in the plan of attaching his own views to the false views of the fathers, an opening to a double patronage—that of the Protestants, in the first place, as interested in all doctrines seeming to be anti-papal; that of the sceptics, in the second place, as interested in the exposure of whatever had once commanded, but subsequently lost, the superstitious reverence of mankind. On this policy, he determined to treat the subject polemically. He fastened, therefore, upon the fathers with a deadly *acharnement*, that evidently meant to leave no arrears of work for any succeeding assailant; and it must be acknowledged that, simply in relation to this purpose of hostility, his work is triumphant. So much was not difficult to accomplish; for barely to enunciate the leading doctrine of the fathers is, in the ear of any chronologist, to overthrow it. But, though successful enough in its functions of destruction, on the other hand, as an affirmative or reconstructive work, the long treatise of Van Dale is most unsatisfactory. It leaves us with a hollow sound ringing in the ear, of malicious laughter from gnomes and imps grinning over the weaknesses of man—his paralytic facility in believing—his fraudulent villany in abusing this facility—but in no point accounting for those real effects of diffusive social benefits from the Oracle machinery, which must arrest the attention of candid students, amidst some opposite monuments of incorrigible credulity, or of elaborate imposture.

As a book, however, belonging to that small cycle (not numbering, perhaps, on *all* subjects, above three score), which may be said to have moulded and controlled the public opinion of Europe through the last five generations, already for itself the work of Van Dale merits a special attention. It is confessedly the *classical* book—the original *fundus* for the arguments and facts applicable to this question; and an accident has greatly strengthened its authority. Fontenelle, the most fashionable of European authors, at the opening of the eighteenth century, writing in a language at that time even more predominant than at present, did in effect employ all his advantages to propagate and popularise the views of Van Dale. Scepticism naturally courts the patronage of France; and in effect that same remark which a learned Belgian (Van Brouwer) has found frequent occasion to make upon single sections of Fontenelle's work, may be fairly extended into a representative account of the whole—"*L'on trouve les mêmes arguments chez Fontenelle, mais dégagés des longueurs du savant Van Dale, et exprimés avec plus d'élégance.*" This *rifaccimento* did not injure the original work in reputation: it caused Van Dale to be less read, but to be more esteemed; since a man confessedly distinguished for his powers of composition had not thought it beneath his ambition to adopt and to remodel Van Dale's theory. This important position of Van Dale with regard to the effectual creed of Europe—so that, whether he were read directly, or were slighted for a more fashionable expounder, equally in either case it was *his* doctrines which prevailed—must always confer a circumstantial value upon the original dissertations, "*De Ethnicorum Oraculis.*"

This original work of Van Dale is a book of considerable extent. But, in spite of its length, it divides substantially into two great chapters, and no more, which coincide, in fact, with the two separate dissertations. The first of these dissertations, occupying one hundred and eighty-one pages, inquires into the failure and extinction of the Oracles; *when* they failed, and *why*, or under what circumstances. The second of these dissertations inquires into the machinery and resources of the Oracles during the time of their prosperity. In the first dissertation, the object is to expose the folly and gross ignorance of the fathers, who insisted on representing the history of the case roundly in this shape—as though all had prospered with the Oracles up to the nativity of Christ; but that, after his crucifixion, and simultaneously with the first promulgation of Christianity, all Oracles had suddenly drooped; or, to tie up their language to the rigour of their theory, had suddenly expired. All this Van Dale peremptorily denies; and, in these days, it is scarcely requisite to add, triumphantly denies; the whole hypothesis of the fathers having literally not a leg to stand upon; and being, in fact, the most audacious defiance to historical records that, perhaps, the annals of human folly present.

Oracles, take them at the very worst, were no otherwise hostile to Christianity than as a branch, or (mathematically speaking) a *function* of Paganism. If, for instance, the Delphic establishment were hateful (as sometimes no doubt it was) to the holy spirit of truth which burned in an apostle, *why* was it hateful? Not primarily in its special character of Oracle, but in its universal character of Pagan temple; not as an authentic distributor of counsels adapted to the infinite situations of its clients—often very wise counsels; but as being ultimately engrafted on the stem of idolatrous religion—as deriving, in the last resort, their sanctions from Pagan deities, and, therefore, as sharing *constructively* in all the pollutions of that tainted source. Now, therefore, if Christianity, according to the fancy of the fathers, could not tolerate the co-presence of so much evil as resided in the Oracle superstition—that is, in the derivative, in the secondary, in the not unfrequently neutralised or even redundantly compensated mode of error —then, *à fortiori*, Christianity could not have tolerated for an hour the parent superstition, the larger evil, the fontal error, which diseased the very organ of vision—which not merely distorted a few objects on the road, but spread darkness over the road itself. Yet what is the fact? So far from any mysterious repulsion *externally* between idolatrous errors and Christianity, as though the two schemes of belief could no more co-exist in the same society than two queen-bees in a hive—as though elementary nature herself recoiled from the abominable *concursus*—do but open a child's epitome of history, and you find it to have required four entire centuries before the destroyer's hammer and crowbar began to ring loudly against the temples of idolatrous worship; and not before five, nay, locally six, or even seven centuries had elapsed, could the better angel of mankind have sung gratulations announcing that the great strife was over—that man was inoculated with the truth; or have adopted the impressive language of a Latin father, that "the owls were to be heard in *every* village hooting from the dismantled fanes of heathenism, or the gaunt wolf disturbing the sleep of peasants as he yelled in winter from the cold, dilapidated altars." Even this victorious consummation was true only for the southern world of civilisation. The forests of Germany, though pierced already to the south in the third and fourth centuries by the torch of missionaries—though already at that time illuminated by the immortal Gothic version of the New Testament proceeding from Ulphilas, and still surviving—sheltered through ages in the north and east vast tribes of idolaters, some awaiting the baptism of Charlemagne in the eighth century and the ninth, others actually resuming a fierce countenance of heathenism for the martial zeal of crusading knights in the thirteenth and fourteenth. The history of Constantine has grossly misled the world. It was very early in the fourth century (313 A.D.) that Constantine found himself strong enough to take his *earliest* steps for raising Christianity to a privileged station; which station was not merely an effect and monument of its progress, but a further cause of progress. In this latter light, as a power advancing and moving, but politically still militant, Christianity required exactly one other century to carry out and accomplish even its eastern triumph. Dating from the era of the very inaugurating and merely local acts of Constantine, we shall be sufficiently accurate in saying that the corresponding period in the fifth century (namely, from about 404 to 420 A.D.) first witnessed those uproars of ruin in Egypt and Alexandria—fire racing along the old carious timbers, battering-rams thundering against the ancient walls of the horrid temples—which rang so searchingly in the ears of Zosimus, extorting, at every blow, a howl of Pagan sympathy from that bad and most howling of antichristian slanderers. So far from the fact being, according to the general prepossession, as though Constantine had found himself able to destroy Paganism, and to replace it by Christianity, on the contrary, it was both because he happened to be far too weak, in fact, for such a mighty revolution, and because he *knew* his own weakness, that he fixed his new capital, as a preliminary caution, upon the Propontis.

There were other motives to this change,* and particu-

* The reader will find me here treading in the footsteps of a former

larly (as I have attempted to show in a separate dissertation) motives of high political economy, suggested by the relative conditions of land and agriculture in Thrace and Asia Minor, by comparison with decaying Italy; but a paramount motive, I am satisfied, and the earliest motive, was the incurable Pagan bigotry of Rome. Paganism for Rome, it ought to have been remembered by historians, was a mere necessity of her Pagan origin. Paganism was the fatal dowery of Rome from her inauguration; not only she had once received a retaining fee on behalf of Paganism, in the mysterious *Ancile* (or supernatural shield), supposed to have fallen from heaven, but she actually preserved this bribe amongst her rarest jewels. She possessed a palladium, such a national amulet or talisman as many Grecian or Asiatic cities had once possessed—a *fatal* guarantee to the prosperity of the state. Even the Sibylline books, whatever ravages they might be supposed by the intelligent to have sustained in a lapse of centuries, were popularly believed, in the latest period of the western empire, to exist as so many charters of supremacy. Jupiter himself in Rome had put on a peculiar Roman physiognomy, which associated him with the destinies of the gigantic state. Above all, the solemn augury of the Twelve Vultures, so memorably passed downwards from the days of Romulus, through generations as yet uncertain of the event, and, therefore, chronologically incapable of participation in any fraud—

essay. As the repetition is brief, and not at all in the same words, and occurring at different periods of time, I have seen no reason to cancel it. A kind interpreter of the case will rather regard it as an argument of my sincerity and self-consistency. The real subject for wonder, as perhaps such an interpreter may be disposed to think, is, that in such hurried essays, the Press always fretting at my irregularities, I did not oftener need to make similar apologies.

an augury *always* explained as promising twelve centuries of supremacy to Rome, from the year 748 down to 452 A.D.—co-operated with the endless other Pagan superstitions in anchoring the whole Pantheon to the Capitol and Mount Palatine. So long as Rome had a worldly hope surviving, it was impossible for her to forget the Vestal Virgins, the College of Augurs, or the indispensable office and the *indefeasible* privileges of the *Pontifex Maximus*, which (though Cardinal Baronius, in his great work, for many years sought to fight off the evidences for that fact, yet afterwards partially he confessed his error) actually availed — historically and *medallically* can be demonstrated to have availed—for the temptation of Christian Cæsars into collusive adulteries with heathenism. Here, for instance, came an emperor that timidly recorded his scruples—feebly protested, but gave way at once as to an ugly necessity. There came another, more deeply religious, or constitutionally more bold, who fought long and strenuously against the compromise. "What! should he, the delegate of God, and the standard-bearer of the true religion, proclaim himself officially head of the false? No; that was too much for his conscience." But the fatal meshes of prescription, of superstitions ancient and gloomy, gathered around him; he heard that he was no perfect Cæsar without this office: and eventually the very same reason which had obliged Augustus not to suppress, but himself to assume, the tribunitian office—namely, that it was a popular mode of leaving democratic organs untouched, whilst he neutralised their democratic functions by absorbing them into his own—availed to overthrow all Christian scruples of conscience, even in the most Christian of the Cæsars. Many years *after* Constantine, the pious Theodosius found himself liteially compelled to become a Pagan pontiff. A *bon mot** circulating amongst the people warned him that, if he left the cycle of imperial powers incomplete, if he suffered the galvanic battery to remain imperfect in its circuit of links, pretty soon he would tempt treason to show its head, and would even for the present find but an imperfect obedience. Reluctantly therefore the emperor gave way: and perhaps soothed his fretting conscience by offering to Heaven, as a penitential litany, that same excuse which Naaman the Syrian offered to the prophet Elijah as a reason for a private personal dispensation. Hardly more possible it was that a camel should go through the eye of a needle, than that a Roman senator should forswear those inveterate superstitions with which his own system of patrician rank and privilege had been riveted for better and worse. As soon would the Venetian senator, the gloomy "magnifico" of St Mark, have consented to renounce the annual wedding of his republic with the Adriatic, as the Roman noble, whether senator, or senator elect, or of senatorial descent, would have dissevered his own solitary stem from the great forest of his ancestral order; and this he must have done by doubting the legend of Jupiter Stator, or by withdrawing his allegiance from Jupiter Capitolinus. The Roman people universally became agitated towards the opening of the fifth century after Christ, when their own twelfth century was drawing near to its completion. Rome had now

* "*A bon mot.*"—This was built on the accident that a certain man whose proper name was *Maximus* stood in notorious circumstances of rivalship to the emperor [Theodosius]: and the bitterness of the jest took this turn—that if the emperor should persist in declining the office of *Pont. Maximus*, or Supreme Pontiff, in that case, "erit Pontifex Maximus;" Maximus (the secret aspirant) shall be our Pontifex—*i. e.*, shall be our Emperor. *So* the words sounded to those in the secret [συνετοῖσι], whilst to others they seemed to have no meaning at all.

reached the very condition of Dr Faustus—having, like *him*, received a known term of prosperity from some dark power; but doomed, like *him*, to hear the revolving hours, one after one, tolling solemnly the summons to judgment, as they exhausted the waning minutes of that fatal day marked down in the contract. The more profound was the faith of Rome in the flight of the Twelve Vultures, once so glorious, now so sad, an augury, the deeper was the depression as the last hour drew near that had been so mysteriously prefigured. The reckoning, indeed, of chronology was slightly uncertain. The Varronian account varied from others. But these were trivial differences, and might tell as easily against them as for them, and did but strengthen the universal agitation. Alaric, in the opening of the fifth century [about 410]—Attila, near the middle [445]—already seemed prelusive earthquakes running before the final earthquake. And Christianity, during this era of public alarm, was so far from assuming a more winning aspect to Roman eyes, as a religion promising to survive their own, that already, under that character of reversionary triumph, this gracious religion seemed, by no fault of its own, a public insult, and this meek religion a clamorous defiance; pretty much as a king sees with scowling eyes, when revealed to him in some glass of Cornelius Agrippa, the phantom procession of that mysterious house which is destined to supplant his own.

Now, from this condition of feeling at Rome, it is apparent not only as a fact that Constantine did not overthrow Paganism, but as a possibility that he could not have overthrown it. In the fierce conflict he would probably have been overthrown himself; and, even for so much as he *did* accomplish, it was well that he attempted it at a distance from Rome. So profoundly, therefore, are the fathers in error, that, instead of that instant victory which they ascribe to Christianity, even Constantine's revolution was slow and merely local. Nearly five centuries, in fact, it cost, and not three, to Christianise even the entire Mediterranean empire of Rome; and the premature effort of Constantine ought to be regarded as a mere *fluctus decumanus**

* "*Fluctus decumanus*:"—Connected with this term, once so well understood, but now (like all things human) hurrying into oblivion, there was amongst the ancients a fanciful superstition; or, until it is proved such, let us call it courteously a popular creed, that wanted the seal and *imprimatur* of science. Has the reader himself any creed whatsoever, or even opinion, as to *waves?* Stars, we all know, are of many colours, and of many sizes—crimson, green, azure, orange, and (I believe, but am not certain) violet. As to size, they range all the way from those grandees up and down the sky, apparently plenipotentiaries of the heavens, or (in the Titanic language of Æschylus) *λαμπροι Δυνασαι*—blazing potentates—all the way down to such as count only amongst the secrets of the telescope: telescopic stars, as imperfectly revealed to the children of man as those children are revealed to *them*. The graduation of stars runs down a Jacob's ladder. Can there be any parallel graduation amongst the billows of old Ocean? The ancients—and perhaps it furnishes not the least conspicuous amongst the many evidences attesting their defect of power to observe accurately enough to meet the purposes of natural philosophy—fancied that there was; and supposing them for the moment right as to the main principle—viz., of a secret law moulding the waves in obedience to some geometric pressure, and expressing itself in some recurrent relation to arithmetic intervals, they must yet have been negligent in excess not to have investigated the relations of the vulgar waves—those, I mean, which apparently escaped the control of the ocean looms. What the ancients held was simply this—that every *tenth* wave was conspicuously larger than the other nine. But in what respect larger? In height was it, or generally in bulk? Did the favoured wave distribute its superiority of size through the three dimensions of space (consequently the three dimensions of that which fills space)—an arrangement which would greatly disturb the apparent (though not the real) advantage on the scale of comparison between the tenth wave and the other nine? or did this privileged tenth wave accumulate its entire advantage upon the one dimension of altitude? Next, as to the nine subordinate waves, defrauded of their fair proportions by unjust novercal nature, were they all equally defrauded, or was a bias towards favouritism manifested here also? And, if unequally endowed, did this inequality proceed *gradatim* and continuously, or discontinuously? And, if continuously,

in the continuous advance of the new religion—one of those ambitious billows which sometimes run far ahead of their fellows in a tide steadily gaining ground, but

---

how did the scale move upwards? Was it by a geometrical progression through a series of multiples, or arithmetically through a series of constant increments? And the tenth wave—a thing which I was nearly forgetting to demand—being always superior in the scale, was it always equally superior? And if not, if the superiority were liable to disturbances, did these disturbances follow any known law? or was this law suspected of leaning towards the well-known Cambridge problem—Given the captain's name, and the price of his knee-buckles, to determine the latitude of the ship.

This question about *the tenth wave*, together with others sent down to us from elder days—such, in particular, as that which respects the venom of the toad—had interested equally myself, the poorest of naturalists, and the late Professor Wilson, among the very best. We both admired, in the highest degree, the impassioned eloquence of Sir Thomas Brown in those works which allowed of eloquence, as in his "Religio Medici," and his "Urn-Burial;" but in his works of pure erudition, he, the corrector of traditional follies (as in his "Vulgar Errors"), sometimes needs correction himself. We had, in Westmoreland, learned experimentally that Shakspere is right, in describing the toad as *venomous*. Venomous it is, to the small extent of diluted nitric acid in burning and discolouring the skin, when irritated—or more probably when greatly alarmed. Several brute creatures, cats in particular, when driven into a frenzy of fear, have been supposed to fall into a self-generated hydrophobia, with full power to inflict it. But grieved should we have been, if we had imagined that the full establishment of this persecution-born venom would ever suggest an argument of palliation to the cruel persecutors of this most inoffensive creature. Aggressive tendencies it has none: not offended, it will never offend. But *the decuman wave* was a more elaborate case. We had heard little else than scoffs at the Greek races who had countenanced such a belief. *Græcia mendax*, in the brief exsibilation from the stage by the stern Roman of all Greek testimony whatsoever, had been the answer of the incredulous. Yet this reference had the effect of suggesting a question favourable to the ancients: might not the phenomenon, in Hibernian phrase, be "*thrue for them?*" The tides in the Mediterranean are, I believe, everywhere in an under-key as compared with those of our angry Atlantic: in the Euripus, or narrow frith between Eubœa (Negropont) and the mainland, there are, by report, none at all. And having confessedly one great difference, why not another?

Professor Wilson, therefore, and myself had imposed it upon ourselves as a duty to investigate this problem. Of all companions

which inevitably recede in the next moment, marking only the strength of that tendency which sooner or later is destined to fill the whole capacity of the shore.

---

that a man *could* have had, with the world stretched out before him to choose from, in any chase after a natural phenomenon, for any purpose, whether of sceptical inquiry or of verification, none was equal to Professor Wilson. He had used his youthful (I may say schoolboy) opportunities indefatigably: he had won all his knowledge, so varied and so accurate, by direct experience, troubling himself little about books,* which in *his* earlier days, had as yet benefited by no reform (though even then on the brink of it). Professor Wilson has himself most powerfully discriminated (see Christopher in his "Aviary," Cant. i.) the two orders of naturalists: those self-formed amongst the fields and forests, on the one hand—on the other, the dry sapless students of books in a closet or a museum. To the former class belonged pre-eminently White of Selborne, Waterton, Audubon, Charles Bonaparte, and those whom Professor Wilson himself indicated as "the two Wilsons," meaning, probably, his own younger brother, James Wilson, and the American Wilson. But we ought *now* to speak of "the three Wilsons:" for the Professor himself, in so far as his other studies had left him time to pursue this science, was the

* I ought in all gratitude to make an emphatic exception for "Bewick's Quadrupeds," a book to which myself, in common with my brothers and sisters, had been more deeply indebted than to any score of books beside in that department of knowledge. But, after all, it was the matchless vignettes of Bewick himself—

"And the skill which he learn'd on the banks of the Tyne"—

that gave such golden value to this book: for the printed text, though I daresay respectable, did not leave a profound impression upon any one of us. The "Birds," in which some of the vignettes struck me as even more beautiful, came to us, however, at a less impressible period. And the "Fables" we never heard of whilst children. Our experience of this delightful artist, on whom rest the benedictions of childhood for ever, was gathered in the years 1794 (when Robespierre might have figured for the Royal Tiger of Bengal), 1795, and 1796. Since then, two entire generations of the human race, with its annual harvests of children, have pursued their flight over the disk of Time. I have elsewhere mentioned "Gulliver" as one of those books which command a mixed audience where children and grown-up men are seen jostling each other; to this list must be added "Bunyan," the "Arabian Nights," "Robinson Crusoe," and "Bewick." Publishers, it seems to me, should pay some regard to this fact in the characteristic embellishments, &c., adapted separately to the two different audiences.

To have proved, therefore, were it even open to proof, that Christianity had been fatal in the way of a magical charm to the Oracles of the world, would have proved no-

---

most vivid, life-like, and realising describer of brute animals, especially birds and fishes. He was not the measurer of proportions in fins and beaks, but the circumstantiator of habits and variable resources under variable difficulties.

Perhaps, in earlier days, Swammerdam should be added to this meritorious catalogue. Of *him* it was said, that, for every one year passed in human society, he had passed three in a ditch amongst frogs. At the time I speak of, our own inquiries concerned a sublimer object!* But, sublime as it might be, *that* formed no attraction to the feelings—morbid, it may be thought, but pathetically morbid—of Professor Wilson. The year of which I speak was (to the best of my recollection) 1826. Consequently, I had already known him most intimately for 17 years; and year by year, as regards the latter seven, there had been growing upon him a deadly recoil of feeling from the sea-shore—as presenting that peculiar gathering of sights and sounds which more than any other awoke phantom resurrections to his own mind of his youthful gifts and physical energies, now annually decaying. We made two separate visits, if not three, to the sea-shore (*i. e.*, the shore of the Frith near Edinburgh), one perhaps in the year already mentioned, and a second some seven years later. One or other of these was to no greater distance than the sands of Portobello; but on that occasion, unfortunately, we met the Yeomanry (of Mid-Lothian, I think), who with some difficulty executed a charge on the very insufficient area of sand exposed at Portobello. This accident did not improve the spirits of Professor Wilson, who was reminded too keenly of the years 1806 and 1810, when he had himself figured most conspicuously in the ranks, first of the Oxford, subsequently of the Ken-

---

* Not so sublime, however, as at first it may be fancied. Charles Lamb explained the cause of this when accounting for some person's disappointment on his first introduction to the sea. This person had vaguely prefigured the case to himself, as though the total object would present itself in all its tumultuous extent. Not that, upon a moment's reflection, he could have expected such a spectacle; but irreflectively he had allowed himself to anticipate, if not such a spectacle, yet an *impression* answerable in grandeur to such a spectacle. Meantime, all that he saw, or should reasonably have hoped to see, was a beggarly section, a fraction of the whole concern; and even for that fraction, the very station of dry land, *from* which he viewed it, reminded him that the ocean was anything but boundless. The ocean pretended to hem in mighty continents; but the naked truth was—that *they* hemmed in *him*.

thing but a perplexing inconsistency, so long as the fathers were obliged to confess that Paganism itself, as a gross total, as the parent superstition (sure to reproduce Oracles

---

dal Volunteers—on both occasions in the light company; for his powers as an athlete turned altogether upon agility, not upon strength. No man was a better judge upon questions of bodily prowess; and no man, at least no gentleman, was better acquainted with the records of the Fancy, as delivered by Mr Pierce Egan, an amateur of first-rate ability. As to mere strength, though always disposed to speak disparagingly of his own powers, he was right, I believe, in undervaluing his own pretensions to the power of hard hitting. What had been sometimes said of Spring, though champion of England for some years, he has often assured me was true of himself—viz., that "he could not make a dint in a pound of butter." But in agility, as manifested in running, leaping, and dancing, he was the Pelides of his time. One striking proof of his supreme excellence as a leaper is implied in this anecdote:—When he was about 20 (Anno 1805), he had started from Oxford at midnight for Moulsey Hurst (50 miles distant, I believe), where some great event was to come off. After this was decided, Wilson, at the request of several friends on the ground, favoured the amateurs with a specimen of his leaping. The crack leaper of the day—I rather think Richmond, a black—witnessed this performance; and, upon hearing the circumstances under which it had been executed—viz., the severe pedestrian effort, and the night's want of sleep—declined to undertake a contest upon any terms. That advantage upon which Lady Hester Stanhope idly nursed a secret vanity, as peculiar to herself and the Bedouins—viz., an instep so highly arched that a rat might have run under her foot—formed one in the system of muscular machinery by which nature had equipped him for unapproachable excellence in one mode of gymnastics. Barely to see him even walk round a table was a pure delight to an eye at all learned in the fluencies of motion. Burke's expression upon the visionary grace of Marie Antoinette—that she hardly seemed to touch the earth—was realised, and became suddenly apprehensible to the sense, in *him*. And through this same structure of foot it was, and the extraordinary strength of his *tendon Achillis*, that he danced with ease and elegance so perfect. Yet he had never received one hour's instruction.

I fear that this preliminary account of my partner in the research may prove disproportioned; for the total result was small and purely negative. In the latter trial we waited and watched from an early stage of a spring tide; but the answer was none. We began by watching for a wave that should seem conspicuously larger than its fellows, and then counted onwards to the 10th, the 20th, the 30th, and so on to the 100th dated from *that*. But we never could detect any overruling principle involving itself

faster than they could be extinguished), had been suffered to exist for many centuries concurrently with Christianity, and had finally been overthrown by the simple majesty of

in the successive swells; and the wind continually disturbed any tendency that we had fancied to a recurrent law. Southey's brother, Tom, a lieutenant in the navy, whom I had once asked for his opinion upon the question, laughed, and said that such a notion must have come from the *log* of the ship Argo. Thus raising the Professor, who really *had* a good deal of nautical skill, and my ignorant self, that had none at all, to the rank of Argonauts. We, however, fancying that the phenomenon might possibly belong to *tideless* waters, subsequently tried the English lakes, some of which throw up very respectable waves when they rise into angry moods. The Cumberland lakes of Bassenthwaite and Derwentwater fell to my share; Windermere, Coniston, and Ulleswater, to Professor Wilson. But the issue of all was emptiness and aerial mockeries; as if the lady of the secret depths—Undina, or some Grecian Naiad,

"Or Lady of the Lake,*
Sole-sitting by the shores of old romance"—

had been playing with our credulity. False, however, as it may be, this image of the tenth wave furnished the ancients with a strong rhetorical expression for any possible excess in any mode of evil. A fiery heat of persecution, a threatening advance of exterminating war, a sudden and simultaneous rush of calamities [as upon Athens in the Peloponnesian War], was termed a *fluctus decumanus* of evil. Perhaps I have too lightly yielded to the temptation of connecting a *personal* interest with my imperfect report of an attempt to investigate the *thing*, or attempt at least to ascertain whether the supposed "thing" had any real root except in the fanciful creeds of Pagan naturalists. Now let us retreat from this digression into the high-road of the discussion upon ORACLES.

* "*Lady of the Lake:*"—Such was the earliest expression of Wordsworth's heavenly image—perhaps the loveliest that poetry can show. By altering the word *lake* to *mere,* he greatly deteriorated the effect: as he partly perceived himself. Why then had he done it? Simply because amongst the dramatic writers of Shakspere's era the phrase *Lady of the Lake* had received a slang meaning, like *Bona roba,* and other disreputable designations for that frail sisterhood. But this meaning (never at any time popularly diffused) had vanished for two entire centuries. So weak was William Wordsworth's reason for this, as for many another tampering with his own text. His first thoughts were almost invariably best. Indeed it is very noticeable that William Wordsworth, in earlier life the most obstinate of recusants, as regarded the arrogant mandates of criticism (and in general rightly so), became, towards the close of his life, most injudiciously indulgent to capricious objectors.

truth that courts the light, as matched against falsehood that shuns it, that fears it, and that hates it.

As applied, therefore, to the first problem in the whole question upon Oracles—*When, and under what circumstances, did they cease?*—the "*Dissertatio*" of Van Dale, and the *Histoire des "Oracles"* by Fontenelle, are irresistible; though not written in a proper spirit of gravity, nor making use of that indispensable argument which I have myself derived from the analogy of all scriptural cases in parallel circumstances.

But the case is far otherwise as concerns the second problem—*How and by what machinery did the Oracles, in the days of their prosperity, conduct their elaborate ministrations?* To this problem no justice at all is done by the school of Van Dale. A spirit of mockery and banter is ill applied to questions that at any time have been centres of fear, and hope, and mysterious awe, to long trains of human generations. And the coarse assumption of systematic fraud in the Oracles is neither satisfactory to the understanding, as failing to meet many important aspects of the case, nor is it at all countenanced by the kind of evidences that have been hitherto alleged. The fathers had taken the course—vulgar and superstitious—of explaining everything sagacious, everything true, everything that by possibility could seem to argue prophetic functions in the greater Oracles, as the product indeed of inspiration, but of inspiration emanating from an evil spirit. This hypothesis of a diabolic inspiration is rejected by the school of Van Dale. Both the power of at all looking into the future, and the fancied source of that power, are dismissed as contemptible chimeras. Upon the first of these dark pretensions I shall have occasion to speak at another point. Upon the other I agree with Van Dale. Yet, even here, the spirit of triumphant ridicule, applied to questions not wholly within the competence of human resources, is displeasing in grave discussions; grave they are by necessity of their relations, howsoever momentarily disfigured by levity, and the unseasonable grimaces of self-sufficient "philosophy." This temper of mind is already advertised from the first to the observing reader of Van Dale by the character of his engraved frontispiece. Men are there exhibited in the act of juggling, and still more odiously as exulting over their juggleries by gestures of the basest collusion, such as protruding the tongue, inflating one cheek by means of the tongue, grinning, and winking obliquely. These vilenesses are so ignoble, that for his own sake a man of honour (whether as a writer or a reader) shrinks from dealing with any case to which they do really adhere; such a case belongs to the province of police courts, not of literature. But, in the ancient apparatus of the Oracles, although frauds and *espionage* did certainly form an occasional resource, the artifices employed were rarely illiberal in their mode, and frequently ennobled by their motive. As to the mode, the Oracles had fortunately no temptation to descend into any tricks that could look like "thimble-rigging;" and as to the motive, it will be seen that this could never be dissociated from some regard to public or patriotic objects in the first place; to which if any secondary interest were occasionally attached, *that* could rarely descend so low as even to an ordinary purpose of gossiping curiosity, but never to a mercenary purpose of fraud. My views, however, on this phasis of the question will speedily speak for themselves.

Meantime, pausing for one moment to glance at the hypothesis of the fathers, I confess myself to be scandalised by its unnecessary plunge into the ignoble. Many sincere Christian believers have doubted altogether of any evil spirits, as existences, warranted by Scripture; that is, as beings whose *principle* was evil ("evil, be thou my good"); others, again, believing in the possibility that spiritual beings had been (in ways unintelligible to us) seduced from their state of perfection by temptations analogous to those which had seduced man, acquiesced in the notion of spirits tainted with evil, but not therefore (any more than man himself) essentially or causelessly malignant. Now, it is well known, and, amongst others, Eichhorn (*Einleitung in das alte Testament*) has noticed the fact, which will be obvious, on a little reflection, to any even unlearned student of the Scriptures who can throw his memory back through a *real* familiarity with those records, that the Jews derived their obstinate notions of fiends and demoniacal possessions (as accounting even for bodily affections) entirely from their Chaldean captivity. Not before that great event in Jewish history, and, therefore, in consequence of that great event, were the Jews inoculated with this Babylonian, Persian, and Median superstition. If Eichhorn and others are right, it follows that the elder Scriptures, as they ascend more and more into the purer atmosphere of untainted Hebrew creeds, ought to exhibit an increasing freedom from all these modes of demoniacal agency. And accordingly so we find it. Messengers of God are often concerned in the early records of Moses; but it is not until we come down to Post-Mosaical records—Job, for example (though that book is doubtful as to its chronology), and the Chronicles of the Jewish kings (whether *Judaic or Israelitish*)—that we first find any allusion to malignant spirits. As against Eichhorn, however, though readily conceding that the agency is not often recognised, I would beg leave to notice, that there is a threefold agency of evil, relatively to man, ascribed to certain spirits in the elder Scriptures; viz., 1. of *misleading* (as in the case of the Israelitish king seduced into a fatal battle by a falsehood originating with a spiritual being); 2. of *temptation;* 3. of calumnious *accusation* directed against absent parties. It is not absolutely an untenable hypothesis, that these functions of malignity to man, as at first sight they appear, may be in fact reconcilable with the general character of a being not malignant, and not evil in any sense, but simply obedient to superior commands: for none of us supposes, of course, that a "destroying angel" must be an evil spirit, though sometimes appearing in a dreadful relation of hostility to *all* parties (as in the case of the chastising angel who checked his wrath at the threshing-floor of Araunah). In commemoration of that merciful intervention from heaven, this threshing-floor was subsequently purchased by the national treasury, and solemnly appropriated to the use of the First Temple, for which it furnished the foundation area. The Temple itself, therefore, built by Solomon 1000 years before Christ, became a monumental record of that suspended wrath which uttered its departing thunders over the homestead of Araunah. But surely the Holy Temple would not have been suffered to commemorate any act of an impure spirit. Waiving, however, all these speculations, one thing is apparent, that the negative allowance, the toleration granted to these later Jewish modes of belief by our Saviour, can no more be urged as arguing any positive sanction to such existences (to *demons*, in the bad sense), than his toleration of Jewish errors and conceits in questions of science. Once for all, it was no purpose of his mission to expose errors in matters of pure curiosity, and in speculations *not* moral, but exclusively intellectual.

To leave the Patristic literature, and to state my own views on the final question argued by Van Dale—"What was the essential machinery by which the Oracles moved?"—I shall inquire, subdividingly,

1. What was the relation of the Oracles (and I would wish to be understood as speaking particularly of the Delphic Oracle) to the religious credulity of Greece?

2. What was the relation of that same Oracle to the absolute truth?

3. What was its relation to the public welfare of Greece?

Into this trisection I shall decompose the coarse unity of the question presented by Van Dale and his Vandals, as though the one sole "issue," that could be sent down for trial before a jury, were the probabilities of fraud and gross swindling. It is not with the deceptions or collusions of the Oracles, as mere matters of fact, that we in this age are primarily concerned, but with those deceptions as they affected the contemporary people of Greece. It is important to know whether the general faith of Greece in the mysterious pretensions of Oracles were unsettled or disturbed by the several agencies at work that naturally tended to rouse suspicion; such, for instance, as these four which follow:—1. eminent instances of scepticism with regard to the assumed prophetic vision of any Oracle, from time to time circulating through Greece in the shape of *bon mots;* or, 2.—which silently amounted to the same virtual expression of distrust—refusals (often more speciously wearing the name of *neglects)* to consult the proper Oracle on some hazardous enterprise of general notoriety and interest; 3. cases of direct failure in the event, as understood to have been predicted by the Oracle, not unfrequently accompanied by tragical catastrophes to the parties misled by this erroneous construction of the Oracle; 4.

(which is, perhaps, the climax of the exposures possible under the superstitions of Paganism) a public detection of known oracular temples doing business on a considerable scale, as accomplices with felons.

Modern appraisers of the oracular establishments are too commonly in all moral senses anachronists. I hear it alleged with some plausibility against Southey's portrait of Don Roderick, though otherwise conceived in a spirit proper for bringing out the whole sentiment of his pathetic situation,* that the king is too Protestant, and too evangelical, after the model of 1800, in his modes of penitential piety. The poet, in short, reflected back, upon one who was too certain in the eighth century to have been the victim of dark popish superstitions, his own pure and enlightened faith. But the anachronistic spirit in which modern sceptics react upon the Pagan Oracles is not so elevating as the English poet's. Southey reflected his own superiority upon the Gothic prince of Spain. But the sceptics reflect their own vulgar habits of mechanic and compendious office business upon the large institutions of the ancient Oracles. To satisfy *them*, the Oracle should resemble a modern coach-office—where undoubtedly you would suspect fraud, if the question, "How far to Derby?"

---

* What *was* this situation? Early in the eighth century after Christ (let us say A.D. 707), Roderick the Goth, King of Spain, taking an infamous advantage from his regal power, was said to have violated the person of Count Julian's daughter—by some historians called Cava. Her father, as the deadliest mode of vengeance open to him, had called in the Mahometan invaders of the Barbary coasts. Roderick, by a deep prophetic instinct, read in vision the desolation which his own perfidious atrocity had let loose upon Spain, his country, and Christianity, his faith, through eight hundred years; descended into hell by means of despair, re-ascended by penitence to earth, fought one mighty battle for the Cross, was beaten, and immediately vanished from earth—leaving no traces for deciphering his mysterious fate.

were answered evasively, or if the grounds of choice beween two roads were expressed enigmatically. But the το λοξον, or mysterious indirectness of the Oracle, was calculated far more to support the imaginative grandeur of the unseen God, and was designed to do so, than to relieve the individual suitor in a perplexity that was seldom of any capital importance. In this way every oracular answer operated upon the local Grecian neighbourhood in which it circulated as one of the impulses which, from time to time, renewed the sense of a mysterious involution in the invisible powers, as though they were incapable of direct correspondence or parallelism with the monotony and slight compass of human ideas. As the symbolic dancers of the ancients, who narrated an elaborate story, "Saltando Hecubam," or "Saltando Loadamiam," interwove the passion of the advancing incidents into the intricacies of the figure—something in the same way, it was understood by all men, that the Oracle did not so much evade the difficulty by a dark form of words, as he revealed his own hieroglyphic nature. All prophets, the true equally with the false, have felt the instinct for surrounding themselves with the majesty of darkness. Look at the Hebrew prophets: never once are *they* direct and without obliquity. And in a religion like the Pagan, so deplorably meagre and starved as to most of the draperies connected with the mysterious and sublime, we must not seek to diminish its already scanty wardrobe. But let us pass from speculation to illustrative anecdotes. I have imagined several cases which might seem fitted for giving a shock to the general Pagan confidence in Oracles. Let me review them.

The first is the case of any memorable scepticism published in a pointed or witty form; as Demosthenes avowed his suspicions "that the Oracle was *Philippising.*" This was about 344 years B.C. Exactly one hundred years earlier, in the 444th year B.C., or the *locus* of Pericles, Herodotus (then forty years old) is universally supposed to have read (which for *him* was to publish) his history. In this work two insinuations of the same kind occur: during the invasion of Darius the Mede (about 490 B.C.) the Oracle was charged with *Medising;* and in the previous period of Pisistratus (about 555 B.C.) the Oracle had been almost convicted of *Alcmœonidising.* The Oracle concerned was the same—viz., the Delphic—in all three cases. In the case of Darius, fear was the ruling passion; in the earlier case, a near self-interest, but not in a base sense selfish. The Alcmœonidæ, an Athenian house hostile to Pisistratus, being exceedingly rich, had engaged to rebuild the ruined temple of the Oracle; and had fulfilled their engagements with a munificence outrunning the letter of their professions, particularly with regard to the quality of marble used in facing or "veneering" the front elevation. Now, these sententious and rather witty expressions gave wings and buoyancy to the public suspicions, so as to make them fly from one end of Greece to the other, and they continued in lively remembrance for centuries.

In the second case—viz., that of sceptical slights shown to the Oracle—there are some memorable precedents on record. Most readers know the ridiculous stratagem of Crœsus, the Lydian king, for trying the powers of the Oracle, by a monstrous culinary arrangement of pots and pans, known (as he fancied) only to himself. But, please your most Lydian majesty, it was known also to your cook, though not perhaps to your chancellor, and therefore to your cook's scullion. Which scullion, if a man, had assuredly told it to his wife—but, if a woman, then by a deadlier necessity to her husband. Generally, the course of the Delphic Oracle under similar insults was, warmly to resent them. But Crœsus, as a king, as a foreigner, and as a suitor of unexampled munificence, was privileged, especially because the ministers of the Delphic temple had doubtless found it easy to extract the secret by bribery from some one of the royal mission. A case, however, much more interesting, because arising between two leading states of Greece, and in the century subsequent to the ruder age of Crœsus (who was about co-eval with Pisistratus, 555 B.C.), is reported by Xenophon of the Lacedæmonians and Thebans. They concluded a treaty of peace without any communication, not so much as a civil notification to the Oracle; *τῳ μεν Θεῳ ουδεν εκοινωσαντο, ὁπως ἡ ειρηνη γενοιτο*—to the god (the Delphic god) they made no communication at all as to the terms of the peace; *αυτοι δε εβουλευοντο*, but they personally pursued their negotiations in private. That this was a very extraordinary reach of presumption, is evident from the care of Xenophon in bringing it before his readers; it is probable, indeed, that neither of the high contracting parties had really acted in a spirit of religious indifference; though it is remarkable of the Spartans, that of all Greek tribes they were the most facile and frequent delinquents under all varieties of foreign temptations to revolt from their hereditary allegiance to their own established yoke of civic usage—a fact which measures the degree of unnatural constraint and tension which the Spartan usages involved; but in this case I rather account for the public outrage to religion and universal usage, by a strong political jealousy lest the provisions of the treaty should transpire prematurely amongst states adjacent to Bœotia—a point forgotten by Xenophon.

Whatever, meantime, were the secret motive to this policy, it did not fail to shock all Greece profoundly. And, in a slighter degree, the same effect upon public feeling followed the act of Agesipolis, who, after obtaining an answer from the Oracle of Delphi, carried forward his suit to the more awfully ancient Oracle of Dodona; by way of trying, as he most impudently alleged, "whether the child agreed with its papa." These open expressions of distrust were generally condemned; and the irresistible proof that they were, lies in the fact that they led to no imitations. Even in a case mentioned by Herodotus, where a man had the audacity to found a colony without seeking an oracular sanction, no precedent was established; though the journey to Delphi must often have been peculiarly inconvenient to the founders of colonies moving westwards from Greece; and the expenses of such a journey, with the subsequent offerings, could not but prove unseasonable at the moment when every drachma was most urgently needed. Charity begins at home, was a thought quite as likely to press upon a Pagan conscience, in those circumstances, as upon our modern Christian consciences under heavy taxation; yet, for all that, such was the regard to a pious inauguration of all colonial enterprises, that no one provision or pledge of prosperity was held equally indispensable by all parties to such hazardous speculations. The merest worldly foresight, indeed, to the most irreligious leader, would suggest this sanction as a necessity, under the following reason:—colonies the most enviably prosperous upon the whole, have yet had many hardships to contend with in their novitiate of the first five years; were it only from the summer failure of water under circumstances of local ignorance, or from the casual failure of crops under imperfect arrangements of culture. Now, the one great qualification for wrestling strenuously with such difficult contingencies in solitary situations, is the spirit of cheerful hope; but, when any room had been left for apprehending a supernatural curse resting upon their efforts—equally in the most thoughtfully pious man and the most crazily superstitious—all spirit of hope would be blighted at once; and the religious neglect would, even in a common human way, become its own certain avenger, through mere depression of spirits and misgiving of expectations. Well, therefore, might Cicero in a tone of defiance demand, "Quam vero Græcia coloniam misit in Ætoliam, Ioniam, Asiam, Siciliam, Italiam, sine Pythio (the Delphic), aut Dodonæo, aut Hammonis oraculo?" An oracular sanction must be had, and from a leading oracle—the three mentioned by Cicero being the greatest;* and, if a minor oracle could have satisfied the inaugurating necessities of a regular colony, we may be sure that the Dorian states of the Peloponnesus, who had twenty-five decent oracles at home (that is, within the peninsula), would not so constantly have carried their money to Delphi. Nay, it is certain that even where the colonial counsels of the greater oracles seemed extravagant, though a large discretion was allowed to remonstrance, and even to very homely expostulations, still, in the last resort, no doubts were felt that the oracle must be right. Brouwer, the Belgic scholar, who has so recently and so temperately treated these subjects ("Histoire de la Civilisation Morale et Religieuse chez les Grecs." 6 tomes: Groningue: 1840), alleges a case (which, however, I do not remember to have met) where the client ventured

* To which at one time must be added, as of equal rank, the Oracle of the Branchides, in Asia Minor. But this had been destroyed by the invading Persians, in retaliation of the Athenian outrages—real or pretended—at Sardis.

to object:—"*Mon roi Apollon, je crois que tu es fou.*" * But cases are obvious which look this way, though not going so far as to charge lunacy upon the lord of prophetic vision. Battus, who was destined to be the eldest father of Cyrene, memorable as the first ground† of Greek intercourse with the Libyan shore of the Mediterranean, so often as he consulted the Delphic Oracle in reference to his eyes, which happened to be diseased, was admonished to prepare for colonising Libya. "Grant me patience," would the peppery Battus reply; "here am I getting into years; and never do I consult the Oracle about my precious eyesight, but you, King Phœbus, begin your old yarn about Cyrene. Confound Cyrene! Nobody knows where it is. But, if you are serious, speak to my son: he's a likely young man, and worth a hundred of old rotten hulks like myself." Battus was provoked in good earnest; and it is well known that the whole scheme went to sleep for several years, until King Phœbus sent in a gentle refresher to the peppery Battus and his islanders, in the shape of failing crops, pestilence, and his ordinary chastisements. The people were roused—the colony was founded—and, after utter failure, was again founded—and the results justified the Oracle. But, in all such cases, and where the remonstrances were least respectful, or where the resistance

* "*Tu es fou:*"—The merely English reader, who is unacquainted with French, must not mistake *fou* for *sot*. *Sot* is the word for *fool;* and the word *fou*, though looking too like that opprobrious term, denotes a form of intellectual infirmity—viz., madness—claiming deeper pity, but also deeper awe and respect.

† "*First ground:*"—In our modern geography, *Egypt* is the first region of Africa to those who enter it from the east. But exactly at that point it is that Grecian geography differs from ours. The Greek Libya, as regarded the Mediterranean coast, coincided with our Africa, except precisely as to Egypt, which (Herodotus tells us) was, or ought to be, regarded as a transitional chamber between Asia and Libya.

of *inertia* was longest, I differ altogether from M. Brouwer in his belief, that the suitors fancied Apollo to have gone distracted. If they ever said so, this must have been merely by way of putting the Oracle on its mettle, and calling forth some *plainer*—not any different—answer from the god, who was essentially enigmatic; for there it was that the doubts of the clients settled, and on that it was the practical demurs hinged. Not because even Battus, vexed as he was about his precious eyesight, distrusted the Oracle, but because he felt sure that the Oracle had not spoken out freely—that the Oracle was in debt to him as regarded plain dealing in a matter of *national* interest and a question of life and death; therefore had he and many others in similar circumstances presumed to linger or to demur. Blind obedience was hard to practise in cases which, being clothed in riddles, might (as a long experience had taught them) be too easily deciphered erroneously. A second edition was what they waited for, corrected and *enlarged*. We have a memorable instance of this policy in the Athenian envoys, who, upon receiving a most ominous doom, but obscurely expressed, from the Delphic Oracle—which politely concluded by saying, "And so get out, you vagabonds, from my temple—don't cumber my decks any longer"—were advised to answer sturdily, "No! we will *not* get out; we mean to sit here for ever, until you think proper to give us a more reasonable reply." Upon which spirited rejoinder, the priestess saw the policy of revising her truly brutal rescript as it had stood originally.*

* At first sight, the reader is apt to wonder why it was that insolence so undisguised should have been allowed to prosper. But in fact all religions have been indulgent to insolence, where the known alternative has been sycophantic timidity. Christianity herself encourages men to

The necessity, indeed, was strong for not acquiescing in the answer of the Oracle, until it had become clearer by revision or by casual illustration. But some were so precipitate as to adopt the first answer in its most literal and apparent sense. As usual, there is a Spartan case of this nature. Cleomenes complained bitterly that the Oracle of Delphi had deluded him, by holding out as a possibility, and under given conditions as a certainty, that he should possess himself of Argos. But the Oracle, agreeably to Pagan casuistry, was justified: there was an inconsiderable place outside the walls of Argos which bore the same name. This was the commonest of dodges amongst the heathen professors of divination. Most readers will remember the case of Cambyses, who had been assured by a legion of oracles that he should die at Ecbatana, generally supposed to be the *Hamadan* of our days, to which northern city, cooled by Caspian breezes, the Shah of Persia retires when Teheran grows too hot. Suffering, therefore, in Syria from a scratch inflicted upon his thigh by his own sabre, whilst angrily sabring a ridiculous quadruped which the Egyptian priests had put forward as a god, Cambyses felt quite at his ease so long as he remembered his vast distance from the mighty capital of Media, to the eastward of the Tigris. The scratch, however, inflamed, for his intemperance had saturated his system with com-

---

"take heaven by storm." In that spirit it was that the Pagan deities, in the persons of their representative idols, submitted to be caned and horsewhipped without open mutiny, and continually to be chained up by one leg, in cases where the gods were suspected of meditating flight to the enemy. Universally, insolence was but an offence of *manner*. Even *that* might have provoked a shade of displeasure, were it not that, more effectually than any other expression of temper, it cured the one unpardonable offence of insincerity, languishing devotion, decay of burning love—to which love, as the one sole pledge of undying loyalty, all frailties were forgiven.

bustible matter; the inflammation spread; the pulse ran high: and he began to feel twinges of alarm. At length mortification commenced; but still he trusted to the old prophecy about Ecbatana, when suddenly a horrid discovery was made—that the very Syrian village at his own head-quarters was known by the pompous name of Ecbatana. Josephus tells a similar story of some man contemporary with Herod the Great. And we must all remember that case in Shakspere, where the first king of the *red* rose, Henry IV., had long fancied his destiny to be that he should meet his death in Jerusalem; which naturally did not quicken his zeal for becoming a crusader. "All time enough," doubtless he used to say; "no hurry at all, gentlemen!" But at length, finding himself pronounced by the doctor ripe for dying, it became a question whether the prophet were a false prophet, or the doctor an incompetent physician. However, in such a case, it is something to have a collision of opinions—the prophet against the doctor. But, behold, it soon transpired that there was no collision at all. It was the Jerusalem chamber, occupied by the king as a bedroom, and extant even yet, to which the prophet had alluded. Upon which his majesty reconciled himself at once to the ugly necessity at hand—

"In that Jerusalem shall Harry die."

The last case—that of oracular establishments turning out to be accomplices of thieves—is one which occurred in Egypt on a scale of some extent; and is noticed by Herodotus. This degradation argued great poverty in the particular temples: and it is not at all improbable that, amongst a hundred Grecian Oracles, some, under a similar temptation, might fall into a similar disgrace: the poverty must often have existed, but without the thieves; and at Delphi constantly the thieves, but without the poverty.

Yet now, as regards even this lowest extremity of disgrace, much more as regards the qualified sort of disrepute attending the three minor cases, one brief distinction puts all to rights. The Greeks never confounded the temple, and household of officers engaged in the temple service, with the dark functions of the presiding god. In Delphi, besides the Great Lady who discharged the life-shaking duties of Pythia, and the priests, with their train of subordinate ministers directly billeted on the temple, there were two orders of men outside, Delphic citizens—the one styled *ἀριστεῖς*, gentlemen of the service; the other *ὅσιοι*, a sort of semi-sanctified members of the temple establishment, wearing a shadowy resemblance to the lay *elders* of the Presbyterian Kirk, whose duty was probably, *inter alia*, to attach themselves to persons of corresponding rank in the retinues of the envoys or consulting clients, and doubtless to extract from them, in convivial moments, all the secrets or general information which the temple required for satisfactory answers. If these outside agents of the great temple personally went too far in their intrigues or stratagems of decoy, the disgrace no more recoiled on the god, than, in modern times, the vices or crimes of a priest can affect the pure spiritual sanctity of the sacrament he dispenses.

Meantime, through these outside ministers—though unaffected by their follies or errors as trepanners—the Oracle of Delphi drew that vast and comprehensive information, from every local nook or recess of Greece, which made it in the end a blessing to the land. The great error is, to suppose the majority of cases laid before the Delphic Oracle strictly questions for *prophetic* functions. Ninety-nine in a hundred respected marriages, state-treaties, sales, purchases, founding of towns or colonies, which demanded no faculty whatever of divination, but the nobler faculty of natural sagacity, that calculates the natural consequences of human acts co-operating with the local circumstances. If ever I should attempt to trace the steps, or to appraise the value, of Grecian civilisation—the mother of civilisation to all the western earth—it will not be difficult to prove that Delphi discharged the functions of a central *bureau d'administration*, a general centre of political information, an organ of universal organisation for the counsels of the whole Grecian race. And that which caused the declension of the Oracles was the loss of political independence and autonomy. After Philip and the day of Chæronea, still more after the Roman conquest, each separate state, having no powers, and therefore no motive, for asking counsel on public interests, naturally confined itself more and more to its humbler local interests of police, or even at last to its family arrangements.

In drawing towards a close upon the great institution of Oracles, I would wish to point the reader's attention to a feature of strong analogy between these mysterious incorporations and that great modern product of high civilisation—the Banking system. Had the ancients any banks, or any apology for banks? Formally and directly they certainly had not; but indirectly they had an imperfect representative of our banks. What was it? First let me ask—What is the primary and elementary function of a bank—of a good, honest, hard-working, industrious bank? Vixere Bankers ante Agamemnona. But their task was simpler; it was—merely to take care of a man's money when he could not take care of it himself. What, because he was drunk? Oh no: but because housebreakers [family-men, as they are called in our flash dictionaries] were in

Greece and circumjacent regions far too plentiful. They swarmed in all quarters of needy Greece.

What an invitation to you and me, when speculating for a rise in our respective capitals, to suspect a supper table left by the sleeping family to take care of itself and also of all the family plate, with a perfect knowledge on our parts that as small a tool as a mason's trowel will introduce us in six minutes to that same abandoned supper-tray. The word τοιχωρυχος, literally wall-borer, or τοιχωρυκτης, wall-underminer, the Greek name for a housebreaker, indicates the brief process through which the Attic burglar seduced and eloped with another man's too charming plate. The artist had but to excavate a peck or two of earth with his trowel; a rabbit's burrow was large enough; this he soon improved and widened, using his own body as a gimlet; and very soon he had gimleted himself down amongst the family rats. Then making free to borrow a rat-hole for a minute, and lying on his back, he soon *whittled* away or chiselled away the slight piece of carious flooring that divided him from the beautiful object (whether gold or silver) that enamoured him. Between Greece and Rome, in this point, how vast the difference! In Rome the houses were built for eternity—twelve to twenty thousand pounds sterling was no uncommon cost, I believe, for the mansion of a senator. In Athens it is notorious that the houses of citizens the most distinguished, Miltiades, and soon afterwards of Themistocles, were little better than hovels. And although it is true that in forty years more, when the star of Pericles began to dawn upon Athens, the houses showed symptoms of improvement, nevertheless, being still built of slight and frail materials, they continued to rest on no massier or deeper foundations than does at this day a Scotch Highland bothy. Stakes or poles, hand-driven into the ground, formed their whole support—not at all stronger than the pegs which hold down the draperies of a soldier's tent. This it was—viz., the make-shift foundation—which so powerfully facilitated the art, or "profession" (as I find it called by one lexicographer) of the housebreaker. In fact the art might be viewed as a mode of *diving:* the Attic burglar dived into the earth on the outside of the walls, and coming up on the other side, found himself comfortably seated in grandmamma's easy-chair. And whilst the access was thus easy at Athens, was thus impossible at Rome, on the other hand, the burglars in the former land swarmed like flies in a hot August with us, and in the latter were rare as hornets. With robbery a thousand times easier, and robbers a thousand times more plentiful*—reason

---

* In fact so plentiful, that even the memorials dearest to their vanity and patriotism—viz., their Battle Trophies—could no otherwise be protected from the rapacity of domestic robbers than by making them of materials which would hardly pay the cost of removal. The Greeks, after any victory of one little rascally clan over another, of Spartans over Thebans, for instance, or (what is more gratifying to imagine) of Thebans over Spartans, used to do two things in the way of self-glorification: first, they chanted a hymn or *pæan* (επαιανιζον), which was *their* mode of singing *Te Deum;* secondly, they erected a trophy, or memorial of their victory, on the ground. But this trophy one might naturally expect to be framed of the most durable materials; whereas, on the contrary, it was framed of the very frailest; viz., firewood, at sevenpence the cart-load; and the best final result that I, for *my* part, can suppose from any trophy whatsoever, would be—that some old woman, living in the neighbourhood of the trophy, went out on favourable nights, and selected fuel enough to warm her poor old Pagan bones through the entire length of a Grecian winter. Why the wood rapidly disappeared, is therefore easy to understand: but not why it had ever been relied on as a durable record. The Greeks, however, who were masters in the arts of varnishing and gilding, reported the whole case in the following superfine terms:—"It is right," said they, "and simply a necessity of our human nature, that we should quarrel intermittingly. We Grecians are all brothers, it is true: but still even brothers must,

enough there was in Athens for banks to take charge of a man's money. And banks, therefore, of the very strongest construction the Greeks had, banks that could stand a military siege, and sometimes *did*. But what was

---

for the sake of health, have a monthly allowance of fighting and kicking. Not at all less natural it is, that the conquerors in each particular round of our never-ending battle should triumph gloriously, and crow like twenty thousand game cocks, each flapping his wings on his own dunghill, armed with spurs according to the Socratic model left us by Plato. An allowance, in short, of shouting and jubilating is but fair. Still all this should have a speedy end. Not only upon the prudential maxim—that he who is the kicking party to-day, will often be the kicked party to-morrow; but also on a moral motive—viz., to forget and forgive. Under these suggestions, it becomes right to raise no memorials of fighting triumphs in any but fugitive materials; not therefore of brass, not therefore of marble, which (says the cunning Greek) would be too durable, which (say I, revising the Greek dissembler) would be too costly, but rather of wood the most worm-eaten, and if it show signs of dry-rot, all the better. Under this limitation our triumph puts on a human and a natural shape. It very soon decays; and typifies our exultation, which decays concurrently." Ay, very plausible and sentimental. But this is an *ex parte* account; purely Grecian. Mine is different. I venture to suggest that the reason for not using brass or copper was, because, in that case, long before the moon had run her circuit, the trophy would have been found in a blacksmith's shop at Corinth or Athens, sold or pawned, at the rate of a drachma a-head for a gang of forty thieves. The *Græculus esuriens* of Juvenal's sketch (taken from the standing-point of Rome) was true for centuries: always he was a knave, a sharp sycophantic knave, that lived by his wits; and yet, multiplying too fast, always in the large majority he was hungry. Through many a generation he was the dominant physician of the earth; he left behind him a body of medical research that is even yet worth studying: he, if nobody else, forestalled Lord Bacon's philosophy, for he at least relied altogether upon experience and tentative approaches; others he healed by myriads; but himself he never succeeded in healing permanently or widely of the disease called hunger. Empty stomachs continued to form the reproach of his art. For the truth was, through centuries, that Greece bred too large a population. Her institutions favoured population too much, whilst her agriculture and commerce tended (but could not establish a sufficient tendency) to repress population. Too constantly, therefore, Greece was *mendax, edax, furax* (mendacious, edacious, furacious), though indisposed to criminal excesses.

the name of these banks? The name? Why, the name of these banks was *temples.* Upon a twofold consideration, temples were eligible as banks. In the first place, any temple whatsoever, being regarded as a monument of reverence and gratitude to a divinity, was naturally made as splendid as the disposable funds would allow. Marble, therefore, or stone at the least, was used in constructing the walls and porticoes. But the great weight of marble and stone obliged the architects to lay them upon deep foundations. Hence it happened that, in such altered circumstances, the alliance of a rat, and the loan of a rat hole, went but a little way towards a prosperous burglary. But there was even a deeper protection to a temple. Being placed under the tutelary care of a divinity, the building enjoyed the *prestige* of consecration. And this kept the most audacious burglar at a distance. His trade was hopeless, he well knew that, against walls so impregnable; and, had it been otherwise, the burglar feared a pursuing curse if he robbed a temple of any peculiar sanctity: he would as little dally with any such dangerous purpose as a Spanish *flibustier* would have joined an English buccaneer in pillaging a shrine of the Virgin. With power ten times multiplied did these grounds of strength apply to an *oracular* temple; most of all to Delphi—known to all princes that were themselves known. It is not surprising, therefore, that Delphi should have become the consecrated *depôt* for incalculable property through many generations. And if the reputation of wealth so enormous drew upon that temple and town occasional threats, or even assaults from a distance, no losses arising in this way could counterbalance, by a thousandth part, the vast amount of conservative aid that this temple must, in so many generations, have dispensed; for Delphi must have been viewed as central to Greece, to the Grecian Islands, in later days to Macedon, Epirus, Thrace, and (in Asia Minor) to regions stretching all the way to the Euphrates.

As a bank of deposit, therefore, Delphi and its illustrious temple discharged a most weighty class of services; and with this class at least Christianity could have had no wish to interfere. No rivalship could here be imagined; no crossing of purposes; no collision of interests. So far it is not any service offering *analogies* to the modern services of banks that Delphi might have claimed; it was the direct, undeniable, and elementary service that any and every bank does or can perform. The service done was not of a nature to involve any social refinements; it was plain and homely as a cudgel; and in fact very like a cudgel: for one of the best uses which the learned have yet discovered in a cudgel is its tendency to mount guard effectually upon a man's pockets; and precisely *that* use was rendered in perfection by the temple of the Oracle at Delphi. A bank, which could not be stormed by Brennus and his Gauls, was manifestly in no danger from the τοιχωρυχος and his trowel.

But mere security, though a great point to achieve in a community where hardly anything was safe from moths that corrupt, or from thieves that break through and steal, was yet far from approaching that mysterious discovery as to the powers of capital, which to all mankind, for many a long century, seemed to involve an impossibility. The exquisite silliness of the ancient doctrine—"that money doth not breed money"—that one gold or silver coin was never known, in any natural process of generation, to produce another gold or silver coin, gagged the utterance—blindfolded the eyes—paralysed the understanding of man through much more than a thousand years. From this doctrine it seemed (in the eyes of our worthy and most stupid ancestors) to radiate as the most irresistible of inferences—that, if any man drew a profit, a something *extra*, from the employment of his money, that profit must take its rise in some unlawful source. The most obvious explanation was, that it arose in fraud. In some way the man must have cheated. This, as most people know, was the theory of Cicero. A man must lie, and must lie pretty strongly [*admodum*], in *his* opinion, before he could reap any gain whatever—the least or most shadowy—from a commercial transaction. And, if Cicero had been made to understand that the distinction between buyer and seller was imaginary, that a buyer was necessarily a seller—a seller necessarily a buyer, and that in every transaction of exchange—the two parties, the party on each side, might gain simultaneously, might gain equally, and not by any metaphysical trick of words, but by a gain expressible in money—he would probably, in excess of wrath, have assaulted his opponent. Any use of capital that should imply such doctrines would, in the Grecian stage of civilisation, have been impossible. Yet, why? Simply because all such uses waited for other concurrent agencies, which must meet in combination before their last potential results could be developed. From that Grecian stage of social progress, in which the showy religion of men, and the pomps of their gay mythologies, had put forth their uttermost strength in the stationary grandeur of temples and the scenical beauty of processions, let us leap by a flight across forty generations to that modern period when the bank of Venice, of Amsterdam, &c., had implied as a cause, and had promoted as an effect, that new birth in the science of capital and its uses which the world has now gazed upon for three centuries and upwards as a gorgeous spectacle towering to the clouds by its multitudinous creations. From this grand station, commanding both stages—the infancy and the maturity of the banking economy, and connecting them into one field of retrospect—let us ask what it is in the upshot that has been gained? In the Grecian infancy of its power, moneyed power (as regards the western regions of the ancient world) was first of all made safe. The temples (and probably in many instances under dim anticipations of future Persian invasions, or even of tumultuary invasions by mere Scythian, German, or Gaulish savages) were built with the strength of fortresses; not meant for the security of money, these massy temples had not the less benefited money. In that cradle of European culture, under the double protection of martial power and of religion, first of all we behold the great productive power of property, as yet, indeed, most slenderly applied to production, but still reposing in absolute safety. Under all this vast advantage, as yet however it slumbers passively, having very little more interest for society than simply as all property, however little employed productively, nevertheless (in the shape of expenditure as an income) unavoidably stimulates production. But at the modern terminus of our long prospect we behold this property no longer inert and lifeless, but waking magically into a twofold life. Money, to the confusion of the incredulous, now, at last, is found to produce money; and this intolerable paradox, as through so long a period it has been held, is accomplished oftentimes through another machinery equally paradoxical. Not the proprietor of the money, in most cases, but an alien as regards any natural relations to the money, reaps the primary benefits from the property; and out of that seeming intrusion into another man's rights, first of all it becomes possible that a bank should create an income for the true proprietor. This man's share of benefit is so far from being encroached upon by the alien employer of his property, that, on the contrary, in the innumerable cases where the owner could not himself be the employer, it is only through this intrusion of an alien party that the bank carves out a triple return—first, for itself; secondly, for the commercial employer; thirdly, for the sedentary and passive proprietor.

Pausing for an instant, let us review the methods through which the bank organises such great results. All the little rills and runnels of surplus income scattered amongst numerous individuals, which in an uncommercial land could not find employment, and would lie as barren accumulation in domestic depositories, tempting the assaults of housebreakers, are converged by banks into large central reservoirs, from which they are speedily returned, through the channels of many commercial or manufacturing men, into the vast field of productive industry. What the bank does is essentially the function of a broker. The bank brings scattered interests into communication, and remote interests into contact. Through this agency, the multitudes who have surplus money, and would be glad to lend it, under any sufficient prospect of seeing it profitably employed, are brought face to face with the multitudes who wish to extend their means of creating such profitable employment. And now, turning back to the great Oracular Temple of Delphi, we may trace more firmly and luminously the direct point of contact, or the more indirect and remote points of analogy, which connect the Delphic Temple with the machineries of banking. In the early and elementary stage of this great organ, we notice (as I remarked above) not so much the analogy, as the direct parity or identity of their public ministrations. A modern bank contemplates, as its initial service, the safe keeping of the money confided to its care. The bank provides a strong building, rooms specially protected against burglars, iron safes, proper attendants, and watchmen, together with the means of rapid and authentic intelligence upon questions connected with the public securities of the national treasury, &c., and is able to distribute these great advantages amongst an immense number of customers, at a cost to each which is little more than nominal. The Delphic Temple, upon terms essentially the same, but very much more costly, indemnified itself for the absolute security (both in its English and its Latin sense)* which it had created.

What more did the bank of Delphi accomplish towards the development of the banking system, than simply to make it safe? Nothing. Then how was I entitled to say, that Delphi & Co. exhibited strong features of analogy to our existing banks, in their most improved state of efficiency? The Bank of England at this day is prepared to stand a siege, if such a necessity should arise, only I fear that she is not victualled; she has not laid in enough of biscuit. However, this is the uttermost extent of her martial capacities: and Delphi could do as much, besides having actually done it. But what further lineaments of sisterly resemblance do we trace in the two banks? This one marked expression at the least we trace—viz., a systematic use of brokerage in the largest extent: by which

* In English we understand by security neither more nor less than *safety; i. e.*, freedom from danger. But in Latin, *securitas* means freedom—not at all from danger, but from the *sense* of danger and its anxieties. A man is therefore in Latin often described as *securus*, whilst on the brink of destruction, if only not conscious of his danger. Milton, in his occasional tendency to draw too emphatically upon the Latin elements in our language, has given to the word *secure* its Roman acceptation; but he has hardly naturalised that use.

term "brokerage" I understand a regular and known machinery for bringing into practical communication with each other, parties that, but for this machinery, were too remote to have learned their reciprocal wants. All people of rank and distinction, throughout Greece and its dependencies or adjacencies, kept up a respectful intercourse with Delphi; and consequently that great bank had the advantage of what might be called *official* reports from every corner of Hellas; and (if need arose) of reports circumstantially minute. Was a high-born lady with ample dowery leading a solitary life, because no suitor of corresponding pretensions existed in her own neighbourhood? The Oracle had a ready means for transmitting this intelligence to a remote quarter, where it would tell effectually. Was a call for colonisation becoming clamorous in some particular region? What more beneficial, or what more easy, than for the Oracle to forward this news by its own channels to a tract of country labouring (through causes casual or local) under an excess of pauperised population? Or, if a chieftain in the north were commencing a sumptuous palace, what should hinder the Oracle from forwarding that intelligence to the architects and decorators of the south? Mr Carlyle's impeachment of Poor-law arrangements, on the ground that they accumulated ploughs and ploughmen in one province, whilst the arable lands needing to be ploughed all lay in some other province, would hardly have existed under Delphi, or not as any subject of complaint where the remedy was so prompt. The brief summary of Delphic administration was this—It moved by *secret* springs: not being visibly or audibly displayed, it irritated no jealousies. Appealing to no *coercive* powers, but purely to moral suasion, it provoked no refractoriness. Combining with the very highest of religious influences that Hellas recognised, it insured a docile and a reverential acceptance for all its directions. And, finally, because this great Delphic establishment held in its hands the hidden reins from *every* province, therefore it was, that out of universal Greece, as a body of wants, powers, slumbering activities, and undeveloped resources, Delphi would have constructed, and *did* construct, so far as her influence escaped the thwarting of cross currents, a system of political watch-work, where all the parts and movements played into a common centre. We must remember that Greece, after all, and allowing for every class of drawbacks, was really the first region upon earth in which (as in our present Christendom) there had formed itself a system of international law, and fixed modes of diplomacy. Compare her, this Greece, with the wretched voluptuaries of Southern Asia from Western Arabia, and Persia to Eastern China, no matter *when*, whether before or after Mahomet. Greece, though beginning with institutions as to women too dangerously Asiatic, was yet never emasculated. Men, aspiring men, were what she still produced. And much of this great advantage she owed apparently to that diffusive Delphic influence through which she nourished and expanded her unity, all parts existing for the sake of each, and each for all, in a degree of which no vestige was ever exhibited by the crazy and effeminate policy of any Asiatic state.

Now, therefore, having laid the foundations of a road for safe footing, let me march to *my* conclusion. The conclusion of the Fathers was the wildest of errors, into which they were misled by the most groundless of preconceptions. They started with the assumption that there was an essential hostility between Christianity and the primary pretensions of Oracles, consequently of Delphi as the supreme Oracle. And one result of this startling error was, that they exacted as a debt from Christianity that *expression* of hostility which, except in a Patristic romance, never had any real existence. The fathers regarded it as a duty of Christianity to destroy Oracles; and, holding that baseless creed, some of them went on to affirm, in mere defiance of history, that Christianity *had* destroyed Oracles. But *why* did the fathers fancy it so special a duty of the Christian faith to destroy Oracles? Simply for these two reasons—viz., that,

1. Most falsely they supposed *prophecy* to be the main function of an Oracle; whereas it did not enter as an element into the main business of an Oracle by so much as once in a thousand responses.

2. Not less erroneously they assumed this to be the inevitable parent of a collision with Christianity. For all prophecy, and the spirit of prophecy, they supposed to be a regal prerogative of Christianity, sacred, in fact, to the true faith by some inalienable right. But no such claim is anywhere advanced in the Scriptures. And even a careless reader will remember one conspicuous case, where a prophet of known hostility to the Hebrew interest and the Hebrew faith, and for that reason invoked and summoned to curse the children of Israel, is nevertheless relied on as a fountain of truth by the Hebrew leaders.

But suppose that there really *were* any such exclusive pretension to prophecy on behalf of Christianity—what *is* prophecy? The Patristic error is here intolerable. In order to make any comparison as to such a gift between the Greek Oracles and Christianity, we must at least be talking of the same thing; whereas nothing can be more extensively distinguished from the vaticinations of the

Pagan Oracle than prophecy as it is understood in the Bible. St Paul is continually referring in his Epistles to gifts of prophecy: but does any man suppose this apostle to mean gifts as to the faculty of prediction? Nobody, of all whom St Paul was addressing, pretended to any qualifications of that nature. A prophet in the Bible nowhere means a foreseer or predicter. It means a person endowed with *exegetic* gifts; that is, with powers of *interpretation* applicable to truth hidden, or truth imperfectly revealed. All profound and scriptural truth may be regarded as liable to misinterpretation, because originally lying under veils of shadowy concealment, many and various. He who removes any one of these varying obscurations—he who displays in his commentaries the gifts of an *exegetes,* or interpreter—is, in St Paul's sense, a prophet. Now, among these obscuring causes, one is time: some features of what is communicated may chance to be hidden by the clouds which surround a distant future; and in that sole case, one case amongst hundreds, the prophet coincides with the predicter. But, in the vast majority of cases, prophecy means the power of interpretation, or of commentary and practical extension, applied to scriptural doctrines; a sense not only irrelevant to the Oracles, but without purpose, or value, or meaning to any Pagan whatever. So that competition from that quarter was the idlest of chimeras. Prophecy, therefore, in any sense ever contemplated by a Christian writer, *could* not be violated or desecrated by any rival pretensions of Paganism, such as the fathers feared; inasmuch as all such pretensions on the part of Paganism were blank impossibilities.

That falsification, therefore, of historic facts, by which the fathers attempted to varnish and mystify the absolute indifference of Christianity to the Oracles, falls away spontaneously, when the motive upon which it moved is exposed as frivolous and childish. Cleared from these gross misrepresentations of the ill-informed, Oracles appear to have fulfilled a most important mission. As rationally might Christianity be supposed hostile to post-offices, or jealous of mail steamers, as indisposed to that oracular mission, of which the noble purpose, stated in the briefest terms, was—to knit the extremities of a state to its centre, and to quicken the progress of civilisation.

Why the Oracles really decayed, I presume arose thus: I have already noticed their loss of high political functions. This loss, though never intentionally offered as a degradation, not the less had that result. During that long course of generations, when princes or republics needed the co-operation of Oracles, that possessed worlds of local information, and that furnished the sanctions of heavenly authority, not at all less than the Oracles needed martial protection—the two powers were seen, or were felt obscurely, acting always in harmony and coalition. With us in Great Britain a man acquires the title of *Right Honourable* by entering the Privy Council as a member. Some honour, or some distinction for the ear or for the eye, corresponding to this, no doubt settled upon the high officers at Delphi. They were probably regarded as honorary members of the national council that in one shape or other advised and assisted the ruler of every state having established relations with Delphi. But these flattering distinctions would cease, or would become mere titular honours, when Delphi lost her connection, and her right of suggestion, and her "voice potential," with the supreme government of her own land. With us, when a man has been presented to the sovereign, he obtains (or used to obtain), from the Lord Chamberlain, a sort of certificate, which said, "Mr Thingamby is known at the Court of St James:" whether known for any good, was civilly suppressed; and this potent recognition enabled Thingamby to present himself as one having on a wedding garment, and admissible at any other court or courtlet whatsoever, except that of Ashantee. Let the reader honestly confess that he envies Thingamby. Now, it is not improbable that the high ministers at Delphi had a power equal to the Lord Chamberlain's, of certifying on behalf of any man going on his travels, were it Pythagoras or Solon, Herodotus or Plato, Anacharsis or Thingamby (every one of whom was a traveller), that the bearer is favourably known at Delphi. In the days of Delphic grandeur, such an introduction would bear a high value at all the surrounding courts; and this value would be multiplied in that age when the successors of Alexander had founded thrones stretching all the way from the Oxus to the Nile. But, after the Roman conquest of Greece and of Macedon, all this would collapse. A large field of economic services would still remain open to the temple; but the atmosphere of sanctity, with the faith in supernatural co-operation, would have suffered a shock. And the local agents, that once in every district had emulously disputed the glory of ranking in the long retinue of the god, and of the great lady seated on the tripod, would no longer find a sufficient indemnification for their labours in the glory of the service. Delphi, like the "Times" newspaper, would have to pay its agents; and the clouded splendours of the Delphic shrine and temple would reflect themselves, as years went on, in the dilapidations of the town. Delphi, the city, must have been the creation of Delphi, the oracular temple; and the dismantlings of both must have gone on under the same impulses, and through corresponding stages; so that either would reflect sufficiently to the other its own ruins and superannuations. When earthly grandeurs, however, were gone, there would still survive a large arrear of humbler and economic services, by which a decent revenue might be secured. And the true reason why the ceasing of Oracles was so variously timed and so vaguely dated, is to be looked for precisely in this variable declension of humbler ministrations, through local ebbs and flows in casual advantages of position. The case recalls to my eye a scene exhibited in certain streets of London very early on a summer morning nearly forty-four years ago. It was high summer, in the year 1814. All the leaders, royal or not royal, in the three immortal campaigns of Moscow (1812), of Leipsic (1813), and of France (1814), were just then in London, and paying a visit of honour to our own Regent. There was the reigning King of Prussia, whom most people likened to "the knight of the rueful countenance." There was the king's sole faithful servant—Blucher. There was the imperial fop, Alexander, and in his train men of sixty different languages; and, distinguished above all others that owed suit and service to this great potentate, rode Platoff, the Hetman of the Cossacks, specially beloved by all men as the most gallant, adventurous, and ugly of Cossacks. These Cossacks, if one might believe the flying rumours, drank with rapture every species of train oil. The London lamps were then lighted with oil; and the Cossacks, it was said, gave it the honour of a decided preference: so that, in streets lying near to the hetman's residence, to the north of Oxford Street, the lamps were observed to burn with a very variable lustre. In such a street, I, and others my companions, returning from a ball, about an hour before sunrise, saw a mimic sketch of the decaying Oracles. Here, close to the hetman's front-door, was a large overshadowing lamp, that might typify the Delphic shrine, but (to borrow a word from kitchen-maids) "black out." It was supposed to have been tapped too frequently by the hetman's sentinels who mounted guard on his Tartar Highness; then, on the other side the street, was a lamp, ancient and gloomy, that might pass for Dodona, throwing up sickly and fitful gleams of *undulating* lustre, but drawing near to extinction. Further ahead was a huge octagon lamp, that apparently never had been cleaned from smoke and fuliginous tarnish, forlorn, solitary, yet grimly alight, though under a disastrous eclipse, and ably supporting the part of Jupiter Ammon—that unsocial oracle which stood aloof from men in a narrow oasis belted round by worlds of sandy wilderness. And in the midst of all these vast and venerable mementoes rose one singularly pert and lively, though not bigger than a farthing rushlight, which probably had singly escaped the Cossacks, as having promised nothing; so that the least and most trivial of the entire group was likely to survive them all.

Briefly, the Oracles went out—lamp after lamp—as we see oftentimes in some festal illumination that one glass globe of light capriciously outlives its neighbour. Or they might be described as melting away like snow on the gradual return of vernal breezes. Large drifts vanish in a few hours: but patches here and there, lurking in the angles of high mountainous grounds, linger on into summer. Yet, whatever might have been their distinctions or their advantages on collation with each other, none of the ancients ever appear to have considered their pretensions to divination or prescience (whether by the reading of signs, as in the flight of birds, in the entrails of sacrificial victims—or, again, in direct spiritual prevision) as forming any conspicuous feature of their ordinary duties. Accordingly, when Cato in the Pharsalia is advised by Labienus to seek the counsel of Jupiter Ammon, whose sequestered oracle was then near enough to be reached without much *extra* trouble, he replies by a fine abstract of what might be expected from an oracle; viz., not predictions, but grand sentiments bearing on the wisdom of life. These representative sentiments, as shaped by Lucan, are fine and noble; we might expect it from a poet so truly Roman and noble. But he dismisses these oracular sayings as superfluous, because already familiar to meditative men. We know them,

> "Scimus"—(says he)
> "Et hæc nobis non altius inseret Ammon."

And no Ammon will ever engraft them more deeply into my heart.

This I mention, when concluding, as a further and collateral evidence against the fathers. For if any mode of prophetic illumination had been the sort of communication reasonably and characteristically to be anticipated from an Oracle, in that case, Lucan would have pointed his artillery from a very different battery, the battery of scorn and indignation. No people certainly *could* be more superstitious than the Roman populace: witness the everlasting *Bos locutus est* of the credulous Livy. Yet, on the other hand, already in the early days of Ennius, we know, by one of his beautiful fragments, that no nation could breed more high-minded denouncers of such misleading follies.

MIRACLES AS SUBJECTS OF TESTIMONY.

HUME's argument against miracles is simply this:—Every possible event, however various in its degree of credibility, must, of necessity, be more credible when it rests upon a sufficient cause lying within the field of what is called *nature*, than when it does not: more credible when it obeys some mechanical cause, than when it transcends such a cause, and is miraculous.

Therefore, assume the resistance to credibility, in any preternatural occurrence, as equal to x, and the very ideal or possible value of human testimony as no more than x —in that case, under the most favourable circumstances conceivable, the argument for and against a miracle, $+ x$ and $- x$, will be equal; the two values will destroy each other, and the result will be $= 0$.

But, inasmuch as this expresses the value of human testimony in its highest or ideal form, a form which is seldom realised in experience, the true result will be different—there will always be a negative result much or little according to the circumstances, but in any case enough to turn the balance *against* believing a miracle.

"Or, in other words," said Hume, popularising his argument, "it will always be more credible that the reporter of a miracle should have told a falsehood, or should himself have been the dupe of appearances, than that a miracle should have actually occurred—that is, an infraction of those natural laws (any or all) which limit what we call experience. For, assume the utmost disinterestedness, veracity, and sound judgment in the witness, with the utmost advantage in the circumstances for giving full play to those qualities; even in such a case the value of affirmative testimony could, at the very utmost, be equal to the negative value on the other side the equation: and the result would be, to keep my faith suspended *in equilibrio*. But, in any real case ever likely to come before us, the result will be worse; for the affirmative testimony will be sure to fall in many ways below its ideal maximum; leaving, therefore, for the final result some excess, much or little, to the negative side of the equation.

SECTION II.

Of the Argument as Affected by the Covert Limitations under which it is presented.

Such is the argument: and, as the first step towards investigating its sanity and its strength—its kind of force, and its quantity of force—we must direct our attention to the following fact; viz., that amongst three separate conditions under which a miracle (or any event whatever) might become known to us, Hume's argument is applied only to one. Assuming a miracle to happen (for the possibility of a miracle is of course left open throughout the discussion, since any argument against *that* would at once foreclose every question about its communicability), then it might happen under three several sets of circumstances, in relation to our consciousness. 1. It might happen in the presence of a single witness—that witness not being ourselves. This case let us call *Alpha.* 2. It might happen in the presence of many witnesses, witnesses to a variable amount, but still (as before) ourselves not being amongst that multitude. This case let us call *Beta.* 3. It might happen in our own presence, and fall within the direct light of our own consciousness. This case let us call *Gamma.*

Now these distinctions are important to the whole extent of the question. For the second case, which is the actual case of many miracles recorded in the New Testament, at once cuts away a large body of sources in which either error or deceit could lurk. Hume's argument supposes the reporter of the miracle to be a dupe, or the maker of dupes—himself deluded, or wishing to delude others. But, in the case of the thousands fed from a few loaves and small fishes, the chances of error, wilful or not wilful, are diminished in proportion to the number of observers,* and Hume's inference as to the declension of the affirmative x, in relation to the negative x, no longer applies, or, if at all, with vastly diminished force. With respect to the third case, it cuts away the whole argument at once in its very radix. For Hume's argument applies to the *communication* of a miracle, and therefore to a case of testimony. But, wherever the miracle falls within direct personal cognisance, there it follows that no question can arise about the value of human testimony. The affirma-

* "*In proportion to the number of observers:*"—Perhaps, however, on the part of Hume, some critical apologist will say, "Doubtless he was aware of that; but still the reporters of the miracle were few. No matter how many were present, the witnesses for us are but the Evangelists." Yes, certainly, the Evangelists; and let us add, all those contemporaries to whom the Evangelists silently appealed. These make up the "multitude" contemplated in the case *Beta.*

tive x, expressing the value of testimony, disappears altogether; and that side of the equation is possessed by a new quantity (viz., a quantity representing ourselves—our own consciousness), not at all concerned in Hume's argument.

Hence it results that, of three possible conditions under which a miracle may be supposed to offer itself to our knowledge, two are excluded from the view of Hume's argument.

SECTION III.

Whether the Second of these Conditions is not Expressly Noticed by Hume.

It may seem that it *is*. But in fact it is not. And (what is more to the purpose) we are not at liberty to consider it any accident that it is not. Hume had his reasons. Let us take all in proper order: 1. that it seems so; 2. that in fact it is not so; and 3. that this is no accident, but intentional.

1. Hume seems to contemplate such a case—viz., *Beta*, the case of a miracle witnessed and attested by a multitude of persons—in the following imaginary miracle, which he proposes as a basis for reasoning. Queen Elizabeth, as everybody will remember who has happened to read Lord Monmouth's Memoirs, died on the night between the last day of 1602 and the first day of 1603:* this could

* *I. e.*, ecclesiastically: the queen died on the night of March 24, in the year which we should *now* (1858) call 1603, but which by every class of careful writers was *then* regarded as 1602. March 24 was the last day of 1602: for *Lady-Day*, or the day of our Lady the Virgin Mary (the day which corresponds by anticipation with December 25, or Christmas Day, so as to allow nine months for the gestation of the Holy Child), is not a *moveable* festival, but fixed unalterably to March 25. This was the opening day, the *Jour de l'An* of Paris, the New-year's-day of England, for the year 1603. And all the days which lie between December 31 of

not be forgotten by the reader, because, in fact, Lord Monmouth, who was one of Her Majesty's nearest relatives (being a younger son of her first cousin Lord Hunsdon), obtained his title and subsequent preferment as a reward for the furious ride he performed to Edinburgh (at that time at least 440 miles distant from London), without taking off his boots, in order to lay the earliest tidings of the great event at the feet of her successor. In reality, never did any death cause so much posting day and night over the high-roads of Europe. And the same causes which made it so interesting, have caused it to be the best dated event in modern history; that one which could least be shaken by any discordant evidence still in arrear. Now, says Hume, imagine the case, that, in spite of all this chronological precision—this precision, and this notoriety of precision—Her Majesty's court physicians should have chosen to propagate a story of her resurrection. Imagine that these learned gentlemen should have issued a *bulletin*, declaring that Queen Elizabeth had been met in Greenwich Park, or at Nonsuch, on May-day of 1603, or in Westminster, two years after, by the Lord Chamberlain when detecting Guy Faux—let them even swear it before twenty justices of the peace; I for one, says Hume, am free to confess that I would not believe them. No, nor, to say the truth, would I; nor would I advise my readers to believe them.

2. Here, therefore, it would seem as if Hume were boldly pressing his principles to the very uttermost—that is, were charging a miracle as untenable, though attested

---

1602 and March 25 of 1603, were written as a fraction—viz., February 10, $\frac{1602}{1603}$, where the denominator expresses the true year, according to our present mode of reckoning. But the reader must understand that this has nothing to do with O. S. *(Old Style)* and N. S. *(New Style)*. It simply expresses the ecclesiastic way of counting opposed to the civil.

by a multitude. But, in fact, he is not. He only seems to do so; for, if no number of witnesses could avail anything in proof of a miracle, why does he timidly confine himself to the hypothesis of the queen's physicians only coming forward? Why not call in the whole Privy Council—or the Lord Mayor and Common Council of London—the Sheriffs of Middlesex—and the Twelve Judges? As to the court physicians, though three or four nominally, virtually they are but one man. They have a common interest, and in two separate ways they are liable to a suspicion of collusion: first, because the same motives which act upon one probably act upon the rest: in this respect, they are under a *common* influence. Secondly, because, if not the motives, at any rate the physicians themselves, act upon each other. In this respect, they are under a *reciprocal* influence. They are to be reasoned about as one individual.

3. As Hume could not possibly fail to see all this, we may be sure that his choice of witnesses was not accidental. In fact, his apparent carelessness marks a very discreet management. His object was, under the fiction of an independent multitude, to smuggle in a virtual unity; for his court physicians are no plural body in effect and virtue, but a mere pleonasm and a tautology.

And in good earnest, Hume had reason enough for his caution. How much or how little testimony would avail to establish a resurrection in any neutral case,* few people would be willing to pronounce off-hand, and, above all, on a fictitious case. Prudent men, in such circumstances,

* By a neutral case is meant, 1st, one in which there is no previous reason, from a great doctrine requiring such an event for its support, to expect a resurrection; 2dly, a case belonging to a period of time in which it is fully believed that miraculous agency has ceased.

would act as the judges in our English courts, who are always displeased if it is attempted to elicit their opinions upon a point of law by an imaginary and collusive case. And very reasonably; for in these fictitious cases all the little circumstances of reality are wanting; and therefore the oblique relations to such circumstances, out of which it is that any sound opinion can be formed. We all know very well what Hume is after in this problem of a resurrection. And his case of Queen Elizabeth's resurrection being a perfectly fictitious case, we are at liberty to do any one of three different things:—either simply to refuse an answer; or, 2dly, to give such an answer as he looks for—viz., to agree with him in his disbelief under the supposed contingency; without, therefore, offering the slightest prejudice to any scriptural case of resurrection: *i. e.*, we might go along with him in his premises, and yet baulk him of his purpose; or, 3dly, we might even join issue with him, and peremptorily challenge his verdict upon his own fiction. For it is singular enough, that a modern mathematician of eminence (Mr Babbage) has expressly considered this very imaginary question of a resurrection, and he pronounces the testimony of *seven* witnesses, competent and veracious, and presumed to have no bias, sufficient to establish such a miracle. Strip Hume's case of the ambiguities already pointed out—suppose the physicians *really* and virtually, as well as speciously and nominally, independent witnesses—not a corporation speaking by one organ—it will then become a mere question of degree between the philosopher and the mathematician—seven witnesses? or fifty? or a hundred? For though none of us (not Mr Babbage, we may be sure) seriously believes in the possibility of a resurrection occurring in these days, as little can any of us believe in the possibility that seven witnesses of honour and sagacity (but say seven hundred) could be found to attest such an event when not occurring.

But the useful result from all this is, that Mr Hume is perfectly aware of the case *Beta* (of last sect.), as a distinct case from *Alpha* or from *Gamma*, though he affects blindness: he is aware that a multitude of competent witnesses, no matter whether seven or seven hundred, is able to establish that which a single witness could not; in fact, that increasing the number of witnesses is able to compensate increasing incredibility in the subject of doubt; that, even supposing this subject a resurrection from the dead, there may be assigned a quantity of evidence (x) greater than *any* resistance to the credibility. And he betrays the fact that he has one eye open to his own jesuitism, by palming upon us an apparent multitude for a real one, thus drawing all the credit he can from the name of a multitude, and yet evading the force which he strictly knew to be lodged in the thing; seeking the reputation of the case *Beta*, but shrinking from its hostile force.

SECTION IV.

Of the Argument as Affected by a Classification of Miracles.

Let us now inquire whether Hume's argument would be affected by such differences in miracles as might emerge upon the most general distribution of their kinds.

Miracles may be classed generally as inner or outer.

1. The inner, or those which may be called miracles for the individual, are such as go on, or may go on, within the separate personal consciousness of each separate man. And it shows how forgetful people are of the very doctrines which they themselves profess as Christians, when we consider, on the one hand, that miracles, in this sense, are

essential to Christianity, and yet, on the other hand, consider how often it is said that the age of miracles is past. Doubtless, in the sense of external miracles, all such agencies *are* past. But in the other sense there are three distinct classes of the supernatural agency, which we are now considering; and these three are held by many Christians; two by most Christians; and the third by all. They are

α.—*Special Providences:* which class it is that many philosophic Christians doubt or deny.

β.—*Grace:* both predisposing [by old theologians called *prevenient**] and effectual.

γ.—*Prayer considered as efficacious.*

Of these three I repeat, that the two last are held by most Christians: and yet it is evident that both presume a supernatural agency. But this agency exists only where it is sought. And even where it *does* exist, from its very nature (as an *interior* experience for each separate consciousness) it is incommunicable. But that does not

---

* "*Prevenient grace:*"—Memorable it is, and striking as a record of the changes worked continually by time, that in a trial before one of our English Ecclesiastical Courts some two or three years ago [the parties to the suit being on the one side, as I think, the Bishop of Exeter, and on the other a reverend gentleman, of whom the solitary wreck or floating spar that remains in the custody of my recollection is a capital A, as the initial letter of his name], the technical term "*prevenient grace*" came forward many a score of times. But how completely this was felt to be a resurrection from the grave, may be judged by the declaration of a leading counsel, a most eminent barrister, who protested against the mysterious phrase as one which, in the whole course of his reading [some little being *sacred*, but a great deal *profane*], he had never once met (or heard of) such a monster:—was it something to drink? or was it something that one would give in charge to a policeman? Now, reader, look into the eleventh book of "Paradise Lost," and you will find it within the first four or five lines. To be available for the purposes of a great poet, the phrase must have been common at that day [1667]: and in every theological work it is as common as the songs of birds in spring.

defeat its purpose. It is of its essence to be incommunicable. And, therefore, with relation to Hume's great argument, which was designed to point out a vast *hiatus* or inconsistency in the divine economy—"Here is a miraculous agency, perhaps, but it is incommunicable: it may exist, but it cannot manifest itself; which defect neutralises it, and defeats the very purpose of its existence"—the answer is, that, as respects these interior miracles, there is no such inconsistency. They are *meant* for the private forum of each man's consciousness: nor would it have met any human necessity to have made them communicable. The language of Scripture is, that he, who wishes experimentally to know the changes that may be accomplished by prayer, must pray. In that way only, and not by communication of knowledge from another, could he understand it as a practical effect. And to understand it not practically, but only in a speculative way, could not meet any religious end, but merely an irreligious curiosity.

As respects one great division of miraculous agency, it is clear, therefore, that Hume's argument does not apply. The arrow glances past: not so much missing its aim, as taking a false one. The failure is not in the executive hand, but in the guiding eye. The *hiatus* which it supposes, the insulation and incommunicability which it charges upon the miraculous as a capital oversight, was part of the design: such mysterious agencies were *intended* to be incommunicable, and for the same reason which shuts up each man's consciousness into a silent world of its own—separate and inaccessible to all other consciousnesses. If a communication is thrown open by such agencies between the separate spirit of each man and the supreme Spirit of the universe, then the end is accomplished: and it is part of that end to close this communication against all other cognisance

So far Hume is baffled. The supernatural agency is incommunicable: it ought to be so. That is its perfection.

2. But now, as respects the other great order of miracles —viz., the *external*—first of all, we may remark a very important subdivision: miracles, in this sense, subdivide into two great leading varieties—1. *Evidential* miracles, which simply *prove* Christianity; 2. *Constituent* miracles, which, in a partial sense, *are* Christianity, as in part composing its substance. And, perhaps, it may turn out that Hume's objection, if applicable at all, is here applicable in a separate way, and with a varying force.

The first class, the evidential miracles, are all those which were performed merely as evidences (whether simply as indications, or as absolute demonstrations) of the divine power which upheld Christianity. The second class, the constituent miracles, are those which constitute a part of Christianity. Two of these are absolutely indispensable to Christianity, and cannot be separated from it even in thought—viz., the miraculous birth of our Saviour, and his miraculous resurrection. The first is essential upon this ground—that unless Christ had united the two natures (divine and human), he could not have made the satisfaction required. For try it both ways: not being human, then, indeed, he might have had power to go through the mysterious sufferings of the satisfaction: but how would that have applied to man? It would have been perfect, but how would it have been relevant? Now try it the other way: not being divine, then indeed any satisfaction he could make would be relevant: but how would it have been possible in a being himself tainted with frailty? It is an argument used by Christianity itself—that man cannot offer a satisfaction for man? The mysterious and supernatural birth, therefore, was essential, as a capacitation for the work to be performed; and, on the other hand, the mysterious death and consequences were essential, as the very work itself.

Now, therefore, having made this distinction, I may observe, that the first class of miracles was occasional and polemic: it was meant to meet a special hostility incident to the birth-struggles of a new religion, and a religion which, for the very reason that it was true, stood opposed to the spirit of the world; of a religion which, in its first stage, had to fight against a civil power in absolute possession of the civilised earth, and backed by seventy legions. This being settled, it follows, that if Hume's argument were applicable in its whole strength to the evidential miracles, no result of any importance could follow. It is clear that a Christianised earth never can want polemic miracles again; polemic miracles were wanted for a transitional state, but such a state cannot return. Polemic miracles were wanted for a state of conflict with a dominant idolatry. It was Christianity militant, and militant with child-like arms, against Paganism triumphant, that needed such weapons, and that used them. But Christianity, in league with civilisation, and resting on the powers of this earth allied with her own, never again can speak to idolatrous man except from a station of infinite superiority. If, therefore, these evidential miracles are incommunicable as respects their grounds of credibility to after generations, neither are they wanted.

Still it will be urged—were not the miracles meant for purposes ulterior to the transitional state? Were they not meant equally for the polemic purpose of confuting hostility at the moment, and of propping the faith of Christians in all after ages? The growing opinion amongst reflecting Christians is, that they were not: that the evidential miracles accomplished their whole purpose in their own age. Something of supernatural agency, visibly displayed, was wanted for the first establishment of a new faith. But, once established, it must be a false faith that could need this external support—the evidential miracles, the polemic credentials of Christianity. Christianity could not unroot itself now, though every trace of evidential miracle should have vanished. Being a true religion, once rooted in man's knowledge and man's heart, it is self-sustained; it never could be eradicated.

But, waiving that argument, it is evident that, whatever becomes of the evidential miracles, Christianity never can dispense with those transcendent miracles which I have called *constituent*,—those which do not so much demonstrate Christianity, as constitute Christianity, and *are* Christianity by a large integral section. Now as to the way in which Hume's argument could apply to these, I shall reserve what I have to say until a subsequent section. Meantime, with respect to the other class, the simply evidential miracles, it is plain, that if ever they should be called for again, then, as to *them*, Hume's argument will be evaded, or not evaded, according to their purpose. If their function regards an individual, it will be no just objection to them that they are incommunicable. If it regards a multitude or a nation, then the same power which utters the miracle can avail for its manifestation before a multitude, as happened in the days of the New Testament, *and then is realised the case* Beta *of Sect. II.* And if it is still objected, that even in that case there could be no sufficient way of propagating the miracle, with its evidence, to other times or places, the answer must be—

1. That supposing the purpose merely polemic, that purpose is answered without such a propagation.

2. That, supposing the purpose, by possibility, an ulterior purpose, stretching into distant ages, even then our modern arts of civilisation, printing, &c., give us advantages which place a remote age on a level with the present as to the force of evidence; and that even the defect of *autopsy* may be compensated by sufficient testimony of a multitude, it is evident that Hume himself felt, by his evasion in the case of the imaginary Elizabethan miracle proposed by himself.

RECAPITULATION.

Now let us recapitulate the steps already made before going on to the rest.

1. I have drawn into notice [Sect. II.] the case *Beta*—overlooked by Hume in his argument, but apparently not overlooked in his consciousness—the case where a multitude of witnesses overrules the incommunicability attaching to a single witness.

2. I have drawn into notice the class of internal miracles—miracles going on in the inner economy of every Christian's heart; for it is essential to a Christian to allow of prayer. He cannot *be* a Christian if he should condemn prayer; and prayer cannot hope to produce its object without a miracle. And to such miracles Hume's argument, the argument of incommunicability, is inapplicable. They do not seek to transplant themselves; every man's personal experience in this respect is meant for himself alone.

3. Even amongst miracles *not* internal, I have shown, that if one class (the merely evidential and polemic) are incommunicable—*i.e.*, not capable of propagation to a remote age or place—they have sufficiently fulfilled their ultimate purpose by their immediate effect. But such

miracles are alien and accidental to Christianity. Christ himself reproved severely those who sought such signs, as a wicked, unbelieving generation; and afterwards he reproved, with a most pathetic reproach, that one of his own disciples who singly, amongst the total brotherhood, demanded such a sign. But, besides these evidential miracles, I noticed also

4. The constituent miracles of Christianity; upon which as regarded Hume's argument, I reserved my remarks to the latter section: and to these I now address myself.

But first I premise this

Lemma:—That an *à priori* (or, as I shall attempt to show, an *à posteriori*) reason for believing a miracle, or for expecting a miracle, will greatly disturb the valuation of x (that is, the abstract resistance to credibility), as assumed in Hume's argument. This is the centre in which, I am satisfied, lurks that πρωτον ψευδος, or primary falsehood, which Hume himself suspected: and I add, that as a vast number of witnesses (according to a remark made in Section II.) will virtually operate as a reduction of the value allowed to x, until x may be made to vanish altogether; so, in the reverse order, any material reduction of value in x will virtually operate exactly as the multiplication of witnesses; and the case *Alpha* will be raised to the case *Beta.*

This *Lemma* being stated as a point of appeal in what follows, I proceed to

SECTION V.

On Hume's Argument as affected by the Purpose.

This topic is so impressive, and indeed awful, in its relation to Christianity, that I shall not violate its majesty by doing more than simply stating the case. All the known or imagined miracles that ever were recorded as flowing from any Pagan origin were miracles—1. of ostentation; 2. of ambition and rivalship; 3. were blank expressions of power; or, 4. were blind accidents. Not even in pretence was any one of them more than that. First and last came the Christian miracles, on behalf of a *moral* purpose. The purpose was to change man's idea of his own nature; and to change his idea of God's nature. Many other purposes might be stated; but all were moral. Now to any other wielder of supernatural power, real or imaginary, it never had occurred, by way of pretence even, that in working miracles he had a moral object. And here, indeed, comes in the argument of Christ with tremendous effect—that, whilst all other miracles might be liable to the suspicion of having been effected by alliance with darker agencies, his only (as sublime moral agencies for working the only revolution that ever was worked in man's nature) could not be liable to such a suspicion; since, if an evil spirit would lend himself to the propagation of good in its most transcendent form, in that case the kingdom of darkness would be "divided against itself."

Here, then, is an *à posteriori* reason, derived from the whole subsequent life and death of the miracle-worker, for diminishing the value of x according to the *Lemma*.

SECTION VI.

On the Argument of Hume as affected by Matters of Fact.

It is a very important axiom of the schoolmen applicable to this case—that, *à posse ad esse non valet consequentia;* you can draw no inference from the possibility of a thing to its reality, but, in the reverse order, *ab esse ad posse,* the inference is inevitable: if it is, or if it ever has been—then of necessity it can be. Hume himself would have admitted, that the proof of any one miracle, beyond all possibility of doubt, at once lowered the—x of his argument (*i. e.*, the value of the resistance to our faith), so as to affect the whole force of that argument, as applying to all other miracles whatever having a rational and an adequate purpose. Now it happens that we have two cases of miracles which can be urged in this view: one *à posteriori*, derived from our historical experience, and the other *à priori*. We will take them separately.

1. The *à priori* miracle I call such—not (as the unphilosophic may suppose) because it occurred previously to our own period, or from any consideration of time whatever, but in the logical meaning, as having been derived from our reason in opposition to our experience. This order of miracle it is manifest that Hume overlooked altogether, because he says expressly that we have nothing to appeal to in this dispute except our human experience. But it happens that we have; and precisely where the possibilities of experience desert us. We know nothing through experience (whether directly personal or historical) of what preceded or accompanied the first introduction of man upon this earth. But, in the absence of all experience, our reason informs us, that he must have been introduced by a supernatural agency. Thus far we are sure. For the sole alternative is one which would be equally mysterious, and, besides, contradictory to the marks of change, of transition, and of perishableness in our planet itself—viz., the hypothesis of an eternal, unoriginated race: *that* is more confounding to the human intellect than any miracle whatever: so that, even tried merely as one probability against another, the miracle would have the advantage. The miracle supposes a supersensual and transcendent cause. The opposite hypothesis supposes effects without *any* cause;

in short, upon any hypothesis, we are driven to suppose—and compelled to suppose—a miraculous state as introductory to the earliest state of nature. The planet, indeed, might form itself by mechanical laws of motion, repulsion, attraction, and central forces. But man could not. Life could not. Organisation, even animal organisation, might perhaps be explained out of mechanical causes. But life could not. Life is itself a great miracle. Suppose the nostrils formed by mechanic agency; still the breath of life could not enter them without a supernatural force. And *à fortiori*, man, with his intellectual and moral capacities, could not arise upon this planet without a higher agency than any lodged in that nature which is the object of our present experience. This kind of miracle, as deduced by our reason, and not witnessed experimentally, or drawn from any past records, I call an *à priori* miracle.

2. But there is another kind of miracle, which Hume ought not to have overlooked, which he has, however, overlooked. He himself observes candidly that *prophecy* is a distinct species of the miraculous; and, no doubt, he neglected the Scriptural Prophecies, as supposing them all of doubtful interpretation; or else believing with Porphyry, that such as are not doubtful, must have been posterior to the event which they point to. It happens, however, that there are some prophecies which cannot be evaded or "refused," some to which neither objection will apply. One I will here cite, by way of example: The prophecy of Isaiah, describing the desolation of Babylon, was delivered about seven centuries before Christ. A century or so *after* Christ, comes Porphyry, and insinuates, that all the prophecies alike might be comparatively recent forgeries! Well, for a moment suppose it: but, at least, they existed in the days of Porphyry. Now, it happens, that more

than two centuries *after* Porphyry, we have good evidence, as to Babylon, that it had not yet reached the stage of utter desolation predicted by Isaiah. Four centuries after Christ, we learn from a father of the Christian Church, who had good personal information as to its condition, that it was then become a solitude; but a solitude in good preservation as a royal park. The vast city had disappeared, and the murmur of myriads: but as yet there were no signs whatever of ruin or desolation. Not until our own nineteenth century was the picture of Isaiah seen in full realisation—then lay the lion basking at noonday—then crawled the serpents from their holes; and at night the whole region echoed with the wild cries peculiar to arid wildernesses. The transformations, therefore, of Babylon have been going on slowly through a vast number of centuries, until the perfect accomplishment of Isaiah's picture. Perhaps they have travelled through a course of more than two thousand years; and from the glimpses we gain of Babylon at intervals, we know for certain that Isaiah had been dead for many centuries before his vision could have even *begun* to realise itself. But then, says an objector, the final ruins of great empires and cities may be safely assumed on general grounds of observation. Hardly, however, if they happen to be seated in a region so fertile as Mesopotamia, and on a great river like the Euphrates. But allow this possibility—allow the natural disappearance of Babylon in a long course of centuries. In other cases the disappearance is gradual, and at length perfect. No traces can now be found of Carthage; none of Memphis; or, if you suppose something peculiar to Mesopotamia, no traces can be found of Nineveh,* or on the other

* Of late, however, fully exposed by Layard, Rawlinson, &c.

side of that region: none of the other great cities—Roman, Parthian, Persian, Median, in that same region or adjacent regions. Babylon only is circumstantially described by Jewish prophecy as long surviving itself in a state of visible and audible desolation: and to Babylon only such a description applies. Other prophecies might be cited with the same result. But this is enough. And here is an *à posteriori* miracle.

Now, observe: these two orders of miracle, by their very nature, absolutely evade the argument of Hume. The incommunicability disappears altogether. The value of—x absolutely vanishes, and becomes $=0$. The human reason being immutable, suggests to every age, renews and regenerates for ever, the necessary inference of a miraculous state antecedent to the natural state. And, for the miracles of prophecy, these require no evidence, and depend upon none: they carry their own evidence along with them: they utter their own testimonies, and they are continually reinforcing them; for, probably, every successive period of time reproduces fresh cases of prophecy completed. But even one, like that of Babylon, realises the case of *Beta* (Sect. II.) in its most perfect form. History, which attests it, is the voice of every generation, checked and countersigned in effect by all the men who compose it.

SECTION VII.

Of the Argument as affected by the particular Worker of the Miracles.

This is the last "moment," to use the language of Mechanics, which I shall notice in this discussion. And here there is a remarkable *petitio principii* in Hume's management of his argument. He says, roundly, that it makes no difference at all if God were connected with the question as the author of the supposed miracles. And why? Because, says he, we know God only by experience —meaning as involved in nature—and, therefore, that in so far as miracles transcend our experience of nature, they transcend by implication our experience of God. But the very question under discussion is—whether God did, or did not, manifest himself to human experience in the miracles of the New Testament. Yet, at all events, the idea of God in itself already includes the notion of a *power* to work miracles, whether that power were ever exercised or not; and as Sir Isaac Newton thought that space might be the sensorium of God, so may we (and with much more philosophical propriety) affirm that the miraculous and the transcendent is the very *nature* of God. God being assumed, it is as easy to believe in a miracle issuing from him as in any operation according to the laws of nature (which, after all, is possibly in many points only the nature of our planet): it is as easy, because either mode of action is indifferent to him. Doubtless this argument, when addressed to an atheist, loses its force; because he refuses to assume a God. But then, on the other hand, it must be remembered that Hume's argument itself does not stand on the footing of atheism. He supposes it binding on a theist. Now a theist, in starting from the idea of God, grants, of necessity, the plenary power of miracles as greater and more awful than man could even comprehend. All he wants is a sufficient motive for such transcendent agencies; but this is supplied in excess (as regards what we have called the *constituent* miracles of Christianity) by the case of a religion that was to revolutionise the moral nature of man. The moral nature—the kingdom of the will—is essentially opposed to the kingdom of nature even by the confession of irreligious philosophers; and, therefore, being itself a supersensual field, it seems more reasonably adapted to agencies supernatural than such as are natural.

GENERAL RECAPITULATION.

In Hume's argument—x, which expresses the resistance to credibility in a miracle, is valued as of necessity equal to the very maximum or ideal of human testimony; which, under the very best circumstances, might be equal to $+ x$, in no case more, and in all known cases less. I, on the other hand, have endeavoured to show—

1. That, because Hume contemplates only the case of a single witness, it will happen that the case *Beta* (of Sect. II.) where a multitude of witnesses exist, may greatly exceed $+ x$; and with a sufficient multitude *must* exceed x.

2. That, in the case of internal miracles—operations of divine agency within the mind and conscience of the individual—Hume's argument is necessarily set aside: the evidence, the $+ x$, is perfect for the individual, and the miraculous agency is meant only for *him*.

3. That, in the case of one primary miracle—viz., the first organisation of man on this planet—the evidence greatly transcends x: because here it is an evidence not derived from experience at all, but from the reflecting reason: and the miracle has the same advantage over facts of experience, that a mathematical truth has over the truths which rest on induction. It is the difference between *must be* and *is*—between the inevitable and the merely actual.

4. That, in the case of another order of miracles—viz., prophecies—Hume's argument is again overruled; because the $+ x$ in this case, the affirmative evidence, is not de-

rived from human testimony. Some prophecies are obscure; they may be fulfilled possibly without men's being aware of the fulfilment. But others, as that about the fate of Babylon—about the fate of the Arabs (the children of Ishmael)—about the fate of the Jews—are not of a nature to be misunderstood; and the evidence which attends them is not alien, but is intrinsic, and developed by themselves (a contingency for which Hume has made no allowance) in successive stages from age to age.

5. That, because the primary miracle in No. 3 argues at least a *power* competent to the working of a miracle, for any after miracle we have only to seek a sufficient *motive.* Now, the objects of the Christian revelation were equal at the least to those of the original creation. In fact, Christianity may be considered as a second creation; and the justifying cause for the *constituent* miracles of Christianity is even to us as apparent as any which could have operated at the primary creation. The *epigenesis,* the secondary birth, was, at least, as grand an occasion as the *genesis,* the original birth. Indeed, it is evident, for example, that Christianity itself could not have existed without the constituent miracle of the Resurrection; because without that there would have been no conquest over death. And here, as in No. 3, $+ x$ is derived—not from any experience, and therefore cannot be controlled by that sort of hostile experience which Hume's argument relies on; but is derived from the reason which transcends all experience; that is, which would be valid—I do not say against the positive case of a hostile experience, but in the neutral or negative case, where all confirmatory experience is wanting.

CASUISTRY.

PART I.

It is remarkable, in the sense of being noticeable and interesting, but not in the sense of being surprising, that casuistry has fallen into disrepute throughout all Protestant lands. This disrepute is a result partly due to the healthier morality which usually* follows in the train of the Protestant faith. So far it is honourable, and an evidence of superior illumination. But, in the excess to which it has been pushed, we may trace also a blind and fanatical reaction of the horror inspired by the abuses of the Popish Confessional. Unfortunately for the interests of scientific ethics, the first cultivators of casuistry had been those who kept in view the professional service of auricular confession. Their purpose was—to assist the reverend confessor in appraising the quality of doubtful

* "*Usually:*"—We Protestants, being generally bigots where we happen to be sincere and earnest, have assumed it as a settled point that, wheresoever Protestant and Popish provinces lie intermingled with each other (as in Germany and in Switzerland), the transition from the first to the second, in all that argues order, industry, social activity, and public welfare, leaves an impression so powerfully advantageous to Protestantism, as to resemble the alternate successions of sunlight and twilight. But candid observers, amongst whom is to be reckoned the late Dr Arnold of Rugby, do not admit the truth of this representation—at least so far as regards Switzerland.

actions, in order that he might properly adjust his scale of counsel, of warning, of reproof, and of penance. Some, therefore, in pure simplicity and conscientious discharge of the duty they had assumed, but others from lubricity of morals or the irritations of sensual curiosity, pushed their investigations into unhallowed paths of speculation. They held aloft a torch for exploring guilty recesses of human life, which it is far better for us all to leave in their original darkness. Crimes that were often all but imaginary, extravagancies of erring passion that would never have been known as possibilities to the young and the innocent, were thus published in their most odious details. At first, it is true, the decent draperies of a dead language were suspended before these abominations: but sooner or later some knave was found, on mercenary motives, to tear away this partial veil; and thus the vernacular literature of most nations in Southern Europe was gradually polluted with revelations that had been originally made in the avowed service of religion. Indeed, there was one aspect of such books which proved even more extensively disgusting. Speculations pointed to monstrous offences, bore upon their very face and frontispiece the intimation that they related to cases rare and anomalous. But sometimes casuistry pressed into the most hallowed recesses of common domestic life. The delicacy of youthful wives, for example, was often not less grievously shocked than the manliness of husbands, by refinements of monkish subtlety applied to cases never meant for religious cognisance—but far better left to the decision of good feeling, of nature, and of pure household morality. Even this revolting use of casuistry, however, did less to injure its name and pretensions than a persuasion, pretty generally diffused, that the main purpose and drift of this science was a sort of hair-splitting process, by which doubts might be applied to the plainest duties of life, or questions raised as to the extent of their obligations, for the single benefit of those who sought to evade them. A casuist was viewed, in short, as a kind of lawyer or special pleader in morals, such as those who, in London, are known as Old Bailey practitioners, called in to manage desperate cases—to suggest all available advantages—to raise doubt or distinctions where simple morality saw no room for either—and generally to teach the art, in nautical phrase, of sailing as near the wind as might be found possible, without absolutely foundering.

Meantime it is certain that casuistry, when soberly applied, is not only a beneficial as well as a very interesting study; but that, by whatever title, it is absolutely indispensable to the *practical* treatment of morals. We may reject the name; the thing we cannot reject. And accordingly the custom has been, in all English treatises on Ethics, to introduce a good deal of casuistry under the idea of special illustration, but without any reference to casuistry as a formal branch of research. Indeed, as society grows complex, the uses of casuistry become more urgent. Even Cicero could not pursue his theme through such barren generalisations as entirely to evade all notice of special cases: and Paley has given the chief interest to his very loose investigations of morality, by scattering a selection of such cases over the whole field of his discussion.

The necessity of casuistry might, in fact, be deduced from the very origin and genesis of the word. First came the general law or rule of action. This was like the major proposition of a syllogism. But next came a special instance or *case*, so stated as to indicate whether it did or did not fall under the general rule. This, again, was exactly the minor proposition in a syllogism. For example, in logic we say, as the major proposition in a syllogism, *Man is mortal.* This is the rule. And then "subsuming" (such is the technical phrase—*subsuming*) Socrates under the rule by a minor proposition—viz., Socrates is a man—we are able mediately to connect him with the predicate of that rule—viz., *ergo*, Socrates is mortal.* Precisely upon this model arose casuistry. A general rule, or major proposition, was laid down: suppose that he who killed any human being, except under the palliations X, Y, Z, was a murderer. Then, in a minor proposition, the special case of the suicide was considered. It was affirmed, or it was denied, that his case fell under some one of the palliations assigned. And then, finally, according to the negative or affirmative shape of this minor proposition, it was argued, in the conclusion, that the suicide was or was not a murderer. Out of these *cases*—*i. e.*, oblique deflexions from the universal rule (which is also the grammarian's sense of the word *case*)—arose *casuistry*.

After morality has done its very utmost in clearing up the grounds upon which it rests its decisions—after it has multiplied its rules to any possible point of circumstantiality—there will always continue to arise cases without end,

* The ludicrous blunder of Reid (as first published by Lord Kames in his "Sketches"), and of countless others, through the last seventy or eighty years, in their critiques on the logic of Aristotle, has been to imagine that such illustrations of syllogism as these were meant for specimens of what syllogism could perform. What an elaborate machinery, it was said, for bringing out the merest self-evident truisms! But just as reasonably it might have been objected, when a mathematician illustrated the process of addition by saying 3 + 4 = 7, behold what pompous nothings! These Aristotelian illustrations were *purposely* drawn from cases not open to dispute, and simply as exemplifications of the meaning: they were intentionally self-evident.

in the shifting combinations of human action, about which a question will remain whether they do or do not fall under any of these rules. And the best way for seeing this truth illustrated on a broad scale, the shortest way, and the most decisive, is—to point our attention to one striking fact; viz., that all law, as it exists in every civilised land, is nothing *but* casuistry. Simply because new cases are for ever arising to raise new doubts whether they do or do not fall under the rule of law, therefore it is that law is so inexhaustible. The law terminates a dispute for the present by a decision of a court (which constitutes our "*common law*"), or by an express act of the legislature (which constitutes our "*statute law*"). For a month or two matters flow on smoothly. But then comes a new case, not contemplated or not verbally provided for in the previous rule. It is varied by some feature of difference. This feature, it is suspected, makes no *essential* difference: substantially it may be the old case. Ay, but that is the very point to be decided. And so arises a fresh suit at law, and a fresh decision. For example, after many a decision and many a statute (all arising out of cases supervening upon cases), suppose that great subdivision of jurisprudence called the Bankrupt Laws to have been gradually matured. It has been settled, suppose, that he who exercises a trade, and no other whatsoever, shall be entitled to the benefit of the Bankrupt Laws. So far is fixed: and people vainly imagine that at length a station of rest is reached, and that in this direction at least the onward march of law is barred. Not at all. Suddenly a schoolmaster becomes insolvent, and attempts to avail himself of privileges as a technical bankrupt. But then arises a resistance on the part of those who are interested in resisting: and the question is raised, whether the calling of a schoolmaster can be legally considered a trade. This also is settled: it is solemnly determined that a schoolmaster is a tradesman. But next arises a case, in which, from peculiar variation of the circumstances, it is doubtful whether the teacher can technically be considered a schoolmaster. Suppose that case settled: a schoolmaster, sub-distinguished as an X Y schoolmaster, is adjudged to come within the meaning of the law. But scarcely is this sub-variety disposed of, than up rises some de-complex case, which is a sub-variety of this sub-variety: and so on for ever.

Hence, therefore, we may see the shortsightedness of Paley, in quoting with approbation, and as if it implied a reproach, that the Mussulman religious code contains "not less than seventy-five thousand traditional precepts." True: but, if this statement shows an excess of circumstantiality in the moral systems of Mussulmans, that result expresses a fact which Paley overlooks—viz., that their moral code is in reality their legal code. It is by aggregation of *cases*, by the everlasting depullulation of fresh sprouts and shoots from old boughs, that this enormous accumulation takes place; and, therefore, the apparent anomaly is exactly paralleled in our own unmanageable superstructure of law, and in the French supplements to their code, which have already far overbuilt the code itself. If names were disregarded, we and the Mahometans are sailing in the very same boat.

Casuistry, therefore, is the science of cases, or of those special varieties which are for ever changing the face of actions as contemplated in general rules. The tendency of such variations is, in all states of complex civilisation, to absolute infinity.* It is my present purpose to state a

* "*To absolute infinity:*"—I have noticed our own vast pile of law, and that of the French. But neither of us has yet reached the alarming

few of such cases, in order to fix attention upon the interest and the importance which surround them. No modern book of ethics can be worth notice, unless in so far as it selects and argues the more prominent of such cases, as they offer themselves in the economy of daily life. For I repeat—that the name, the word casuistry, may be evaded, but the thing cannot; nor *is* it evaded in our daily conversations.

1. *The Case of the Jaffa Massacre.*—No case in the whole compass of casuistry has been so much argued to and fro—none has been argued with so little profit; for, in fact, the main elements of the moral decision have been left out of view. Let me state the circumstances:—On the 11th of February, 1799, Napoleon, then, and for seven months before, in military possession of Egypt, began his march from Cairo to Syria. His object was to break the force of any Turkish invasion, by taking it in fractions. It had become notorious to every person in Egypt, that the Porte rejected the French pretence of having come for the purpose of quelling Mameluke rebellion—the absurdity of which, apart from its ludicrous Quixotism, was evident in the most practical way, viz., by the fact, that the whole revenues of Egypt were more than swallowed up by the pay and maintenance of the French army. What could the Mamelukes have done worse? Hence it had become certain that the Turks would send an expedition to Egypt; and Napoleon viewing the garrisons in Syria as the advanced guard of

---

amount of the Roman law, under which the very powers of social movement threatened to break down. Courts could not decide, advocates could not counsel, so interminable was becoming the task of investigation. This led to the great digest of Justinian. But, had Roman society advanced in wealth, extent, and social development, instead of retrograding, the same result would have returned in a worse shape. The same result now menaces England, and will soon menace her much more.

such an expedition, saw the best chance for general victory in meeting these troops beforehand, and destroying them in detail. About nineteen days brought him within view of the Syrian fields. On the last day of February he slept at the Arimathea of the Gospel. In a day or two later his army was before Jaffa (the Joppa of the Crusaders)—a weak place, but of some military interest,* from the accident of being the very first fortified town to those entering Palestine from the side of Egypt. On the 4th of March this place was invested; on the 6th, barely forty-eight hours after, it was taken by storm. This fact is in itself important; because it puts an end to the pretence so often brought forward, that the French army had been irritated by a long resistance. Yet, supposing the fact to have been so, how often in the history of war must every reader have met with cases where honourable terms were granted to an enemy merely on account of his obstinate resistance? But then here, it is said, the resistance was wilfully pushed to the arbitration of a storm. Even that might be otherwise stated; but, suppose it true, a storm in military law confers some rights upon the assailants which else they would not have had—rights, however, which cease with the day of storming. Nobody denies that the

* "*Of some military interest:*"—It is singular that some peculiar interest has always settled upon Jaffa, no matter who was the military leader of the time, or what the object of the struggle. From Julius Cæsar, Joppa enjoyed some special privileges and immunities; about a century after, in the latter years of Nero, a most tragical catastrophe happened at Joppa to the Syrian pirates, by which the very same number perished as in the Napoleon massacre—viz., something about 4000. In the 200 years of the Crusades, Joppa revived again into military verdure. The fact is, that the shore of Syria is pre-eminently deficient in natural harbours, or facilities for harbours; those which exist have been formed by art, and after severe contest with the opposition of nature. Hence their extreme paucity, and hence their disproportionate importance in every possible war.

French army might have massacred all whom they met in arms at the time, and during the agony of storming. But the question is, Whether a resistance of forty-eight hours could create the right, or in the least degree palliate the atrocity, of putting prisoners to death in cold blood? Four days after the storming, when all things had settled back into the quiet routine of ordinary life, men going about their affairs as usual, confidence restored, and, above all things, after the faith of a Christian army had been pledged to these prisoners that not a hair of their heads should be touched, the imagination is appalled by this wholesale butchery—even the apologists of Napoleon are shocked by the amount of murder, though justifying its principle. They admit that there were two divisions of the prisoners—one of fifteen hundred, the other of two thousand five hundred.* Their combined amount is equal to a little army; in fact, *numerically*, it repeats pretty exactly that noble little army of ours which opened the great Titan war waged with Napoleon, by winning the battle of Maida in Calabria. They composed a force equal to about six English regiments of infantry on the common establishment. Every man of these four thousand soldiers, chiefly brave Albanians—every man of this little army was basely, brutally, in the very spirit of abject poltroonery, murdered—murdered as foully as the infants of Bethlehem; resistance being quite hopeless, not only because they had surrendered their arms, but also because, in reliance on Christian honour, they had quietly submitted to have their hands confined with ropes behind their

* But this was a merely popular computation, adapted to ordinary circumstances, which rendered punctilious accuracy useless, or, unless with a special justifying purpose, pedantic. The true number massacred was 4200; counting by the common military scale, that means seven battalions.

backs. If this blood did not lie heavy on Napoleon's heart in his dying hours, it must have been because a conscience originally callous had been seared by the very number of his atrocities.

Now, having stated the case, let me review the casuistical apologies put forward. What, it is demanded, was to be done with these prisoners? What *could* be done? There lay the difficulty. Could they be retained in confinement, according to the common usage with regard to prisoners? No; for there was a scarcity of provisions, barely sufficient for the French army itself. Could they be transported to Egypt by sea? No; for two English line-of-battle ships, the Theseus and the Tiger, each (I believe) carrying eighty guns, were cruising in the offing, and watching the interjacent seas of Egypt and Syria. Could they be transported to Egypt by land? No; for it was not possible to spare a sufficient escort; besides, this plan would have included the separate difficulty as to food. Finally, then, as the sole resource left, could they be turned adrift? No; for this was but another mode of saying, "Let us fight the matter over again; reinstate yourselves as our enemies; let us leave Jaffa *re infectâ*, and let all begin again *de novo*" —since, assuredly, say the French apologists, within a fortnight or less from that date, the prisoners would have been swelling the ranks of those Turkish forces whom Napoleon had reason to expect in front.

Before taking one step in reply to these arguments, let me cite two parallel cases from history: already for themselves separately the cases are interesting; and they have an *occasional* interest beside appropriate to the casuistical difficulty before us, as showing how other armies, not Christian, have treated the self-same difficulty in practice. The first shall be a leaf taken from the great book of

Pagan experience; the second from Mahometan: and both were cases, be it observed, in which the parties called on to cut the knot had been irritated to madness by the parties concerned in their decision.

1. *The Pagan Decision.*—In that Jewish war of more than three years' duration, which terminated in the memorable siege and destruction of Jerusalem, two cities on the Lake of Gennesaret were besieged by Vespasian. One of these was Tiberias; the other Tarichæ. Both had been defended with desperation; and from their peculiar situation upon water, and amongst profound precipices, the Roman battering apparatus had not been found applicable to their walls. Consequently the resistance and the loss to the Romans had been unexampled. At the latter siege Vespasian was present in person. Six thousand five hundred had perished of the enemy. A number of prisoners remained, amounting to about forty thousand. What was to be done with them? A great council was held, at which the commander-in-chief presided, assisted (as we shall soon find Napoleon to have been) by his whole staff. Many of the officers were urgent for having the whole put to death; they used the very arguments of the French—"that, being people now destitute of habitations, they would infallibly persecute into war, by daily importunities, any cities which might receive them;" fighting, in fact, henceforward upon a double impulse—viz., the original one of insurrection, and a new one of revenge. Vespasian was sensible of all this; and he himself remarked, that, if they had any indulgence of flight conceded, they would assuredly abuse that indulgence into a malicious advantage against its magnanimous authors. But still, as an answer to all objections, as a paramount argument, he insisted on the solitary fact, that he had pledged the Roman faith for the se-

curity of their lives; "and to offer violence, after he had given them his right hand, was what he could not bear to think of." Such are the simple words ascribed to him. In the end, overpowered by his council, Vespasian made a sort of compromise. Twelve hundred, as persons who could not have faced the hardships of captivity and travel, he gave up to the sword. Six thousand select young men were transported as labourers into Greece, in fact, as *navvies*, with a view to Nero's scheme, then in agitation, for cutting through the Isthmus of Corinth; the main body, amounting to thirty thousand, were sold for slaves; and all the rest, who happened to be subjects of Agrippa,* as a mark of courtesy to that prince, were placed at his disposal. Now, in this case it will be alleged that, perhaps, the main feature of Napòleon's case was not realised—viz., the want of provisions. Every Roman soldier carried on his shoulder a load of seventeen days' provisions, expressly in preparation for such dilemmas; and Palestine was then rank with population gathered into towns. This objection will be noticed immediately; but, meantime, let it be remembered that the prisoners personally appeared before their conquerors in far worse circumstances than the garrison of Jaffa, except as to the one circumstance (in

* "*Of Agrippa:*"—*i. e.*, not that Agrippa who married the sole daughter of Augustus Cæsar—*he* had long been in his grave—but of Herod Agrippa, grandson to that original Herod, who seems to have been as pretty a murderer, and as tiger-like as any ruffian that you would wish *not* to meet in a lonely lane. His ambition might seriously have seemed to form a bright model for the future sepoy. At Bethlehem he showed them how to murder infants valiantly; but subsequently he improved, for he rose to the bright idea of murdering grown-up women—his wife Mariamne for one, and even men—Mariamne's brother, and two of his own sons. This man history denominates Herod the Great; obviously for his artistic merit as a first-rate murderer, since of other accomplishments he had confessedly none at all.

which both parties stood on equal ground) of having had their lives guaranteed. For the prisoners of Gennesaret were chiefly aliens and fugitives from justice, who had no national or local interest in the cities which they had tempted or forced into insurrection; they were clothed with no military character whatever; in short, they were pure vagrant incendiaries; or, in short (to say the worst thing possible), they were the *budmashes* of Syria, which means (as our sepoy apocalypse has taught us), the houseless ruffians of Asiatic cities, such as Delhi, the ferocious but cowardly Ishmaels of imperfect civilisation. And the populous condition of Palestine availed little towards the execution of Vespasian's sentence; nobody in that land would have bought such prisoners; nor, if they would, were there any means available, in the agitated state of the Jewish people, for maintaining their purchase. It would therefore be necessary to escort them to Cæsarea, as the nearest Roman port for shipping them; thence, perhaps, to Alexandria, in order to benefit by the corn vessels; and from Alexandria the voyage to remoter places would be pursued at great cost and labour—all so many objections exactly corresponding to those of Napoleon, and yet all overruled by the single consideration of a Roman (viz., a Pagan) right hand pledged to the sacred fulfilment of a promise. As to the twelve hundred old and helpless people massacred in cold blood, as regarded themselves it was a merciful doom, and one which many of the Jerusalem captives afterwards eagerly courted. But still it was a shocking necessity. It was felt to be such by many Romans themselves; Vespasian, not yet emperor, was in that instance overruled; but with a beneficial effect, that perhaps long outlived that transitory Flavian family. For the horror which settled upon the mind of Titus, his eldest son, from that very case, made *him* tender of human life ever after; made him anxiously merciful, through the great tragedies which were now beginning to unrol themselves; and although *he* personally was an apparition of brightness and of vernal promise that passed away too early for his own generation, nevertheless, through succeeding generations his example availed to plant kindness and mercy amongst imperatorial virtues.

2. *The Mahometan Decision.*—The Emperor Charles V., at different periods, twice invaded the piratical states in the north of Africa. The last of these invasions, directed against Algiers, failed miserably, covering the emperor with shame, and strewing both land and sea with the wrecks of his great armament. But six years before, he had conducted a most splendid and successful expedition against Tunis, once the seat of mighty Carthage; but then occupied by Heyradin Barbarossa, a valiant corsair, and a prosperous usurper. Barbarossa had an irregular force of fifty thousand men; the emperor had a veteran army, but not acclimatised, and not much above one-half as numerous. Things tended, therefore, strongly to an equilibrium. Such were the circumstances—such was the position on each side: Barbarossa, with his usual adventurous courage, and with Mahometan insolence, was drawing out of Tunis in order to assail the assailant; precisely at that moment occurred the question of what should be done with the Christian slaves. A stronger case cannot be imagined: they were ten thousand fighting men; and the more horrible it seemed to murder so many defenceless people, the more dreadfully did the danger strike upon the imagination. It was their number which appalled the conscience of those who speculated on their murder; but precisely that it was the formidable number, when pressed

upon the recollection, which appalled the prudence of their Moorish masters. Barbarossa himself, familiar with bloody actions, never hesitated for a moment about the proper course; "massacre to the last man" was *his* proposal. But his officers thought otherwise; they were brave men; "and," says Robertson, "they all approved warmly of his intention to fight. But, inured as they were to scenes of bloodshed, the barbarity of his proposal filled them with horror; and Barbarossa, from the dread of irritating *them*, consented to spare the lives of the slaves." Now, in this case, the penalty attached to mercy, on the assumption that it should turn out unhappily for those who so nobly determined to stand the risk, cannot be more tragically expressed, than by saying that it *did* turn out unhappily. We need not doubt that the merciful officers were otherwise rewarded; but for this world, and for the successes of this world, the ruin was total. Barbarossa was defeated in the battle which ensued; flying pell-mell to Tunis with the wrecks of his army, he found these very ten thousand Christians in possession of the fort and town; they turned his own artillery upon himself; and his overthrow was sealed by that one act of mercy—so unwelcome from the very first to his own Napoleonish temper.

Thus we see how this very case of Jaffa had been settled by Pagan and Mahometan casuists, where courage and generosity happened to be habitually prevalent. Now, turning back to the pseudo-Christian army, let us very briefly review the arguments for *them*. First, there were no provisions. But how happened that? or how is it proved? Feeding the prisoners from the 6th to the 10th inclusively of March, proves that there was no instant want. And how was it, then, that Napoleon had run his calculations so narrowly! The prisoners were just 33 per cent. on the total French army, as originally detached from Cairo. Some had already perished of that French detachment; and in a few weeks more, one-half of it had perished, or six thousand men, whose rations were hourly becoming disposable for the prisoners. Secondly (a most important consideration!), resources must have been found in Jaffa; if not, why not? But, thirdly, if Jaffa were so ill provisioned, how had Jaffa ever dreamed of standing a siege? And knowing its condition, as Napoleon must have done from deserters and otherwise, how came he to adopt so needless a measure as that of storming the place? Three days must have compelled it to surrender upon any terms, if it could be really true that, after losing vast numbers of its population in the assault (for it was the bloodshed of the assault which originally suggested the interference of the aides-de-camp*), Jaffa was not able to allow half-rations

* "*Aides-de-camp:*"—Their names were, to the best of my remembrance, Croisier, and a Pole, whose name began with *Sulky*, and no doubt it ended in *iski* or *owski*. Or, according to the witty suggestion of the late Lord Robertson (a Scottish judge), for a *general* Polish name that should save all trouble of special and individual punctilios, you might call him Count *Cask-o'-Whisky*. The mention of these young men, both of whom came to a premature end, through consequences growing out of this diabolical massacre, reminds me of some subordinate incidents connected with the main event that merit a distinct notice. These two officers (upon what errand I could never certainly ascertain, if it were not to invite the Albanians to a timely surrender, upon such terms as must have been conceded to so large a body of men in possession of such manifest advantages) found the enemy occupying an immense barrack. From windows innumerable, and from openings drilled by the men for the momentary purpose, were levelled muskets without end at the two young emissaries. The story tells itself. The aides-de-camp were apparently no fire-eaters: but it is fair to recollect that even men, who were such habitually and by a second nature, would not have acknowledged any call for putting forth their gallantry on this occasion. What had they been sent for? Not surely to say, Albanians, come out and be killed! An idiot would not have surrendered such advantages for defence, without understanding that he was to receive some equivalent in return. The

even to a *part* of its garrison for a few weeks. What was it meant that the whole of this garrison should have done, had Napoleon simply blockaded it? Through all these

two officers, therefore, were perfectly right in the silent overture which they made: having no common language for expressing their message more distinctly, they hung out a white handkerchief. Now is *that* a conventional symbol of pacific overtures, or is it not? If not, we British are sadly to blame: for a number of heavy-built Chinese have carried in their stern quarters, ever since 1842, some leaden remembrances of ours, which we were obliged to fire after them when running away from our white flag, and for having previously fired upon that flag. If we had not punished the brutes for refusing to receive the sole symbol agreed upon amongst nations for requesting a suspension of arms, we should not have delivered our important message, which concerned the whole Chinese people, to the end of the century. Had the Albanians fired upon the two bearers of this symbol, they would rightfully have suffered the death of criminals. *Not* firing, and voluntarily resigning all the means which they possessed for a desperate defence, such as must have cost the French two thousand lives at the least, they were understood to have made a bargain—to have sold a present advantage for a reversionary gain. Napoleon must have this as well as they: perfectly he knew beforehand that this would be, and could not *but* be, the result of that else unintelligible mission which he had imposed upon his *aides*. Yet, as soon as they went back to head-quarters, and reported what had passed, he pretended to fall into a violent passion, and in order to colour this simulated rage with an air of sincerity, he upbraided the young men in such terms of insult as impelled both to seek death. Sulkowski's particular fate I do not recollect; only the fact that he soon perished: Croisier courted and found *his* in the act of suddenly leaping on a wall or conspicuous eminence at the very moment when the gunners on the walls of Acre were presenting their port-fires; Napoleon, who saw the action, loudly commanded him to come down: but the sound of earthly commands had now become an empty terror for the poor aid-de-camp; he heard a deeper summons from a paramount Commander in other worlds; and in the next moment he was blown to atoms. Napoleon was, as regards moral capacities, even for common generosity, much more for magnanimity, about the poorest creature ever known. He knew himself to have been grossly in the wrong as regarded the two *aides*, and yet he was never able to summon self-conquest enough to beg their pardon. Meantime, what had he really expected of them? Simply this: he had counted on it as a certainty that between two parties, unable to communicate freely from want of a common language, hot misunderstandings would arise, and that amongst so many impatient tempers, and so much boiling youthful blood, shots in

contradictions we see the truth looming large, as the sun from behind a mist: it was not because provisions failed that Napoleon butchered four thousand young men in cold

---

showers would be fired; and the two aides-de-camp would perish. This was what he expected from them: and he meant to use this colourable pretence of a violated international usage as a summary plea for putting to death every man of the Albanians. Cruel was his disappointment when he found himself suddenly stripped of this anticipated plea, and, on the contrary, bound by a horrid pledge to some disgusting act of merciful indulgence. His first words of reproach to these two members of "his family" (such is the technical language) acknowledged this result. His very complaint, as against *them*, confessed by implication his obligation as regarded the Albanians. They (the two aides-de-camp) had landed him in difficulties inextricable. But, if he were still free to shoot the Albanians, how had they landed him in any difficulty at all? In the very torrent of his wrath he confessed the debt contracted to the enemy; and the wrath was solely on account of that debt. Yet, after all, he contrives, under cover of the feeble moral sense existing in the French army, to trample on this confessed contract. He calls together the leading officers of the army: he propounds the case, and the separate difficulties which met each variety of actions. The extra trouble, and the sacrifices, which would have accompanied any attempt on the part of eleven thousand men, having before them the bloody labours of a siege the most desperate, to watch and tend more than four thousand captives, were glaringly manifest: and under the temptations to perfidy, which disclosed themselves too highly and broadly, the French sense of honour was not strong enough to hold: the storm was mighty, and the anchors of their good faith all drove, and "came home."

The closing scene is frightful: it might well be left to the reader's imagination, were it not for an incident which adds a crest and novelty of preternatural foulness to a drama which already offered a scenical display of wrong that Abana and Pharpar could never wash away, and no Jordan will ever cleanse. The Albanians, all young, of ages ranging from eighteen to twenty-two, easily divined their coming fate. Easily they read in the conscious eyes of their guilty jailers the horror which rose before them. No man can hear without affliction a case, where, without the pretence of any crime, so ample a capacity of joy and ebullient life was summoned in one hour to take their last look of a sun that pours down upon Syria such eternity of splendour. Scarcely to have tasted from the cup of life, before it was torn from their grasp by hellish fraud, and all the while to feel their unexhausted energies jubilating along their youthful veins, was an atrocity and an anomaly of suffering for which the bare ordinary justice and truthfulness of human nature has not left and

blood; it was because he wished to signalise his entrance into Palestine by a sanguinary act, such as might strike panic and ghastly horror far and wide, might resound

---

gate open once in five centuries. They were shot down by platoons; and of course, in such a mode of executing the sentence, it happened unavoidably that a considerable number were not mortally wounded, or not so wounded as to cause instant death, or, in some instances, not wounded at all. Of these, some were despatched by a second, some by a third, *fusillade*. But a few, a dwindling arrear, escaped the bullets after all. And from this sad arrear, sighing, supplicating, languishing, rose up, as from a closing grave, the last narrowing scene of anguish, that furnished the last stings of torment, on the one side, to departing agony, and, on the other, to any repenting accomplice perhaps the first-born stings of remorse. Some, by those same bullets which had spared their persons, found their bonds cut asunder, and themselves suddenly liberated. Could not even this poor relic of the ghastly crowd have found mercy? No; mercy in no case; but for these was reserved a separate and parting fraud. The prisoners, having no other refuge, saw one (though but momentary) in the sea. The weltering billows might at least hide them from their enemies: those hellish faces, triumphing and laughing through the gathering mists of death, they might at least shut out. Not so: not thus were they to be dismissed. The Syrian sea is an inhospitable chamber of the great central Christian lake. Nothing rose to view but a barren rock. To this the despairing few swam out. Boats there were none for pursuit; and had the Albanians maintained their hold till night, the merciful darkness would have covered their return to land, and possibly their final evasion. But this was not to be: the French, if they could not pursue, could still persecute. Seeing the risk, they saw also a means for baffling it. By significant gestures they notified to the tenants of the rock an entire amnesty as regarded the past. What was done was done, and could not be recalled; but, for the future, let the fugitive prisoners put their trust in French honour, and come back to land. The fugitives did so; they came back—some trusting, some doubting. But strictly impartial was their welcome on shore. To the trusting there was no special favour; to the doubting no separate severity. All were massacred alike; and in one brief half-hour a loose scattering of soil rose as a winding-sheet over the forty-two hundred corpses, that heaved convulsively here and there for a moment, and then all was still.

Frenchmen, this atrocity belongs to the holy soil of Palestine. Bethlehem is near, and sees it. Jerusalem is not far off, and reports it to the heavens. That man errs who believes that such deeds perish. They are found again in other generations. And so long as France makes the author of that awful crime her idol, so long she makes his deeds her own.

through Syria as well as Egypt, and might paralyse the nerves of his enemies. Fourthly, it is urged that, if he had turned the prisoners loose, they would have faced him again in his next battle. How so? Prisoners without arms? But then, perhaps, they could have retreated upon Acre, where it is known that Djezzar, the Turkish pacha, had a great magazine of arms. That might have been dangerous, if any such retreat had been open. But surely the French army, itself under orders for Acre, could at least have intercepted the Acre route from the prisoners. No other remained but that through the defiles of Naplous. In that direction, however, there was no want of men. Beyond the mountains cavalry only were in use; and the prisoners had no horses, nor equestrian training, nor habits of acting as cavalry. In the defiles it was riflemen who were wanted, and the prisoners had no rifles; besides which, the line of the French operations never came near to that route. Then, again, if provisions were universally so scarce, how were the disarmed prisoners to obtain them (which the French allege that they would have done, if turned adrift), on the simple allegation that they had fought unsuccessfully against the French!

But, finally, one conclusive argument there is against this damnable atrocity of Napoleon's, which, in all future lives of him, one may expect to see noticed—viz., that if the circumstances of Palestine were such as to forbid the ordinary usages of war, if (which I am far from believing) want of provisions made it indispensable to murder prisoners in cold blood—in that case a *Syrian war* became impossible to a man of honour; and the guilt commences from a higher point than Jaffa. If mercy were notoriously impossible in a Syrian war, in that case none but a ruffian would be found to offer his services for such a war.

Already at Cairo, and in the elder stages of the expedition, planned in face of such afflicting necessities, we read the counsels of a murderer; of one carrying appropriately such a style of warfare towards the ancient country of the Assassins; of one not an apostate merely from Christian humanity, but from the lowest standard of soldierly honour. He and his friends abuse the upright and ill-used Sir Hudson Lowe as a jailer. But better a thousand times over to be a jailer, and faithful to one's trust, than to be the cut-throat of unarmed men.

One consideration remains, which I reserve to the end; because it has been universally overlooked, and because it is conclusive against Napoleon, even on his own hypothesis of an absolute necessity. In Vespasian's case—the case of having given his right hand as the symbolic pledge of an engagement to show mercy—it does not appear that he had gained anything for himself, or for his army, by his promise of safety to the enemy whose lives had been guaranteed, and who, on the faith of that guarantee, had surrendered their arms: he had simply gratified his own feelings, by holding out prospects of final escape. But Napoleon had absolutely seduced the four thousand men from a situation of power, from vantage-ground, by his treacherous promise. And when the French apologists plead—"If we had dismissed the prisoners, we should soon have had to fight the battle over again"—they totally forget the state of the facts: they had not fought the battle at all: they had literally evaded the battle as to these prisoners: as many enemies as could have faced them *de novo* (viz., four thousand and two hundred), which constituted the temptation, so many had they bought off from fighting. Forty-two centuries of armed men, brave and despairing, and firing from windows, must have made prodigious havoc: and this havoc the French evaded by a trick, by a perfidy, perhaps unexampled in the annals of honourable warfare.*

II. *Piracy.*—It is interesting to trace the revolutions of moral feeling. In the early stages of history we find piracy in high esteem. Thucydides tells us that ληστεια, or robbery, when conducted *at sea* (*i. e.*, robbery on non-Grecian people), was held in honour by his countrymen through elder ages. And this, in fact, is the true station, this point of feeling for primitive man, from which we ought to view the robberies and larcenies of savages. Captain Cook, though a good and often a wise man, erred exceedingly in this point. He took a plain Old Bailey view of the case; and very sincerely believed (as all sea-captains ever have done), that a savage must be a bad man, who would purloin anything that was not his own. Yet it is evident that the poor child of uncultured nature, who saw strangers descending, as it were from the moon, upon his aboriginal forests and lawns, must have viewed them under the same angle as the Greeks of old. They were no part of any system to which he belonged; and why should he not plunder them? By force if he could: but, where that was out of the question, why should he not take the same credit for an undetected theft that the Spartan gloried in taking?† To be detected was both shame and loss; but he was certainly entitled to any

---

* The French have learned since then, by the bloody experience of 1830 and of 1848 in Paris, what is the fearful power of street and house firing.

† It is singular that this Spartan glory from non-detection exists in full blow amongst ourselves: the resurrectionist, or body-snatcher, is, or was, regarded as a public benefactor and an ally of science, if undetected; being detected, he was punished severely by the magistrate, and had to fly for his life from the mob.

glory which might seem to settle upon success, not at all less than the more insolent and conceited savage of Grecian Sparta. Besides all which, amongst us civilised men the rule obtains universally—that the state and duties of peace are to be presumed until war is proclaimed.* Whereas, amongst rude nations, war is understood to be the rule—war, open or covert, until suspended by express contract. War is the natural state of things for all, except those who view themselves as brothers by natural affinity, by local neighbourhood, by common descent, or who make themselves brothers by artificial contracts. Peace needs a proclamation. Captain Cook, who overlooked all this, should have begun by arranging a solemn treaty with the savages amongst whom he meant to reside for any length of time. This would have prevented many an angry broil then, and since then: it would also have prevented his own tragical fate. Meantime the savage is calumniated and misrepresented, for want of being understood.

There is, however, amongst civilised nations a mode of piracy still tolerated, or which *was* tolerated in the last war, but is now ripe for extinction. It is that war of private men upon private men, which goes on under the name of privateering. Great changes have taken place in our modes of thinking within the last twenty-five† years; and the greatest change of all lies in the thoughtful spirit which we now bring to the investigation of all public questions. I have no doubt at all that, when next a war arises at sea, the whole system of privateering will be con-

* The public proclamation with man civilised, first of all, opens and inaugurates war. It is peace, until otherwise ordered. But with the savage logic is reversed; the very opposite case obtains: war is so entirely the natural state of man with man, that it needs a special, resonant, and thundering contract to make it otherwise.

† This, let me admonish the reader, was written about twelve years ago.

demned by the public voice. And the next step after that will be, to explode all war whatsoever, public or private, upon commerce. War will be conducted *by* belligerents and *upon* belligerents exclusively. To imagine the extinction of war itself, in the present stage of human advance, is, I fear, idle. Higher modes of civilisation—an earth more universally colonised—the *homo sapiens* of Linnæus more developed, and other improvements, must pave the way for *that:* but amongst the earliest of those improvements will be the abolition of war carried into quarters where the spirit of war never ought to penetrate. Privateering will be abolished. War, on a national scale, is often ennobling, and one great instrument of pioneering for civilisation; but war of private citizen upon his fellow, in another land, is always demoralising.

III. *Usury.*—This ancient subject of casuistry I place next to *piracy*, for a significant reason: the two practices have both changed their public reputation as civilisation has advanced, but inversely—they have exactly interchanged their places. Beginning in honour, piracy has ended in infamy: and at this moment it happens to be the sole offence against society in which *all* the accomplices, without pity or intercession, let them be ever so numerous, are punished capitally. Elsewhere, we decimate, or even centesimate: here, we are all children of Rhadamanthus. Usury, on the other hand, beginning in utter infamy, has travelled upwards into considerable esteem; and Mr "10 *per shent*" stands a very fair chance of being pricked for sheriff next year; and, in one generation more, of passing for a great patriot. Charles Lamb complained that, by gradual changes, not on his part, but in the spirit of refinement, he found himself growing insensibly into "an indecent character." The same changes which carry some downwards, carry others up; and Shylock himself will soon be viewed as an eminent martyr or confessor for the truth as it is in the Alley. Seriously, however, there is nothing more remarkable in the history of casuistical ethics, than the utter revolution in human estimates of usury. In this one point the Hebrew legislator agreed with the Roman—Deuteronomy with the Twelve Tables. Cicero mentions that the elder Cato being questioned on various actions, and how he ranked them in his esteem, was at length asked, *Quid fœnerari?* —how did he rank usury? His indignant answer was, by a retorted question, *Quid hominem occidere?*—what do I think of murder? In this particular case, as in some others, we must allow that our worthy ancestors and forerunners upon this terraqueous planet were enormous blockheads. And their "exquisite reason" for this opinion on usury was quite worthy of Sir Andrew Aguecheek:—"Money," they argued, "could not breed money: one guinea was neither father nor mother to another guinea: and where could be the justice of making a man pay for the use of a thing some supposed equivalent, which that thing could never produce?" But, venerable blockheads, that argument applies to the case of him who locks up his borrowed guinea. Suppose him *not* to lock it up, but to buy a hen, and the hen to lay a dozen eggs; one of those eggs will be so much per cent.; and the thing borrowed has then produced its own *fœnus*. A still greater inconsistency was this: Our ancestors would have rejoined—that many people did not borrow in order to produce (*i. e.*, to use the money as capital); but in order to spend (*i. e.*, to use it as income). In that case, at least, the borrowers must derive the *fœnus* from some other fund than the thing borrowed: for, by the supposition, the thing borrowed has been spent. True; but on the same principle these ancestors ought to have forbidden every man to sell any article whatsoever to him who paid for it out of other funds than those produced by the article sold. Mere logical consistency required this: it happens, indeed, to be impossible; but that only argues their entire non-comprehension of their own doctrines.

The whole history of usury teems with instruction: 1st, comes the monstrous absurdity in which the proscription of usury anchored; 2dly, the absolute compulsion, and downright unevadable pressure of realities in forcing men into a timid abandonment of their own ridiculous doctrines; 3dly, the unconquerable power of sympathy, which humbled all minds to one level, and forced the strongest no less than the feeblest intellects into the same infatuation of stupidity. The casuistry of ancient moralists on this question, especially of the scholastic moralists, such as Suarez, &c.—the oscillations by which they alternately relaxed and tied up the law, just as their erring conscience or the necessities of social life happened alternately to prevail—would compose one of the interesting chapters in this science. But the Jewish relaxation is the most amusing: it coincides altogether with the theory of savages as to property, as a thing made sacred from robbery only by a special treaty. All men on earth, except Jews, were held to be fair subjects for usury; not as though usury were a just or humane practice: no—it was a belligerent practice: but then all foreigners in the Jewish eye were enemies, for the same reason that the elder Romans had one common term for an enemy and a stranger. And it is probable that many Jews at this day, in exercising usury, conceive themselves to be seriously making war, in a privateering fashion, upon Christendom, and practising reprisals on the Gentiles for the capture of Jerusalem by Titus.

IV. *Bishop Gibson's Chronicon Preciosum.*—Many people are aware that this book is a record of prices, so far as they were recoverable, pursued through six centuries of English history. But they are not aware that this whole inquiry is simply the machinery for determining a casuistical question. The question was this:—An English college—but I cannot at this moment say in which of our universities—had been founded in the reign of Henry VI., and between 1440 and 1460; probably it might be King's College, Cambridge.* Now, the statutes of this college, whatever be its name, make it imperative upon every candidate for a fellowship to swear that he does not possess an estate in land of inheritance, nor a perpetual pension, amounting to *five pounds per annum.* It is certain, however, that the founder did not mean superstitiously so much gold or silver as made *nominally* the sum of five pounds, but so much as virtually represented the five pounds of Henry VI.'s time—so much as would buy the same quantity of ordinary comforts. Upon this, therefore, arose two questions for the casuist:—(1.) What sum did substantially represent, in 1706 (the year of publishing the "Chron. Preciosum"), that nominal £5 of 1440? (2.) Supposing this ascertained, might a man with safe conscience retain his fellowship by swearing that he had not £5 a-year, when perhaps he had £20, provided that £20 were proved to be less in efficacy than the £5 of the elder period? Verbally this was perjury: was it such in virtue, and for the responsibilities of the conscience?

The Chronicle is not, as by its title the reader might suppose, a large folio: on the contrary, it is a small octavo of less than 200 pages. But it is exceedingly interesting,

* Eton, which everybody knows from Gray's "Ode" to have been certainly founded by Henry VI., is in close connection with King's College.

very ably reasoned, and as circumstantial in its illustrations as the good bishop's opportunities allowed him to make it. In one thing he was more liberal than Sir William Petty, Dr Davenant, &c., or any elder economists of the preceding generation; he would have statistics treated as a classical or scholar-like study; and he shows a most laudable curiosity in all the questions arising out of his main one. His answer to *that* is as follows: 1. That *£5* in Henry VI.'s time contained forty ounces of silver, whereas in Queen Anne's it contained only nineteen ounces and one-third; so that, in reality, the *£5* of 1440 was, even formally, as to weight of silver, without needing to plead its virtuality, rather more than £10 of 1706. 2. As to the efficacy of £10 in Henry VI.'s reign: upon reviewing the main items of common household (and therefore of common academic) expenditure, and pursuing this review through bad years and good years, the bishop decides that it is about equal to *£25* or £30 of Queen Anne's reign. Sir George Shuckburgh has since treated this casuistical problem more elaborately (see the "London Philosophical Transactions"): but Bishop Gibson it was who, in his "Chronicon Preciosum," first broke the ice.

After this, he adds an ingenious question upon the apparently parallel case of a freeholder swearing himself worth 40s. per annum as a qualification for an electoral vote: ought not he to hold himself perjured in voting upon an estate often so much below the original 40s. contemplated by Parliament, for the very same reason* that a collegian is *not* perjured in holding a fellowship, whilst, in

---

* *"For the very same reason:"*—The reader may fail to see this. Let him consider that the point of conscience is exactly reversed for the two men: for the college man it is to prove his poverty, for the freeholder to prove his wealth.

fact, he may have four or five times the nominal sum privileged by the founder? The bishop says *no;* and he distinguishes the case thus: the college £5 must always mean a virtual £5—a £5 in efficacy, and not merely in name. But the freeholder's 40s. is not so restricted; and for the following reason—that this sum is constantly coming under the review of Parliament. It is clear, therefore, from the fact of not having altered it, that Parliament is satisfied with a merely nominal 40s., and sees no reason to alter it. True, it was a rule enacted by the Parliament of 1430; at which time 40s. was even in weight of silver equal to 80s. of 1706; and in virtue or power of purchasing equal to £12 at the least. The qualification of a freeholder was, therefore, much lower in Queen Anne's days than in those of Henry VI. But what of that? Parliament, it must be presumed, sees good reason why it *should* be lower. And, at all events, till the law operates injuriously, there can be no reason to alter it.

A case of the same kind with those argued by Bishop Gibson has oftentimes arisen in trials of larceny—I mean in construing that enactment which fixed the minimum for a capital offence. This case is noticed by the bishop; and juries of late years habitually took the casuistry into their own hands. They were generally held to act with no more than a proper humanity to the prisoner; but still people thought such juries, in the extreme rigour of ethics, incorrect. Whereas, if Bishop Gibson is right, who allows a man to swear positively that he has not £5 a-year, when nominally he has much more, such juries were even technically right. However, this point is now, by Sir Robert Peel's reforms, adjusted in conformity to the equities of the case, and so as to meet the noble sensibilities of juries more thoughtful, and the Christian scruples of those who are jealous not only of human life, but of human suffering in every degree. But there are other cases, and especially those which arise, not between different times, but between different places, which will often require the same kind of casuistry as that which is so ably applied by the good and learned bishop.

V. *Suicide.*—It seems passing strange that the main argument upon which Pagan moralists relied in their unconditional condemnation of suicide—viz., the supposed analogy of our situation in life to that of a sentinel mounting guard, who cannot, without a capital offence, quit his station until called off by his commanding officer—is dismissed with contempt by a Christian moralist—viz., Paley. But a stranger thing still is, that the only man who ever wrote a book in palliation of suicide should have been not only a Christian, not only an official minister and dignitary of a metropolitan Christian church, but also a scrupulously pious man. I allude, as the reader will suppose, to Dr Donne, Dean of St Paul's, one of the subtlest intellects that England has produced. His opinion is worthy of solemn consideration. Not that I myself would willingly diminish, by one hair's weight, the reasons against suicide; but it is never well to rely upon ignorance or inconsideration for the defence of any principle whatever. Donne's notion was (a notion, however, adopted in his earlier years), that as we do not instantly pronounce a man a murderer upon hearing that he has killed a fellow-creature, but, according to the circumstances of the case, pronounce his act either murder, or manslaughter, or justifiable homicide, so, by parity of reason, suicide is open to distinctions of the same or corresponding kinds; that there may be such a thing as self-homicide not less than self-murder, culpable self-homicide, and justifiable self-homicide. Donne called his Essay by the Greek name *Biathanatos*,* meaning *violent death*. But a thing equally strange, and a blasphemy almost unaccountable, is the fancy of a Prussian or Saxon baron, who wrote a book to prove that Christ committed suicide, for which he had no other argument than this: that, in fact, Christ had surrendered himself unresistingly into the hands of his enemies, and had in a manner wilfully provoked his own death. This, however, describes the case of every martyr that ever was or can be. It is the very merit and grandeur of the martyr, that he proclaims the truth with his eyes open to the consequences of proclaiming it. Those consequences are connected with the truth, but not by a natural link: the connection is by means of false views, which it is the very business of the martyr to destroy. And, if a man founds my death upon an act which my conscience enjoins, even though I am aware and fully warned that he will found my death upon it, I am not, therefore, guilty of suicide. For, by the supposition, I was obliged to the act in question by the highest of all obligations—viz., moral obligation—which far transcends all physical obligation; so that, whatever

* This word, however, which occurs nowhere, that I remember, except in Lampridius, one of the Augustan historians, is there applied to Heliogabalus; and means, not the act of suicide, but a suicidal person. And possibly Donne, who was a good scholar, may so mean it to be understood in his title-page. Heliogabalus, says Lampridius, had been told by the Syrian priests that he should be *biathanatos*—*i. e.*, should commit suicide. He provided, therefore, ropes of purple and of gold intertwisted, that he might hang himself imperatorially. He provided golden swords, that he might run himself through as became Cæsar. He had poisons enclosed in jewels, that he might drink his farewell heel-taps, if drink he must, in a princely style. Other modes of august death he had prepared. Unfortunately all were unavailing; for he was murdered, and dragged through the common sewers by ropes, without either purple or gold in their base composition. The poor fellow has been sadly abused in history; but, after all, he was a mere boy, and as mad as a March hare.

excuse attaches to a physical necessity, attaches, *à fortiori*, to the moral necessity. The case is, therefore, precisely the same as if he had said, "I will put you to death, if the frost benumbs your feet." The answer is, "I cannot help this effect of frost." Far less can I help revealing a celestial truth. I have no power, no liberty, to forbear. When a wing of an army persists in regression exactly as its antagonist endeavours to force it into action, and still wheels away, turning upon the centre as a pivot, it is technically said to *refuse* itself. To a kindling enthusiasm for a truth simply great by its effects, a man may often refuse himself. But if the truth is doubly great—great by its origin, great by its tendency—sometimes it will not submit to be refused. And, in killing me, he punishes me for a mere necessity of my situation and of my secret knowledge.

It is urged that brutes never commit suicide—except, indeed, the salamander, who has been suspected of loose principles in this point, but suspected merely under an old traditional conceit, founded in misinterpretation of equivocal appearances; and I myself know a man who constantly affirmed that a horse of his had committed suicide, by violently throwing himself from the summit of a precipice. "But why," as I still asked him—"why should the horse have committed felony on himself? Were oats rising in the market?—or was he in love?—or vexed by politics?—or could a horse, and a young one rising four, be supposed to suffer from *tædium vitæ?*"* Meantime, as respects

* I have since known other cases of the same class. But all alike were chargeable upon the precipice. There are instances on record of hounds in nearly an entire pack being carried headlong over a precipice, in perhaps the mere moral enthusiasm of hostile pursuit. But the horses (all young) went over under mere ignorance of the ground, and consequent *physical* inability to check their own impetus.

the general question of brute suicides, two points must be regarded:—1. that brutes are cut off from the vast world of moral and imaginative sufferings entailed upon man; 2. that this very immunity presupposes another immunity—

"A cool suspense from pleasure and from pain,"

in the far coarser and less irritable animal organisation which must be the basis of an insulated physical sensibility. By *insulated* I mean, not extended through the unlimited propagation of *sympathy*. Brutes can neither suffer from intellectual passions, nor even, as I imagine, from very complex derangements of the nervous system; so that in them the motives to suicide, the temptations to suicide, are prodigiously diminished. Nor are they ever alive to "the sublime attractions of the grave." It is, however, a humiliating reflection, that, if any brutes can feel such aspirations, it must be those which are under the care of man. Doubtless the happiness of brutes is sometimes extended by man; but also, too palpably, their misery.

Why suicide is not noticed in the New Testament is a problem yet open to the profound investigator.

VI. *Duelling.*—No one case, in the vast volume of casuistry, is so difficult to treat with justice and reasonable adaptation to the spirit of modern times as this of duelling. For, as to those who reason all upon one side, and never hearken in good faith to objections or difficulties, such people convince nobody but those who were already convinced before they began. At present (1839) society has for some years been taking a lurch to one side *against* duelling; but inevitably a reaction will succeed; for, after all, be it as much opposed as it may to Christianity, duelling performed such important functions in society as now constituted—I mean through the sense of instant personal accountability which it diffused universally amongst gentlemen, and all who have much sensibility to the point of honour—that, for one life which it took away as an occasional sacrifice, it saved myriads from outrage and affronts—millions from the anxiety attached to inferior bodily strength. However, it is no part of my present purpose to plead the cause of duelling, though pleaded it must be, more fairly than it ever has been, before any progress will be made in suppressing it.

But the point which I wish to notice at present is the universal blunder in treating this subject of duels about the Romans and Greeks. They, it is alleged, fought no duels; and occasion is thence taken to make very disadvantageous reflections upon us, the men of this Christian era, who, in defiance of our greater light, *do* fight duels, or at least *did* so. Lord Bacon himself is duped by this enormous blunder, and founds upon it a long speech in the Star-Chamber.

Now, in the first place, who does not see that, if the Pagans really *were* enabled by their religion to master their movements of personal anger and hatred, the inevitable inference will be to the huge disadvantage of Christianity. It would be a clear case. Christianity and Paganism have been separately tried as means of self-control: Christianity has flagrantly failed; Paganism succeeded universally; not having been found unequal to the task in any one known instance.

Oh, reader! these are gross falsehoods. A profounder error never existed. No religious influence whatever restrained the Greek or the Roman from fighting a duel. It was purely a civic influence, and it was sustained by this remarkable usage—in itself a standing opprobrium to both Greek and Roman—viz., the unlimited license of tongue allowed to anger in the ancient assemblies and senates. This liberty of foul language, this perfect license to Billingsgate, in its utmost extravagance, operated in two ways: 1. Being universal, it took away all ground for feeling the words of an antagonist as any personal insult; so the offended man had rarely a motive for a duel. 2. The anger was thus less acute; yet, if it *were* acute, then this Billingsgate resource furnished an instantaneous valve for expectorating the wrath. Look, for example, at Cicero's orations against Mark Antony, or against Catiline, or against Piso. This last person was a senator of the very highest rank, family, connections; yet, in the course of a few pages, does Cicero, a man of letters, polished to the extreme standard of Rome, address him by the elegant appellations of "filth," "mud," "carrion" *(projectum cadaver)*. How could Piso have complained? It would have been said, "Oh, there's an end of republican simplicity, if plain speaking is to be put down." And then it would have been added invidiously, "Better men than ever stood in *your* shoes have borne worse language. Will *you* complain of what was tolerated by Africanus, by Paulus Æmilius, by Marius, by Sylla?" Who could reply to that? And why should Piso have even wished to *call out* his foul-mouthed antagonist? On the contrary, a far more genial revenge awaited him than any sword could have furnished. Pass but an hour, and you will hear Piso speaking; it will then be *his* turn—every dog has his day; Piso will lay the lash into the scurrilous dog; and, though not quite so eloquent as his malignant enemy, he is yet eloquent enough for revenge; or, if he runs short, he can borrow from Tully what will meet the necessities of the moment; he is eloquent enough to call Cicero "filth," "mud," "carrion."

No; the reason of our modern duelling lay deeper than all that; it lies in the principle of *honour*—a direct product of chivalry—as that was in part a product of Christianity. The sense of honour did not exist in Pagan times. Bare natural equity, and the municipal laws—those were the two moral forces under which men acted. Honour applies to cases where both those forces are silent. And precisely because the ancients had no such sense, and because their revenge emptied itself by the basest of vomitories—viz., foul speaking and license of tongue—was it that the Greeks and Romans had no duelling. It was no glory to them that they had not, but the foulest blot on their moral grandeur.

PART II.

"Celebrare domestica facta."—HOR.

In a former notice of casuistry, I touched on such cases only as were of public bearings, or such as (if private) were of rare occurrence and of a tragical standard. But ordinary life, in its most domestic paths, teems with cases of difficult decision; or, if not always difficult in the decision of the abstract question at issue, difficult in the accommodation of that decision to immediate practice. A few of these more homely cases, intermixed with more public ones, I will now select and review; for, according to a remark in my first paper, exactly as social economy grows more elaborate, does the demand sympathetically strengthen for such circumstantial morality. As man advances, casuistry advances. Principles are the same; but the abstraction of principles from accidents and circumstances becomes a work of more effort. Aristotle, in his "Nicomachean Ethics," has not one case; Cicero, three hundred years after, has a few; Paley, eighteen hundred years after Cicero, has many. Seneca, I think, has a few more than Cicero. In particular, he it was that first of all introduced for public discussion the very trying and afflicting collision between your private duties to a man who in past times has done you many eminent services, and your public duties of hostility against that same man considered as a traitor to the state. Such a case is in itself a proof and an exemplification of a remark which I made just now—viz., that "*as man advances, casuistry advances.*"

There is also something in place as well as in time—in the people as well as the century—which determines the amount of interest in casuistry. I once heard an eminent person delivering it as an opinion, derived from a good deal of personal experience, *that of all European nations, the British was that which suffered most from remorse;* and that, if internal struggles during temptation, or sufferings of mind after yielding to temptation, were of a nature to be measured upon a scale, or could express themselves sensibly to human knowledge, the annual report from Great Britain, its annual balance-sheet, by comparison with those from continental Europe, would show a large excess. At the time of hearing this remarkable opinion I, the hearer, was young, and I had little other ground for assent or dissent than such general impressions of national differences as I might happen to have gathered from the several literatures of Christian nations. These were of a nature to confirm the stranger's verdict; but these were not sufficient. Since then, I have had occasion to think closely on that question. I have had occasion to review the public records of Christendom; and, beyond all doubt, the public conscience, the international conscience, of a people, is the reverberation of its private conscience. History is but the converging into a focus of what is moving in the domestic life below; a set of great circles expressing and summing up, on a representative dial-plate, the motions of many little circles in the machinery within. Now history, what may be called the Comparative History of Modern Europe, countersigns the traveller's opinion.

"So then," says a foreigner, or an Englishman with foreign sympathies, an Englishman who has undergone a French mercurial salivation, and has imported (as the one great result of a continental training) the brilliant art of shrugging his shoulders—"so, then, the upshot and amount of this doctrine is, that England is more moral than other nations." "Well," I answer, "and what of that?" Observe, however, that the doctrine went no further than as to conscientiousness; the principle out of which comes sorrow for all violation of duty, out of which comes a high standard of duty. Meantime both the "sorrow" and the "high standard" are very compatible with a lax performance. So that there was no such ostentatious pretension advanced as my opponents represent. But, suppose that I *had* gone as far as the objector supposes, and had ascribed a moral superiority every way to England, what is there in *that* to shock probability? Whether the general probability from analogy, or the special probability from the circumstances of this particular case? We all know that there is no general improbability in supposing one nation, or one race, to outrun another. The modern Italians have excelled all nations in musical sensibility, and in genius for painting. They have produced the largest quantity of good music. And four of their supreme painters have perhaps not been approached hitherto by the painters of *any* nation. That facial structure, again, which is called the Caucasian, and which, through the ancient Greeks, has travelled westward to the nations of Christendom, and through *them* (chiefly through the British) has become the transatlantic face, is, past all disputing, the finest type of the "human face divine" on this planet. And most other nations, Asiatic or African, have hitherto put up with this insult; except, indeed, the Kalmuck Tartars, who are highly indignant at our European vanity in this matter; and some of them, says Bergmann, the German traveller, absolutely howl with rage, whilst others only laugh hysterically, at any man's having the insanity to prefer the Grecian features to the Kalmuck. Again, amongst the old pagan nations, the Romans seem to have had "the call" for going ahead; and they fulfilled their destiny in spite of all that the rest of the world could do to prevent them. So that, far from being an improbable or unreasonable assumption, superiority (of one kind or other) has been the prevailing tendency of this and that nation, at all periods of history.

Still less is the notion tenable of any special improbability applying to this particular pretension. For centuries has England enjoyed — 1. civil liberty; 2. the Protestant faith. Now, in those two advantages are laid the grounds, and the presumptive arguments for a superior morality. But watch now the inconsistency of men: ask any one of these men who dispute this English pretension *mordicus;* ask him, or bid an Austrian serf ask him, what are the benefits of Protestantism, and what the benefits of liberty, that he should risk anything to obtain either. Hear how eloquently he insists upon their beneficial results, severally and jointly; and notice that he places foremost among those results a pure morality. Is he wrong? No: the man speaks bare truth. But what brute oblivion he manifests of his own doctrine, in taxing with arrogance any people for claiming one of those results *in esse*, which he himself could see so clearly, and postulate so fiercely, *in posse!* Talk no more of freedom, or of a pure religion, as fountains of a moral pre-eminence, if those who have possessed them in combination for the longest space of time may not, without arrogance, claim the vanward place amongst the nations of Europe.

So far as to the presumptions, general or special; so far as to the probabilities, analogous or direct, in countenance of this British claim. Finally, when we come to the proofs, from fact and historical experience, we might appeal to a singular case in the records of our Exchequer; viz., that for much more than a century back, our "Gazette" and other public advertisers have acknowledged a series of anonymous remittances from those who, at some time or other, had appropriated public money. I understand that no corresponding fact can be cited from foreign records, or was ever heard of on the Continent. Now, this is a direct instance of that compunction which our travelled friend insisted on. But I choose rather to throw myself upon the general history of Great Britain, upon the spirit of her policy, domestic or foreign, and upon the notorious records of her public morality. Take the case of public debts, and the fulfilment of contracts to those who could not have compelled the fulfilment; We, we, we first set this precedent. All nations have now learned that honesty in such cases is eventually the best policy; but this they learned from our experience, and not till nearly all of them had tried the other policy. We it was who, under the most trying circumstances of war, maintained the sanctity from taxation of all foreign investments in our funds. Our conduct with regard to slaves, whether in the case of slavery or of the slave-trade—how prudent it may always have been, we need not inquire; as to its moral principles, they went so far ahead of European standards, that we were neither comprehended nor believed. The perfection of romance was ascribed to us by all who did not reproach us with the perfection of Jesuitical knavery. Finally, looking back to our dreadful conflicts with the three conquering despots of modern history, Philip II. of Spain, Louis XIV., and Napoleon, we may incontestably boast of having been single in maintaining the general equities of Europe by war upon a colossal scale, and by our councils in the general congresses of Christendom.

Such a review would amply justify the traveller's remarkable *dictum* upon the principle of remorse, and therefore of conscientiousness, as existing in greater strength amongst the people of Great Britain. On the same scale of proportions we may assume, in such a people, a keener sensibility to moral distinctions; more attention to shades of difference in the modes of action; more anxiety as to the grounds of action. In the same proportions among the same people, we may assume a growing and more direct regard to casuistry; which is precisely the part of ethics that will be continually expanding, and continually throwing up fresh questions. Not as though a moral principle could ever be essentially doubtful; but that the growing complexity of *human* actions will make it more and more difficult in judgment to detach the principle from the circumstances; or, in practice, to determine the application of the principle to the facts. It will happen, therefore, as Coleridge used to say happened in all cases of importance, that extremes meet: for casuistical ethics will be most consulted by two classes the most opposite to each other—by those who seek excuses for evading their duties, and by those who seek a special fulness of light for fulfilling them.

CASE I.—HEALTH.

Strange it is, that moral treatises, when professing to lay open the great edifice of human duties, and to expose its very foundations, should not have begun with, nay, should not have noticed at all, those duties which a man owes to himself; and, foremost amongst them, the duty of cultivating his own health. For it is evident, that, from mere neglect of that one personal interest, which is at once a duty and a right, with the very best intentions possible, all other duties whatever may languish, or even become impossible; for good intentions exist in all stages of efficiency, from the fugitive impulse to the realising self-determination. In this life, the elementary blessing is health. What! do I presume to place it before peace of mind? Far from it; but I speak of the *genesis;* of the succession in which all blessings descend; not as to time, but the order of dependency. All morality implies free agency; it presumes beyond all other conditions an agent who is in perfect possession of his own volitions. Now, it is certain that a man without health is not uniformly master of his own purposes. He is not always, and in an absolute sense, a free agent. Often he cannot be said either to be *in* the path of duty or *out* of it; so incoherent are the actions of a man forced back continually from the objects of his intellect and choice upon some alien objects dictated by internal wretchedness. It is true that, by possibility, some derangements of the human system are not incompatible with happiness; and a celebrated German author of the last century, Von Hardenberg—better known by his assumed name of Novalis—maintained, that certain modes of ill health, or valetudinarianism, were pre-requisites towards certain modes of intellectual development. He drew this refinement from his own case. But the ill health to which he pointed could not have gone beyond a luxurious indisposition; nor the corresponding intellectual purposes have been other than narrow, fleeting, and anomalous. Inflammatory action, in its early stages, is sometimes connected with voluptuous sensations; so is the preternatural stimulation of the liver. But these states, as pleasurable states, are transitory. All fixed derangements of the health are doubly hostile to the moral energies; first, through the intellect, which they debilitate unconsciously in many ways; and, next, both consciously and semi-consciously, through the will. The judgment is, perhaps, too clouded to fix upon a right purpose; the will too enfeebled to pursue it.

Two general remarks may be applied to all interferences of the physical with the moral sanity: 1. That it is not so much by absolute subtractions of time that ill health operates upon the serviceableness of a man, as by its lingering effects upon his temper and his animal spirits. Many a man has not lost one hour of his life from illness, whose faculties of usefulness have been most seriously impaired through gloom, or untuned feelings. 2. That it is not the direct and known risks to our health which act with the most fatal effects, but the semi-conscious condition, the atmosphere of circumstances, with which artificial life surrounds us. The great cities of Europe, perhaps London beyond all others, under the modern modes of life and business, create a vortex of preternatural tumult, a rush and frenzy of excitement, which is fatal to far more than are ever heard of as express victims to that system.

The late Lord Londonderry's* nervous seizure was no solitary or rare case. So much I happen to know. I am well assured by medical men of great London practice, that the case is one of growing frequency. In Lord Londonderry it attracted notice for reasons of obvious personal interest, as well as for its tragical catastrophe. But the complaint, though one of modern growth, is well known, and comes forward under a most determinate type as to symptoms among the mercantile class. The original predisposition to it lies permanently in the condition of London life, especially as it exists for public men. But the immediate exciting cause, which fires the train always ready for explosion, is invariably some combination of perplexities and deadly anxieties, such as are continually gathering into dark clouds over the heads of great merchants; sometimes only teasing and molesting, sometimes menacing and alarming. These perplexities are generally moving in counteracting paths; some progressive, some retrograde. There lies a man's safety; moving on opposite tacks, these anxieties will not often be confluent. But at times it will happen that all meet at once; and then

* This expression—late Lord Londonderry—now (1858) means the *third* lord, him that was Lord Stewart, having earned that earlier of his titles by the severe (almost the unexampled) service of watching the expenditure of the subsidy voted by Parliament to Sweden; which subsidy Bernadotte (the greatest rogue, "pure and simple," that even Gascony has ever turned out) anxiously tried to pocket, without doing the work that these wages represented. But Lord Stewart (then Sir Charles Stewart) watched the rogue, until he (the rogue) was obliged to sit down and cry. Lord Stewart, on the death of his brother, succeeded him in the title of Londonderry; and at present he (the third Lord Londonderry) is "the late Lord Londonderry." But when this was written, many years ago, the second Lord Londonderry, whom so many of us remember as Lord Castlereagh, and who committed suicide in 1822, was the late Lord Londonderry.

comes a shock such as no brain already predisposed by a London life is strong enough (but more truly let us say, coarse enough) to support.

Lord Londonderry's case was precisely of that order: he had been worried by a long session of Parliament, which adds the crowning irritation in the interruption of sleep. The nervous system, ploughed up by intense wear and tear, is denied the last resource of natural relief. In this crisis, already perilous, a new tempest was called in —of all the most terrific—the tempest of anxiety; and from what source? Anxiety from fear is bad; from hope delayed is bad; but worst of all is anxiety from responsibility, in cases where disease or weakness makes a man feel that he is unequal to the burden. The diplomatic interests of the country had been repeatedly confided to Lord Londonderry; he had justified that confidence; and he had received affecting testimonies of the honour and gratitude due to such services. A very short time before his fatal seizure, he had occasion to pass through Birmingham; he stopped only for the purpose of changing horses; yet, in that brief interval, an expression of public enthusiasm, unpremeditated, but unanimous, had reached him; and it affected him the more because Lady Londonderry was with him. At a moment when all the gentlemen of the place were assembled on 'Change, close to his inn, he had witnessed the whole assembly—no mob, but the collective good sense of the place—by one impulse standing bareheaded in his presence: a tribute of disinterested homage which affected him powerfully, and which was well understood as offered to his foreign diplomacy. Under these circumstances, could he bear to transfer the business of future negotiation? Could he suffer to lapse into other hands, as a derelict, the consummation of that task which thus far he had so prosperously conducted? Was it in human nature to do so? He felt the same hectic of human passion which Lord Nelson had felt in the very gates of death, when some act of authority was thoughtlessly suggested as belonging rightfully to his successor—"Not whilst I live, Hardy; not whilst I live." Yet, in Lord Londonderry's case, it was indispensable, if he would not transfer the trust, that he should rally his energies instantly; for a new Congress was even then assembling. There was no delay open to him by the nature of the case; the call was—*Now, now*, my lord, just as you are, with those shattered nerves and that overworked brain, take charge of interests the most complex in Christendom; in fact, of interests which *are* those of total Christendom.

This struggle, between a nervous system too grievously shaken, and the *instant* demand for energy seven times intensified, was too much for any generous nature. A merely ceremonial embassy might have fulfilled its mission even under these drawbacks; but not this embassy. Anxiety supervening upon nervous derangement was bad; anxiety through responsibility was worse; but, through a responsibility created by grateful confidence, anxiety was an appeal through the very pangs of martyrdom. No brain could stand such a siege. Lord Londonderry's gave way; and he fell with the tears of the generous, even where they might happen to differ from him greatly in politics.

Meantime, this case, belonging to a class generated by the furnace of a London life, was in some quarters well understood even then; *now*, it is generally known that, had remedies more potent and more active been applied, or had the sufferer been able to stand up under his torture until the cycle of the successive symptoms had begun to come round, he might have been saved. The treatment is now well understood; but even then it was understood by some physicians; amongst others by that Dr Willis who had attended George III. In several similar cases overpowering doses had been given of opium, or of brandy; and usually a day or two had carried off the oppression of the brain by a tremendous reaction.

Amongst the Quakers (who may be regarded as a monastic people) anomalous forms of nervous derangement are developed; the secret principle of which turns not, as in these London cases, upon feelings too much called out by preternatural stimulation, but upon feelings too much repelled and driven in. Morbid suppression of deep sensibilities must lead to states of disease equally terrific, and possibly even less tractable; not so sudden and critical it may be, but more settled and gloomy. I speak not of any physical sensibilities, but of those which are purely moral—sensibilities to poetic emotions, to ambition, to social gaiety, or to impassioned and exalted love. Quaker philosophy takes notice of no possible emotions, however modified or ennobled, as more or other than as morbid symptoms of a morbid derangement. Accordingly, it is amongst the young men and women of this body that the most afflicting cases under this eccentric type occur. Even for children, however, the systematic repression of all ebullient feeling must be perilous; and would be more so, were it not for that marvellous flexibility by which nature adapts herself to all changes—whether imposed by climate or by situation—by inflictions of Providence, or by human spirit of system.

These cases I point to as formidable mementos—*monumenta sacra*—of those sudden catastrophes which either ignorance of what concerns the health, or neglect in the midst of knowledge, may produce. Any mode of life in London, or not in London, which trains the nerves to a state of permanent irritation, prepares a *nidus* for disease; and unhappily not for chronic disease only, but for disease of that acute order which finishes the struggle almost before it is begun. In such a state of habitual training for morbid action, it has happened—that one and the same week has seen the victim apparently well, and in his grave.

These, indeed, are extreme cases: though still such as threaten many more than they actually strike; for, though uncommon, they grow out of very common habits. But even the ordinary cases of unhealthy action in the system are sufficient to account for perhaps three-fourths of all the disquiet and bad temper which disfigure daily life. Not one man in every twenty-five is perfectly clear of some disorder, more or less, in the digestive system—not one man in fifty enjoys the absolutely normal state of that organ; and upon that depends the daily cheerfulness, in the first place, and through that (as well as by more direct actions) the sanity of the judgment. To speak strictly, not one man in a hundred is perfectly sane even as to his mind. For, though the greater disturbances of the mind do not take place in more than one man of each thousand,* those slighter shades that settle on the judgment, which daily bring up molesting thoughts such as a man would gladly banish, thoughts imperiously irritating at the moment, and wearing to the animal spirits—these derangements are universal.

From the greater alike and the lesser, no man can free

* "*One man of each thousand:*"—In several nations that has been found to be the average proportion of the insane. But this calculation has never been made to include all the slighter cases. It is not impossible that at some periods the whole human race may have been partially insane.

himself but in the proportion of his available knowledge applied to his own animal system, and of the surrounding circumstances, as constantly acting on that system. Would I, then, desire that every man should interrupt his proper studies or pursuits for the sake of superintending a medical discipline applied to his own case? Not at all: nor is that requisite. The laws of health are as simple as the elements of arithmetic or geometry. It is required only that a man should open his eyes, to perceive the great elementary forces which support health.

They are these: 1. the *blood* requires motion; 2. the great central organ of the *stomach* requires exercise and adaptation of diet: 3. the *nervous system* requires regularity of repose. In those three functions of sleep, diet, exercise, is contained the whole economy of health. All three, of course, act and react upon each other: and all three are wofully deranged by a London life—above all, by a parliamentary life. As regards the first point, it is probable that any torpor, or even *lentor* in the blood, such as scarcely expresses itself sensibly through the pulse, renders that fluid less able to resist the first actions of disease. As to the second, a more complex subject, luckily we benefit not by our own brief experience exclusively; every man benefits practically by the traditional experience of ages, which constitutes the culinary experience in every land and every household. The inheritance of knowledge, which every generation receives, as to the salubrity of this or that article of diet, operates continually in preventing dishes from being brought to table. Every man wonders, on reading the long list of edible substances forbidden by the Mosaic law, how the ordinary Jew could find time to watch this long prohibitory tariff. But *that* was done for him by proxy. The butcher was bastinadoed who offered for sale any prohibited article. The buyer was therefore without anxiety. The same good office is performed for us all, Jews and Gentiles, by old traditional maxims embodied in immemorial usages. Each man's separate experience adds something to arm him against the temptation when it is offered; and again, the traditional experience far oftener intercepts the temptation. As to the third head, *sleep*, this of all is the most immediately fitted by nature to the relief of the brain and its exquisite machinery of nerves:—it is the function of health most attended to in our navy; and of all it is the one most painfully ravaged by a parliamentary life.

It would seem, therefore, that the three central forces of health—viz., *motion*, *rest*, and *temperance* (or, by a more adequate expression, *adaptation to the organ*)—are, in a certain gross way, taught to every man by his personal experience. The difficulty is—as in so many other cases—not for the understanding, but for the will; not to know, but to execute.

Now, here steps in casuistry with two tremendous suggestions, sufficient to alarm any thoughtful man, and rouse him more effectually to the performance of his duty.

First, that under the same law (whatever that law may be) which makes (or which is generally thought to make) suicide a crime, must the neglect of health be a crime. For thus stand the two accounts:—By suicide you have cut off a *portion unknown* from your life: years it may be, but possibly only days. By neglect of health you have cut off a *portion unknown* from your life: days it may be, but also by possibility years. So the practical result may be the same in either case; or, by possibility, the least is suicide. "Yes," you reply, "the *practical* results; but not the purpose—not the intention: *ergo*, not the crime." Certainly not: in the one case the result arises from absolute predetermination, with the whole energies of the will; in the other, it arises *in spite* of your will (meaning your choice)—it arises out of human infirmity. But still the difference is as between choosing an act for its own sake, and falling into it from strong temptation. I do not pretend to know whether, or in what extent, suicide may be a crime. All *that* is wrapped in clouds. But this is certain—that, in so far as it is criminal, habitual neglect of health must partake of that criminality.

Secondly, that in every case of duty unfulfilled, or duty imperfectly fulfilled, in consequence of illness, languor, decaying spirits, &c., there is a high probability (under the age of sixty-five almost a certainty) that a part of the obstacle is due to self-neglect. No man that lives but loses some of his time from ill health, or at least from the incipient forms of ill health—bad spirits, or indisposition to exertion. Now, taking men even as they are, statistical societies have ascertained that, from the ages of twenty to sixty-five, ill health, such as to interrupt daily labour, averages from seven days to about fourteen per annum. In the *best* circumstances of climate, occupation, &c., one fifty-second part of the time perishes to the species—in the *least* favourable, two such parts. Consequently, in the forty-five years from twenty to sixty-five, not very far from a year perishes on an average to every man—to some very much more. A considerable part even of this loss is due to neglect or mismanagement of health. But this estimate records only the loss of time in a pecuniary sense; which loss, being powerfully restrained by self-interest, will be the least possible under the circumstances. The loss of energy, as applied to duties not connected with any self-interest, or also as applied to the culture of happiness, will be far more. In so far as that loss emanates from defect of spirits, or other modes of vital torpor, such as neglect of health has either caused or promoted, and such as care might have prevented, in so far the omission is chargeable to our own responsibility, and is a modification of suicide more certainly criminal than that act of which it is the modification: because suicide *may* have, at any rate, one mode of palliation to plead [I do not even guess in what proportion of cases it *has* that plea]; whereas wilful neglect of health never has it. Many men fancy that the slight injuries done by each single act of intemperance are like the glomeration* of moonbeams upon moonbeams—myriads will not amount to a positive value. Perhaps they are wrong; possibly every act—nay, every separate pulse or throb of intemperate sensation—is numbered in our own after actions; reproduces itself in some future perplexity; comes back in some reversionary shape that injures the freedom of action for all men, and makes good

* *Glomeration.*—"Rather a pedantic word, I should imagine," says Mr Snarl, critic-general for two parishes. No, Mr Snarl: not at all pedantic, unless moonbeams are pedantic. Let me presume to point out, even to the Snarlian intellect, a beauty in Virgil (as also in other Latin poets), which hitherto has escaped notice. What does *glomerare* mean? Not simply to *aggregate* or *coacervate;* but to do this after a certain model or fashion. What fashion? Why, what is it that you mean by a *glomus,* from which word the verb *glomero* is a derivative? The English word for *glomus* was in elder days a *bottom;* which term still survives in the old English of Lancashire and Yorkshire. And I believe that Shakspere alluded to this technical word in the mystery of *weaving,* when he styled one of his characters in the "Midsummer Night's Dream," *Bottom the weaver.* The *glomus* was a little wooden implement; of what exact shape I do not know; but, when covered with worsted (or cotton, I presume), it presented a spiral circumvolution of the thread. Now the aerial curvetings of a horse with his fore legs, the pawings which he describes in the air, exactly repeat the spiral windings of the thread upon the *glomus.* And thence it is that Virgil describes a fiery horse as attempting *gressus glomerare superbos*—to wind as it were his haughty curvetings round some imaginary *glomus* made out of air or moonshine.

men afflicted. At all events, it is an undeniable fact, that many a case of difficulty, which in apology for ourselves we very truly plead to be insurmountable by our existing energies, has borrowed its sting from previous acts or omissions of our own; it might *not* have been insurmountable, had we better cherished our physical resources. For instance, of such a man it is said, he did not assist in repelling an injury from his friend or his native land. "True," says his apologist, "but you would not require him to do so when he labours under paralysis?" "Certainly not; but perhaps he might *not* have laboured under paralysis, had he uniformly practised abstinence."*

Let not the reader suspect me of the Popish doctrine, that men are to enter hereafter into a separate reckoning for each separate act. That reckoning, we Protestants believe, no man could stand; and that some other resource must be had than any personal merits of the individual. But still we should recollect that this doctrine, though providing a refuge for past offences, provides none for such offences as are committed deliberately, with a prospective

---

* With respect to the management of health, although it is undoubtedly true that, like the "primal charities," in the language of Wordsworth, in proportion to its importance it shines alike for all, and is diffused universally—yet not the less, in every age, some very obstinate prejudices have prevailed to darken the truth. Thus Dryden authorises the conceit, that medicine can never be useful or requisite, because

"God never made his work for man to mend."

To mend! No, glorious John, neither physician nor patient has any such presumptuous fancy; we take medicine to mend the injuries produced by our own folly. What the medicine mends is not God's work, but our own. The medicine is a *plus* certainly; but it is a *plus* applied to a *minus* of our own introducing. Even in these days of practical knowledge, errors prevail on the subject of health, which are neither trivial nor of narrow operation. Universally, the true theory of digestion, as partially unfolded in Dr Wilson Philip's experiments on rabbits, is as

view to the benefits of such a refuge. Offend we may, and we must; but then our offences must come out of mere infirmity—not because we calculate upon a large allowance being made to us, and say to ourselves, *We can do our penitence hereafter: at present let us take out our allowance.*

Casuistry, therefore, justly, and without infringing any truth of Christianity, urges the care of health as the basis of all moral action, because, in fact, of all *perfectly voluntary* action. Every impulse of bad health jars or untunes some string in the fine harp of human volition; and because a man cannot be a moral being but in the proportion of his free agency, therefore it is clear that no man can be in a high sense moral, except in so far as through health he commands his bodily powers, and is not commanded by them.

CASE II.—LAWS OF HOSPITALITY IN COLLISION WITH CIVIC DUTIES.

Suppose the case, that, taking shelter from a shower of rain in a stranger's house, you discover proofs of a connection with smugglers. Take this for one pole of such

---

far mistaken, and even inverted, that Lord Byron, when seeking a diet of easy digestion, instead of resorting to animal food broiled and underdone, which all medical men know to be the most digestible food, took to a vegetable diet, which requires a stomach of extra power. The same error is seen in the common notion about the breakfast of ladies in Elizabeth's days, as if fit only for ploughmen; whereas it is *our* breakfasts of slops which require the powerful organs of digestion. The same error, again, is current in the notion that a weak watery diet is fit for a weak person. Such a person peculiarly requires solid food. It is also a common mistake to suppose that, because no absolute illness is caused by daily errors of diet, these errors are practically cancelled. Cowper the poet delivers the very just opinion, that all disorders of a *function* (as, suppose, the secretion of bile), sooner or later, if not corrected, cease to be functional disorders, and become organic; that is, in plain English, beginning with injury to the mere *office* of any organ, they end by attacking its substance.

case, the trivial extreme; then, for the other pole, the greater extreme, suppose the case, that, being hospitably entertained, and happening to pass the night in a stranger's house, you are so unfortunate as to detect unquestionable proofs of some dreadful crime, say murder, perpetrated in past times by one of the family. The principle at issue is the same in both cases—viz., the command resting upon the conscience to forget private consideration and personal feelings in the presence of any solemn duty; yet merely the difference of degree, and not any at all in the kind of duty, would lead pretty generally to a separate practical decision for the several cases. In the last of the two, whatever might be the pain to a person's feelings, he would feel himself to have no discretion or choice left. Reveal he must; not only, if otherwise revealed, he must come forward as a witness, but, if not revealed, he must denounce—he must lodge an information, and that instantly; else even in law, without question of morality, he makes himself a party to the crime—an accomplice after the act. That single consideration would with most men at once cut short all deliberation. And yet, even in such a situation, there is a possible variety of the case that might alter its complexion. If the crime had been committed many years before, and under circumstances which precluded all fear that the same temptation or the same provocation should arise again, and with no lurking chance that an innocent person should fall under suspicion, most reflecting people would think it the better course to leave the criminal to his conscience. Often in such denunciations it is certain that human impertinence, and the spirit which sustains the habit of gossip, and mere incontinence of secrets, and vulgar craving for being the author of a sensation, have far more often led to the publication of the offence, than any concern for the interests of morality.*

On the other hand, with respect to the slighter extreme —viz., in a case where the offence is entirely created by the law, with no natural turpitude about it, and besides (which is a strong argument in the case) enjoying no special facilities of escaping justice—no man in the circumstances supposed would have a reason for hesitating. The laws of hospitality are of everlasting obligation; they are equally binding on the host and on the guest. Coming under a man's roof for one moment, in the clear character of guest, creates an absolute sanctity in the consequent relations which connect the parties. That is the popular feeling. The king in the old ballads is always represented as feeling that it would be damnable to make a legal offence out of his own venison which he had eaten as a guest. There is a cleaving pollution, like that of the Syrian leprosy, in the act of abusing your privileges as a guest, or in any way profiting by your opportunities as a guest to the injury of your confiding host. Henry VII., though a prince, was no gentleman; and in the famous case of his dining with Lord Oxford, and saying at his departure, with reference to an infraction of his recent statute, "My lord, I thank you for my good cheer, but my attorney must speak with you," Lord Oxford might have justly retorted, "If he does, then posterity will speak pretty plainly with your grace;" for it was in the character of Lord Oxford's guest that he had learned the infraction of his law. Meantime, the general rule, and the *rationale* of the rule, in such cases,

* Most confessions in prison fall within this category. They are special luxuries to all parties, especially to the criminal, whose only vexation is, that he cannot make ten confessions; since ever after he becomes a pet, and is regularly fattened up for the scaffold.

appears to be this: whenever there is, or can be imagined, a sanctity in the obligations on one side, and only a benefit of expediency in the obligations upon the other, the latter must give way. For the detection of smuggling (the particular offence supposed in the case stated), society has an express and separate machinery maintained. If their activity droops, that is the business of government. In such a case, government is entitled to no aid from private citizens; on the express understanding that no aid must be expected, has so expensive an establishment been submitted to. Each individual refuses to participate in exposure of such offences, for the same reason that in some towns he refuses to keep the street clean even before his own door—he has already paid for having such work discharged by proxy.

CASE III.—GIVING CHARACTERS TO SERVANTS WHO HAVE MISCONDUCTED THEMSELVES.

No case so constantly arises to perplex the conscience in private life as this—which, in principle, is almost beyond solution. Sometimes, indeed, the coarse realities of law step in to cut that Gordian knot which no man can untie; for it is an actionable offence in Great Britain to give a character wilfully false. That little fact at once exorcises all aerial phantoms of the conscience. True: but this coarse machinery applies only to those cases in which the servant has been guilty in a way amenable to law. In any case short of *that*, no plaintiff would choose to face the risks of an action; nor could he sustain it; the defendant would always have a sufficient resource in the vagueness and large latitude allowed to opinion when estimating the qualities of a servant. Almost universally, therefore, the case comes back to the forum of conscience. Now in that forum how stands the pleading? Too certainly, we will suppose, that the servant has not satisfied your reasonable expectations. This truth you would have no difficulty in declaring; here, as much as anywhere else, you would feel it unworthy of your own integrity to equivocate—you open your writing-desk, and sit down to tell the mere truth in as few words as possible. But then steps in the consideration, that to do this without disguise or mitigation, is oftentimes to sign a warrant for the ruin of a fellow-creature—and that fellow-creature possibly penitent, in any case thrown upon your mercy. Who can stand this? In lower walks of life, it is true that mistresses often take servants without any certificate of character; but in higher grades this is notoriously uncommon, and in great cities dangerous. Besides, the candidate may happen to be a delicate girl, incapable of the hard labour incident to such a lower establishment. Here, then, is a case where conscience says into your left ear, *Fiat justitia, ruat cœlum*—"Do your duty and defy consequences." Meantime, into the right ear conscience says, "But mark, in that case possibly you consign this poor girl to prostitution." Lord Nelson, as is well known, was once placed in a dilemma* equally trying; on one side, an iron tongue sang out from the commander-in-chief (Sir Hyde Parker), *retreat;* on the other, his own oracular heart sang to him, *advance.* How he decided is well known; and the words in which he proclaimed his decision ought to be emblazoned for ever as the noblest of all re-

---

* "*Once placed in a dilemma:*"—On the first expedition against Copenhagen (in 1801). He was unfortunately second in command; his principal, a brave man in person, wanted moral courage—he could not face responsibility in a trying shape. And had he not been blessed with a disobedient second in command, he must have returned home *re infectâ.*

corded repartees. Waving his hand towards the admiral's ship, he said to his own officers, who reported the signal of recall, "You may see it; I cannot; you know I am blind on that side."* Oh, venerable blindness! immortal blindness! None so deaf as those who will not hear; none so gloriously blind as those who will not see any danger or difficulty—who have a dark eye on that side, whilst they reserve another blazing like a meteor for honour and their country's interest. Most of us, I presume, in the case stated about the servant, hear but the whispering voice of conscience as regards the truth, and the thundering voice as regards the poor girl's interest. In doing this, however, we (and doubtless others) usually attempt to compromise the opposite suggestions of conscience by some such jesuitical device as this. We dwell pointedly upon those good qualities which the servant really possesses, and evade speaking of any others. But how, if minute, searching, and circumstantial inquiries are made by way of letter? In that case, we affect to have noticed only such as we can answer satisfactorily, passing the dangerous ones as so many rocks, *sub silentio*. All this is not quite right, you think, reader. Why, *no*; so think we; but what alternative is allowed? "Say, ye severest, what would ye have done?" In very truth, this is a dilemma for which casuistry is not a match; unless, indeed, casuistry as armed and equipped in the school of Ignatius Loyola. But that is with us reputed a piratical casuistry. The whole estate of a servant lies in his capacity of serving; and often if you tell the truth, by one word you ruin this estate for

* He had lost an eye; I forget whether at Teneriffe, or subsequently at Aboukir.

ever. Meantime, a case very much of the same quality, and of even greater difficulty, is

CASE IV.—CRIMINAL PROSECUTION OF FRAUDULENT SERVANTS.

Any reader, who is not deeply read in the economy of English life, will have a most inadequate notion of the vast extent to which this case occurs. I am well assured (for my information comes from quarters *judicially* conversant with the question), that in no other channel of human life does there flow one-hundredth part of the forbearance and the lenity which are called into action by the relation between injured masters and their servants. I am informed that, were every third charge pursued effectually, half the courts in Europe would not suffice for the cases of criminality which emerge in London alone under this head. All England would, in the course of five revolving years, have passed under the torture of *subpœna*, as witnesses for the prosecution or the defence. This multiplication of cases arises from the coincidence of hourly opportunity with hourly temptation, both carried to the extreme verge of possibility, and generally falling in with youth in the offenders. These aggravations of the danger are three several palliations of the crime, and they have weight allowed to them by the indulgent feelings of masters in a corresponding degree; not one case out of six score that are discovered (while, perhaps, another six score go undiscovered) being ever prosecuted with rigour and effect.

In this universal laxity of temper lies an injury too serious to public morals; and the crime reproduces itself abundantly under an indulgence so Christian in its motive, but unfortunately operating with the full effect of genial culture. Masters, who have made themselves notorious by indiscriminate forgiveness, might be represented symbolically as gardeners watering and tending luxuriant crops of weeds or poisonous herbs in hot-beds or forcing-houses. In London, many are the tradesmen who, being reflective as well as benevolent, perceive that something is amiss in the whole system. In part the law has been to blame, stimulating false mercy by punishment disproportioned to the offence. But many a judicious master has seen cause to suspect his own lenity as more mischievously operative even than the law's harshness, and as an effeminate surrender to luxurious sensibilities. Those have not been the severest masters whose names are attached to fatal prosecutions: on the contrary, three out of four have been persons who looked forward to general consequences —having, therefore, been more than usually thoughtful, were, for that reason, likely to be more than usually humane. They did not suffer the less acutely, because their feelings ran counter to the course of what they believed to be their duty. Prosecutors often sleep with less tranquillity, during the progress of a judicial proceeding, than the objects of the prosecution. An English judge of the last century, celebrated for his uprightness, used to balance against that pity so much vaunted for the criminal, the duty of "a pity to the country." But private prosecutors of their own servants often feel both modes of pity at the same moment.

For this difficulty a book of casuistry might suggest a variety of resources, not so much adapted to a case of that nature already existing, as to the prevention of future cases. Every mode of trust or delegated duty would suggest its own separate improvements; but all improvements must fall under two general heads—first, the diminution of temptation, either by abridging the amount of trust reposed; or, where that is difficult, by shortening its duration, and multiplying the counter-checks: secondly, by the moderation of the punishment in the event of detection, as the sole means of reconciling the public conscience to the law, and diminishing the chances of impunity. There is a memorable proof of the rash extent to which the London tradesmen, at one time, carried their confidence in servants. So many clerks, or apprentices, were allowed to hold large balances of money in their hands through the intervals of their periodical settlings, that during the Parliamentary War multitudes were tempted, by that single cause, into absconding. They had always a refuge in the camps. And the loss sustained in this way was so heavy, when all payments were made in gold, that to this one evil suddenly assuming a shape of excess, is ascribed, by some writers, the first establishment of goldsmiths as bankers.*

Two other weighty considerations attach to this head—1. The known fact that large breaches of trust and embezzlements are greatly on the increase, and have been since the memorable case of Mr Fauntleroy. America is, and will be for ages, if the law of extradition should remain unchanged [*written* in 1846], a city of refuge for this form of guilt. 2. That the great training of the conscience in all which regards pecuniary justice and fidelity to engagements, lies through the discipline and *tyrocinium* of the

* "*First establishment of goldsmiths as bankers:*"—Goldsmiths certainly acted in that capacity from an earlier period. But from this era, until the formation of the Bank of England in 1696, they entered more fully upon the functions of bankers, issuing notes which passed current in London.

humbler ministerial offices—those of clerks, book-keepers, apprentices. The law acts through these offices, for the unconfirmed conscience, as leading-strings to an infant in its earliest efforts at walking. It forces to go right, until the choice may be supposed trained and fully developed. That is the great function of the law; a function which it will perform with more or less success, as it is more or less fitted to win the cordial support of masters.

CASE V.—VERACITY.

Here is a special "title" (to speak with the civil lawyers), under that general claim put in for England with respect to a moral pre-eminence amongst the nations. Many are they who, in regions widely apart, have noticed with honour the English superiority in the article of veneration for truth. Not many years ago, two Englishmen, on their road overland to India, fell in with a royal *cortége*, and soon after with the prime minister and the crown prince of Persia. The prince honoured them with an interview: both parties being on horseback, the conversation was therefore reduced to the points of nearest interest. Amongst these was the English character. Upon this the prince's remark was—that what had most impressed him with respect for England and her institutions was, the remarkable spirit of truth-speaking which distinguished her sons; as supposing her institutions to grow out of her sons, and her sons out of her institutions. And, indeed, well he might have this feeling by comparison with his own countrymen: Persians have no *principles* apparently on this point—all is impulse and accident of feeling. Thus the journal of the two Persian princes in London, as lately reported in the newspapers, is one tissue of falsehoods: not, most undoubtedly, from any purpose of deceiving, but from the overmastering habit (cherished by their whole training and experience) of repeating everything in a spirit of amplification, with a view to the *wonder* only of the hearer. The Persians are notoriously the Frenchmen of the East; the same gaiety, the same levity, the same want of depth both as to feeling and principle. The Turks are supposed to be much nearer to the English: the same gravity of temperament, the same meditativeness, the same sternness of principle. Of all European nations, the French is that which least regards truth. The whole spirit of their private memoirs and their anecdotes illustrates this. To point an anecdote or a repartee, there is no extravagance of falsehood that the French will not endure. What nation but the French would have tolerated that monstrous fiction about La Fontaine, by way of illustrating his supposed absence of mind—viz., that, on meeting his own son in a friend's house, he expressed his admiration of the young man, and begged to know his name. The fact probably may have been that La Fontaine was not liable to any absence at all: apparently this "distraction" was assumed, as a means of making a poor sort of sport for his friends. Like many another man in such circumstances, he saw with half an eye, and entered into the fun which his own imaginary forgetfulness produced. But, were it otherwise, who can believe so outrageous a self-forgetfulness as that which would darken his eyes to the very pictures of his own hearth? Were such a thing possible, were it even real, it would still be liable to the just objection of the critics—that, being incredible in appearance, even as a fact it ought not to be brought forward for any purpose of wit, but only as a truth of physiology, or as a fact from the records of a surgeon. The "*incredulus odi*" is too strong in such cases, and it adheres to three out of every four French anecdotes. The French taste is, indeed, anything but good in all that department of wit and humour. And the ground lies in their national want of veracity. To return to England—and having cited an oriental witness to the English character on this point, let me now cite a most observing one in the West. Kant, in Königsberg, was surrounded by Englishmen and by foreigners of all nations—foreign and English students, foreign and English merchants; and he pronounced the main characteristic feature of the English as a nation to lie in their severe reverence for truth. This from him was no slight praise; for such was the stress he laid upon veracity, that upon this one quality he planted the whole edifice of moral excellence. General integrity could not exist, he held, without veracity as its basis; nor that basis exist without superinducing general integrity.

This opinion, perhaps, many beside Kant will see cause to approve. For myself I can truly say, never did I know a human being, boy or girl, who began life as a habitual undervaluer of truth, that did not afterwards exhibit a character conformable to that beginning; such a character as, however superficially correct under the steadying hand of self-interest, was not in a lower key of moral feeling as well as of principle.

But out of this honourable regard to veracity in Immanuel Kant branched out a principle in casuistry which most people will pronounce monstrous. It has occasioned much disputing backwards and forwards. But, as a practical principle of conduct (for which Kant meant it), inevitably it must be rejected, if for no other reason than because it is at open war with the laws and jurisprudence of all Christian Europe. Kant's doctrine was this; and the illustrative case in which it is involved, let it be remembered, is his own:—So sacred a thing, said he, is truth, that if a murderer, pursuing another with an avowed purpose of killing him, were to ask of a third person by what road the fugitive had fled, that person is bound to give him true information. And you are at liberty to suppose this third person a wife, a daughter, or under any conceivable obligations of love and duty to the fugitive. Now this is monstrous; and Kant himself, with all his parental fondness for the doctrine, would certainly have been recalled to sounder thoughts by these two considerations—

1. That by all the codes of law received throughout Europe, he who acted upon Kant's principle would be held a *particeps criminis*—an accomplice before the fact.

2. That, in reality, a just principle is lurking under Kant's paradox; but a principle translated from its proper ground. Not truth, individual or personal—not truth of mere facts, but truth doctrinal—the truth which teaches, the truth which changes men and nations—this is the truth concerned in Kant's meaning, had he explained his own meaning to himself more distinctly. With respect to that truth, wheresoever it lies, Kant's doctrine applies; that all men have a right to it; that perhaps you have no right to suppose of any race or nation that it is not capable of receiving it; and, at any rate, that no circumstances of expedience can justify you in keeping it back.*

* It is remarkable enough that Kant was once nearly illustrating his own imaginary case. A murderer pursued him for three miles on the high-road with the design of operating; but, being a very religious man, on second thoughts, and in deference to a point of casuistry, he preferred murdering a little girl; and thus it happened that the transcendental philosopher escaped.

CASE VI.—THE CASE OF CHARLES I.

Many cases arise from the life and political difficulties of Charles I. But there is one so peculiarly pertinent to an essay which entertains the general question of casuistry, its legitimacy, and its value, that with this, although not properly a domestic case, or only such in a mixed sense, I shall conclude.

No person has been so much attacked for his scruples of conscience as this prince; and what seems odd enough, no person has been so much attacked for resorting to books of casuistry, and for encouraging literary men to write books of casuistry. Under his suggestion and sanction, Saunderson wrote his book on the obligation of an oath (for which there was surely reason enough in days when the democratic tribunals were forcing men to swear* to an *etcetera)*; and, by an impulse originally derived from *him*, Jeremy Taylor wrote his "Ductor Dubitantium" (*i. e.*, "Guide to the Scrupulous"), Bishop Barlow his "Cases of Conscience," &c.

For this dedication of his studies Charles has been plentifully blamed in after times. He was seeking evasions for plain duties, say his enemies. He was arming himself for intrigue in the spirit of Machiavel. But now turn to his history, and ask in what way any man could have extricated himself from that labyrinth which invested his path *but* by casuistry. Cases the most difficult are offered for his decision; peace for a distracted nation in 1647, on terms which seemed fatal to the monarchy; peace for the same nation under the prospect of war rising up again during the Isle of Wight treaty in 1648, but also under

* Which, however, is untruly stated by all historians.

the certainty of destroying the Church of England. On the one side, by refusing, he seemed to disown his duties as the father of his people. On the other side, by yielding, he seemed to forget his coronation oath, and the ultimate interests of his people; to merge the future and the reversionary in the present and the fugitive. It was not within the possibilities that he could so act as not to offend one-half of the nation. His dire calamity it was, that he must be hated, act how he would, and must be condemned by posterity. Did his enemies allow for the misery of this internal conflict? Milton, who never appears to more disadvantage than when he comes forward against his sovereign, is indignant that Charles should have a conscience, or plead a conscience, in a public matter. Henderson, the celebrated Scotch theologian, came post from Edinburgh to London (whence he went to Newcastle), expressly to combat the king's scruples. And he also (in his private letters) seems equally enraged as Milton, that Charles should pretend to any private conscience in a state question.

Now let us ask, what was it that originally drove Charles to books of casuistry? It was the deep shock which he received, both in his affections and his conscience, from the death of Lord Strafford. Everybody had then told him, even those who felt how much the law must be outraged to obtain a conviction of Lord Strafford, how many principles of justice must be shaken, and how sadly the royal word must suffer in its sanctity—yet all had told him that it was expedient to sacrifice that nobleman. One man ought not to stand between the king and his alienated people. It was good for the common welfare that Lord Strafford should die. Charles was unconvinced. He was sure of the injustice, and perhaps he doubted even of the expedience. But his very virtues were armed against his peace. In all parts of his life self-distrust and diffidence had marked his character. What was he, a single person, to resist so many wise counsellors, and in a representative sense to resist the nation ranged on the other side? He yielded, and it is not too much to say that he never had a happy day afterwards. The stirring period of his life succeeded—the period of war, camps, treaties. Much time was not allowed him for meditation. But there is abundant proof that such time as he had always pointed his thoughts backwards to the afflicting case of Lord Strafford. This he often spoke of as the great blot—the ineffaceable transgression of his life. For this he mourned in penitential words yet on record. To this he traced back the calamity of his latter life. Lord Strafford's memorable words, "Put not your trust in princes, nor in the sons of princes," rang for ever in his ear. Lord Strafford's blood lay like a curse upon his throne.

Now, by what a pointed answer, drawn from this one case, might Charles have replied to the enemies I have noticed—to those, like so many historians since his day, who taxed him with studying casuistry for the purposes of intrigue—to those, like Milton and Henderson, who taxed him with exercising his private conscience on public questions.

"I had studied no books of casuistry," he might have replied, "when I made my capital blunder in a case of conscience.

"I did not insist on my private conscience; wo is me that I did not: I yielded to what was called the public conscience, in that one case which has proved the affliction of my life, and which, perhaps, it was that wrecked the national peace."

A more plenary answer there cannot be to those who suppose that casuistry is evaded by evading books of casuistry. That dread forum of conscience will for ever exist as a tribunal of doubt and difficulty. The discussion must proceed on some principle or other, good or bad; and the only way for obtaining light is by clearing up the grounds of action, and applying the principles of moral judgment to such facts or circumstances as most frequently arise to perplex the understanding, or the affections, or the conscience.

GREECE UNDER THE ROMANS.

WITH A

REFERENCE TO MR GEORGE FINLAY'S WORK UPON THAT SUBJECT.

What is called *Philosophical History* I believe to be yet in its infancy. It is the profound remark of Mr Finlay—profound as I myself understand it—*i. e.*, in relation to this philosophical treatment, "That history will ever remain inexhaustible." How inexhaustible? Are the *facts* of history inexhaustible? In regard to the *ancient* division of history with which he is there dealing, this would be in no sense true; and in any case it would be a lifeless truth. So entirely have the mere facts of Pagan history been disinterred, ransacked, sifted, that except by means of some chance medal that may be unearthed in the illiterate East (as of late towards Bokhara), or by means of some mysterious inscription, such as those which still mock the learned traveller in Persia, northwards near Hamadan (Ecbatana), and southwards at Persepolis, or those which distract him amongst the shadowy ruins of Yucatan (Uxmal, suppose, and Palenque)—once for all, barring these pure godsends, it is hardly "in the dice" that any downright novelty of fact should remain in reversion for this nineteenth century. The merest possibility exists, that in Armenia, or in a Græco-Russian monastery on Mount Athos, or in Pompeii, &c., some authors hitherto *ανεκδοτοι* may yet be concealed; and by a channel in that degree improbable, it is possible that certain new facts of history may still reach us. But else, and failing these cryptical or subterraneous currents of communication, for us the record is closed. History in that sense has come to an end, and is sealed up as by the angel in the Apocalypse. What then? The facts *so* understood are but the dry bones of the mighty past. And the question arises here also, not less than in that sublimest of prophetic visions, "Can these dry bones live?" Not only can they live, but by an infinite variety of life. The same historic facts, viewed in different lights, or brought into connection with other facts, according to endless diversities of permutation and combination, furnish grounds for such eternal successions of new speculations as make the facts themselves virtually new, and virtually endless. The same Hebrew words are read by different sets of vowel points, and the same hieroglyphics are deciphered by keys everlastingly varied.

To me, I repeat that oftentimes it seems as though the *science* of history were yet scarcely founded. There will be such a science, if at present there is not; and in one feature of its capacities it will resemble chemistry. What is so familiar to the perceptions of man as the common chemical agents of water, air, and the soil on which we tread? Yet each one of these elements is a mystery to this day; handled, used, tried, searched experimentally, combined in ten thousand ways—it is still unknown; fathomed by recent science down to a certain depth, it is still probably by its destiny unfathomable. Even to the end of days, it is pretty certain that the minutest particle of earth—that a dew-drop scarcely distinguishable as a separate object—

that the slenderest filament of a plant—will include within itself secrets inaccessible to man. And yet, compared with the mystery of man himself, these physical worlds of mystery are but as a radix of infinity. Chemistry is in this view mysterious and spinosistically sublime—that it is the science of the latent in all things, of all things as lurking in all. Within the lifeless flint, within the silent pyrites, slumbers an agony of potential combustion. Iron is imprisoned in blood. With cold water (as every child is now-a-days aware) you may lash a fluid into angry ebullitions of heat; with hot water, as with the rod of Amram's son, you may freeze a fluid down to the temperature of the Sarsar wind, provided only that you regulate the pressure of the air. The sultry and dissolving fluid shall bake into a solid, the petrific fluid shall melt into a liquid. Heat shall freeze, frost shall thaw; and wherefore? Simply because old things are brought together in new modes of combination. And in endless instances beside, we see in all elements the same Panlike latency of forms and powers, which gives to the external world a capacity of self-transformation, and of *polymorphosis* absolutely inexhaustible.

But the same capacity belongs to the facts of history. And I do not mean merely that, from subjective differences in the minds reviewing them, such facts assume endless varieties of interpretation and estimate, but that objectively, from lights still increasing in the science of government and of social philosophy, all the primary facts of history become liable continually to new presentations, to new combinations, and to new valuations of their moral relations. I have seen some kinds of marble, where the veinings happened to be unusually multiplied, in which human faces, figures, processions, or fragments of natural scenery, seemed absolutely illimitable, under the endless variations or inversions of the order, according to which they might be combined and grouped. Something analogous takes effect in reviewing the remote parts of history. Rome, for instance, has been the object of historic pens for twenty centuries (dating from Polybius); and yet hardly so much as twenty years have elapsed since Niebuhr opened upon us almost a new revelation, by re-combining the same eternal facts, according to a different set of principles. The same thing may be said, though not with the same degree of emphasis, upon the Grecian researches of the late Ottfried Mueller. Egyptian history again, even at this moment, is seen stealing upon us through the dusky twilight in its first distinct lineaments. Before Young, Champollion, Lepsius, and the others who have followed on their traces in this field of history, all was outer darkness; and whatsoever we *do* know or *shall* know of Egyptian Thebes will now be recovered as if from the unswathing of a mummy. Not until a flight of three thousand years has left Thebes the Hekatompylos a dusky speck in the far distance, have we even *begun* to read her annals, or to understand her revolutions.

Another instance I have now before me of this new historic faculty for resuscitating the buried, and for calling back the breath to the frozen features of death, in Mr Finlay's work upon the Greeks as related to the Roman Empire. He presents us with old facts, but under the purpose of clothing them with a new life. He rehearses ancient stories, not with the humble ambition of better adorning them, of more perspicuously narrating, or even of more forcibly pointing their moral, but of extracting from them some new meaning, and thus forcing them to arrange themselves, under some latent connection, with other phenomena now first detected, as illustrations of some great principle or agency now first revealing its importance. Mr Finlay's style of intellect is appropriate to such a task; for it is subtle and Machiavelian. But there is this difficulty in doing justice to the novelty, and at times I may say with truth to the profundity of his views, that they are by necessity thrown out in continued successions of details, are insulated, and, in one word, *sporadic*. This follows from the very nature of his work; for it is a perpetual commentary on the incidents of Grecian history, from the era of the Roman conquest to the commencement of what Mr Finlay, in a peculiar sense, calls the Byzantine Empire. These incidents have nowhere been systematically or continuously recorded; they come forward by casual flashes in the annals, perhaps, of some church historian, as they happen to connect themselves with his momentary theme; or they betray themselves in the embarrassments of the central government, whether at Rome or at Constantinople, when arguing at one time a pestilence, at another an insurrection, or at a third an inroad of barbarians. It is not the fault of Mr Finlay, but his great disadvantage, that the affairs of Greece have been thus discontinuously exhibited, and that its internal changes of condition have been never treated except indirectly, and by men *aliud agentibus*. The Grecian *race* had a primary importance on our planet; but the Grecian name, represented by Greece considered as a territory, or as the political seat of the Hellenic people, ceased to have much importance, in the eyes of historians, from the time when it became a conquered province; and it declined into absolute insignificance after the conquest of so many other provinces had degraded Hellas into an arithmetical unit, standing amongst a total amount of figures, so vast and so much more dazzling to the ordinary mind. Hence it was that in ancient times no complete history of Greece, through all her phases and stages, was conspicuously attempted. The greatness of her later revolutions, simply as changes, would have attracted the historian; but, as changes associated with calamity and loss of power, they repelled his curiosity, and alienated his interest. It is the very necessity, therefore, of Mr Finlay's position, when coming into such an inheritance, that he must splinter his philosophy into separate individual notices; for the records of history furnish no grounds for more. *Spartam, quam nactus est, ornavit.* That ungenial province, which he has obtained by lot, he has beautified by his culture and treatment. But this does not remedy the difficulty for ourselves, in attempting to give a representative view of his philosophy. General abstractions he had no opportunity for presenting; consequently we have no opportunity for valuing; and, on the other hand, single cases selected from a succession of hundreds, would not justify any *representative* criticism, more than the single brick, in the old anecdote of Hierocles, would serve representatively to appraise the house.

Under this difficulty as to the possible for myself, and the just for Mr Finlay, I shall adopt the following course. So far as the Greek people collected themselves in any splendid manner with the Roman Empire, they did so with the eastern horn of that empire, and in point of time from the foundation of Constantinople as an eastern Rome, in the fourth century, to a period not fully agreed on; but for the moment I will say with Mr Finlay, up to the early part of the eighth century. A reason given by Mr Finlay for this latter date is, that about that time the Grecian blood, so widely diffused in Asia, and even in Africa, became finally detached by the progress of Mahometanism and Mahometan systems of power, from all further concurrence or coalition with the views of the Byzantine Cæsar. Constantinople was from that date thrown back more upon its own peculiar heritage and jurisdiction, of which the main resources for war and peace lay in Europe, and (speaking by the narrowest terms) in Thrace. Henceforth, therefore, for the city and throne of Constantine, resuming its old Grecian name of Byzantium, there succeeded a theatre less diffusive, a population more concentrated, a character of action more determinate and jealous, a style of courtly ceremonial more elaborate as well as more haughtily repulsive, and universally a system of interests, as much more definite and selfish, as might naturally be looked for in a nation now everywhere surrounded by new thrones gloomy with malice, and swelling with the consciousness of youthful power. This new and final state of the eastern Rome Mr Finlay denominates the Byzantine Empire. Possibly this use of the term thus limited may be capable of justification; but more questions would arise in the discussion than Mr Finlay has thought it of importance to notice. And for the present I shall take the word *Byzantine* in its most ordinary acceptation, as denoting the local empire founded by Constantine in Byzantium, early in the fourth century, under the idea of a translation from the old western Rome, and overthrown by the Ottoman Turks in the year 1453. In the fortunes and main stages of this empire, what are the chief arresting phenomena, aspects, or relations to the greatest of modern interests? I select by preference these:—

I. First, this was the earliest among the kingdoms of our planet *which connected itself with Christianity.* In Armenia, there had been a previous *state* recognition of Christianity. But *that* was neither splendid nor distinct. Whereas the Byzantine Rome built avowedly upon Christianity as its own basis, and consecrated its own nativity by the sublime act of founding the first provision ever attempted for the poor, considered simply as poor (i. e., *as objects of pity, not as instruments of ambition).*

II. Secondly, *as the great ægis of western Christendom*, nay, the barrier which made it possible that any Christendom should ever exist, this Byzantine Empire is entitled to a very different station in the enlightened gratitude of us Western Europeans from any which it has yet held. I do not scruple to say, that, by comparison with the services of the Byzantine people to Europe, no nation on record has ever stood in the same relation to any other single nation, much less to a whole family of nations, whether as regards the opportunity and means of conferring benefits, or as regards the astonishing perseverance in supporting the succession of these benefits, or as regards the ultimate event of these benefits. A great wrong has been done for ages; for we have all been accustomed to speak of the Byzantine Empire with scorn,* as chiefly known by its effeminacy; and the greater is the call for a fervent palinode.

III. Thirdly, in a reflex way, as the one great danger which overshadowed Europe for generations, and against which the Byzantine Empire proved the capital bulwark,

* "*With scorn:*"—This has arisen from two causes: one is the habit of regarding the whole Roman Empire as in its "decline" from so early a period as that of Commodus; agreeably to which conceit, it would naturally follow that, during its latter stages, the Eastern Empire must have been absolutely in its dotage. If already declining in the second century, then, from the tenth to the fifteenth, it must have been paralytic and bedridden. The other cause may be found in the accidental but reasonable hostility of the Byzantine court to the first Crusaders, as also in the disadvantageous comparison with respect to manly virtues between the simplicity of these western children, and the refined dissimulation of the Byzantines.

Mahometanism may rank as one of the Byzantine aspects or counterforces. And if there is any popular error applying to the history of that great convulsion, as a political effort for revolutionising the world, some notice of it will find a natural place in connection with these present trains of speculation.

Let me, therefore, have permission to throw together a few remarks on these three subjects—1. on the remarkable distinction by which the eldest of Christian rulers proclaimed and inaugurated the Christian basis of his empire; 2. on the true but forgotten relation of this great empire to our modern Christendom, under which idea I comprehend Europe, and *reversionally* the whole continent of America; 3. on the false pretensions of Mahometanism, whether advanced by itself or by inconsiderate Christian speculators on its behalf. I shall thus obtain this advantage, that some sort of unity will be given to my own glances at Mr Finlay's theme; and, at the same time, by gathering under these general heads any dispersed comments of Mr Finlay, whether for confirmation of my own views, or for any purpose of objection to his, I shall give to those comments also that kind of unity, by means of a reference to a common purpose, which I could not have given them by citing each independently for itself.

I. First, then, as to that memorable act by which Constantinople (*i. e.*, the Eastern Empire) connected herself for ever with Christianity—viz., the recognition of pauperism as an element in the state entitled to the maternal guardianship of the state. In this new principle, introduced by Christianity, we behold a far-seeing or proleptic wisdom, making provision for evils before they had arisen; for it is certain that great expansions of pauperism did not exist in the ancient world. A pauper population is a disease peculiar to the modern or Christian world. Various causes latent in the social systems of the ancients prevented such developments of surplus people. But does not this argue a superiority in the social arrangements of these ancients? Not at all; they were atrociously worse. They evaded this one morbid affection by means of others far more injurious to the moral advance of man. The case was then everywhere as at this day it is in Persia. A Persian ambassador to London or Paris might boast that, in his native Irân, no such spectacles existed of hunger-bitten myriads as may be seen everywhere during seasons of distress in the crowded cities of Christian Europe. "No," would be the answer, "most certainly not; but why? The reason is, that your accursed form of society and government *intercepts* such surplus people, does not suffer them to be born. What is the result? You ought, in Persia, to have three hundred millions of people; your vast territory is easily capacious of that number. You *have* —how many have you? Something less than eight millions." Think of this, startled reader. But, if *that* be a good state of things, then any barbarous soldier who makes a wilderness is entitled to call himself a great philosopher and public benefactor. This is to cure the headache by amputating the head. Now, the same principle of limitation to population *à parte ante,* though not in the same savage excess as in Mahometan Persia, operated upon Greece and Rome. The whole Pagan world escaped the evils of redundant population by vicious repressions of it beforehand. But under Christianity a new state of things was destined to take effect. Many protections and excitements to population were laid in the framework of this new religion, which, by its new code of rules and impulses, in so many ways extended the free agency of human beings.

Manufacturing industry was destined first to arise on any great scale under Christianity. Except in Tyre and Alexandria (see the Emperor Hadrian's account of this last), there was no town or district in the ancient world where the populace could be said properly to work. The rural labourers worked a little—not much; and sailors worked a little; nobody else worked at all. Even slaves had little more work distributed amongst each ten than now settles upon one. And in many other ways, by protecting the principle of life, as a mysterious sanctity, Christianity has favoured the development of an excessive population. There it is that Christianity, being answerable for the mischief, is answerable for its redress. Therefore it is that, breeding the disease, Christianity breeds the cure. Extending the vast lines of poverty, Christianity it was that first laid down the principle of a relief for poverty. Constantine, the first Christian potentate, laid the first stone of the mighty overshadowing institution since reared in Christian lands to poverty, disease, orphanage, and mutilation. Christian instincts, moving and speaking through that Cæsar, first carried out that great idea of Christianity. Six years was Christianity in building Constantinople, and in the seventh she rested from her labours, saying, "Henceforward let the poor man have a haven of rest for ever; a rest from his work for one day in seven; a rest from his anxieties by a legal and fixed relief." Being legal, it could not be open to disturbances of caprice in the giver; being fixed, it was not open to disturbances of miscalculation in the receiver. Now, first, when first Christianity was installed as a public organ of government (and first owned a distinct political responsibility), did it become the duty of a religion which assumed, as it were, the *official* tutelage of poverty, to proclaim and consecrate that function by some great memorial precedent. And, accordingly, in testimony of that obligation, the first Christian Cæsar, on behalf of Christianity, founded the first system of relief for pauperism. It is true, that largesses from the public treasury, gratuitous corn, or corn sold at diminished rates, not to mention the *sportulæ* or stated doles of private Roman nobles, had been distributed amongst the indigent citizens of Western Rome for centuries before Constantine; but all these had been the selfish bounties of factious ambition or intrigue.

To Christianity was reserved the inaugural act of public charity in the spirit of charity. We must remember that no charitable or beneficent institutions of any kind, grounded on disinterested kindness, existed amongst the Pagan Romans, and still less amongst the Pagan Greeks. Mr Coleridge, in one of his lay sermons, advanced the novel doctrine, that in the Scripture is contained all genuine and profound statesmanship. Of course he must be understood to mean, in its capital principles; for, as to subordinate and executive rules for applying such principles, these, doubtless, are in part suggested by the local circumstances in each separate case. Now, amongst the political theories of the Bible is this, that pauperism is not an accident in the constitution of states, but an indefeasible necessity; or, in the scriptural words, that "the poor shall never cease out of the land." This theory, or great canon of social philosophy, during many centuries, drew no especial attention from philosophers. It passed for a truism, bearing no particular emphasis or meaning beyond some general purpose of sanction to the impulses of charity. But there is good reason to believe that it slumbered, and was meant to slumber, until Christianity arising and moving forwards should call it into a new life, as a principle suited to a new order of things. Accordingly, we have seen of late that this scriptural dictum—"The poor shall never cease out of the land"—has terminated its career as a truism (that is, as a truth, either obvious on one hand, or inert on the other), and has wakened into a polemic or controversial life. People arose who took upon them utterly to deny the scriptural doctrine. Peremptorily they challenged the assertion that poverty must always exist. The Bible said that it was an affection of human society which could not be exterminated; the economist of 1800 said that it was a foul disease which must and should be exterminated. The scriptural philosophy said, that pauperism was inalienable from man's social condition, in the same way that decay was inalienable from his flesh. "I shall soon see *that*," said the economist of 1800, "for as sure as my name is Malthus, I will have this poverty put down by law within one generation, if there's a law to be had in the courts of Westminster." The Scriptures have left word, that, if any man should come to the national banquet, declaring himself unable to pay his contribution, that man should be accounted the guest of Christianity, and should be privileged to sit at the table in thankful remembrance of what Christianity had done for man. But Mr Malthus left word with all the servants, that, if any man should present himself under those circumstances, he was to be told, "the table is full" (*his* words, not mine); "go away, good man." Go away! Mr Malthus? Whither? In what direction?—"Why, if you come to *that*," said the man of 1800, "to any ditch that he prefers: surely there's good choice of ditches for the most fastidious taste." During twenty years—viz., from 1800 to 1820—this new philosophy, which substituted a ditch for a dinner, and a paving-stone for a loaf, prevailed and prospered. At one time it seemed likely enough to prove a snare to our own aristocracy—the noblest of all ages. But that peril was averted, and the further history of the case was this: By the year 1820, much discussion having passed to and fro, serious doubts had arisen in many quarters; scepticism had begun to arm itself against the sceptic; the economist of 1800 was no longer quite sure of his ground. He was now suspected of being fallible; and what seemed of worse augury, he was beginning himself to suspect as much. To one capital blunder he was obliged publicly to plead guilty. What it was, I shall have occasion to mention immediately. Meantime it was justly thought that, in a dispute loaded with such prodigious practical consequences, good sense and prudence demanded a more extended inquiry than had yet been instituted. Whether poverty would ever cease from the land, might be doubted by those who balanced their faith in Scripture against their faith in the man of 1800. But this at least could not be doubted—that as yet poverty *had* not ceased, nor indeed had made any sensible preparations for ceasing, from any land in Europe. It was a clear case, therefore, that, howsoever Europe might please to dream upon the matter, when pauperism should have reached that glorious euthanasy predicted by the alchemist of old and the economist of 1800, for the present she must deal actively with her own pauperism on some avowed plan and principle, good or evil—gentle or harsh. Accordingly, along the line of years between 1820 and 1830, inquiries were made through our consuls of every state in Europe, what *were* those plans and principles. For it was justly said—"As one step towards judging rightly of our own system, now that it has been so clamorously challenged for a bad system, let us learn what it is that other nations think upon the subject, but above all what it is that they *do.*" The answers to our many inquiries varied considerably; and some amongst the most enlightened nations appear to have adopted the good old plan of *laissez faire*, giving nothing from any public fund to the pauper, but authorising him to levy contributions on that gracious allegoric lady, Private Charity, wherever he could meet her taking the air with her babes. This reference appeared to be the main one in reply to any application of the pauper; and for all the rest they referred him generally to the "ditch," or to his own unlimited choice of ditches, according to the approved method of public benevolence published in 4to and in 8vo by the man of 1800. But there were other and humbler states in Europe, whose very pettiness had brought more fully within their vision the whole machinery and watchwork of pauperism, as it acted and reacted on the industrious poverty of the land, and on other interests, by means of the system adopted in relieving it. From these states came many interesting reports, all tending to some good purpose. But at last, and before the year 1830, amongst other results of more or less value, three capital points were established, not more decisive for the justification of the English system in administering national relief to paupers, and of all systems that reverenced the authority of Scripture, than they were for the overthrow of Mr Malthus, the man of 1800. These three points are worthy of being used as buoys in mapping out the true channels, or indicating the breakers on this difficult line of navigation; and I now rehearse them. They may seem plain almost to obviousness; but it is enough that they involve all the disputed questions of the case.

First, that, in spite of the assurances from economists, no progress whatever had been made by England, or by any state in this world, which lent any sanction to the hope of ever eradicating poverty from society.

Secondly, that, in absolute contradiction to the whole hypothesis relied on by Malthus and his brethren, in its most fundamental doctrine, a legal provision for poverty did *not* act as a bounty on marriage. There went to wreck the basis of the Malthus philosophy. The experience of England, where the trial had been made on the largest scale, was decisive on this point; and the opposite experience of Ireland, under the opposite circumstances, was equally decisive. And this result had made itself so clear by 1820, that even Malthus (as I have already noticed by anticipation) was compelled to publish a recantation as to this particular error, which in effect was a recantation of his entire theory.

Thirdly, that, according to the concurring experience of all the most enlightened states in Christendom, the public suffered least (not merely in molestation, but in money), pauperism benefited most, and the growth of pauperism was retarded most, precisely as the provision for the poor had been legalised as to its obligation, and fixed as to its amount. Left to individual discretion, the burden was found to press most unequally; and, on the other hand, the evil itself of pauperism, whilst much less effectually relieved, nevertheless, through the irregular action of this relief, was much more powerfully stimulated.

Such is the abstract of our latest public warfare on this great question through a period of nearly fifty years. And the issue is this: starting from the contemptuous defiance of the scriptural doctrine upon the necessity of making provision for poverty as an indispensable element in civil communities (*the poor shall never cease out of the land*), the economy of the age has lowered its tone by graduated descents, in each one successively of the four last *decennia*. The philosophy of the day, as to this point at least, is at length in coincidence with Scripture. And thus the very extensive researches of this nineteenth century, as to pauperism, have reacted with the effect of a full justification upon Constantine's attempt to connect the foundation of his empire with that new theory of Christianity upon the imperishableness of poverty, and upon the duties corresponding to it.

Meantime, Mr Finlay denies that Christianity had been raised by Constantine into the religion of the state; and others have denied that, in the extensive money privileges conceded to Constantinople, he contemplated any but political principles. As to the first point, I apprehend that Constantine will be found not so much to have shrunk back from fear of installing Christianity in the seat of supremacy, as to have diverged in policy from our modern *methods* of such an installation. My own belief is, that, according to *his* notion of a state religion, he supposed himself to have conferred that distinction upon Christianity. With respect to the endowments and privileges of Constantinople, they were various; some lay in positive donations, others in immunities and exemptions; some again were designed to attract strangers, others to attract nobles from old Rome. But, with fuller opportunities for pursuing that discussion, I think it might be possible to show, that, in more than one of his institutions and his decrees, he had contemplated the special advantage of the poor considered *as* poor; and that, next after the august distinction of having founded the first Christian throne, he had meant to challenge and fix the gaze of future ages upon this glorious pretension—viz., that he first had executed the scriptural injunction to make a provision for the poor, as an order of society that by laws immutable should "never cease out of the land."

II. Let me advert to the value and functions of Constantinople as the tutelary genius of western or dawning Christianity.

The history of Constantinople, or more generally of the eastern Roman Empire, wears a peculiar interest to the children of Christendom; and for two separate reasons—first, as being the narrow isthmus or bridge which connects the two continents of ancient and modern history, and *that* is a philosophic interest; but, secondly, which in the very highest degree is a practical interest, as the record of our earthly salvation from Mahometanism. On two horns was Europe assaulted by the Moslems: first, last, and through the largest tract of time, on the horn of Constantinople; there the contest raged for more than eight hundred years; and by the time that the mighty bulwark fell (1453), Vienna and other cities near the Danube had found leisure for growing up; Hungary had grown up; Poland had grown up; so that, if one range of Alps had slowly been surmounted, another had now embattled itself against the westward progress of the Crescent. On the westward horn, *in* France, but *by* Germans, once for all Charles Martel had arrested the progress of the fanatical Moslem almost in a single battle; certainly a single generation saw the whole danger dispersed, inasmuch as within that space the Saracens were effectually forced back into their Spanish lair. This demonstrates pretty forcibly the difference of the Mahometan resources as applied to the western and the eastern struggle. To throw the whole weight of that difference, a difference in the result as between eight centuries and thirty years, upon the mere difference of energy in German and Byzantine forces, as though the first did, by a rapturous fervour, in a few revolutions of summer, what the other had protracted through nearly a millennium, is a representation which defeats itself by its own extravagance. To prove too much, is more dangerous than to prove too little. The fact is, that vast armies and mighty nations were continually disposable for the war upon the city of Constantine; nations had time to arise in juvenile vigour, to grow old and superannuated, to melt away, and totally to disappear, in that long struggle on the Hellespont and Propontis. It was a struggle which might often intermit and slumber; armistices there might be, truces, or unproclaimed suspensions of war out of mutual exhaustion; but peace there could *not* be, because any resting from the duty of hatred between races that reciprocally seemed to lay the foundations of their creed in a dishonouring of God, was impossible to aspiring human nature. Malice and mutual hatred, I repeat, became a duty in those circumstances. Why had they *begun* to fight? Personal feuds there had been none between the parties. For the early caliphs did not conquer Syria and other vast provinces of the Roman Empire, because they had a quarrel with the Cæsars who represented Christendom; but, on the contrary, they had a quarrel with the Cæsars because they had conquered Syria; or, at the most, the conquest and the feud (if not always lying in that exact succession as cause and effect) were joint effects from a common cause, which cause was imperishable as death or the ocean, and as deep as are the fountains of life. Could the ocean be altered by a seafight, or the atmosphere be tainted for ever by an earthquake? As little could any single reign or its events affect the feud of the Moslem and the Christian; a feud which could not cease unless God could change, or unless man (becoming careless of spiritual things) should sink to the level of a brute.

These are considerations of great importance in weighing the value of the Eastern Empire. If the cause and interest of Islamism, as against Christianity, were undying, then we may be assured that the Moorish infidels of Spain did not reiterate their trans-Pyrenean expeditions after one generation—simply because they *could* not. But we know that on the south-eastern horn of Europe they *could*, upon the plain argument that for many centuries they *did*. Over and above this, I am of opinion that the Saracens were unequal to the sort of hardships bred by cold climates; and *there* lay another repulsion for Saracens from France, &c., and not merely the Carlovingian sword. We children of Christendom show our innate superiority to the children of the Orient upon this scale or tariff of acclimatising powers. We travel as wheat travels, through all reasonable ranges of temperature; they, like rice, can migrate only to warm latitudes. They cannot support our cold, but we *can* support the countervailing hardships of their heat. This cause alone would have weatherbound the Mussulmans for ever within the Pyrenean cloisters. Mussulmans in cold latitudes look as much out of their element as sailors on horseback. Apart from which cause, we see that the fine old Visigothic races in Spain found them full employment up to the reign of Ferdinand and Isabella, which reign first created a kingdom of Spain; in that reign the whole fabric of their power thawed away, and was confounded with forgotten things. Columbus, according to a local tradition, was personally present at some of the latter campaigns in Grenada: he saw the last of them. So that the discovery of America may be used as a convertible date with that of extinction for the Saracen power in wéstern Europe. True that the overthrow of Constantinople had forerun this event by nearly half-a-century. But then I insist upon the different proportions of the struggle. Whilst in Spain a province had fought against a province, all Asia militant had fought against the eastern Roman Empire. Amongst the many races whom dimly we decry in those shadowy hosts, tilting for ages in the vast plains of Angora, are seen latterly pressing on to the van two mighty powers, the children of Persia and the Ottoman family of the Turks. Upon these nations—the one heretical, the other orthodox, and more accurately Mahometan than Mahomet, both now rapidly decaying—the faith of Mahomet has ever leaned as upon her eldest sons; and these powers, both the right and the wrong, the Byzantine Cæsars had to face in every phasis of Moslem energy, as it revolved from perfect barbarism, through semi-barbarism, to that crude form of civilisation which Mahometans can support. And through all these transmigrations of their power, we must remember that they were under a martial training and discipline, never suffered to become effeminate. One set of warriors after another *did*, it is true, become effeminate in Persia: but, upon that advantage opening, always another set stepped in from Torkistan or from the Imaus. The nation, as individuals, melted away; the Moslem armies were immortal.

Here, therefore, it is, and standing at this point of my review, that I complain of Mr Finlay's too facile compliance with historians far beneath himself. He throws away his own advantages: oftentimes his commentaries on the past are ebullient with subtlety; and his fault strikes me as lying even in the excess of his sagacity applying itself too often to a basis of facts, quite insufficient for supporting the superincumbent weight of his speculations. But in the instance before us he surrenders himself too readily to the ordinary current of history. How would *he* like it, if he happened to be a Turk himself, finding his nation thus implicitly undervalued? For clearly, in undervaluing the Byzantine resistance, he *does* undervalue the Mahometan assault. Advantages of local situation cannot *eternally* make good the deficiencies of man. If the Byzantines (being as weak as historians would represent them) yet for ages resisted the whole impetus of Mahometan Asia, then it follows, either that the Crescent was correspondingly weak, or that, not being weak, she must have found the Cross pretty strong. The *facit* of history does not here correspond with the numerical items.

Nothing has ever surprised me more, I will frankly own, than this coincidence of authors in treating the Byzantine Empire as feeble and crazy. On the contrary, to me it is clear that some secret and preternatural strength it must have had, lurking where the eye of man did not in those days penetrate, or by what miracle did it undertake our universal Christian cause, fight for us all, keep the waters open from freezing us up, and through nine centuries prevent the ice of Mahometanism from closing over our heads for ever? Yet does Mr Finlay describe this empire as labouring, in A.D. 623, equally with Persia, under "internal weakness," and as "equally incapable of offering any popular or national resistance to an active or enterprising enemy." In this Mr Finlay does but agree with other able writers; but he and they should have recollected, that hardly had that very year 623 departed, even yet the knell of its last hour was sounding upon the winds, when this effeminate empire had occasion to show that she could clothe herself with consuming terrors, as a belligerent both defensive and aggressive. In the absence of her great emperor,* and of the main imperial forces, the golden capital herself, by her own resources, routed and persecuted into wrecks a Persian army that had côme down upon her by stealth and a fraudulent circuit. Even at that same period, she advanced into Persia more than a thousand miles from her own metropolis in Europe, under the blazing ensigns of the cross, kicked the crown of Persia to and fro like a tennis-ball, upset the throne of Artaxerxes, countersigned haughtily the elevation of a new *Basileus* more friendly to herself, and then recrossed the Tigris homewards, after having torn forcibly out of the heart and palpitating entrails of Persia whatever trophies that empire had formerly, in her fire-worshipping stage, wrested from herself. These were not the acts of an effeminate kingdom. In the language of Wordsworth we may say—

> "All power was given her in the dreadful trance;
> Infidel kings she wither'd like a flame."

Indeed, no image that I remember can do justice to the first of these acts, except that Spanish legend of the Cid, which tells us that, long after the death of the mighty cavalier, when the children of those Moors who had fled from his face whilst living were insulting the marble statue above his grave, suddenly the statue raised its right arm, stretched out its marble lance, and drifted the heathen dogs like snow. The mere sanctity of the Christian champion's sepulchre was its own protection; and so we must suppose that, when the Persian hosts came by surprise upon Constantinople—her natural protector being absent by three months' march—simply the golden statues of the mighty Cæsars, half rising on their thrones, must have

* *Heraclius;* which name ought not to have the stress laid on the antepenultimate *(rac)*, but on the penultimate *(i)*.

caused that sudden panic which dissipated the danger. Hardly fifty years later, Mr Finlay well knows that Constantinople again stood an assault—not from a Persian hourrah or tempestuous surprise, but from a vast expedition, armaments by land and sea, fitted out elaborately in the early noontide of Mahometan vigour—and that assault also, in the presence of the caliph and the crescent, was gloriously discomfited. Now if, in the moment of triumph, some voice in the innumerable crowd had cried out, "How long shall this great Christian breakwater, against which are shattered into surge and foam all the mountainous billows of idolaters and misbelievers, stand up on behalf of infant Christendom?" and if from the clouds some trumpet of prophecy had replied, "Even yet for eight hundred years!" could any man have persuaded himself that such a fortress against such antagonists—such a monument against such a millennium of fury—was to be classed amongst the weak things of the earth? This oriental Rome, it is true, equally with Persia, was liable to sudden inroads and incursions. But the difference was this—Persia was strongly protected in all ages by the wilderness on her main western frontier; if this were passed, and a hand-to-hand conflict succeeded, where light cavalry or fugitive archers could be of little value, the essential weakness of the Persian Empire then betrayed itself. Her sovereign was then assassinated, and peace was obtained from the condescension of the invader. But the enemies of Constantinople—Goths, Avars, Bulgarians, or even Persians—were strong only by their weakness. Being contemptible, they were neglected; being chased, they made no stand; being prostrate, they capitulated; and *thus* only they escaped. They entered like thieves by means of darkness, and escaped like sheep by means of dispersion. But, if caught, they were annihilated. No; I resume my thesis; I close this head by reiterating my correction of history; I re-affirm my position, that in eastern Rome lay the salvation of western and central Europe; in Constantinople and the Propontis lay the *sine quâ non* condition of any future Christendom. Emperor and people *must* have done their duty; the result, the vast extent of generations surmounted, furnish the triumphant demonstration. Finally, indeed, they fell, king and people, shepherd and flock; but by that time their mission was fulfilled. And doubtless, as the noble Palæologus lay on heaps of carnage, with his noble people, as life was ebbing away, a voice from heaven sounded in his ears the great words of the Hebrew prophet, "Behold! YOUR WORK IS DONE; your warfare is accomplished."

III. Such, then, being the unmerited disparagement of the Byzantine government, and so great the ingratitude of later Christendom to that sheltering power under which themselves enjoyed the leisure of a thousand years for knitting and expanding into strong nations; on the other hand, what is to be thought of the Saracen anti-Byzantines? Everywhere it has passed for a lawful postulate, that the Saracen conquests prevailed, half by the feebleness of the Roman government at Constantinople, and half by the preternatural energy infused into the Arabs by their false prophet and legislator. In either of its faces, this theory is falsified by a steady review of facts. With regard to the Saracens, Mr Finlay thinks, as I do, and argues, that they prevailed through the *local*, or sometimes the *casual*, weakness of their immediate enemies, and rarely through any strength of their own. We must remember one fatal weakness of the imperial administration in those days, not due to men or to principles, but entirely to nature and the slow growth of scientific improvements—viz., the difficulties of locomotion. As respected Syria, Egypt, Cyrenaica, and so on to the most western provinces of Africa, the Saracens had advantages for moving rapidly which the Cæsar had not. But is not a water movement speedier than a land movement, which for an army never has much exceeded fourteen miles a-day? Certainly it is; but in this case there were two desperate defects in the imperial control over that water service. To use a fleet, you must have a fleet; but their whole naval interest had been starved by the intolerable costs of the Persian war. Immense had been the expenses of Heraclius, and annually decaying had been his Asiatic revenues. Secondly, the original position of the Arabs had been better than that of the emperor in every stage of the warfare which so suddenly arose. In Arabia the Arabs stood nearest to Syria, in Syria nearest to Egypt, in Egypt nearest to Cyrenaica. What reason had there been for expecting a martial legislator at that moment in Arabia, who should fuse and sternly combine her distracted tribes? What blame, therefore, to Heraclius, that Syria—the first object of assault, being also by much the weakest part of the empire, and immediately after the close of a desolating war—should in four campaigns be found indefensible? We must remember the unexampled abruptness of the Arabian revolution. The year six hundred and twenty-two, by its very name of Hegira, does not record a triumph, but a humiliation. In that year, therefore, and at the very moment when Heraclius was entering upon his long Persian struggle, Mahomet was yet prostrate, and his destiny was doubtful. Eleven years after—viz., in six hundred and thirty-three—the prophet was dead and gone; but his *first* successor was already in Syria as a conqueror. Such had been the velocity of events. The Persian war had then been finished by three years, but the exhaustion of the empire had perhaps, at that moment, reached its maximum. I am satisfied that ten years' repose from this extreme state of collapse would have shown us another result. Even as it was, and caught at this enormous disadvantage, Heraclius taught the robbers to tremble, and would have exterminated them, if not baffled by two irremediable calamities, neither of them due to any act or neglect of his own. The first lay in the treason of his lieutenants. The governors of Damascus, of Aleppo, of Emesa, of Bostra, of Kinnisrin, all proved traitors. The root of this evil lay, probably, in the disorders following the Persian invasion, which had made it the perilous interest of the emperor to appoint great officers from amongst those who had a local influence. Such persons it might have been ruinous too suddenly to set aside; as, in the event, it proved ruinous to employ them. A dilemma of this kind, offering but a choice of evils, belonged to the nature of any Persian war; and that particular war was bequeathed to Heraclius by the management of his predecessors. The second calamity was even more fatal; it lay in the composition of the Syrian population, and its original want of vital cohesion. For no purpose could this population be united; they formed a rope of sand. There was the distraction of religion—Jacobites, Nestorians, &c.; there was the distraction of races — slaves and masters, conquered and conquerors, modern intruders mixed, but not blended with, aboriginal mountaineers. Property became the one principle and ground of choice between the two governments. Where was protection to be had for *that?* Barbarous as were the Arabs, they saw their present advantage. Often it would happen from the position of the armies, that *they* could, whilst the emperor could not, guarantee the instant security of land or of personal treasures; the Arabs could also promise, sometimes, even a total immunity from taxes; generally a diminished scale of taxation; always a remission of arrears; none of which concessions could be listened to by the emperor, partly on account of the public necessities, partly from jealousy of establishing operative precedents. For religion, again, protection was more easily obtained in that day from the Arab, who made war on Christianity, than from the Byzantine emperor, who was its champion. What were the different sects and subdivisions of Christianity to the barbarian? Monophysite, Monothelite, Eutychian, or Jacobite, all were to him as the scholastic disputes of noble and intellectual Europe to the camps of gipsies. The Arab felt himself to be the depositary of one sublime truth, the unity of God. His mission, therefore, was principally against idolaters. Yet even to *them* his policy was to *sell* toleration of idolatry and Polytheism for tribute. Clearly, as Mr Finlay hints, this was merely a provisional moderation, meant to be laid aside when sufficient power was obtained; and it *was* laid aside, in after ages, by many a wretch like Timor or Nadir Shah. Religion, therefore, and property once secured, what more had the Syrians to seek? And if to these advantages for the Saracens we add the fact, that a considerable Arab population was dispersed through Syria, who became so many emissaries, spies, and decoys in the service of their countrymen, it does great honour to the emperor, that through so many campaigns he should at all have maintained his ground; and this at last he resigned only under the despondency caused by almost universal treachery.

The Saracens, therefore, had no great merit even in their earliest exploits; and the *impetus* of their movement forwards, that principle of proselytism which carried them so strongly "ahead" through a few generations, was very soon brought to a stop. Mr Finlay, in my mind, does right to class these barbarians as "socially and politically little better than the Gothic, Hunnish, and Avar monarchies." But, on consideration, the Gothic monarchy embosomed the germs of a noble civilisation; whereas the Saracens have never propagated great principles of any kind, nor attained even a momentary grandeur in their institutions, except where coalescing with a higher or more ancient civilisation.

Meantime, ascending from the earliest Mahometans to their prophet, what are we to think of *him*? Was Mahomet a great man? I think not. The case was thus: the Arabian tribes had long stood ready, like dogs held in a leash, for a start after distant game. It was not Mahomet who gave them that impulse. But next, what was it that hindered the Arab tribes from obeying the impulse? Simply this, that they were always in feud with each other; so that their expeditions, beginning in harmony, were sure to break up in anger on the road. What they needed was, some one grand compressing and unifying principle, such as the Roman found in the destinies of his city. True; but this, you say, they found in the sublime principle that God was one, and had appointed them to be the scourges of all who denied it. Their mission was to cleanse the earth from Polytheism; and, as ambassadors from God, to tell the nations, "Ye shall have no other gods but me." That was grand; and *that* surely they had from Mahomet. Perhaps so; but where did he get it? He stole it from the Jewish Scriptures, and from the Scriptures no less than from the traditions of the Christians. Assuredly, then, the first projecting *impetus* was not impressed upon

Islamism by Mahomet. This lay in a revealed truth; and by Mahomet it was furtively translated to his own use from those oracles which held it in keeping. But possibly, if not the *principle* of motion, yet at least the steady conservation of this motion was secured to Islamism by Mahomet. Granting (you will say) that the launch of this religion might be due to an alien inspiration, yet still the steady movement onwards of this religion, through some centuries, might be due exclusively to the code of laws bequeathed by Mahomet in the Koran. And this has been the opinion of many European scholars. They fancy that Mahomet, however worldly and sensual as the founder of a pretended revelation, was wise in the wisdom of this world; and that, if ridiculous as a prophet (which word,* however, did not mean *foreteller*, but simply revealer of truth), he was worthy of veneration as a statesman. He legislated well and presciently, they imagine, for the interests of a remote posterity. Now, upon that question let us hear Mr Finlay. He, when commenting upon the steady resistance offered to the Saracens by the African Christians of the seventh and eighth centuries—a resistance which terminated disastrously for both sides—the poor Christians being exterminated, and the Moslem invaders being robbed of an indigenous working population, naturally inquires what it was that led to so tragical a result. The Christian natives of these provinces were, in a political condition, little favourable to belligerent

* I have already (viz., in the paper on "Oracles") had occasion to notice the erroneous limitation of the word *Prophecy*, as if it meant only, or chiefly, that revelation which draws away the veil of futurity. But in the great cardinal proposition of Islamism this correction is broadly enunciated—There is one God, and Mahomet is his Prophet. Now, in the narrow sense of prediction, Mahomet disclaimed the gift of prophecy as much as of miracles.

efforts; and there cannot be much doubt that, with any wisdom or any forbearance on the part of the intruders, both parties might soon have settled down into a pacific compromise of their feuds. Instead of this, the scimitar was invoked and worshipped as the sole possible arbitrator; and truce there was none, until the silence of desolation brooded over those once fertile fields. How savage was the fanaticism, and how blind the worldly wisdom, which could have co-operated to such a result! The cause must have lain in the unaccommodating nature of the Mahometan institutions, in the bigotry of the Mahometan leaders, and in the defect of expansive views on the part of their legislator. He had not provided even for other climates than that of his own sweltering sty in the Hedjas, or for manners more polished, or for institutions more philosophic, than those of his own sun-baked Ishmaelites. "The construction of the political government of the Saracen Empire," says Mr Finlay, "was imperfect, and shows that Mahomet had neither contemplated extensive foreign conquests, nor devoted the energies of his powerful mind to the consideration of the questions of administration which would arise out of the difficult task of ruling a numerous and wealthy population, possessed of property, but deprived of equal rights." He then shows how the whole power of the state settled into the hands of a chief priest—systematically irresponsible. When, therefore, that momentary state of responsibility had passed away from the Mahometans, which was created (like the state of martial law) "by national feelings, military companionship, and exalted enthusiasm," the administration of the caliphs became "far more oppressive than that of the Roman Empire." It is in fact an insult to the majestic Romans, if we should place them seriously in the balance with savages like the Saracens. The Romans were essentially the leaders of civilisation, according to the possibilities then existing; for their earliest usages and social forms involved a high civilisation, whilst promising a higher: whereas all Moslem nations have described a petty arch of national civility—soon reaching its apex, and rapidly barbarising backwards. This fatal gravitation towards decay and decomposition in Mahometan institutions, which at this day exhibit to the gaze of mankind one uniform spectacle of Mahometan ruins, all the great Moslem nations being already in a *Strulbrug** state, and held erect only by the colossal support of Christian powers, could not, as a *reversionary* evil, have been healed by the Arabian prophet. His own religious principles would have prevented *that*, for they offer a permanent bounty on sensuality; so that every man who serves a Mahometan state faithfully and brilliantly at twenty-five, is incapacitated at thirty-five for any further service, by the very nature of the rewards which he receives from the state. Within a very few years, every public servant is usually emasculated by that unlimited voluptuousness which equally the Moslem princes and the common Prophet of all Moslems countenance as the proper object, and indeed the sole object, of human pursuit, not on earth only, but in the future of paradise. Here is the mortal ulcer of Islamism, which can never cleanse itself from death and the odour of death. A political ulcer would or might

* To any reader who happens to be illiterate, or not extensively informed, it may be proper to explain, that *Strulbrugs* were a creation of Dean Swift. They were people in an imaginary world, who were afraid of dying; and who had the privilege of lingering on through centuries when they ought to have been dead and buried, but suffering all the evils of utter superannuation and decay; having a bare glimmering of semi-consciousness, but otherwise in the condition of mere vegetables.

have found restoration for itself; but this ulcer is higher and deeper:—it lies in the religion, which is incapable of reform: it is an ulcer reaching as high as the paradise which Islamism promises, and deep as the hell which it creates. I repeat, that Mahomet could not effectually have neutralised a poison which he himself had introduced into the circulation and life-blood of his Moslem economy. The false prophet was forced to reap as he had sown. But an evil, which is certain, may be retarded; and ravages, which tend finally to confusion, may be limited for many generations. Now, in the case of the African provincials which I have noticed, we observe an original incapacity in Islamism, even at its meridian altitude, for amalgamating with any *superior* (and therefore any Christian) culture. And the specific action of Mahometanism in the African case, as contrasted with the Roman economy which it supplanted, is thus exhibited by Mr Finlay in a most instructive passage, where every negation on the Mahometan side is made to suggest the countervailing *positive* usage on the side of the Romans. O children of Romulus! how noble do you appear, when thus abruptly contrasted with the wild boars that desolated your vineyards! "No local magistrates elected by the people, and no parish priests connected by their feelings and interests both with their superiors and inferiors, bound society together by common ties; and no system of legal administration, independent of the military and financial authorities, preserved the property of the people from the rapacity of the government."

Such, we are to understand, was *not* the Mahometan system; such *had* been the system of Rome. "Socially and politically," proceeds the passage, "the Saracen Empire was little better than the Gothic, Hunnish, and Avar monarchies; and that it proved more durable, with almost equal oppression, is to be attributed to the powerful enthusiasm of Mahomet's religion, which tempered for some time its avarice and tyranny." The same sentiment is repeated still more emphatically at p. 468:—"The political policy of the Saracens was of itself utterly barbarous; and it only caught a passing gleam of justice from the religious feeling of their prophet's doctrines."

Thus far, therefore, it appears that Mahometanism is not much indebted to its too famous founder; it owes to him a principle—viz., the unity of God—which, merely through a capital blunder, it fancies peculiar to itself. Nothing but the grossest ignorance in Mahomet, nothing but the grossest non-acquaintance with Greek authors on the part of the Arabs, could have created or sustained the delusion current amongst that illiterate people—that it was themselves only who rejected Polytheism. Had but one amongst the personal enemies of Mahomet been acquainted with Greek, *there* was an end of the new religion in the first moon of its existence. Once open the eyes of the Arabs to the fact, that Christians had anticipated them in this great truth of the divine unity, and Mahometanism could only have ranked as a subdivision of Christianity. Mahomet would have ranked only as a Christian heresiarch or schismatic; such as Nestorius or Marcian at one time, such as Arius or Pelagius at another. In his character of *theologian*, therefore, Mahomet was simply the most memorable of blunderers, supported in his blunders by the most unlettered*

* "*Most unlettered:*"—Viz., at the era of Mahomet. Subsequently, under the encouragement of great caliphs, they became confessedly a learned people. But this cannot disturb the sublime character of their ignorance, at that earliest period when this ignorance was an indispensable co-operating element with the plagiarisms of Mahomet, or the generation of a new religion.

of nations. In his other character of *legislator*, we have seen that already the earliest stages of Mahometan experience exposed decisively his ruinous imbecility. Where a rude tribe offered no resistance to his system, for the simple reason that their barbarism suggested no motive for resistance, it could be no honour to prevail. And where, on the other hand, a higher civilisation had furnished strong points of repulsion to his system, it appears plainly that this pretended apostle of social improvements had devised or hinted no readier mode of conciliation, than by putting to the sword all dissentients. He starts as a theological reformer, with a fancied defiance to the world which was no defiance at all, being exactly what Christians had believed for six centuries, and Jews for six-and-twenty. He starts as a political reformer, with a fancied conciliation to the world, which was no conciliation at all, but was sure to provoke imperishable hostility wheresoever it had any effect at all.

I have thus reviewed some of the more splendid aspects connected with Mr Finlay's theme; but that theme, in its entire compass, is worthy of a far more extended investigation than my own limits will allow, or than the historical curiosity of the world (misdirected here, as in so many other cases) has hitherto demanded. The Greek race, suffering a long occultation under the blaze of the Roman Empire, into which for a time it had been absorbed, but again emerging from this blaze, and re-assuming a distinct Greek agency and influence, offers a subject great by its own inherent attractions, and separately interesting by the unaccountable neglect which it has suffered. To have overlooked this subject, is one amongst the capital oversights of Gibbon. To have rescued it from utter oblivion, and to have traced an outline for its better illumination, is the peculiar merit of Mr Finlay. His greatest fault is —to have been careless or slovenly in the niceties of classical and philological precision. His greatest praise, and a very great one indeed, is—to have thrown the light of an *original* philosophic sagacity upon a neglected province of history, indispensable to the *arrondissement* of Paganism in its latest stages, and of anti-Paganism in its earliest.

END OF SEVENTH VOLUME.

CPSIA information can be obtained
at www.ICGtesting.com
Printed in the USA
LVHW110807120522
718525LV00003B/48

9 783375 000752